BETH KERY
ONLY FOR
YOU

headline
ETERNAL

First published in ebook in Great Britain in 2014
by HEADLINE ETERNAL
An imprint of HEADLINE PUBLISHING GROUP

First published in paperback in Great Britain in 2015
by HEADLINE ETERNAL
An imprint of HEADLINE PUBLISHING GROUP

Published by arrangement with Berkley Publishing Group,
A member of Penguin Group (USA) LLC,
A Penguin Random House Company

2

Cataloguing in Publication Data is available from the British Library

ISBN 978 1 4722 1103 3

Offset in Sabon by Avon DataSet Ltd, Bidford-on-Avon, Warwickshire

Printed and bound by CPI Group (UK) Ltd, Croydon, CR0 4YY

Headline's policy is to use papers that are natural, renewable and recyclable
products and made from wood grown in well-managed forests and other
controlled sources. The logging and manufacturing processes are expected
to conform to the environmental regulations of the country of origin.

HEADLINE PUBLISHING GROUP
An Hachette UK Company
338 Euston Road
London NW1 3BH

www.headlineeternal.com
www.headline.co.uk
www.hachette.co.uk

Acknowledgments

I'd like to thank my editor, Leis Pederson, from the bottom of my heart for putting up with all my author angst and worry about my babies. She's stuck by me through thick and thin, highs and lows, laughter and inevitable frustrations. I think the stories are better for it too. Mahlet, you are the most awesome beta reader . . . *romance reader par excellence* in general. My deepest gratitude for your selfless, smart assistance and feedback. Ed, thank you as always for standing by me, a solid, steady, reassuring touchstone. You not only help me with all those pesky business questions and weird, mundane writing queries, like . . . "what's this thing that surrounds a door called?" but you are a part of every single one of my heroes. Last and most importantly, thank you, reader, for having faith in the books and characters. You are amazing.

ONLY FOR YOU

One

TWO AND A HALF YEARS AGO

His final project for the benefit ball cast admiring looks at her many reflections as she sashayed out of the room. Not without good reason, Seth acknowledged with wry amusement as he glanced at the Alien Ice Queen's ass gloved in a clinging blue gown. The starlet paused in the act of appraising herself from all angles.

She had ample opportunity to adore herself in the luxurious but garish dressing room where they stood. No less than a dozen gilded mirrors adorned the suite, including a large one on the ceiling. Daphne DeGarro, the heiress-turned-reality-show-star and hostess for the Cancer Research Benefit Ball, had opened several rooms in her Hollywood Hills mansion that night for the transformation of her guests. She'd reserved her risqué, decadently decorated dressing room for Seth, however. Earlier that evening, Daphne had led him to it with a sly grin. Seth had made her his first project, turning her into a magnificent, sexually flagrant Marie Antoinette, his creative instincts sparked by the woman's opulent bad taste and brassy beauty. The benefit ball for cancer research was now in full swing in an almost equally gaudy ballroom and downstairs terrace.

Seth was the last special effects makeup artist to finish. He was weary. He'd done his part for tonight. Between him and fourteen of his regular staff and two eager interns from Hightower Special Effects Studio, they'd completed nearly two hundred characters in costume and makeup. The price of their labor, in addition to the use of Hightower's extensive costume-and-makeup collection, was a hefty donation to the Cancer Research Fund by each client. Daphne DeGarro might have been in love with herself, but she was shrewd. Hollywood players would pay a sizable chunk of cash to be turned into a fearsome fairy-tale creature or glamorous fantasy character for one magical night.

Perhaps the young actress noticed his gaze lingering on her backside in one of the many mirrored reflections, because she turned to him.

"Aren't you attending the ball, Seth?" she asked.

"No, I'm done for the night," Seth replied, briskly zipping up an airbrush case and returning it to his kit. Realizing he still had on the tinted glasses he wore when he did an application, he shoved them impatiently back on his head.

"That's all it was then? Work?" the Ice Queen asked. He paused warily, hearing the hint of seduction in her tone. She'd drunk too much champagne while he was doing her application. He glanced up. She was arching her back slightly, highlighting her ample, airbrush-frosted breasts beneath the low-cut gown. Earlier, he had offered to glue the edges of the gown—her nipples were bound to pop over the edge at any moment—but his offer had been flatly refused. Apparently the possibility was something she hoped for rather than dreaded.

She was a temptation, all right, but one he'd grown well accustomed to denying himself. Seth liked women a lot.

Just not the actress variety.

He resumed packing his kit methodically. He knew firsthand the level of infatuation a woman could get for a man who could turn her into a breathtaking vision. He tried to recall her name, but quickly gave up. What difference did it make? Seth avoided women possessed of fame fever. This particular ingenue was burning with it, which had perhaps been his inspiration for the Ice Queen makeup.

She could use a little something to cool her down.

"No. Not just work. It's my art as well," he replied levelly, sliding some paints into his kit.

"I hope you're pleased with your creation then. I know I am. I feel so honored to have been touched by the best," the Ice Queen said tremulously. When he didn't look up, because he had a damn strong suspicion she was feathering her fingertips across the top of her breasts and peekaboo nipples, he heard a resigned sigh.

"I see. All the rumors about you not fraternizing with the talent are true then. Shame."

The door closed.

He exhaled in relief and shut his kit briskly in preparation to leave as well. Eight members of his staff had volunteered to stay and assist with prosthetic and costume removal after the ball. A delivery service had been hired to pick up all the costumes and gear left at Daphne's house tomorrow.

He paused next to one of several iced buckets of champagne in the room and poured himself half a glass. He rarely drank champagne—or any alcohol, really. He'd developed a dislike for the stuff at an early age after seeing firsthand its effects on his father and two uncles in his home village, Isleta Pueblo. It had been a long, trying night though. Usually a script and his creative instincts drove his work. Tonight, he'd been driven largely by vanity and questionable taste.

He drained the flute, finding the cold, dry liquid cleared his mental cobwebs better than he would have expected.

He caught his reflection in one of the gilded mirrors, a tall man holding a delicate flute in a large hand. Next to the feminine flounces and pastel shades of green, gold and blue décor that surrounded him, he looked especially out of place, a bull in a china shop . . . a savage in the midst of contrived artifice.

It was the paradox of his life that those unlikely, big hands contributed to the subtlety, artistry and nuance of Hollywood's grand façade.

He couldn't wait to leave. He set down the flute. A small amount of peace and a large steak were awaiting him at home. Even though it was the weekend and almost nine thirty in the evening, it was early for him to be taking off. He was looking forward to a little R and R.

He swung open the door to the hallway and halted abruptly at the sight of a young woman's pale, startled face—a face he definitely did not know. In the distance, however, he heard a voice he recognized all too well.

Shit. Cecilia.

"Why is she playing coy?" Cecilia was saying, sounding out of breath. "Half my client list is here tonight. I haven't got time to play hide-and-seek with her. What makes your girlfriend think she's so important?"

"I told you," a man said in a bored tone. "She claims I'm not her boyfriend anymore."

The girl stared at Seth with huge green eyes. At first, he thought she was stunned. He quickly realized she *was* dazed, but also nearly panicked. Reacting purely on instinct, he reached for her hand and pulled her into the room with him. She came without hesitation, spinning into him in a motion that bizarrely struck Seth like a dance move between familiar partners. Her back was to his front as he reached around her and silently shut the door. He could tell by the sound of their footsteps that Cecilia and her companion had rounded the corner of the hallway in the distance. Very gently, he turned the lock. His fingers lingered on the metal while his other hand continued to clasp the woman's hand in the vicinity of her waist.

For several seconds, they just stood there, utterly still as he half-embraced her, staring at the door and listening. He heard the sound of door after door opening and shutting as Cecilia and the man carried out their search.

"What have you done now?" Cecilia Arends, one of the most

successful agents in Hollywood, continued. Cecilia was smart and savvy. Seth and she had gone out a few times. Cecilia had made it clear she wanted more than a few dates. He regrettably didn't return the interest, and he had been friendly but frank with her about it. Cecilia was *way* too attached to her cell phone and doing business, even while they were on a date. When Seth took off from work, he relished his private life, his freedom and anonymity. Cecilia had infringed on his privacy via her celebrity deal making while at candlelit dinners—or finally—during an intimate moment following sex. He'd ended things with her the next day.

He hadn't been avoiding Cecilia—until tonight, that is—but he hadn't been seeking her out either.

"Did she catch you at it with another girl?" Cecilia was saying. "I've told you all along Gia won't stand for your antics. She's too smart for her own good and values her opinion far too much for someone so young. Good *God*," Cecilia added in a beleaguered, distracted tone. "*Look* at this décor." A door snapped shut. "Who does Daphne DeGarro think she is, the Whore of Babylon? You'd think with that much money, she could buy herself some taste."

The searchers' footsteps drew nearer. Instead of being concerned, Seth looked down at the girl distractedly. She possessed gleaming, golden brown hair that was gathered at her neck in a thick braid. He unlocked his gaze from the way the light hit the richly colored strands, and he watched dispassionately as the doorknob turned. His inner elbow pressed against the young woman's shoulder and neck. She was cuddled against the middle of his body like a pea in a pod, the pressure of her against him slight, but . . . nice. He sensed her tensing and holding her breath as the doorknob rattled. He, on the other hand, inhaled deeply. The clean, fresh scent of soap and tangerines tickled his nose. Sexual awareness flickered down his spine, the charged, wholly unexpected scenario perhaps amplifying the sensation.

The knob twisted back into place.

"It's locked. Let's go back down to the party. Maybe she's turned up there again," the male said in an irritated tone.

When the voices began to fade, the young woman turned and looked over her shoulder. She stared at his face as if rapt. The silence stretched. She blinked and seemed to come back to herself.

"Thank you," she said earnestly. "I didn't think I'd run into anyone I knew tonight."

He arched his eyebrows, extremely curious and a little wary. He drank in the vision of her face. "Cecilia Arends is one of the most sought-after agents in Hollywood. What does she want with you?"

She shrugged uneasily under the costume armor she wore. A light pink stain spread on the cheek turned toward him. Realizing she was still sheltered by his body, he lowered his arm from the door reluctantly and straightened. She stepped to the side, but he noticed with a sense of satisfaction that she didn't move far off. He'd liked having her next to him. He dropped her hand and scowled slightly.

His gaze lowered over her with growing interest. She'd been costumed as Joan of Arc. Whoever had done her makeup had been smart enough to apply hardly any paint. The typecasting was perfect. The girl had the intelligent gaze and radiant, fresh glow one might imagine the virgin warrior to possess . . . although Seth somehow doubted a saint would possess such a pink, delectable mouth. There was an interesting tilt to her light green eyes; beautifully shaped, high cheekbones added a hint of regal haughtiness to her otherwise girl-next-door pretty face. He found it striking, the unexpected and exotic combined with all that rosy, creamy freshness. There was something very frank and honest about her gaze. He'd have said she possessed a tomboy quality if he didn't find her to be utterly feminine.

"It's actually Tommy who is responsible for the search party," she said, interrupting his unexpected and increasingly lustful thoughts. Never let it be said that one night you might randomly open a door and see an incredible, singular woman standing there.

"So you're *not* one of Cecilia's clients?" he pressed.

Something flickered across her face. She shook her head adamantly. "No. I came with my old college roommate. She's an intern for—"

She abruptly halted her rapid, anxious speech, lush lips falling open. Eyes the color of a newly opened leaf lowered slowly over his face and body, and then widened. "Are . . . are *you* Seth Hightower?" she asked in a strangled voice.

"Yes."

White teeth scraped across her lower lip. Seth felt his body tingle and tighten. Her mouth was a hundred times the temptation of the Ice Queen's flagrantly displayed ass and breasts.

"Your friend is an intern with my company? Liza," he stated calmly rather than asked.

The young woman's face went tellingly blank.

"What makes you think that?" she hedged, the spark of panic returning to her eyes.

He nodded once at her Joan of Arc costume. "That's a costume from my collection. Only one of my staff could have given it to you. And I brought just two interns tonight, Liza being the only female. Last I heard, they didn't allow males and females to share rooms at UCLA," he said, the vision of Liza's résumé springing into his mind's eye in perfect detail.

Anxiety and regret flickered across her face.

"I'm sorry. Please don't be angry with Liza for bringing me and loaning me the costume. It's my fault. I begged her to let me come tonight. I'm only visiting her in Los Angeles for a few days, and I wanted to see her at work. She's been vibrating with excitement because she won the internship with you. She says you're the absolute best in the special effects–makeup business. She's been walking on air."

"Are you trying to flatter your way out of this?" he asked. For a second, her anxious expression intensified. Then her gaze sharpened on his face. She smiled slowly, her anxiety apparently evaporating.

Funny. Most people couldn't tell when he was joking.

"I just wouldn't want Liza to get in trouble because of me," she said, her smile lingering. "No one else wanted the Joan of Arc costume, and as you can see, Liza wasted no time on my makeup. I did my own hair. Do you . . . disapprove of my makeup?" she asked cautiously.

He realized he'd been scowling again as he tried to discern the trick of magic to her face. He kept telling himself not to stare at her, but he couldn't seem to help himself.

"No. It would have been a mistake on her part to paint you," he admitted gruffly. "Liza showed good taste in that. Or maybe that was your doing? Are you an artist, as well?"

She pulled a face. "Sort of. I doubt *you'd* think so."

"What did you study at UCLA?"

"History," she said, suddenly beaming.

He smiled and glanced down at her Joan of Arc costume in admiring amusement. "Appropriate. You still haven't told me why Cecilia and that man were looking for you. Why were you running from them?"

She blinked, her smile faltering. He felt a little regret at using a technique he'd learned during his days in Army intelligence—indulge in a light, warm moment of banter and then spring the loaded question calmly on the unwary.

"Oh . . . yes. That," she said breathlessly, glancing around the room. For the first time, Seth realized she'd been staring almost as fixedly at him for the last few moments as he had been staring at her. He raised his eyebrows, waiting for an answer.

"I'm not sure why Cecilia joined the hunt, exactly. She's Tommy's agent, so maybe she thinks it's her duty," she said vaguely.

"The man was Tommy?" he clarified, nodding toward the hall-way. "Your boyfriend?"

"My *ex*-boyfriend," she corrected. She seemed to realize how fierce she'd sounded because she sighed, and her stare started bouncing off every surface of the room again, except for his face. "I've been very stupid," she said, the four words striking him like a regretful confession.

"Have you?" he asked after a pause. "Or has he?"

"*He* has," she agreed. "But I was naïve enough to believe his act. I came to Los Angeles from New York during a break from work to visit Liza. I thought I'd surprise Tommy. I surprised him, all right," she added bitterly under her breath. "He clearly hadn't been expecting me to walk in while he was entertaining another woman in bed two nights ago. I hadn't realized how convenient this long-distance romance was for him." Her eyes sprang wide as if she was shocked she'd blurted something so intimate to a stranger. "I'm making it sound a lot more melodramatic than it was," she assured him. "We hadn't been seeing each other long or anything. We weren't serious. Obviously, it was no great loss."

"We're all young once," he said quietly. "It's not a crime."

She gave him a lopsided grin, her gaze slowly moving over his face. He was struck by the focus of her observation. Her smile turned fascinated . . . a little . . . *fey*. He felt his muscles tighten under that enigmatic perusal.

"Forgive me for saying so," she said softly. "But I can't imagine you ever seeming young and stupid."

"I was. Trust me." He frowned as a thought occurred to him. "So I'm Liza's ancient employer, is that it?"

She laughed. "God, no. I didn't mean that at all. It's just Liza respects you so much—so does every member of your staff I've met here tonight—and everyone knows about your success in the film business. You'd been nominated for two Academy Awards before you even turned thirty."

"And never won once by thirty-two," he replied wryly.

"It's just a matter of time," she said warmly. "I've also heard how intimidating you can be. Not from Liza, of course," she added hastily. "My point is, I doubt you'd ever be fooled by a man like Tommy Valian."

He blinked. "*Tommy V* is your ex-boyfriend? The lead singer from Crime Fix?" he asked, referring to the popular rock band. "How did you ever meet him?"

She shook her head, and he had the impression she didn't think the topic was even worthy of pursuing. "At a Broadway play one very unlucky night." She gave him a sheepish look. "I was clearly struck stupid by fame. If you're a fan, I hate to break it to you, but Tommy's lyrics are about a thousand times more poetic and smart than he could ever imagine being in his finest moment."

He saw the sparkle in her eyes, glad to see she was far, far from being in any distressing straits over the likes of Tommy Valian. He smiled full-out at the evidence. She blinked, looking startled. He waved over at the seating area he'd been using for a makeup station. "Have a drink with me?"

His smile fell when she didn't immediately respond, and her gaze roved over the garish dressing room. Would she say no? Was she just being polite, chatting it up with her friend's *ancient* boss?

He looked into the depths of her eyes. At six feet four inches, he looked down at most people. He suddenly felt like the big bad wolf, considering swallowing Red whole, and he had the distinct impression the girl was thinking the same thing . . . and was liking her thought. Another wave of simple, undiluted lust, the likes of which he wasn't sure he'd ever experienced in his life, surged through him. Was it wishful thinking on his part, that spark of fascinated interest in her eyes? The beguiling curve of her mouth, as she smiled, was like a caress where it counted.

No. This kind of unexpected magic was rarely one-way, at least in Seth's limited experienced with it.

"Well . . . a girl's got to do *something* while she's in hiding, right?"

He raised his eyebrows in amused agreement. She went ahead of him. He followed, leaving the door locked behind them.

"Champagne, ice water or soda?" he asked when they approached the seating area and impromptu bar that had been set up on a long table.

"Champagne, please," Gia said, thankful Seth's back was turned as she began the ungraceful process of sitting in the armor. The costume was lightweight, but still, she felt like a stiff-jointed eighty-year-old in it. To make matters worse, a dozen large mirrors scattered around the room were showcasing her ungainly maneuvering from every angle. Precisely how many mirrors did a person require? Zero, given the ridiculous way *she* looked at the moment. Just Gia's luck, to be dressed this way when unexpectedly having a run-in with an extremely handsome, attractive man. She'd been curious about Seth Hightower ever since she'd first learned about him from Liza. He was reputed to be a brilliant artist, but also a bit of a lone wolf. Meeting the real man had amped her interest up to fascination. Her heart had lurched against her breastbone in flat-out shock when she had stood panicked in that hallway a moment ago and turned to stare into his inscrutable face.

Her favorite sculpture had come to life.

She noticed the champagne bottle looked dwarfed in his large hand. She was fascinated by his arms beneath the short-sleeved white T-shirt he wore. He had to possess the most impressive biceps she'd ever seen. He suddenly jerked to a halt while reaching for a glass. She couldn't quite interpret the dangerous slant of his dark brows as he turned to regard her, but her heart seemed to recognize why. It leapt into overtime.

No *wonder* Liza thought Seth Hightower was intimidating.

"What?" Gia asked, freezing in the act of trying to prop her awkwardly armored body up against some cushions.

"Liza just turned twenty-five," he said slowly. "How old are you?"

She stared at him in blank befuddlement. Why was he bringing up her friend's age? A thought suddenly struck her.

"Are you worried I'm not old enough?" she asked, a grin breaking free.

"Are you?"

Somehow, his suspicion thrilled her. *He's asking if you're of age, but* not *for drinking.* She couldn't swear the thought that popped into her head was true, but it certainly *felt* that way. Seth appealed to her in an elemental way she'd never before experienced, and she didn't want him to find *her* lacking in return. Unlike Tommy Valian, Seth was in his thirties, a man in his prime, both physically and in his career and life. And unlike Tommy, when Seth had looked at her earlier, she'd felt like the exact opposite of a naïve ingénue.

"Don't worry. I'm plenty old enough," she assured him, repressing a smile because he was looking so fierce. He merely raised one dark eyebrow and waited. She realized he expected an answer to his question. "I told you I was Liza's roommate in college. We're of an age. Do you expect me to show you ID?" she teased him.

His stare bore into her. She forced herself not to blink or flinch. His tension suddenly dissipated. He turned to pour her champagne. The sound of the liquid flowing into the flute seemed unusually sensual to her. The effervescence from the bubbles seemed to transfer to her, causing a tingle of excitement between her thighs.

"Cecilia said your name is Gia?"

"Yes. Gia Harris," she said, surprised and a little embarrassed to realize she hadn't even thought to tell him her name.

He came toward her, holding out the flute. As he handed it to her, a small smile ghosted his lips, perhaps an apology for his former sternness. He had a very hard, very sexy mouth. It fascinated her, to see something she'd grown used to being eternally frozen now animated with life. His face was well-proportioned, bold and . . . somehow *beautiful*, as well, although in a thoroughly masculine way Gia wasn't sure she'd ever experienced in real life.

He sat down on the couch, a good portion of the center cushion separating them.

At the start of their conversation, she was equal parts nervous and excited, so she decided it was best to just focus on his face. As compelling it was, it forced all her worries into the background. Worries about the crucial juncture she was experiencing in her career, about her uncertainty about her life . . . about what she was so uncharacteristically doing here, behind a locked door with a virile stranger.

Gia wasn't the type to become enraptured. She didn't dream; she made plans. Even as a child, she'd been practical.

But she had to admit, as she stared into Seth Hightower's indomitable, handsome face, that for the first time in her life, she was utterly entranced. Perhaps it was the amber flecks amid the golden brown of his irises that were sending electrical impulses to her nerves, making her skin feel tingly and sensitive, her lungs and throat tight and uncooperative in their usual tasks. The light touch of his forearm on her neck earlier, as they'd stood so close at the door, had garnered almost every ounce of her attention, even with Cecilia Arends and Tommy searching for her just inches away.

"I hope you don't think it's odd for me to tell you this," she began tentatively, after they'd talked for a while. She was reclining on the pillows, having found a relatively comfortable position in the armor. "But during the summer I turned sixteen, I traveled across the country with my mother from San Diego to New York by car. I tried to live on the West Coast with my mom and my new

stepfather after my parents' divorce and my mom's remarriage, but
it didn't work. I told her it was because I'm a New Yorker at heart.
I have the city and the seasons in my bones, but in reality . . ."

She faded off.

"You didn't get along well with your new stepfather? Or your
mother?" Seth asked, his gravelly baritone sending prickles of pleasure along the back of her neck.

Gia grimaced regretfully. "Let's just say I couldn't abide by
some of my mother's life choices. At the time it was a bigger deal
than it is now. She was a very talented attorney when she was with
my dad and me. I was used to seeing her as a smart, together, accomplished woman. She threw away all of her potential, her
career—everything—to become a La Jolla trophy wife." She noticed that Seth remained very still as he watched her, his golden
eyes trained on her with a complete—and thrilling—focus. "It
was sort of hard to see, for a girl forming her own ambitions and
goals for the future, that's all," she explained ruefully. "Besides, it
was like a watershed summer for me. Developmentally. But that's
not the point," she said apologetically, recognizing she was ram-
bling. "I begged my mom to drive me back to Dad's instead of fly.
I was in my Jack Kerouac stage," she grinned. "Driving across the
country sounded very romantic to me. Mom humored me because
it kept me with her for a few days longer . . . and maybe I wanted
that too. It was a wonderful trip, just my mom and me and the long
hours on the road with the country unfolding in front of us. You
can't help but bond under those circumstances, you know? We'd
been going through some real mom-daughter drama—we *still* go
through some mom-daughter drama—but that trip . . . well, it's a
kind of touchstone for us, a wonderful memory both of us cherish,"
she trailed off wistfully.

Noticing Seth's unwavering, palpable attention on her, she hastened to continue. "In New Mexico, we stopped at one of those
roadside gas stations and stores that sell everything. I was stretch-

ing my legs and looking at some of the artwork from local artists that was on sale there, and I saw this very subtle, masterfully carved and painted sculpture of a man." Her gaze flickered over his face; she suddenly felt uncharacteristically shy. "And it just blew me away. The face. Even though the expression was so impassive, it spoke volumes to me. I bought it with all the money I had in my purse, ignoring my mother's protests. I still have it today, in my Manhattan apartment."

Seth looked vaguely amused and puzzled. "You thought I'd consider it odd for you to tell me that?"

When she recalled her meandering approach to the topic, she laughed. She'd wandered far from the central point. "No, but now you will because of my lame storytelling skills, right? My whole point is: You look like it. The carving. It's why I keep staring at you . . . I think . . ." she faded off awkwardly.

He calmly took a swallow of the water he was drinking, but kept his gaze on her. Panther eyes. That's what they reminded her of. Hypnotic. Beautiful. Warm, but also . . .

Dangerous.

"Were you near Albuquerque?" he asked.

"Uh . . . yeah, I think we were."

"There's a good chance it *was* my face, then," he said, deadpan.

"What?" she asked, laughing. She hadn't expected him to say that. She'd just thought the resemblance was an odd coincidence and wanted to offer some kind of lame excuse for why she kept gawping at him.

He shrugged his broad shoulders. "I grew up on the Isleta Pueblo Indian Reservation near there. My mother was an artist, and she used both my brother and me as models at various times. I'd have to see it to be sure, but given the time period, it's more likely me than Jake. We look alike, but my brother is a lot older than me—almost a whole generation. Jake would have been long gone by the time period you're talking about. Mom did painted wooden carvings as well as watercolors and pottery, and she sold her work at local stores."

She shook her head in disbelief. "If you're saying there's an actual chance that it's you, then it's *definitely* you. I immediately noticed it when I first saw you, but thought it was too unlikely to be true. I didn't think that man could be real." She glanced away, embarrassed she'd muttered the private thought out loud. "I just met you tonight, but I've been looking at your face all this time. That's just . . . weird."

"Weird?"

"Not in a bad way," she assured quickly.

He was handsome, but his smile transformed his hard features to drop-dead gorgeous. Her mouth hung open at the vision. Her gaze dropped over him, despite her mental command to keep her eyes in her head. His body was big, but lean, long and rangy. He exuded strength, and not only from his personality. His near-black hair was a tousled, sexy glory. Despite the finger-combed negligence of the style, the strands were smooth and shiny. It fell several inches past his chin. Her fingertips itched to touch it.

He took a long draw on his water, and Gia guiltily glanced away. She'd been gawking. Again.

"So if you decided you were a New York girl at heart, how come you came to Los Angeles for college?" he asked quietly.

"I got a good scholarship here," Gia explained, thankful he'd offered a safe topic. "I'll probably always feel a little out of place in California, but I had a good college experience."

"I know what you mean about feeling out of place."

She nodded. "I can imagine living on the reservation was a different world from Hollywood."

"I spent quite a few years in the Army and was based in several places in the Middle East and Germany, as well. But even with all the places I've lived, I felt like a being from a different planet coming to Hollywood." He smiled slightly in memory. "Luckily, I liked the work so much that I've adapted reasonably well to the alien environment."

"You don't regret it? Making your life here?" she asked him, leaning forward and grimacing slightly because the stiff breastplate pinched at her waist.

"Once in a while, but not too often. This is my dream job. To do it, I need to be here."

"You must meet dozens of wannabe actors and models and the like every day, people who have migrated here with stars in their eyes," she mused softly. "Do they ever ask your advice while you're doing their makeup?"

"About betting on the ten-billion-to-one lottery called Fame?" he asked dryly.

"You did it."

"No. I bet on my art. If fame was part of the bargain, I'd be miles away."

For a moment, they sat in silence as his low, gruff voice replayed in her head with absolute certainty.

"You never told me what you did for a living in New York. Something to do with your major?" he asked, setting aside his empty water glass. "You lit up when you mentioned you studied history."

Her gaze flickered across to a golden clock on a nearby table. It had taken them an hour and twenty minutes to get to the dreaded topic.

"My work does have to do with history." She smiled at him and took the final sip out of her second glass of champagne. He arched his brows, waiting for her to continue. Silently demanding it, actually. While they talked, Gia had grown accustomed to some of his expressions. She sighed. "You can't expect someone a few years out of undergrad to be as proud of her job as a person like you. New York isn't the easiest place in the world to rise up the ranks—not that Hollywood is either," she conceded.

His black eyebrows slanted. "Did you think I was bragging or something?" he asked, looking vaguely bemused.

"Of course not. I've had to pry every detail of your work life out of you, you're so closemouthed about the whole thing. You'd think you were a spy or something, as hard as it is to get specifics out of you," she joked, ignoring his narrowed stare. "I just meant couldn't you give me the courtesy of letting me remain interesting in your eyes just a little longer by not asking me career questions?"

"There's nothing you could say that could make you un-interesting."

Her laughter faded at his quick, confident reply along with the frank male heat in his golden eyes.

"What do you have on under that armor?" he asked suddenly.

Her eyes widened in surprise at his unexpected question. A smile flickered across his mouth, as if he'd read her stunned reaction. "You've got to be uncomfortable. I wanted to bring it up earlier, but I was selfish. I didn't want you to leave in order to change, for fear you wouldn't come back."

Heat flooded her cheeks at his compliment. "Oh . . . a tank top and shorts . . . along with the costume's pants."

He stood and set down his empty glass. He held out his hand to her. "Come on," he urged. "Let's get you out of it."

Two

His hand swallowed hers. Some of the uncertainty and strangling sexual tension she was feeling fractured when one of the joints in the armor squeaked in protest as he pulled her up off the couch. She met his stare and snorted with laughter. Smiling, he tapped on the back of her shoulder matter-of-factly.

"Turn around, Tin Man."

She spun around, every nerve in her body attuned to his presence behind her. He drew her braid over her shoulder. Had he pinched at the rope of hair, as if to better feel the texture of the strands? The small hairs on the back of her nape stood on end, hinting to her that he had. She waited with bated breath. He found the fastening at the back of her neck. His fingertips brushed a tiny fragment of her skin.

"It's funny," she said shakily. "People always focus on the makeup application. Nobody ever talks about the work involved in taking everything off."

His hand lowered and she felt him loosen the fastening at her upper back. The armor began to part.

"That's because it's the messy, boring cleanup after the party. Usually," he added gruffly under his breath.

Cool air rushed across her upper back, even as a hot flood of excitement hit her brain.

Usually. Had he meant she was the exception?

His fingertips brushed against her tank top as he pried apart the costume. She'd found the armor inflexible and awkward when Liza had pulled and pried it onto her earlier. Seth maneuvered the thin metal plates as if they were soft silk. After only seconds, he peeled the upper portion with the breastplate off her arms and chest. She took a deep inhalation of relief at the freedom, her breasts rising. It suddenly struck her just how briefly clad she was beneath the costume. It hadn't felt like that before, when she'd stripped for Liza to dress her. She rubbed her bare arms nervously as he moved behind her again. She grasped for a safe topic.

"It's very generous of you to volunteer for the Cancer Research Fund. Do you do it every year?" she asked.

"For the past several years, yeah." She wanted to turn around and see what he was doing behind her, but she was worried her expression would betray her anxiety.

"It's quite a contribution on your part, volunteering not only all of your expertise, but all the tools of your trade as well," she said.

"It's not just my contribution," he said. She heard the sound of metal clinking and realized he was setting aside the piece of armor. "My staff volunteers their time and skill as well. I don't force them to do it, but it's a worthwhile cause. And very much needed."

She turned her chin over her shoulder. She'd heard something in his voice just then.

"Do you know someone with cancer?" she asked tentatively. His stare burned into her.

"I *did*," he said after a pause. "My sister-in-law. She's gone now."

"I'm sorry," she murmured sincerely.

"It was much more of a loss for my niece. Alice was all Joy had. Except me."

"That's no small thing, I'm sure."

She forced herself to break his steady stare and face forward again. She heard him set aside the breastplate and move behind her.

"So . . . you know Cecilia Arends?" she asked, mentally damning the tremor in her voice. She was entirely too aware of Seth Hightower. The air around them seemed thick and charged.

"Why would you ask that?" he asked. For a second, she struggled to recall what they were talking about. He'd slipped long fingers beneath the waist strap of the costume. Pieces of armor were fastened over the pants and had to be removed, one part at a time. She felt the give in the armor, and he placed the hooplike pannier that covered her hips on a nearby chair. She jumped when he placed one hand on her inner thigh a second later.

"Spread your legs," he prompted gruffly.

Her eyes widened. She could tell by the location of his voice that he'd knelt behind her. An invisible tendril tickled her clit and a rush of warmth went through her sex. She strained to catch the thread of their former topic of conversation.

"It's just . . . you spoke earlier like you knew Cecilia," she said, gulping as she parted her thighs. When he didn't speak immediately, she turned cautiously and looked over her shoulder. He *was* kneeling behind her, his head at the level of her lower back. His bent legs looked long and very powerful. She could clearly see the pair of blue-tinted glasses on top of his dark, silky hair from this angle. He glanced up and met her stare as he tossed aside the armor plate he'd just removed from a thigh.

"I know her."

"Do you know her well?"

"Well enough," he said, reaching for the fastening on her other thigh.

Her brows creased as a thought struck her. "Were you *hiding* from Cecilia? When you heard her coming down the hallway. Is that why you helped me? Because you didn't want to be found either?"

"It wasn't the only reason."

"I see," she said slowly. "So you're laconic on topics outside of your work and accomplishments."

He glanced up sharply. "I'm not involved with Cecilia Arends," he said, holding her stare levelly. "Or anyone, for that matter."

Warmth rushed through her. He had understood what she needed to know. She turned back around. Cecilia Arends was beautiful and successful. She was polished and experienced, and closer to Seth's age. It wouldn't surprise her at all if there were some kind of history between the two of them. Lots of women must lust after Seth Hightower. He was very good-looking, true, but there was something about his stoicism and sheer male power that was like waving a red flag of challenge at a female.

"Why not?" she wondered, a little stunned to realize she'd spoken the thought out loud.

His hand slid beneath the fastener at her lower leg. Her eyes sprang wide when he palmed what felt like her entire calf with his big hand. "Why not *what*? Lift your heel a little," he requested.

She followed his urging, cursing the lurch of her heart inspired by his touch. He slipped the bootie attached to the foot covering— the *sabaton*—off of her.

"Why aren't you involved with anyone? I mean, is it by choice or circumstance?" she persisted.

"Circumstance. The one called I'm-too-damn-busy."

She laughed softly. "I can imagine. Have you ever done a Rill Pierce film?" she asked as he touched her other calf and she tracked every subtle nuance of his long fingers on her flesh.

"No. But I'd like to. What makes you ask? Foot up," he directed. She lifted her foot obligingly. He slid off the bootie, but then his fingers returned, briefly cupping and stroking the naked heel of her bare foot in a fleeting caress. Electricity tingled through her at the unexpected, shockingly erotic touch. He urged her to put her foot down.

"Oh . . . because I knew someone who received his scholarship while I was at UCLA, and I went and heard Pierce speak once. He's very talented. Both of you are sort of . . . men's men. I was thinking you two might work well together."

When he didn't immediately speak, she twisted her chin around anxiously. He came up behind her, going from kneeling to towering over her in a second. The vision of him rising behind her like some kind of intimidating, steely phantom ascending fast from the floor froze her breath in her lungs.

No. Seth Hightower was no ghost, nor was he just a favorite sculpture. He was a vibrant, primal, flesh-and-blood man.

"Men's men?" he repeated, standing close enough that she could see those thousands of pinpricks of amber that made his eyes whiskey-colored instead of just brown.

She nodded, temporarily speechless. He quirked a brow in a silent query.

"Big. Reserved." She hesitated. "Simmering."

"Simmering?" he said, his gaze moving slowly over her face and fastening on her lips.

"Yeah. Like something is frothing just beneath the surface, and you might . . . blow at any second," she whispered.

The silence stretched.

"Take off the pants," he said quietly.

"*What?*"

"You heard me. They're part of the costume. I want to keep it all together, or there's a chance things will get misplaced tomorrow when the delivery service comes to get them. I'll look around after I pack this and see if I can't find a robe for you."

He turned away and started to gather the armor parts. Gia was a little floored. He *was* interested in her, wasn't he? He was extremely hard to read at times. But then she recalled that squeeze of her braid, the obvious male heat in his eyes when he studied her just now, not to mention that tingling stroke on her heel.

No. She wasn't misreading him.

Her pulse began to leap in her throat as she fumbled with the fastenings on the loose pants. She drew them off and folded them. Turning around slowly, she saw Seth methodically packing the armor into a duffel bag, his back to her. She approached him.

"Here you go," she said.

"Thanks."

He barely turned from his task as he accepted the pants. Feeling very exposed in a pair of low-rise, boy-cut black briefs and a tank top, not to mention confused by Seth's intense focus elsewhere, she wandered back to the seating area. *Should she take this opportunity to go?* she wondered anxiously as she tugged at the shorts. Liza had told her to wear something brief that hugged the body. The black shorts were extremely tight. She looked down at herself anxiously. Why hadn't she noticed the way they outlined her sex before? Maybe she should sit down on the couch and put a pillow over her hips until Seth returned with the robe? She jerked on the fabric again, only to have the waistband creep down beneath the bottom of her tank top and expose the skin of her lower belly.

She wasn't wearing a bra. That fact hadn't bothered her at all when Liza had been costuming her earlier, even when a few of her coworkers came into the room in search of adhesive or a prosthetic or a certain hair color for a beard and mustache.

Seth was a professional as well, she reassured herself, as she once again looked at the back of him.

And no. She didn't want to leave.

She loved the way he looked, the way he moved. He wore a pair of jeans, a white T-shirt, a supple black leather vest, a thick platinum watch that struck her as very masculine on his strong forearms, and a pair of sturdy leather work boots. She was struck by how he moved with such graceful economy, despite his largeness.

She was also struck by how good his butt looked in his jeans.

He turned around, and she again was staring into his unyielding face. She forced her fussing hands to her sides. His gaze dropped slowly over her, and Gia felt a pleasant pressure in her body dipping in tandem with it. His stare lowered over her belly and hips and lingered between her thighs. Something hot leapt into his eyes.

So much for her concern that he'd changed his mind about finding her attractive.

His gaze wandered back up her body, scoring her. Her breasts suddenly felt very heavy and . . . obvious.

He took three steps toward her, and Gia swore her heart jumped directly into her throat.

"What about the rest?" he asked gently, one dark brow slanting.

"These"—she waved stupidly at her shorts and shirt—"are mine. They aren't part of the costume."

"I know," he said, coming closer still. "Do you want to take them off too?"

The ensuing silence throbbed in her ears. Her heart chugged like a restrained locomotive. *This is really going to happen.* Her clit prickled in anticipation.

"Yes," she replied honestly through numb lips.

He just nodded, holding her stare. Was he a magician, the way he hypnotized her?

"Take off the top first."

It felt very difficult to draw a breath, as if the air in the room had become too thick for her lungs to process. She was very aroused, but still . . . she hesitated.

"How many times have you said that to a woman after removing a costume or makeup?" she managed to ask because her tongue had gone very thick.

"Seriously?" he asked, eyebrows arched. She nodded. "Never. Do you believe me?"

"Yes," she whispered. Naïve or not, she trusted her instincts. Plus, she knew about Seth from Liza. If this were par for the course for him, Liza would have told her. "Would you believe I've never agreed to something like this before?" she croaked, her fingers playing with the bottom of her tank top.

He took another step and came to a halt. "It never crossed my mind to doubt it."

She gave him a shaky, grateful smile.

Shocked by her uncharacteristic brazenness, she pulled her tank top up over her swollen lungs and aching breasts.

His breath stuck as she dropped the tank top to the floor. She stared at him, seemingly transfixed. He stepped closer, drinking in the image of her. He laid his hand on the smooth expanse of skin above her left breast. She trembled beneath him. He felt the delicate beating of her heart. His gaze leapt to meet her stare.

"You're very lovely," he muttered, his voice breaking slightly.

Her lips parted. It was the sweetest temptation. He couldn't remove his eyes from the vision of her mouth, or how desire glazed her springtime eyes. His hand lowered over a firm breast. Her skin was like warm silk. He cradled her breast and lifted it slightly, arousal shooting through him at the sensation of her firmness and weight. A soft moan slipped past her lips. He feathered his thumb over her nipple and felt her bead against his fingertip.

"Seth?" she whispered, sounding almost as awed as he felt. He heard her wonder, but also her need for reassurance.

"*Shhh,*" he growled. "It's going to be okay."

He'd never touched a woman so intimately without having even kissed her first. Gia's mouth was an indescribable temptation. He was enjoying prolonging the anticipation of tasting her, of sinking into her sweetness . . . of debauching that innocent mouth just a little. The thought made his cock twitch and stiffen into a heavy ache.

He continued to caress her breast and finesse the nipple as he ran his other hand over her smooth shoulder and arm. He spread his hand along her back and made a study of the graceful slope of her spine and petal-soft skin. Much to his satisfaction, he felt her skin roughen beneath his touch. She leaned forward, her mouth craning up toward him.

"Stay still," he said. She blinked, and he realized intense arousal had made him sound harsh. He'd been chaining himself like never before as he sat on the couch with her, waiting on a knife's edge for the addictive vision of her smile. Removing the costume and having her exquisite body revealed to him bit by bit had been a fierce trial. He'd needed the moment of carefully packing the costume to bring himself under control. Turning around and seeing her standing there, so lovely and vulnerable, had smashed that control to bits. She'd called it like a pro earlier. He *was* about to explode in unregulated lust.

She reached for him, but he gently placed her arms back at her side. He resumed stroking her soft skin and taut curves.

"Let me touch you for a moment. I'm enjoying this," he explained quietly when he saw her bemusement. "Are you?"

"God, yes," she whispered.

He leaned down until their faces were only inches apart. "You're so beautiful," he said gruffly, as if telling her an intimate secret. He felt her tremble beneath his hands. "Your mouth is killing me. I can't wait to taste you." He held both her breasts in his hands and lifted them slightly, peering down to examine the fat, pink, erect nipples between his dark fingers. His cock lurched against the confines of his clothing. "Everywhere," he assured her, as hunger clawed at him deeper.

She gave a muffled moan and reached up to touch his hair. Her fingers delved into the strands greedily. His scalp prickled in awareness. A cascade of sensation flowed down his body, tickling the root of his cock. Blood pulsed into his flesh. He growled and encircled her in his arms. She cried out softly in surprise when he lifted her off her feet. He set her atop a nearby low ottoman. She steadied herself by grasping his shoulders.

They were at the same height now. He ran both his hands along her back and the sides of her ribs while he stared directly into her face.

"Look at you," he whispered thickly.

She blinked and glanced to the side into one of several mirrors. He stared at her face while she watched the reflection of him massaging and caressing her back and waist and breasts. Her skin was incredibly smooth, pale with peachy-pink undertones. His hands couldn't seem to get enough of touching her taut planes and lush curves. The blush on her cheeks deepened as she watched in the mirror while he molded her to his hands.

"You're so big," she whispered, trailing his hands with her gaze, as though caught in a spell. He captured one of her breasts and shaped it to his palm.

"You're so little. But you fit me perfectly." He feathered her nipple with his forefinger, and she gasped.

"Your fingers are calloused."

He paused, worried he was making her uncomfortable, his rough fingers against her silky skin—

"It feels so good," she said in a rush, and he resumed stroking her, stepping closer. He pressed his cock between the juncture of her thighs. She was a sweet, soft harbor, and he was hard. So hard. He gritted his teeth as the hurt in him mounted. Her grip tightened on his shoulders.

He pressed his mouth to her neck and smooth shoulder, intent on ravishing her. Over her shoulder, he saw a reflection of her from behind, his hands on the back of her waist, his mouth moving hungrily on her elegant neck, strands of his dark hair spilling on her shoulder. Relishing the anticipation, he slowly peeled the shorts over her bottom and partially down her thighs. The vision of her pale, taut ass in the reflection sent a sharp spike of sexual anticipation through him.

"Seth?" Her shaky query made him straighten and look into her face. "Kiss me. *Please*."

"Part your lips," he demanded, lust beginning to cut at him relentlessly.

He watched her with a feral stare as she opened her mouth. He cupped her buttocks and pressed her tight against him. His cock lurched viciously at the sensation.

"Jesus, you're sweet," he grated out, massaging her ass. He plucked at her plump lower lip hungrily and groaned. "You should be punished for having a mouth like this," he told her, smiling slightly as he nibbled at her. "You've been making me crazy with it all night."

"I have?" she asked, her breath falling across his lips. "I was wondering if you were affected at all." She bit at his lower lip, and he groaned roughly.

"I haven't been affected like this for a long, long time," he assured her, grinding his erection against her as blatant evidence. She moaned. Surrendering to the inevitable, he slid his tongue into her mouth, savoring and claiming at once.

God, it was good. He'd known she would be delicious, and she'd surpassed his expectations. He dipped into her wet heat with a firm, suggestive rhythm, coaxing her to join him. He sucked, calling another moan from her throat. Still gripping her ass in his hands, he moved her against him in a mind-blowing rhythm. She joined him in the subtle sexual dance, gyrating her hips against his erection and tangling her tongue with his.

He was going to eat her alive. Her singular taste was doing strange things to him. He reluctantly released her ass. Framing her jaw with his hands, he molded her mouth to his, sucking and piercing and stroking, his lust sharp and exposed.

"This is going to be so good," he grated out at the same time he gripped her braid and pulled. She arched her neck back willingly. He pressed his mouth to her throat, the tiny whimpers vibrating against his lips maddening him. His mouth closed over her fluttering pulse as he took her breasts in his hands again. She jerked her hands on his shoulders as if she'd just remembered she had them. Frantically, she began pushing at his vest, her fingers burrowing beneath the crew neck of his T-shirt. Her obvious desire made him see red for a moment.

He leaned up and gathered both her wrists, lifting her hands off him. It was hard enough to keep his head without her hands stroking and rubbing his skin and her nails scratching his nerves into a frenzy. He held her stare as he pushed her hands to her middle back.

"Stay still now while I touch you," he said. "Keep your hands here."

He waited for a moment, studying her reaction to his demand closely. She watched him with huge eyes, her lips and cheeks flushed, her high, firm, pink-tipped breasts rising and falling as she panted shallowly. Slowly, he released her. A small smile of approval shaped his mouth when she kept her wrists at the middle of her back. Even though her eyes were wary, her mouth flickered with returned warmth.

"That's right, I only want to make you feel good," he assured her gruffly next to her lips as their breath mingled and he ran his hands along her sides, stroking her with his fingertips. She quaked. He ground his teeth together. Her excitement was like a stimulant in his blood. His brain pounded with it.

Unable to resist, he cupped her ass again, holding her stare, his cock pulsing as he shaped her flesh to his palms. His mouth curled into a snarl. She bit off a whimper. He forced the shorts down her legs. When they fell to her ankles, she stepped out of them. He held her steady with his hands at her hips and ass, plucking and nipping at her lush lips. He dipped his tongue between them, still watching her. She moaned feverishly.

"Are you getting wet?" he asked, between biting at her sweet lips.

"Yes," she whispered hotly, craning forward slightly to catch his mouth. "Let me touch you."

"Tonight we'll focus on you," he rasped, sinking his tongue into the warm, velvety depths of her mouth again. "I could spend a lifetime focusing on you."

His hands settled on her hips, and he looked down at her, eating up the vision of her pale, smooth skin, slender waist and curving hips. Her legs were long, the muscles toned. His nostrils flared as he stared at the light-brown trimmed thatch of hair between shapely thighs. He tightened his hold on her and brought her against him. She ground her hips against his cock, gyrating subtly, stroking him through his clothing. He lightly swatted a plump ass cheek, watching her reaction. She blinked in surprise. She wasn't used to being spanked. Vivid color bloomed in her cheeks.

But she liked it, he thought with savage triumph.

He lifted his head, still watching her, and slid his hand down the crack of her ass and between her thighs.

"Spread your legs," he said tensely. She responded wordlessly.

He growled low in his throat as his seeking fingers were coated in warm honey. He pierced her with his finger. She whimpered.

"You weren't acting. You're warm and wet, and *so* tight," he said through a clenched jaw as he stroked her.

"Oh God," she said shakily, a wild, helpless expression on her face. "I don't know why I'm doing this."

"Because you wanted to take a risk," he said, biting gently at her bee-stung lower lip. He touched the side of her breast with his free hand and found a hard nipple, pinching at it as he continued to plunge his finger into her drenched, snug sheath. "And because we wanted each other. Period." He kissed her again, hard and deep. She moaned into his mouth, the vibrations thrilling his nerves. She flexed her hips against his cock, grinding herself against him, and made a wild sound of frustration. For a second, his vision darkened.

When his haze of lust cleared, he was holding her in his hands just above her waist, his arm muscles rigid, and the tip of her breast was in his mouth. His tongue lashed at a puckering nipple, and miraculously, she tightened more for him. She squirmed against him, thrashing his nerves, gasping his name in quiet desperation. Her fingers dug into his hair and scratched his scalp, making him growl against her firm, soft flesh. Her nipple popped out from be-tween his lips, the vision of the glistening, dark pink flesh only adding to his madness. He couldn't wait to get inside her.

Instead, he pulled her an inch higher against his body and transferred his attention to her other breast. As much as his cock hurt, he couldn't resist the allure of tasting as much of her as he could.

Jesus.

He'd lifted her against him as if she weighed nothing, his desire single-minded. The feeling of his hot, wet mouth enclosing her nipple and his firm suck made her hips jerk in arousal like an elec-trical shock had gone through her. His tongue pressed and laved at the sensitive nipple. She writhed against his solid body, helpless in the grip of undiluted lust and pleasure. He tugged gently on the crest with his mouth, his tongue a warm, wet lash one moment, gentle and coaxing the next.

Gia gripped at his head mindlessly, sensation flooding her con-sciousness. Trying desperately to ground herself from this dizzying descent into the very core of desire, she opened her eyes. Instead, seeing the image of them together plunged her straight into the center of lust. She gasped, staring into one of the mirrors at the vision of Seth holding her against him, ravishing her.

He was completely dressed and she was naked. Her face was flushed; her expression dazed. Her feet dangled several inches off the ottoman as he took his fill of her. His hands looked dark and masculine gripping her feminine curves.

It was the very image of a woman being debauched by a man, and thoroughly loving it. Yet there was nothing depraved about it. His desire was concentrated and unrelenting, but . . . *pure* somehow.

She said his name when he released her aching nipple from his taut suck and transferred to her other breast, still holding her up like a feast for his mouth, pressing her to him. She had the impression that although he was unusually powerful, it was his desire that gave him the strength to hold her suspended that way.

He was a man determined to get his fill.

The thought fired her. She squirmed against him, aroused even more by the feeling of his cock through his clothing. It was like the rest of him, big and hard and frothing her senses. Her hunger mounting, she reached downward, finding his waistband. She ripped at his button fly savagely, wild to undress him. His low, guttural groan thrilled her. His lips slipped over her nipple, his tongue lingering in a caress. Then he was moving and setting her down gently on the couch.

She stared up at him, panting. He watched her while he reached into his back pocket and withdrew his wallet. Dazedly, she realized he was retrieving a condom.

He finished what she'd started, drawing up the hem of his T-shirt over a taut, ridged belly and unfastening his jeans. He shoved them roughly around his thighs. Her breath froze. He wore a pair of boxer briefs beneath the jeans, the cloth looking starkly white against his olive-toned, hair-sprinkled, powerful thighs. Gia was no expert on men's underwear, but Seth's possessed a front panel that seemed to be made to accommodate his size. She could see the outlines of his cock through the clinging cotton. The staff was thick and long, heavy enough to fall forward several inches and tent the fabric. The crown was fat, the cap clearly defined even through the boxer briefs.

She stared, enthralled.

Even as his fingers slipped beneath the waistband of the underwear, she reached forward and caressed the tempting, swollen head through the fabric. His cock jumped at her touch. She encircled the head and gave a small, erotic tug on the base of the crown.

She looked up into his face and smiled.

A muscle jumped in his rigid cheek. He jerked the cotton down over his erection to his thighs. He straightened before her, his gaze on her, scorching.

"Go on," he said quietly, but she needed no encouragement. Her hand already encircled him. A thrill shot through her. He was warm and hard and pulsing. She squeezed him tight experimentally. He grunted softly as she pistoned her fist up and down the stalk for a moment. She felt his avid gaze on her from above. It mounted her excitement. Fascinated by the sensation of him—the sheer weight and texture—she wrapped her other hand around the fleshy crown, using her fingers to trace the succulent rim. One swollen vein ran the length of his cock, amply feeding his arousal, and she followed that with a fingertip as well. He groaned, low and rough. She began to pump the staff while she continued to make a study of the head with her fingertips. She leaned forward on the couch, spellbound. Her lips parted.

He hissed. She blinked in surprise because he was suddenly moving, sitting on the couch next to her.

He lifted her onto his thighs. With a hand on the back of her head, he immediately pushed her down to his mouth. She moaned feverishly as their tongues rubbed and dueled and tangled. He tasted so good. His kiss drugged her. He was so hot, sending up her fever of excitement.

He opened his hand along the side of her head and jaw and sealed their kiss.

"I have to have you now," he declared gruffly.

"I have to have you too," she squeaked, glancing down at his lap. His heavy erection had fallen against his belly and T-shirt.

"Hold it up for me," he instructed her quietly, hastily tearing open the condom package. She reached for the base of the staff. He shaved. The edge of her hand pressed against round, firm testicles, the skin over them tautly drawn. She found the sensation exciting. She found *everything* about him exciting. When he'd unrolled the clear condom most of the way down, she moved her hand. She couldn't resist running her hand over his balls curiously.

He groaned and reached for her hips.

"Come here," he growled.

She raised up over him, her knees on the couch beside his hips, trying to adjust to him. He took control, guiding her with one hand spread on her hip and buttock, the other fisting his cock.

"Right there," he mumbled thickly when she was suspended over him. "Stay still a moment." Her hands on his shoulders, she watched with bated breath as he reached between her thighs. He sunk his forefinger into her channel.

Her thighs quivered and she bit off a moan. Almost immediately, he withdrew, his finger coated in her juices. He used the ridge of the lubricated finger to give her clit a firm rub.

"*Oh.*" Her hips flexing against the delicious pressure. He watched her narrowly for a moment while he expertly rubbed her clit and she gasped in pleasure.

"You're more than ready," he said. Gia agreed wholeheartedly. He cupped her hip again. She gritted her teeth in unbearable excitement as she watched him present the head of his cock to her slit. She pushed with her hips, forcing her tissues to part for his hard

flesh. The crown slid into her. She moaned uncontrollably. The
pressure was intense.

"It's okay, be patient," he urged, obviously sensing how hard
she was pushing . . . how huge her hunger to have him inside her
was. He grasped her hips with both hands and bounced her very
gently with his tensed arms. She found it intensely exciting. After
a moment, he paused. He cupped her ass in his palms and lifted her
buttocks, parting her further.

Their moans twined as she eased down on the rigid staff.

She looked into his face while she lowered down onto his cock,
but he was watching their sexes fuse. His face was a paradox of
profound, wild lust and rigid restraint. She was on top, but he was
in control. His arm muscles bunched round and tight as he took
much of her weight with his hold on her ass and hips. He didn't
shove her down onto his cock, but nevertheless, his stark determination to be inside her was clear.

She whimpered at the increasing feeling of fullness and pressure, unprecedented for her.

He paused with only inches to go and met her stare. It wasn't
an apology she saw in his gaze precisely, but it was a bid for understanding. And she *did* understand. Who could deny the storm of
need that had swept them both into its grip?

He gripped her ass and flexed his hips, sinking his cock to the
hilt. She cried out shakily. He lowered his hold, clutching her buttocks from below. He never paused, but immediately began lifting
and lowering her weight while he subtly pumped his hips up and
down in a wicked counter rhythm. Gia could only imagine her
expression at that moment. Was it the look of thrilled terror and
sharp excitement a person gets when a roller-coaster ride crests and
then abruptly drops? She opened her mouth—

"*Don't* scream, Gia," Seth said sharply.

At the last second, she choked off her scream and made a sort of muffled wail instead. He never paused fucking her with short, powerful strokes. She bounced on top of him, her entire world rocking. She stared into his face helplessly. He looked hard and strained, his jaw clenched.

"I just don't want anyone to interrupt this," he said to explain his harsh command.

"God no," she said wildly. "Oh my *God*," she muttered disbelievingly when he thrust into her with more force and their skin slapped together tautly. The almost unbearable friction was turning into a delicious, hot burn. She tightened her hold on his shoulders and pumped against him, desperate to increase the tension building in her.

"That's right," he said thickly, and suddenly he was hugging her waist, leaning forward slightly and gathering her to him. Their rhythm hardly broke, but suddenly his mouth was on her neck, hot and possessive, his teeth scraping against her sensitive skin and fueling her fire. He'd taken the undisputed lead again, hugging her to him, lifting her up and down on his cock with his hold on her waist. He brought her higher up on his cock and plunged back into her, her ass popping in his lap. He repeated that wicked stroke again and again. Gia hugged his rock-hard shoulders as pleasure pounded into her.

He was relentless. She loved it. She felt his chin move on her shoulder. He thrust her down on his staff and made a harsh sound of pleasure. He lifted her, and she heard him groan gutturally. Staring dazedly over his shoulder, she looked at the image in a mirror behind her, facing Seth. It was a reflection of a reflection. He was fixedly watching in the mirror in front of him as his cock plunged in and out of her.

She should have been insulted, but she wasn't. Instead, she joined him in watching, captivated by the erotic image. His cock looked ruddy and flagrant next to her pale buttocks and thighs. She made a choked sound of arousal and leaned back slightly, keening softly at the new angle . . . still watching in the mirror. He searched her face. Suddenly he paused in his wicked pace and glanced over his shoulder. Their gazes met in the mirror.

He, too, knew she'd been watching them.

For an electric few seconds, he held her down in his lap, his cock fully embedded in her, her stare melded to his. She saw a slight snarl shape his mouth, and then he was turning back to her, leaning back on the couch. His hands moved back to her hips and ass, and he was driving back into her again and again, slamming her down into his lap with a strange combination of raw force and a subtle, yet precise, circular motion of both of their hips. It pushed her right to the edge of climax.

"You liked watching it, too, didn't you, Bright Eyes?" he growled between white clenched teeth.

For a moment, she couldn't answer. She was overwhelmed by the hard, relentless friction of his cock. The frantic, fast slaps of their bodies crashing together beat like a warning tattoo in her ears, matching her heartbeat . . . surpassing it.

"Answer me," he said as she continued to rise and fall over him like a bobbing cork in a raging sea. She was going to drown in the storm of it.

"Yes," she managed, her nails biting into his shoulders. "I loved it."

His right-handed grip on her ass shifted to her hip. His thumb reached around the front of her. He rubbed her clit with a bull's-eye precision. Orgasm crashed into her, sending jagged shudders of pleasure through her flesh.

"That's right. Give in to it," she heard him say tautly, as if from a distance.

His mouth clamped on her breast, his tongue laving her nipple with a hard pressure. She cried out sharply in surprised bliss as her climax amplified impossibly higher.

* * *

It was like starting out thinking you'd take a nice little pleasure cruise and instead finding yourself on the adventure of a lifetime.

Feeling Gia convulse around his cock as she came sent him straight into a sexual berserk. Pleasure pounded at him from all directions, her whimpers and cries of release cutting through his sexual haze like piercing missiles. He boiled in a vat of need.

He shouldn't have done it, but he was mindless with arousal in those seconds. A deep, insistent voice called out to him to claim her even more thoroughly. He didn't think about it at the moment. It wasn't rational. Only monumental lust and desire could have given him the strength and will to do it. When the teeth-gnashing spasms of her clamping channel eased some, and her sweet cries slowed, he lifted his head from her breast and gathered her in his arms. Barely suppressing a vicious curse, he lifted her off his cock.

She cried out as if in pain.

"*Shhh,*" he soothed, although his voice hardly sounded calming, but rough from his restraint and rising misery. He gently heaved her supple, soft body onto the couch, her back on the cushions, her hips next to his, her legs still draping across his lap.

"Seth?" she asked. She sounded disoriented from her climax and his abrupt altering of her position. He lifted her legs off of him high enough so he could stand and move between them.

"Don't worry, I'm coming right back," he assured with grim amusement. "There's no way this is going to end until I'm back inside your sweet little pussy. Spread your thighs," he urged, moving between her legs and coming down over her. She followed his instructions, but he was helping, parting her long legs to accommodate him as he placed one knee between the back of the sofa and her hip. Before he braced his arms, he glanced between her thighs and bit off a snarl.

The vision of her exposed pink, glossy sex was like mainlining a stimulant into his blood. He knew only one thing: an absolute mandate to *get back in there*.

One leg bent and still on the floor, he placed a hand next to her head, bracing himself. He guided the head of his cock into her slit.

A shudder of pleasure quaked his flesh as he drove back into her.

"God," he moaned gutturally. His harsh exclamation twined with her shaky cry. Bracing himself with both hands, he began to drive into heaven. Pleasure hazed his consciousness. He focused on her face with effort. She watched him with a wild, fierce expression, her beautiful eyes shining. Her pink lips parted. He wanted to sink his tongue into that tempting target. He wanted to taste her everywhere and absorb her cry . . . Claim it as his.

It was cutting at him that he couldn't do those things *and* take his fill of her all at once. He was helpless at the eye of the inferno, and for now, the most he could do was burn. Might as well submit to the firestorm.

Using his boot for traction on the floor, he rocketed into her. She mewled with pleasure, gripping onto his hips and using her strength to drive him harder, higher, faster, her head lifting off the couch.

"Seth."

Her head fell back, bouncing on the cushions. Her entire body was jolted with the strength of his possession. He saw her gaze focus on the ceiling, a stunned expression combining with her rapturous one. She was *watching* them again, this time on that damn mirror on the ceiling. The distilled arousal shining in her eyes was too much. He felt that dreaded, yet longed-for tingling in his balls.

"We look good together, don't we?" he snarled as he thrust deep inside her.

She yelped, her eyes going wide. He thought he might under-stand why. He'd never felt so heavy, so swollen with need. She gripped onto his ass and pulled him to her with surprising strength, using her hold to tilt her hips up.

Jesus.

He barely cut off a throat-tearing roar, muffling it to a groan as orgasm slashed through him. His body was paralyzed for a mo-ment as it roared through him. Acting purely on instinct, he began to move again when the first wave passed, fucking her while he came and staring down at her face. She cried out sharply. His eyes rolled into the back of his head when he felt her squeezing him while he ejaculated.

God bless it, she was perfect. She was coming for him again.

She stared at the enthralling image of Seth taking her without constraint. She hardly recognized herself. Could that wanton, shameless female whose body quaked against the couch cushions as she submitted wholly to a near stranger *really* be Gia Harris?

She knew the second when he began to feel the urge to finally explode. She *saw* it. His expression grew even fiercer. In the mirror, she saw his smooth, muscular buttocks contract extra-tight, super-powering his already strong thrusts. Her body jolted as he rocketed into her. It was so much—*he* was—and yet she wanted *more*. She tilted her hips back and spread her legs wider in the air, offering everything. Sliding her hands over ridged muscle and narrow hips, she gripped the dense, flexing muscles of his ass greedily, squeezing his buttocks and pushing him to her.

When she looked up at herself in the reflection on the ceiling, her expression was wild. Then she saw nothing as she clamped her eyelids shut. His rough groan combined with the sensation of his cock convulsing high inside her made her muscles strain tight. His pelvis ground against her outer sex in a subtle circular motion, sending a jolt of pressure through her clit.

Then he was fucking her again, and all thought left her as she climaxed.

The next thing she knew he was nuzzling her ear and kissing her temple and cheek. She opened her eyes sluggishly. Seth lifted his head and met her stare. His eyes were light and dark at once, she realized muzzily, like the night sky lit by thousands and thousands of glowing stars.

"That was . . ." She faded off because her lips felt strange and uncooperative, and her throat was sore—perhaps from holding in tearing screams of pleasure?

Besides, words failed her.

"It was amazing," he finished for her without hesitation. The sound of his deep, gruff voice and absolute certainty made her focus on his compelling face.

"I've never done anything like that before," she said honestly. What had just occurred slowly started to penetrate her haze of arousal and tickle at rational thought.

"You don't witness falling stars every day," he said dryly.

"You mean it's only going to happen once?" she asked worriedly, lifting her head off the cushion.

"*Shhh,*" he hushed, a small smile ghosting his mouth. He brushed her hair back from her face. His gentle caress should have soothed her. Instead, his cherishing touch, lambent stare and god-awful-sexy smile made desire flicker across her nerves like heat lightning on the night sky. Encroaching logic slinked back into the shadows.

He leaned down and brushed his lips against hers. She inhaled the intoxicating, male scent coming off his skin and wondered what the hell was happening to her.

"The rarity I was referring to is you and me together. What just happened is going to happen many, *many* more times," he assured her before he covered her mouth with his.

Gia never could claim that he'd broken that promise. It *did* happen again and again later that night and the next morning in Seth's bed at his attractive and comfortable Silver Lake home.

He'd also said he would call her after she returned to New York. That was a promise Seth Hightower never kept.

Three

~~~

Seth had promised himself he'd be free for Charles Trew's visit at three o'clock, no matter what catastrophe occurred in the makeup room today. Luckily, his partner in Hightower Special Effects—his niece, Joy—had promised to cover for him for the meeting.

Charles was an old friend from their Army intelligence days, and was now the assistant district attorney in charge of Special Operations for the County of Los Angeles. Seth could immediately tell from Charles's brisk manner on the phone that he wasn't calling to get together to watch a football game, rehash their old Army days and shoot the shit. No, Seth had a sinking feeling his friend was calling him for a consultation.

It wasn't that Seth was against helping out for a good cause when the situation arose. He'd done it before. There weren't that many ex-intelligence operatives who possessed Seth's specific skills for disguise, after all. It was just that he was on the final day of a grueling schedule. Not for just any movie either, but a high-budget zombie flick. They were reshooting two short, but major, scenes that involved a lot of special effects makeup. A horde of zombies and free time just didn't go hand in hand, not for the co-head of the makeup department.

Seth finally peeled off a silicone throat-and-chest prosthetic from an actress and replaced it carefully on a stand. He glanced up and saw Charles walking toward his station.

"That's it, Sherry. You're officially back to being a human for good. Thanks for all your patience, and congrats on finishing up," he told the actress.

"Thanks, Seth. You too. It's been so great working with you. I hope I get the chance to work with you on another project sometime soon. Good luck with the rest of the day, and I'll see you at the party later?"

"Sure," Seth said when Sherry went on tiptoe and gave him a brief hug and kiss.

Activity in the lab was high today, given their tight final-day shooting schedule. Seth saw Charles approaching in the midst of the chaos. Without a spec of blood and gore on his conservative suit and with his meticulously neat, modernized crew cut, Charles looked like zombie bait approaching.

Sherry turned to go and halted, smirking slightly when she noticed Charles's startled expression as he stared at her. She unhurriedly finished buttoning her "bloody" costume shirt over her bare breasts and walked away.

Charles whistled softly under his breath and met Seth's amused stare.

"I knew I should have gone into showbiz instead of law school after the Army. You have all the luck," Charles mumbled, still gazing after the departing actress. "Who *was* that? Anyone I should know?"

"I doubt Cara thinks so," Seth replied, referring to Charles's wife of eight years and Seth's friend.

"I didn't mean should I *get* to know her. I meant is she famous? I couldn't recognize her with her hair under wraps like that and all the paint."

"I doubt you'd be able to come up with an identification by

staring at her tits and ass," Seth said without an ounce of inflection in his voice.

"Yeah, but it never hurts to scan the whole territory," Charles replied, turning to him with a broad grin. Seth chuckled and began scrubbing his hands and forearms briskly in a nearby sink. He'd bunked with Charles in basic training and served with him for three out of his five years in Army Human Intelligence in Iraq and Afghanistan. It was enough time in the trenches for Charles to know when Seth was ribbing him and when he wasn't.

"Is Joy around?" Charles asked. He'd met Seth's niece on several occasions. Seth had told him during their recent phone conversation that he'd asked Joy to join him in heading Hightower Special Effects.

"She's doing some fabrication for me so I could meet with you." Seth toweled off and stuck out his hand in a belated greeting.

Charles shook it warmly. "Which I can't thank you enough for in advance. If you can help us out with this in any way, there are quite a few others who will be lining up to thank you as well."

"Let's go over to my office and talk. I assume this is top secret business?" Seth asked dryly, but to no effect. Charles had become distracted yet again. A few feet away, a female extra had whipped off her robe in preparation for a prosthetic application. Charles stared as she stood there wearing nothing but a nearly nonexistent G-string, while one of Seth's female artists started to paint adhesive on her chest with a brush in preparation for an application.

Charles sighed and waved Seth in front of him. "I really did pick the wrong job," he said resignedly.

Charles sat in front of Seth's desk in the ad hoc office he shared with Joy, cradling a cup of coffee between his bent legs. The din of the makeup room was muffled to a hum in here, but they still spoke in low voices. As Charles began talking, an uncomfortable, tight feeling had started to rise in Seth's chest. He had a feeling he knew why Charles was visiting him.

Knew *who* this whole meeting was about. He found himself both dreading and wishing for Charles to just say her name out loud.

"I was wondering if you were working on the McClarin case," Seth told Charles quietly after they'd talked for ten minutes. "I haven't noticed your name in the papers. Nice job on the indictment."

"We didn't get him for a fraction of what we wanted to pin on him. We're glad to have *something* solid to get Sterling McClarin out of circulation. So are the feds. The FBI is still building their own case for suspected white-collar crimes involving that multibillion-dollar cult of his. Both Madeline and the FBI are hoping our case will discredit him with the public and his followers, and witnesses will start to come forward as things begin to crumble around McClarin," Charles explained, referring to Madeline Harrington, his boss, the Los Angeles County district attorney. "But we haven't nailed McClarin yet. There's a little matter of the trial. And if you've been reading the papers or caught the news, you must realize what a media frenzy it's turning into."

"Thanks to your high-profile witness," Seth said, frowning.

Charles's gaze flickered up to meet his. "Exactly. The darling and icon of young adults across the globe, Gia Harris." Charles flourished his hand drolly before he took a sip of coffee. "McClarin sure screwed himself big time by giving in to temptation with Harris in his vicinity."

There. Her name had been said out loud. This *was* about Gia. Seth took a long draw on his water.

"Have you ever worked with her on a movie?" Charles asked.

"No," Seth replied shortly.

He had suspected the day would arise when he came face-to-face with Gia again. She was an actress—a truth she'd glaringly omitted on that single electrical night they'd spent together two years ago.

Since then she'd made the leap from Broadway to Hollywood and rocketed to the top of the A-list after her debut role in a legendary blockbuster young adult film. She'd rapidly moved on to more adult roles and huge stardom. He'd wondered if he would ever run into her again. He'd assumed if he did, it would be on a movie set or a chance meeting at a party or something. Not that Seth partied with the Hollywood elite much. He tended to avoid glamorous bashes like the plague.

He would never have guessed in a million years that he would run up against the vivid memory of Gia under these bizarre circumstances.

"Did you hear what happened yesterday?" Charles asked.

Seth nodded soberly. "She's had a mob of reporters and photographers hounding her ever since the news broke about her being your star witness against Sterling McClarin. A high-profile young movie star testifying in a lurid trial involving the forty-year-old charismatic leader of a modern day 'religion' raping the fourteen-year-old daughter of two of his followers? It's got all the makings of a media frenzy. Gia can't go into hiding because she began filming this week on a blockbuster Joshua Cabot movie. Yesterday, a couple of overeager members of the press drove her car off the road."

Charles nodded grimly.

"Is she okay?" Seth asked quietly.

"Yeah. Her driver was a little beat up, but Gia wasn't hurt physically. Whether it got to her mentally is another matter. She's been through a lot in the past few months. I'm glad you've been following the case. Saves me the effort of explaining the background."

Seth quirked his brows in sarcastic amusement. "Everybody in the country is following it. This thing is bigger than the O.J. Simpson spectacle. It's being shoved down our throat by the media everywhere we turn. You'd have to live in a hole not to know about the New Temple and Sterling McClarin and how Hollywood's sweetheart is taking part in his downfall."

Charles nodded. "Therein lies the problem. Everybody in the country is following it. What's worse, my boss is concerned that an 'accident' like what occurred yesterday could potentially be more than what it seems."

Seth sat forward. "You suspect Gia Harris was run off the road intentionally?"

"We don't have any proof of that. But the New Temple has some avid followers and a long reach," he said, referring to McClarin's pseudoreligious organization.

Seth scowled. Didn't he know it?

"Can't you get Harris into protective custody or something?" Seth asked.

"She has police protection, something she's really starting to resent now that she started shooting a film. She's not really a candidate for the U.S. Marshall's Witness Security Program. There isn't any kind of tangible threat to her life. Even if she were a candidate, she'd never agree to leaving her career and starting over again in Boise, Idaho, or Amarillo, Texas."

"And give up all her fame and fortune?" Seth asked with grim amusement. "Not likely."

"Exactly. And Sterling McClarin is no godfather of organized crime or a gangbanger. More like a spider. He's not going to whack a witness, especially when it's someone as high profile as Gia Harris, and the world has both of them under a microscope right now. He knows as well as anyone how bad that'd make him look. Sterling McClarin and the New Temple have a lot of tentacles in the show business community, though. A disturbing amount. The DA—and the FBI on a more-removed level—is more concerned about one of McClarin's minions 'influencing' our witness in some way to change her testimony than actually eliminating her altogether."

"Either that, or engineer some scenario to make Gia look bad in the public eye," Seth said.

"You've got it. You probably know that circumstances being what they are, there were huge challenges for jury selection. Judge Halloran has already selected a jury and alternates, although the trial probably won't begin for three to five weeks. The jury has repeatedly been instructed by Halloran about avoiding media and any queries about the case, but with a furor this loud, we're worried a juror would have to be a hermit not to be influenced."

"It seems to me McClarin and his followers were hard at work trying to defame Gia *before* jury selection," Seth said with a sharp look, referring to a recent rumor that had been circulated in the tabloids about Gia having a drug problem. It'd died out quickly enough.

"You caught that, huh?"

Seth nodded. "There's no truth to the rumors, right?" he asked. He somehow doubted that fresh, beautiful girl could ever succumb to drug addiction, but who knew? Hollywood was a cruel, ruthless place to exist. Many couldn't survive it.

"No. We've been fortunate in that. Harris has a squeaky-clean record. Even the smallest smudge on it might have been fuel for the defense team."

Seth took a sip of water, considering. "McClarin *is* a spider. A big, nasty, dangerous one," Seth stated unequivocally. He noticed Charles's upraised brows at his venom. "One of McClarin's 'knights' tried to recruit Joy's husband."

"Everett Hughes?" Charles asked, looking startled by the news. Seth nodded, distractedly studying his water glass.

Joy was his niece, but she was more like his younger sister. They were much closer in age than most uncles and nieces. For years, they'd been the only family each other had. Joy had married superstar Everett Hughes almost a year ago. Seth had never made it a secret that he thought it wise to avoid actors in the romantic arena, especially ones of Everett Hughes's caliber. He hadn't hesitated to warn Joy of the potential pitfalls. Movie stars were a different breed from everyday humanity, in his considerable experience. Fortunately, Everett was one in a million—a megastar with his feet planted firmly on the ground and a family-and-friends structure that had insulated him from the pitfalls of narcissism and sycophantic followers. It had been an unlikely match, and one that Seth hadn't approved of initially. He couldn't complain at the end result though. Joy was euphorically happy with Everett, and if Joy was happy, Seth was. Still, he'd been personally offended at even the slightest chance of the shadow of the New Temple darkening Joy's world.

Not that it had ever been a remote possibility, Everett had reminded him repeatedly with exacerbated, pointed irony.

Still, neither Joy nor Everett suspected the subtly dangerous threat a cult like the New Temple represented. Not like Seth did.

Gia Harris wasn't family. She was a far cry from it. Seth barely knew her, aside from being inexplicably powerfully attracted to her one night years ago. He didn't *want* to be concerned for Gia like he had been for Joy.

But he was.

"Everett didn't realize he was dealing with a New Temple higher-up, until he was offered instant exclusive entry into the inner secrets of the Golden Realm . . . that fantasyland every initiate is brainwashed into craving like it's crack," Seth added derisively.

"Hughes would be the perfect recruitment idol. Scary to consider it ever happening, actually. Good thing Hughes has a head on his shoulders and recognized what was going on."

"The DA is right to worry about your witness. And not just because of the overlap of the God complex and star complex. McClarin might be subtler than having her fitted for cement shoes, but he'd likely find some way to influence either her or the public. Bribes. Blackmail. A setup for bad publicity. Most celebrities aren't as impervious as my nephew-in-law. Trust me on that."

"So you'll help us?" Charles asked quietly.

Seth hesitated. "Like before . . . on the Mianaco case?" Mianaco was easily recognized from the press surrounding his trial, but he was no Gia Harris. It would be a challenge to disguise one of the most recognizable faces in the country.

It was a face *he'd* certainly never forget.

"You're getting the gist of it," Charles said with a grin.

Seth had not only helped out Charles and Madeline in the past but also consulted and assisted the FBI. Many of his friends and coworkers in Army intelligence had gone into legal, criminal investigation and intelligence-related work after leaving the Army. Surgical alteration and disguise were being used more and more in sticky proceedings, given the pervasiveness of camera phones, social media and surveillance equipment on almost every corner. It was becoming increasingly difficult for a marked man or woman to merely disappear from one location and reappear unnoticed in another.

Seth was no longer a government employee, but given his unique skill set and background in intelligence, people he knew who worked in investigative and legal capacities sometimes asked for his expert help. Usually a consultation and conference with the organization's disguise expert was all that was required, but on a few notable occasions, Seth had been more deeply involved.

"Things are getting way too hot for Gia to stay in L.A. and go on her merry way," Charles said. "The trial won't begin for several weeks, at the earliest. Until then, we want her to fall off the map. In order to make Gia Harris disappear, though, we need you."

"What about the movie she's doing?"

Charles grunted softly and shifted in his chair. "Luckily,

Madeline has a far reach in the show business community. She was a sorority sister with Joshua Cabot's wife, and they still socialize on occasion. She's been in conference with Cabot, who has opened talks with United Studio. They've agreed to put off production of *Interlude* until Gia has gotten through the bulk of her testimony."

Seth whistled softly under his breath. "That took some major power-brokering."

"They agreed to put it off, but only for a short period of time. Certainly not much longer than it takes to shoot the scenes Gia isn't in."

Still, Seth was too familiar with the movie industry not to realize what a sacrifice even a "short period of time" was. If anything, it indicated how irreplaceable they thought Gia was for the leading role.

That part didn't surprise him. He clearly saw her face in his mind's eye—her light. She'd fascinated him from the start. Apparently, millions of people agreed with him. They couldn't get enough of her face on the big screen.

And Gia couldn't get enough of the high of giving it to them. She'd been working almost nonstop ever since she came to Hollywood two years ago.

"Well? Will you help us, Seth?" Charles asked.

Seth frowned, unwilling to commit to something so . . .

Big.

"I thought it was par for the course that Hollywood highfliers suddenly had a problem with their memory when it came to testifying about anything they saw in a case that could compromise their career . . . or their life. Why's Gia doing this?"

"She *is* very ambitious, so I can't really say for sure. She personally knew McClarin's victim, so she likely relates. The victim's mother is her hairdresser, and Gia would go to their private residence to have her hair done. That's when she witnessed the rape. Gia's a relative newcomer, especially given her current status on the Hollywood A-list. She's only twenty-four years old. Maybe she hasn't absorbed some of the nastier habits of Hollywood yet. Truth be told, I'd be sorry to see the day that happens . . . if it does ever occur," Charles mused.

A flash of familiar anger went through Seth, but he quickly repressed it. He'd thought Gia was twenty-five two years ago, that night they slept together. He'd thought that because Gia had *made* him think that. The day after she'd flown back to New York, he'd learned the truth. Liza, his intern, had innocently revealed that Gia had misled him. Apparently, Gia was somewhat of a prodigy. She'd skipped several grades in elementary and high school. Yes, she'd graduated from college at the same time as Liza, but she was nearly three years younger. She'd been twenty-two, *not* twenty-five, on that night he'd let his guard down and made love to her like a man possessed.

Did two or three years really make all that much difference?

To Seth it did. He didn't like being lied to. He didn't know which of Gia's lies of omission bothered him more—the fact that she'd misled him about her age or the fact that she belonged to the profession he routinely avoided when it came to sex, relationships and romance. Yes, she'd worked on Broadway at the time, and not in films, but she was already being sought out for the title role in *Glory Girl*, her film debut. He had good reason to believe she had omitted the truth about her profession on purpose.

Seth didn't do actresses. And most people who worked with him, including Gia's friend Liza, knew that.

"If she really is that ambitious, maybe she doesn't regret all the press. It wouldn't be the first time in history an actress thrived on publicity," Seth said.

"She can't have wanted what happened to her and her driver yesterday, being run off the road like that . . . Seth?" Charles prodded, and Seth realized he'd become lost in his thoughts. "We could really use you on this."

"I don't think it's a good idea, Charles." He nodded toward the door and the makeup room. "You saw what I'm dealing with out there."

"You said on the phone this is the final day for shooting this movie," Charles said. Seth rolled his eyes, both resigned and frustrated, he'd revealed that tidbit of information before he knew exactly what Charles wanted.

Charles chuckled, knowing he'd caught him out. "Will you just meet us for a consultation at least? Madeline really wants you," he persisted, leaning across the desk and handing Seth a card. Seth glanced stonily at the card with the Los Angeles County district attorney's address on it. "Tomorrow at noon?"

"Does Gia Harris know what you're planning?" Seth asked pointedly.

Charles shook his head. "No, and she's not going to like it when we tell her. Especially the part about Madeline maneuvering to have her shooting postponed. But given what happened yesterday, we've got to convince her that it's not feasible—or safe—for her to continue as if everything is normal. A lot is hanging on Gia's testimony, not only for us, but for the feds' future case."

Seth didn't want to see Gia Harris again.

He *did*. Too much. Which is precisely why he *shouldn't*.

But dammit, this meeting with Charles had started alarms blaring in his head. Yes, he'd rather avoid Gia.

But he didn't want to see her hurt or blackmailed either.

Or dead.

How responsible and guilty would he feel if he learned something had happened to her and he could have helped prevent it?

He frowned and stood. "I have a really bad feeling I'm going to regret this," he informed Charles pointedly as he shoved the card into his jeans.

* * *

Gia gave a little sigh of relief when the deputy du jour stopped following her ten feet away from the conference room door. She was starting to feel like she'd acquired a permanent shadow. It was damn disconcerting.

God curse narcissistic wack jobs for interfering with my life.

The bitter thought and a dozen similar ones flew through Gia's head as she walked across the threshold of the conference room attached to Madeline's office. She thought she'd become accustomed to facing off with lawyers and judges and the formidable Los Angeles County district attorney. But there were two men sitting at the oval conference table tonight that sent a shock through her.

Shit.

"Joshua." She said the director's name numbly, pausing at the entry to the room. "Dan . . . uh, Mr. Arden," she amended, blushing. She'd met the superpowerful movie producer and United Studio executive twice, but his silver-gray full head of hair and the aura of prestige, power and money that surrounded him seemed to discourage first-name usage.

What were the director and executive producer of her next movie doing *here*, in Madeline's offices? Was she in trouble for causing an increase in security, on and around the film set all this week?

Joshua Cabot stood at her entrance, along with Arden, the assistant DA Charles Trew, and an FBI agent she'd met briefly, called Alex Demonico. Gia knew the FBI wasn't officially involved in the state's case against Sterling McClarin, but it had been made clear to her that a lot was riding on the success of the state's prosecution for a potential future federal indictment.

Madeline Harrington, the Los Angeles County DA, remained seated, although she gave Gia a warm smile. Gia had come to learn that Madeline stood up for no one but her presiding judge.

"We thought it would be helpful to have Joshua and Dan here to discuss your future plans," Charles Trew said enigmatically.

"I don't understand," Gia said, putting her purse down in an empty chair and sitting at the same time everyone else did. She looked at Madeline Harrington bemusedly. She'd learned in the past months that Madeline was sharp as a honed knife and just as dangerous, should the occasion arise, but also surprisingly motherly and compassionate at times.

"After what happened yesterday," Madeline said gently, "you must realize things can't go on like this. The media shitstorm is only going to get worse the closer we get to the trial."

"What do you mean *things can't go on*?" Gia asked warily, glancing at a compassionate-looking Joshua Cabot and a stony-faced Dan Arden. "My life can't go on? My job? I don't understand. Why are you here, Joshua?"

Joshua Cabot had a nice face. She'd thought so from the first time she'd met him. Yes, she'd been influenced by his brilliance and reputation as a director, but his warm, fond expression when he'd spoken about his four daughters had utterly convinced Gia that she would be working with a decent man. Dan Arden, in comparison to Joshua, looked far less compassionate. His expression had settled into one of resigned annoyance.

"Maddie has a point, Gia," Joshua said. Gia raised her eyebrows at the familiar usage of the district attorney's name. She gave Madeline a pointed, disbelieving glance.

"Joshua and I go way back," Madeline admitted to Gia with a smile at the director.

"So that gives you the right to plot with him about my life behind my back?" Gia asked incredulously.

"Retract the claws, dear," Madeline said without any heat. "I'm thinking about your health and well-being."

"You're thinking about getting my testimony without any major hitches," Gia corrected.

Madeline smiled. "You're right. Your health and well-being relate directly to the health and well-being of my case, though. And Alex's too, indirectly," she said, glancing at the FBI agent, who nodded. "But believe it or not, I'd rather you remained in one piece for personal reasons as well. I'm busy enough as it is without having to deal with unwanted guilt if something happens to you because of this media circus," she said wearily. She noticed Gia's stubborn expression. "I know I told you at the start of all this that I'd try to make this as painless as possible for you. But circumstances alter all the time, Gia. We have to be flexible, given the changing atmosphere."

"*Why* did you call them here?" Gia demanded under her breath. God, what if the studio took steps to break her contract? She wouldn't put it past them. Who wanted to deal with all the trouble, inconvenience and loss of time and money Gia was bound to bring them, embroiled in this trial as she was?

Charles Trew leaned forward, elbows on the table. "It's too risky to keep you in L.A., Gia."

"I can't just pick up and leave," she exclaimed.

"We're not talking about anything permanent," Madeline soothed. "But given the way things are escalating, everyone agrees that in the three weeks leading up to the trial, we need you out of this pressure cooker. Gone. Before something explodes in our faces."

"Locked up in a hotel room somewhere? *No.* I've told you all, I hate confinement. I start to feel like I'm going crazy being penned inside for any more than a day or two. And what about the movie—"

"Joshua and Mr. Arden have kindly agreed to arrange things so that your scenes can be postponed," Madeline said.

There. The bomb had been dropped. Her skin tingled in anxiety. She met Joshua's stare.

"But you can't do that," she said softly, stunned. "It will cost the studio hundreds of thousands of dollars—"

"And a hell of a lot *more* inconvenience," Arden interrupted succinctly, glowering at her. Gia clamped her mouth shut, mortified by the movie executive's harsh chastisement. Madeline cleared her throat in the uncomfortable silence that followed and gave Charles a significant glance.

"The bottom line is, the studio understands the complexity of this situation and is willing to make allowances for it," Charles smoothed.

"I'm so sorry," Gia told Joshua. "I didn't have any choice in any of this."

Arden made a huffing sound and shifted restlessly in his chair. Gia was sure she knew what he was thinking. *You could have said you weren't* certain *it was Sterling McClarin you saw getting up off a bruised and stunned teenage girl. You could have said, "I just don't recall" or "I can't say for certain it was McClarin."*

You could have lied.

But she couldn't. And therein lay the problem.

"Of course, you didn't have any choice."

She looked up into Joshua Cabot's sympathetic face. She hoped he read the monumental gratefulness for his words in her gaze. He nodded slightly and gave her a small reassuring smile before he turned his attention to Charles Trew.

"How do you plan on making one of the most recognizable faces in the country disappear until the legal proceedings begin?"

Someone rapped firmly on the door. It opened and a Los Angeles County deputy stepped inside.

"Mr. Hightower is here," the deputy said to Charles. Charles stood, a satisfied expression on his face.

"Ah, good. Hopefully, here is the man who can answer your question, Joshua."

Surely fate had overserved its share of shock in the past twenty-four hours. Gia had been rattled around in her car and frantic with worry for her bruised driver, Jim. She'd suffered the unpleasant shock of seeing Joshua Cabot and Dan Arden sitting at the conference table.

It seemed, however, that fate wasn't finished with her yet. She stared in ragged disbelief as Seth Hightower stalked into the conference room.

Four

Charles immediately began to make introductions as Seth approached the table. In the seconds that followed, everything became strangely surreal for Gia, both hazy and hyperfocused at once. She stared at Seth's tall, rangy form as he shook hands with Madeline Harrington and greeted Charles familiarly. Charles introduced him to Alex Demonico. Seth hadn't noticed Gia yet, or was his averted gaze intentional? Not understanding what the hell was happening only added to her disorientation. Joshua Cabot stood and grinned broadly as he shook hands with Seth.

"No need to introduce us," Joshua assured Charles, shaking Seth's hand heartily. "Dan and I are very familiar with Seth. It's been too long, hasn't it?" Joshua asked Seth enthusiastically.

"Since our days on *Maritime*," Seth agreed, referring to the blockbuster multiple–Oscar-Award-winning film. His quiet, gruff baritone set Gia's nerves to prickling. She'd forgotten his voice. Or she hadn't, really. How could she? The intervening years had made her think she'd imagined the tangible impact of it on her body though. She rubbed her forearms anxiously, willing away the goose bumps that had arisen.

"Seth," Dan Arden greeted, extending a hand.

"The best special effects–makeup artist in the business," Joshua told Madeline, as if he were bragging about one of his daughters. "He won the Academy Award for his work on *Maritime*."

"One of many *Maritime* won," Seth said dryly under his breath, and it all came rushing back to Gia: his compelling, handsome face, the way he waved aside praise, the easy, graceful movement of his big male body, his vibrant, powerful presence, the way his golden brown eyes pierced straight through her . . .

"Have you had the opportunity to work with Gia yet?" Joshua asked when Seth turned and pinned her with his stare. Gia's lungs locked. His face was a mask. *Oh my God*. He didn't even *recognize* her. They'd spent a night of wild, abandoned, intense passion together two years ago, and he stared at her like she was a stranger.

Why should she be surprised? She *had* given him her number.

A number he'd never once put to use.

"I've never had the pleasure, no," Seth said. He extended his hand. Gia's stunned brain screamed at her to *move*.

"Hello," she managed, lifting her arm. His large hand enclosed hers and something flickered in his eyes: there and gone.

He *hadn't* forgotten. Her sudden certainty of that only made this bizarre situation worse.

"Do you mind?" Seth asked, pointing at the empty chair next to her.

"No, of course not," she lied. He rolled back the chair and started to sit. She saw her purse at the last second and reached for it. As she snatched the purse away, the back of her hand brushed against his jean-covered ass cheek and the top of a rock-hard thigh. Embarrassment flooded her.

"Sorry," she mumbled as he finished sitting, her gaze flickering anxiously to his face. His expression didn't give much away—just as she recalled—but beneath the impassive surface, she sensed his amusement.

Annoyed at his smugness while she was reeling in shock, she shoved the cursed purse into her lap and slouched in her chair. Charles launched into his reason for inviting Seth Hightower—of all people—into these proceedings. As curious as she was, she was having trouble attending to his explanation. Her brain was zipping with wild thoughts and out-of-control speculations. She stared at

Charles, but her consciousness was attuned to Seth's nearby presence, like iron to a powerful magnet. Still, she was so curious about how the hell Charles Trew knew Seth and why he was being called in to consult on her case, she barely managed to get the gist of things.

"That's your plan?" Gia asked disbelievingly after a minute. "Disguise me as another person and whisk me off into the mountains for three weeks?"

"You've insisted that you can't abide being confined, Gia. After what happened yesterday, there's no doubt we have to get you out of L.A. You have a very recognizable face, so no matter where we send you, we need Seth. We have the added advantage that because of his background in military intelligence, Seth is very familiar with security and safety issues. He's helped us out in sticky situations in the past."

Gia stared at Seth. *You never told me you were in military intelligence,* she accused him in the privacy of her mind. His poker face and ability to look straight through a person suddenly made more sense.

"And you agreed to this?" she asked Seth, her voice flat with shock.

"Not yet."

Gia blinked at his rapid, quiet reply.

"I said I'd come for this meeting. That's all I agreed to with Charles," he finished, glancing away from her. He looked grim.

Madeline addressed Joshua, who looked a little bemused by Seth's appearance and how the meeting was proceeding.

"Seth has worked for us before," Madeline told Joshua with a sly grin. "He's worked with some of Alex's associates at the FBI too. I'll bet you didn't realize the intersection between our worlds until tonight."

"It makes sense, now that I think of it," Joshua said slowly, studying Seth. "Seth has told me a little about his background in

Army intelligence. And I've seen him transform the most familiar faces in the world into a person I'd never recognize in a million years. If anyone can make Gia drop off the map, it's him."

"Excuse me," Gia said sharply, anxiety simmering in her stomach that was about to escalate to a boil. "We're talking about my life here. You're all planning it as if I'm not even relevant. I haven't agreed to any of this, and yet you've already altered film production—something I completely disagree about doing—and are making plans for me to go into hiding when I specifically told you I wouldn't do it," she said directly to Madeline. Madeline opened her lips to reply but someone else spoke first.

"Your movie will still get made eventually. Maybe you should get your priorities straight. Not even one of Joshua's movies is worth sacrificing your safety. Neither is all the free publicity," Seth said.

Gia turned to him, gaping in astonishment. The trace of dark sarcasm in his quiet voice had struck her like a lash.

"I don't know why I'm defending myself to you," she grated out between clenched teeth. "But Madeline and Charles both agree that McClarin is too smart to do anything as stupid as trying to have me hurt or killed so that I can't testify. The reason I don't want to hide out is because I have obligations, professional and otherwise. It's *not* because I'm wild about the idea of having my private life completely robbed from me, being constantly ambushed by photographers or being run into the ditch and having my driver injured."

Seth shrugged. She knew he was wearing his hair shorter now in comparison to that night two years ago. A while back, she'd watched her television in subdued fascination as he won an Oscar for *Maritime*. His hair was still longish, though, silky in texture and artlessly sexy. In the back, it brushed his collar. The style emphasized the stark, masculine angles of his face and remarkable eyes.

His heavy-lidded stare and bland expression as he studied her now didn't fascinate her, though. Instead, it swelled her anger and sense of helplessness.

"You may not have planned for any of that to happen, but who could have?" Seth said quietly. "Surely you must see things are getting out of hand. It'd be unwise to dig your heels in because you weren't the one to orchestrate all the details of this particular part of your life, Gia."

Even her ears turned hot. She could feel the tips of them burning, just like the rest of her. He had *no idea* what she'd been going through for the past five months. But what was worse, her lungs had frozen at the sound of him saying her name in that familiar, quiet caress. For a few strained seconds, she remained locked in his gaze.

Panther eyes.

The charged thought was followed almost immediately by another unwelcome one.

Why didn't you call me, you bastard?

Something gave slightly in his rigid features. Gia wondered if her thought had been so blistering, he'd caught the bitter gist of it. Besides, she had a pretty good idea why he hadn't called. It was stupid to dwell on one misguided night of wild sex. She needed to move on. She *had* moved on.

"And what about when I come out of hiding?" she asked levelly, facing the others. "It's going to be a zoo all over again. Nothing will have changed."

"We're not going to be able to alter what happens during the trial. We can do something about right now," Charles said. "The smart thing to do now is to get *you* out of the fire, Gia."

Dan Arden checked his watch. "I have to be going. Madeline, will you *please* get my secretary the trial schedule you promised you'd give me tonight? We'll need that to coordinate all these changes with as little cost and hassle to the studio as possible."

Madeline gave him a long-suffering smile. "I'm sorry I couldn't give it to you tonight, Dan. Judge Halloran has about a thousand different factors he has to take into consideration before setting a date. I'll get you a tentative agenda as soon as I can, but like I said, courtroom proceedings are *not* fixed in stone. We might need Gia at a moment's notice, and she'll have to be available."

The studio executive grimaced. Gia knew he was usually in the position of telling others they'd have to wait and be ready at a moment's notice, according to his demands. Arden grunted farewell to Joshua Cabot and left the conference room, slamming the door behind him. *What a jackass.* Irritated by the studio executive's pout over circumstances she couldn't control, Gia suppressed her pang of guilt much easier this time around.

Madeline didn't bother to hide a sound of mixed disgust and relief when Arden vacated the room. Joshua Cabot gave her a knowing grin.

"You should consider yourself lucky, Maddie. You don't have to deal with him 24-7." He sighed and checked his watch. "I should probably get going as well."

"Thank you for coming, Joshua . . . and for *everything*," Gia said sincerely as he walked around the table toward her.

"Don't thank me," Joshua said, leaning down to kiss her cheek. "And don't worry about the movie. Seth is right. It'll get made. If Dan didn't have such high hopes for it—and for you in the role—he wouldn't have agreed to any of this," Joshua assured her with a droll grin. "In the meantime, look at it this way: You've been granted an unexpected vacation. Try to use it to your advantage and relax a little. You look exhausted."

Madeline smiled broadly after Joshua left, seemingly more at ease with just the five of them left around the table. "I've seen your work before, Seth, and I know firsthand the miracles you can do. But do you really think you can make *that* look like an everyday woman on the street?" She glanced significantly at Gia.

Gia's eyes widened. It was bad enough that Charles, Alex and Madeline were all staring at her like she was under a microscope. The worst part was the way Seth's stare moved over her face dispassionately. His gaze flickered down to her breasts. Gia's spine stiffened in mounting annoyance. She all but bared her teeth.

"I can do it," Seth said definitively after a moment.

"And *will* you?" Madeline purred.

He arched his brows. "Will I?" he asked Gia.

She looked at the others, who were watching her expectantly. She made a sound of frustration. Every time she thought she was ultimately cornered and helpless, this situation got worse.

Then the image of Jeannie Salinger—McClarin's victim—popped into her head. Gia would escape McClarin's tentacles long before Jeannie ever would.

"Just the one time? A disguise to get me out of Los Angeles unnoticed?" Gia clarified.

"No," Charles said, eyeing Seth warily. "You say you have a problem with confinement. Of course, we prefer that you stay in a secure place as much as possible. But if you do go out at all in the next three weeks, you'll have to look like someone other than Gia Harris. This story is news nationwide. It's even making headlines in Canada, Europe and South America. Seth? What do you say?"

Seth didn't reply, his expression like stone.

"Wait," Gia said, sensing the subtext to Charles and Seth's exchange. "If I have to be disguised every time I step outside, then . . ." Gia trailed off, giving Seth an uneasy sideways glance.

"Seth will have to be with you the entire time, yes," Alex Demonico said.

Gia blinked in surprise when the FBI agent suddenly spoke.

"I realize I have no say in any of this," Demonico said, "but we have a lot riding on your testimony for eventually bringing down McClarin *and* the influence of the New Temple. Charles thinks it's a good idea. Plus, Seth is trained in security. After studying his file and hearing stellar reports about what he's done with some of my colleagues," Alex added, giving Seth a pointed glance, "I've agreed with Charles and Madeline's plans."

"Seth?" Charles asked tentatively. "I realize the length of time required was one detail I left out yesterday. But you could use a break after wrapping up on your latest movie, couldn't you? You told me yesterday Joy is taking a vacation. Why don't you? I know we're asking a lot, and the compensatory consultant's fee the DA's office offers is practically nothing, but . . ."

"I haven't helped out in the past because of the *pay*," Seth said dryly when Charles faded off. Charles chuckled.

Gia looked at Seth, stunned. *Surely* he wouldn't agree to this. It would save her having to say no to the whole thing if he would just refuse. He had his work and his life. And dammit, why would he sacrifice so much of his time and energy for a woman he didn't even have an interest in calling following mind-blowing sex?

As usual, she had difficulty reading his face.

"I know of an ideal place where we could go," Seth said.

Gia's heart jumped. She hadn't expected him to say that.

"It's true that no place in the country will be completely uncontaminated by this news story," Seth said slowly, "but I know of a place that will be more resistant than most. Much more," Seth directed his attention to Charles and Alex. "It's a secluded house in the Shawnee National Forest in southern Illinois, near a little town called Vulture's Canyon—it's not even on most maps. I know about it through my niece and Everett Hughes as well as Everett's sister, Katie, and her husband, Rill Pierce. The house I'm referring to has a state-of-the-art security system. I'm a friend of the owner—a man named John Corcoran. He's blind, and he has several good reasons to be vigilant about security. One, years ago he was the victim of a break-in and vowed to keep his wife safe and protected at all costs. Two, his wife is Jennifer Turner, so he has excellent cause for making sure her privacy and security are kept intact."

"Jennifer Turner, the actress?" Gia asked. Jennifer Turner had been at the top of her game for years now and was showing no signs of slowing down. She was one of the most respected, sought-after actresses in the business.

Seth nodded. "She and John live there during the summers, but I happen to know it's vacant right now. I'll have to check with John about whether or not we can use it, but I don't foresee any problem. Jennifer starts work soon on location in Spain. John plans to accompany her."

"And no one has ever bothered Jennifer Turner at this house?" Madeline asked, curious.

"Both John and Jennifer will tell you they've never once had a problem there. It's like falling into a time warp going to Vulture's Canyon. Even if the residents ever did figure out who Gia was—and they *won't*," he added with utter confidence, "they wouldn't care. They're a very practical sort. The only use they'd ever have for Hollywood tabloids is picking up crap or covering the floor while they're painting or sculpting. They tend to be the hippie-artist, isolationist types. And if there's one thing they respect, it's their own and other people's privacy."

"You're actually considering *doing* this?" Gia asked him the question that had been scalding her brain ever since he'd mentioned having a place for them to hide.

Seth inhaled slowly, an unreadable expression on his face. "If you can make the sacrifice to do the right thing, I imagine I can."

She continued to regard him with suspicious bemusement.

"That girl Sterling McClarin raped is willing to face her worst fears in a public venue in order to get justice," he said. "McClarin needs to be put away, once and for all. His influence needs to be shut down in this town and beyond. To do that, we need a healthy, intact Gia Harris. It's that simple. I'll do my part. I just finished a shoot. I have the time."

Gia exhaled, sensing defeat. In that moment, Seth had said the one thing that could convince her. He understood McClarin was a poison that needed to be controlled.

"Gia?" Charles prodded.

Gia looked from Charles's to Madeline's expectant faces, then at Seth's impassive one. How did he really feel about the idea of spending the next three weeks with her? How did she feel about doing the same with Seth Hightower, the man who had taken her to heaven—repeatedly—and then discarded her like used tissue afterward?

Stop thinking about that. That night is irrelevant to this situation.

It's certainly *irrelevant to Jeannie Salinger.*

She threw up her hands. She couldn't believe the twists and turns her life was taking her on lately. "Fine. What the hell. It doesn't look like I'm going to be able to get off this roller coaster anytime soon."

"Just buckle up and enjoy the ride as best you can," Seth said.

She whipped her head around, going still when she saw the glint of a dare in his golden eyes.

"It's all settled then," Madeline said, seemingly not noticing the brittle tension between Seth and her. It was probably all in her mind, anyway, Gia thought irritably, as relaxed as Seth looked. "We'll work out all the details right now, but Gia you should prepare to leave town tomorrow morning."

"Tomorrow morning. Of course," Gia said, rolling her eyes. What could surprise her at this point?

"And don't bother to bring many clothes," Seth said.

"What?" she asked, forgetting her weary, aloof attitude over the fact that her life was not her own.

"No dresses or frilly little blouses. Leave all your makeup behind," he said, his gaze dipping fleetingly down to the front of the feminine floral blouse she was wearing with jeans. Gia experienced his stare like a flickering, teasing pressure across her skin and breasts.

"You won't need any of those things, because I'll be disguising you as a teenage boy." He scowled slightly, his cool gaze lingering on her chest. "With some luck and a really good breast binder, I just might be able to pull it off too."

Five

The next morning, Seth waited patiently in the cluttered rear storage room of Studio K on Melrose Avenue. His longtime friend and owner of the salon, Karen Leads, had been briefed only on what she needed to know about Seth's scheme with Gia. Karen had many famous clients and knew the advantages of keeping her mouth closed. Karen owned the exclusive salon and had arrived before normal operating hours to help him with his plan. She'd let Seth and another accomplice in through the back door.

The idea was that anyone following Gia—and there was sure to be several—would think Gia had just scheduled a quick pickup of products at Karen's salon before it opened.

He glanced at Leti Fishmann, a UCLA geology graduate student, fussing with her fuchsia scarf in a nearby mirror. Both his niece, Joy, and he occasionally hired Leti for part-time modeling work. In addition, Leti walked Joy and Everett's rambunctious golden retriever, Marley. Leti was a friend and could be trusted with the minimal information they'd given her. Yesterday Gia had suggested that they use the woman who worked as her body double for the red-herring role in their little escapade, but Seth had nixed that idea. He'd rather have someone like Leti, who cared more about her doctoral dissertation than the possibility of landing a plum role in some future television or film production. He wanted someone immune to bribery. Despite Gia's scowl when he'd said that yesterday, he'd remained insistent on not using Gia's body double. They were not going to use a struggling Hollywood actress he didn't know, and certainly didn't trust, for such a crucial role in their escape from Los Angeles.

Leti was wearing the print dress, jean jacket, newsboy cap and eye-catching fuchsia scarf Seth had specified in yesterday's planning session with Charles and Gia. Seth had provided her with a brown wig that had been styled in a haphazard bun just below the cap.

"How do I look?" Leti asked him distractedly.

"Pretty good, once you put on the glasses, especially," someone said breathlessly.

Seth glanced around to see who'd answered, his stare sticking on Gia Harris as she entered the room. As they had agreed upon the day before, she wore the precise same outfit as Leti. She whipped off her sunglasses, her light green eyes betraying her wariness and anxiety over their clandestine venture.

Or over seeing him again. Seth couldn't be sure.

Duplicate *that* face? he thought bitterly, his gaze on Gia. Not a chance, Seth said to himself with a trace of bitter annoyance. The past two years had only made her more beautiful, if that was possible.

"She'll pass from a distance, anyway," Seth said, standing and scrutinizing Gia's form and outfit closely. "Turn around," he told her.

He saw the flash of anger in her eyes. He quirked up one brow in an amused, sardonic expression. "Please."

Something flickered across her features. It struck him that he'd told Gia the same thing before, on that damn night in Daphne DeGarro's tacky dressing room.

He'd instructed her to "turn around" a few times before their night together was over.

He clamped his teeth tight as erotic memories rushed him. Gia reluctantly turned around. He forced himself to focus, inspecting her closely.

"Were you followed?" he asked Gia, stepping over to Leti,

where he made some quick adjustments to her wig to better match
Gia's hairstyle.

"Jim is positive we were," Gia reported. "By a black SUV and
a dark green Lexus, at the very least."

"I'm Gia, by the way," she added tensely, crossing the room to
shake Leti's hand.

"Leti Fishmann," Leti returned.

"Thank you so much for helping us out with this."

"I'm glad to do it," Leti said. His adjustment complete, Seth
dropped his hands from her wig. Leti gave him a big smile. "Both
Seth and Joy have helped me out too many times to count."

"Joy is your niece, right?" Gia clarified, her gaze on Seth.

He nodded.

"Well, I'm very grateful," Gia said, her eyes pinging back and
forth between Seth and Leti.

"You'd better get going," Seth told Leti. He handed her the
salon bag of products they'd prepared earlier.

"Keep your face averted to the right," Gia instructed Leti as she
handed her the sunglasses she had just removed. "They're parked
on both sides of Melrose, a half block behind my driver, Jim."

Leti nodded in understanding. "Good luck, both of you. See
you, Seth," Leti said, going up on her tiptoes. He lowered his head,
and she gave him a brief kiss on the cheek. She hurried out of the
room to the salon.

Gia and he were alone for the first time since their impulsive
tryst more than two years ago. His glaze slid over to her. There
were light purple smudges beneath her eyes, which made her green
eyes look huge and a little haunted. No, not haunted. *Hunted*. He'd
agreed with Joshua Cabot's assessment last night. She looked exhausted. He didn't know if it was the upcoming McClarin trial and
this press debacle or her frantic work schedule, but the fresh girl
he'd met years back was starting to show signs of stress.

"You definitely trust her?" Gia asked quietly, nodding in the direction where Leti had just departed.

He nodded.

"She's clearly not an actress then," Gia said darkly. When he didn't respond, her eyes flashed. "Are you and she . . . ?" She waved her hand, frowning.

"No. Leti's a friend. Even if I didn't trust her and Karen, though, they have limited information. We've compartmentalized the knowledge of what we're doing, keeping things on a need-to-know basis. Even Karen isn't going to stick around to see your final disguise. *I'm* the only one who will know that. Leti and Karen only know that you and I met here this morning. No one knows where we'll go from here, except for us, Charles, Alex and Madeline."

She stared at him with a mixture of annoyance, anxiety and defiance. He stepped toward her. Her eyes widened. Without a word, he removed the newsboy cap she wore and dug his fingers into the rich, dense coils of the artfully sloppy bun at her neck. She made a choked sound of disbelief and outrage in her throat, but he cut her off before she could speak.

"I don't suppose you'd let Karen cut this, would you?" he asked gruffly, finding several pins and matter-of-factly pulling them out.

"My hair?" she asked in a stunned voice.

He looked down into her eyes. He'd never seen a purer, clearer shade of green. "I told you I was going to transform you into a boy. If you don't let Karen cut it, I'll have to bind it tightly under a cap before I put on the wig," he said as he withdrew the last pin, and the long, golden brown tresses began to fall around her shoulders. He resisted a strong urge to grab a fistful of the glorious stuff. He stiffened slightly when he inhaled the familiar fruity scent of tangerines. She hadn't changed shampoos.

"It'll be itchy and uncomfortable for you," he added.

She stepped away from him.

"I'm afraid I don't have any choice," she said. "I don't think they'd be pleased if I showed up on the set of *Interlude* with my hair all chopped off. It wouldn't fit the part, and I'd rather not wear a wig everyday for shooting."

He shrugged and turned away. He hadn't really thought she would agree to it. Gia Harris cut off those famous flowing locks? Not likely.

"Why do you look so smug?" she demanded.

He turned around, a little surprised by her fierceness. She glared at him.

"I'm not smug," he said. "I just had already figured you'd consider the part for *Interlude* first and foremost."

"Because I'm a shallow, self-centered actress, right?" He just looked at her, refusing to rise to the bait. "Okay," she said, clawing at the knot in her scarf and whipping it off as if she were throwing down a gauntlet. "Why don't I take the first cut through this bullshit," she said, her low voice vibrating with restrained feeling. "Knowing you, you'd go the next three weeks together and never say a word about what happened two years ago at that cancer benefit. Do you really think that's *normal*, Seth?"

He glanced wryly back at the chair and table he'd arranged in preparation for her makeup. "I'd have trouble finding anything about this whole thing that's *normal*."

Her eyes seemed to blaze as she took a step toward him. "I know how much you have a thing about avoiding actresses in your personal life. Liza told me."

"I know. She told you before we ever met that night, didn't she?"

Gia blinked. "I . . . I don't remember."

"You're lying," Seth replied levelly, turning to the chair and picking up the breast binder with subtle shoulder padding that he'd brought. "Liza told me she'd mentioned to you beforehand that I avoided actresses in my personal life."

"Why *do* you?" she demanded suddenly, as if her curiosity had trumped her anger. Not that she still wasn't pissed. Her indignation had flushed her cheeks and lips. He yanked his gaze away from her mouth. "How can you be so self-righteous about such a blatant prejudice? It's unfair to the women you work with, day in and day out."

"A lot of people don't mix business and pleasure. It's not surprising. Besides, you're changing the subject," he said, unzipping the binder. "You knew that night I avoided actresses, and that's why you didn't tell me you were a working Broadway actress—one who had a hit big enough to attract a Hollywood agent like Cecelia Arends," he added, unable to fully disguise his sarcasm. "*That's* why Cecelia was annoyed at Tommy Valian that night. Because he'd alienated the girl she was desperate to sign, and eventually *did* sign. *That's* why she was chasing after you. A casting agent had already earmarked you for the part in *Glory Girl*. Cecelia was in hot pursuit. That's what you were avoiding telling me that night."

"I never lied to you."

"Sometimes lies of omission are even more blatant than telling a falsehood."

"You misled me as well," she accused in a shaking voice. "According to Liza—and Cecelia, for that matter—things were a lot more serious between Cecelia and you than you led me to believe."

"I can't help it if that's what Cecilia thought. I was being honest when I said I wasn't involved with her. Time has proven that, hasn't it?"

"Well, I was being honest that night too. Or as much as I could have been honest around a man with irrational prejudices about a profession."

"Or about an age?" he muttered darkly. First confusion and then guilt flickered across her face. He had to say this about Gia, lying didn't come naturally to her. He must have been half-crazed with lust that night not to notice her sleight of hand.

"What?" she asked breathlessly, recovering. "You're upset because of my age? *Seriously?*"

"You lied about it. You made me think you were Liza's age," he said, repressed anger starting to pulse in his veins.

"I was twenty-two then. You were ten years older. What's the big deal?"

He grimaced slightly. "You're worshipped by a horde of infatuated teenage boys and girls. After you hit it big, I felt . . . *indecent* realizing I'd been with you."

"It's not my fault if my first movie was a young adult hit. *I'm* almost twenty-five right now. I was a consenting adult when we were together. And for your information, you *were* indecent that night. So was I," she added darkly.

He snarled, irritated at her flippancy. Or honesty. Or the heat that flashed through him at her reply. He couldn't say which. "Don't try and deny you didn't mislead me about your age on purpose."

She choked on incredulous laughter. "Oh my God. I can't believe how unreasonable you are. I wasn't a teenager! Is *that* really why you didn't call me?"

"You had my number as well."

The silence swelled. Frustration spiked through him. He hadn't meant to betray the fact that he'd half-hoped she would call, even after he'd learned she'd misled him. Damn her for forcing his hand. She just stared at him, her lips parted in amazement. He closed his eyes briefly.

"That's all in the past," he said, getting ahold of himself. "We can either deal with this situation that we're in or not, no matter how *odd* it is. We have more important things to think about right now." He held up the breast binder. "Can you go and put this on please? It's a binder, but a shaper too. It'll give you more of the outline of a boy. You can change over there. I've put the clothes I want you to wear behind the screen. I'll ask Karen to go back and help you with the binder. You'll need it." He pointed at a dark green folding screen across the room.

Maybe she'd realized all this rehashing of a night better left forgotten wasn't for the best, no matter how angry she was. She grabbed the binder but paused beside him instead of walking behind the screen.

"Just tell me this. Did that night have anything to do with you accepting this consultation?" she asked in a low voice that vibrated with emotion.

"Did it have anything to do with you agreeing to it?"

Her face stiffened. She merely stalked behind the screen.

It looked as if neither of them was willing to tip their hand on *that* volatile topic.

A couple of hours later, Seth noticed Gia sitting forward and staring out the window as he merged onto I-40 East.

"Where are we going?" she asked him with a bewildered look.

"I told you yesterday. The Shawnee National Forest in Illinois."

"But . . . what airport are we flying out of?"

"You left last night before Charles and I made a few alterations to the plan."

"*What* changes?" she asked him, her tone ominous. He glanced sideways at her and did a double take. He had to hand it to himself; he'd done a better female-to-male makeup job on Gia than he had for the Oscar nod he'd earned for turning a famous actress into an equally infamous male rock star a few years back. A seventeen- or eighteen-year-old belligerent male teenager glared back at him from the passenger seat. The wig was a little lighter than Gia's normal hair color, featuring blond highlights. It was a high-quality human hairpiece, the style suited to trendy youth. It swirled and

waved around her cheeks, ears and neck in a carefree, beachy style.
The wig fit her head almost perfectly, making adhesive unneces-
sary. The body shaper had added a few inches to her waist and
flattened her chest out, if not ideally, then adequately. Gia's breasts
were not insignificant. They weren't huge, but they weren't small
either.

In fact, they were perfect.

Petal-soft, thrusting and firm with large, exquisitely sensitive
pink nipples. How well he remembered how those nipples felt beneath his fingers . . . under his laving tongue. Unwelcome arousal
shot through Seth.

Again.

He shifted uneasily in the driver's seat.

Her breasts had been the one doubt he'd had about the transformation.

Things had worked out though. The slight shoulder padding
and firm ribbing in the shaper, along with Gia's naturally slender
figure, gave the impression of a whipcord-lean male torso beneath
a Hurley T-shirt and plaid overshirt. He'd darkened her peaches-
and-cream complexion into a golden tan that would suit a beach-
loving teenage boy. He'd neutralized her hallmark pink mouth into
a much more innocuous pink-beige. The shadowing of her jaw with
slight whisker stubble just beneath short brown sideburns was a
particularly brilliant move on his part.

He had transformed Gia Harris into a boy worthy of the cover
of *Tiger Beat*, Seth thought amusedly, taking pains to hide his
smile.

Of course, the sunglasses were a must. He'd brought contacts
for her in his kit, but he didn't want her to be unnecessarily uncomfortable on the trip. There was something about Gia's large, long-
lashed eyes that screamed of the feminine. Or at least to Seth they
did.

Bright Eyes.

He scowled at the intrusive thought and focused on answering her question.

"Your disguise was going to be too much of a hassle with airport security, and we didn't trust any private pilots well enough to hire them on such short notice. Besides, airports are blanketed with surveillance cameras. It seems as if things have gone well with Leti fooling your followers for the time being, but if something goes amiss, an airport would be the worst place for us to be. It's better just to steer clear of them altogether. So we're driving to Illinois instead of flying."

"Driving," she repeated flatly.

"It'll be nostalgic," he reasoned before shooting a significant glance in her direction. "You can relive your Jack Kerouac days."

He noticed her sharp intake of breath. Seth grimaced. It had been unfair to make a reference to that intimate conversation they'd had years ago about that cross-country trip with her mother, given the fact that he'd made a point of saying that was all in the past.

"We're taking the southern route?" she asked incredulously, staring at the highway.

"Yeah," he replied, his gaze safely on the road in front of him. "I thought we'd even do a few parts of Historic Route 66."

He didn't look at her for several silent seconds, but he felt her gaze on his profile.

"How long will it take?" she asked.

"It depends. Are you going to take a turn driving?"

"Okay," she agreed.

"Then if you're game, we'll drive straight through. I put some toiletries in a bag in the back so we can clean up on stops. Each of us can sleep while the other is driving. There are some pillows and blankets in the backseat as well. If we do that, we should get there sometime tomorrow afternoon. We'll put up with a little discomfort now, but we'll be in Jennifer's comfortable beds all that much sooner."

"Fine," she mumbled, sounding so edgy and bewildered, his heart went out to her a little. "Can you turn on the radio, please?"

He wordlessly did what she asked, finding a soft-rock station.

"Okay?" he asked.

She made a muffled sound of assent.

Neither his motorcycle nor his little Nissan GT-R were appropriate for a cross-country road trip where comfort was essential. He'd borrowed an SUV from a good friend named Alexi who was a cinematographer and was out of town on location. Gia tilted the passenger seat all the way back in the roomy vehicle and turned her head determinedly away from him.

For the thousandth time in the past twenty-four hours, he sensed her disquietude and irritation simmering in the air between them. He exhaled some of his own agitation and focused on the road.

"How can you act so blasé about all this?"

He blinked at her sudden question. He thought she'd fallen asleep. Her head was still turned away from him.

"How do you think I should act? It's a situation. I'm dealing with it," he said bemusedly.

She made a disgusted sound. His response had clearly just annoyed her more. "It's only three weeks, Gia. Is it that hard for you to take a break?"

She whipped her head around, causing her sunglasses to go slightly askew. "Why are you determined to make this all about my job? You are constantly suggesting I'm some kind of fame-aholic."

He stared at the road, choosing his words carefully. "I'm sorry if I'm mistaken, but from what I've gathered while working in the industry and from the checkout-counter tabloids, you've been on a meteoric rise ever since we first met. If you *have* taken a break, it would have been a miracle, with everything else you've accomplished in the past several years."

"So, being ambitious is my crime. When is the last time *you* took a three-week break, Seth?"

When he didn't respond, because he was mentally grasping for the answer, she made a disgusted sound. "That's what I thought," she said scathingly. "My crime is being an *actress*, not a hard worker. I suppose when you're an *artist* like you, they call it *creative drive*, and when you're a film actress like me, it's just dirty, scheming ambition."

She jerked her arm into the backseat and grabbed a pillow. Throwing it down on the reclined seat with force, she again turned a stiff back to him.

After twenty or so minutes, her rigid posture seemed to loosen, her body growing suppler. Seth suspected she slept. He inhaled slowly, forcing his clamped jaw and tense muscles to unclench.

Why had he agreed to this crazy scheme when he knew how much she could get to him . . . when he knew how much he didn't *want* her to? The obvious answer immediately popped into his head. It didn't sit well with him, having the shadow of that insidious cult and its dangerous leader cast over Gia. It made him edgy to think of the press spying on her . . . hounding her.

It made no sense. Why should he care or worry so much about a woman he hardly knew? He couldn't go around saving every female who got herself in trouble in this soul-sucking industry. There weren't enough minutes in the day.

She rustled in the seat next to him. He frowned. Her soft sigh tickled the skin of his ear.

Had she actually accused him of being blasé about this?

What a freaking joke.

Gia couldn't breathe. Someone was holding her down, crushing her, keeping her from running. No, it wasn't some*one*, it was some-

thing. She clawed for air, grasping for release, but her own body seemed to be responsible for her suffocation. Her lungs refused to expand.

"Gia!" a deep voice said sharply. "Wake up."

It was a command she followed without thinking. Her eyelids flew open. Bright sunlight flooded into her vision. She squinted dazedly, but her lungs were finally free. She gasped for air.

Seth Hightower stared down at her from behind the wheel of the vehicle, his face rigid, his eyes narrowed dangerously. She lay on her side, facing him. Her lungs froze again at the uncompromisingly stark image of him. It took her a few seconds to register where he was staring with blazing eyes. She looked down slowly. The T-shirt she wore was bunched up around her chest. Everything came back to her sleep-addled brain in a rush: the need for escape from Los Angeles, Seth's disguise . . . the rigid shaper she wore like a corset.

Shit.

She held the concealed zipper of the rigid garment between her fingers. In her sleep, she'd ripped it down to her belly button in a desperate bid for a full breath of air. Her breasts crowded into the opening of the stiff garment, bursting to be free. A light coat of perspiration glazed the swells of flesh and the valley between them.

One pink nipple had popped into the opening.

It belatedly struck her what she'd seen on Seth Hightower's face just then. It was something she hadn't seen in over two years.

It had been unguarded, distilled lust.

Six

She shoved her T-shirt down over the lewd display of her plumped breasts, sitting up and gasping for air. The seat belt jerked her back.

She stared at an open field. A prickly-looking, colorful blanket of desert shrubs, flowers and cacti covered the ground all the way to the rust-colored mountains and a craggy butte in the far distance. They were stopped in a desolate rear parking lot. She glanced behind her and saw a 1950s-style roadside diner.

"Where are we?" she croaked, dazedly fumbling for the seat adjuster. She realized her sunglasses lay in her lap.

"Do you always take part in wrestling matches in your sleep?" Seth asked baldly.

She blinked, swallowing thickly. Was that unsettlement, concern or lingering lust in his tone? The thought struck her that he had good reason to ask about her sleeping habits. They'd certainly never slept on that wild night years ago. They'd had far more crucial things to attend to than rest. That volatile thought, in combination with the memory of Seth's blatantly lustful stare just now, left her feeling raw.

"No, but I usually don't sleep in torture devices like this thing you made me wear," she said, glaring down at her rumpled T-shirt and then at Seth. She jerked the sides of the overshirt closed, feeling exposed . . . and not just because of unintentionally baring her breasts to him. She immediately regretted her sharp tone when she saw him flinch slightly and his scowl deepen. She leaned her forehead into her palm.

"I'm sorry for snapping," she mumbled, her cheeks still burning. The silence pressed down on her. "I haven't been sleeping all that well lately. I went down deeper than I expected just now, and this thing was making me feel like I couldn't breathe . . ." she faded off, waving vaguely at the restrictive device she wore—not because Seth *made* her. Because *her* life was spinning out of control. That wasn't *his* fault. He was helping her, sacrificing his time, talent and energy for something he was far from obligated to do. When he didn't respond for several seconds, she glanced over at him uneasily. He peered at her from beneath a lowered brow.

"Have you not been sleeping because you're worried about the people watching your house?"

She stared out the front window blindly, her mouth falling open. Is *that* why she'd gone under so deeply in sleep for the first time in what felt like months? Because she'd felt safe, with Seth next to her?

"Someone tried to break into a rear window at my house a few weeks ago. That's why police protection was ordered," she said in a cracking voice.

"Jackals."

She turned sharply. His mouth was pressed into a hard line. Gratitude rushed through her at the edge of anger in his tone. His reaction surprised her. So did her gratefulness in the face of it. Madeline, Charles and the sheriff's-department deputies who had been sent to protect her were all kind enough but *forbearing* about the whole thing. It was as if they thought dozens of reporters watching her every move, being run off the road and home break-ins were par for the course, given this situation. Sometimes she felt as if the deputies, especially, had a condescending attitude, like, *Well, what did you expect, given the choices you've made? You sought out fame and fortune—well, now you've found it along with all the crap that goes with it. Deal with it, girly.*

She hadn't realized until now just how desperate that unspoken message was making her.

Yes, she was used to living in the public eye, and she accepted there were significant downsides to her chosen profession. But no one had openly acknowledged this different, constant, aggressive invasion of her private world since Sterling McClarin had been arrested and she'd been publicly identified as a primary witness against him. Certainly no one had labeled it as succinctly as Seth had just now with one furious, disdainful word.

"Yesterday Charles said you live alone, although your driver is on the grounds in a carriage house. Is there usually someone there with you though?" Seth asked.

"No," she murmured, a little surprised by his question. She got what he was asking. She'd never considered that he didn't know what her relationship status was. It only made sense. She didn't know his either. She'd certainly had a bitter moment of wondering about it in the back of the hair salon when the pretty, friendly Leti had kissed him, but then he'd denied it. She glanced over at him presently, once again unable to stop herself. He looked annoyingly good, all lean, long sexy male. His masculinity was palpable. She couldn't help but breathe it in in the confines of the SUV, couldn't stop being rattled by it. He wore a simple black T-shirt and jeans.

And a belt.

She hadn't noticed that belt when he applied her makeup, but his shirt hem had caught on the silver tooled buckle when he sat in the driver's seat earlier. She couldn't stop herself from stealing glances at his lap as they exited Los Angeles, finding the image of his long, powerful bent legs, flagrantly male crotch and that damn sexy belt buckle next to his flat lower belly a powerful pull on her consciousness.

He gripped his hands on the leather wheel, and her attention fractured even more. She'd loved his hands, even back then. She could have become addicted to the way he touched her. Unlike two years ago during their tryst, he now wore a ring on his left middle finger, a silver tooled one that looked . . . *exciting* next to his swarthy skin and masculine knuckles. That ring had a little surprise to it on the underside. He'd used it like a tool of his trade while he was applying her makeup earlier. Now she couldn't stop thinking about it.

"What about your parents? Has your mother been up to see you, give you a little support during all this?" Seth asked, pulling her thoughts back to the present moment.

Gia shook her head and scratched her neck beneath the wig, grimacing. It was starting to itch, especially after perspiring during her "wrestling match," as Seth had labeled it.

"Mom hates the press mob."

"There are few who would love it to the degree you've been subjected."

You would hate it worst of all. The thought jumped into her brain. There was something about Seth that had made her think it. He exuded independence. He certainly sidestepped the limelight. There was something so essentially private, solitary . . . even enigmatic about him.

A lone wolf personified.

"Some reporters have knocked on my mom's door in La Jolla and even followed her at the grocery store, trying to get an interview about me," Gia explained wearily. "Mom and Stephen—her husband—were outraged. So was I." She frowned slightly. Her mother also possessed that condescending attitude she'd ascribed to her police guards, but in a more crystallized form. While it wasn't the cops' place to give their opinion on her job, Gia's mom certainly believed it was her right to lecture Gia on her choice of working in the Hollywood film industry.

She saw Seth's dark look and knew he'd noticed her frown.

"My dad came out and stayed with me for a couple weeks after McClarin was arrested. He was very supportive, but let's face it. No one loves living in a fishbowl."

"There's no one who'll support you regularly?" Seth asked.

She felt his steady gaze on her cheek as she stared out the window and shook her head. "No one loves living in a fishbowl," she repeated quietly. That pretty much said it all, didn't it? Seth, of all people, would certainly understand that. Isn't that part of why he avoided actresses? She inhaled shakily, attempting to banish her anxious thoughts. "You never said where we were."

"On the far side of Kingman," he said.

She looked over her shoulder at the retro diner and the sun-gilded, starkly beautiful desert landscape. A smile broke free. "I remember this, from my trip with Mom. I can't believe you got us all the way to Arizona already."

"You were out like a light for four hours, until you started fighting there at the end. You *must* have been sleep-deprived. Do you want to go in and get something to eat?"

"Yes," she agreed. She hadn't eaten all day, and it was almost two o'clock in the afternoon. It would help to center her, to get some food in her belly. All this chaos in her life was making her feel rootless and strange. She started to reach for the door handle, stopping short when Seth lightly gripped her upper arm.

"I need to touch you up," he said. "And get you back in."

Understanding struck her, along with a flash of embarrassment, when he glanced down at her chest.

"Does it really matter here? Can't I just take off the binder? No one will recognize me."

"If we are going to do this, we can't do it halfway. You have to be in full disguise every time you're in public. Do you really think the people in this diner have never heard of you? That they couldn't potentially recognize you? Doing this all the way is the *only* way we're going to keep you under wraps."

She sighed in resignation.

"Would you rather stay in the car while I go and get us some food?" he asked.

"I'd like to go to the bathroom and wash up a little."

"I figured," he replied reasonably. "If we can get you back to boy status, you can stretch your legs and enjoy your dinner before we take on the next stretch of road. Instead of thinking of the disguise as a burden, you might think of the freedom it'll give you to be someone else besides Gia Harris."

"Okay," she agreed. What was the point of all this secrecy if she blew her own cover on their first stop on the road?

"Lean your seat back all the way again. I don't want anyone to see what we're doing."

Something in his deep, gruff voice made her skin prickle. His words had sounded illicit. Or her hyperactive libido had made them sound that way. She hesitated. Closing the binder wasn't really a one-person job. His friend, the owner of the salon—Karen Leader—had helped her get it on earlier, before she'd closed up her shop and left. Gia hadn't thought about the fact that for the rest of the trip, Seth was the only person who could do it. He wore sunglasses. His face was impassive, but she had the strangest feeling he was as aware of the seething tension between them as she was.

She touched the seat-adjuster button and reclined all the way back again. She felt very vulnerable, but also . . . *excited* for some damn reason.

Seth unbuckled his seat belt. Her breath caught when he reached over and did the same to hers, his actions brisk and matter-of-fact.

"I'm just going to retouch your face first," he explained, reaching into the backseat and extracting a small black bag. He must have packed it for roadside purposes with supplies specifically for her disguise. The first thing he did was exchange his sunglasses for the blue-tinted ones. When he'd done her makeup earlier in the back of the salon, it had come back to her in a rush that she'd seen them resting on his head that night two years ago. He seemed to only wear the unusual—not to mention very sexy glasses—for makeup applications.

He brushed her cheek with a soft brush, his expression intent and focused. It felt different in this position than it had while she'd been sitting in the swivel chair in the back of Karen's salon. This time was far more intimate, inside the confines of an automobile and lying back. Seth peered down at her as he worked, his mouth set in a hard, stern line, although his lips were as shapely and sensual looking as always. She recalled vividly how he'd consumed her with utter confidence and skill.

He'd done everything with a bone-deep sense of mastery. He'd been completely in control during lovemaking, but his dominance hadn't offended her, only excited.

A moment later, he leaned closer and dragged a cool, damp brush against her sensitive lower lip, back and forth, back and forth. Her clit tickled in awareness. Against her will, she had a graphic image pop into her head of him using the brushes, which he wielded so deftly, on her sex.

She focused on his face, startled at the uncalled for, potently erotic fantasy. His dark brows slanted. He lowered the brush. Her muscles tensed in anticipation, suspecting what was coming next because he'd done it during her original application, much to her unsettlement.

He gently cupped her jaw with his big hand, loosely covering her lower face. There was a smooth onyx stone on that silver ring, not on the top, as most decorative stones would be worn, but beneath the band on the palm side. He used it now with mind-blowing, subtle precision to smooth the makeup on her lips. She held her breath, the ache at her core mounting. He met her stare.

She only took a ragged lungful of air when he leaned back, wiped off the stone and his hands with a moist towelette, and put away his brushes. Then he was turning back to her.

"We have to get you back in now," he said gruffly. She was barely able to nod. Had she done something terrible in another lifetime that she was being forced to endure such torture now?

He lifted her T-shirt several inches and slid a hand beneath it, then paused, the slight pressure of his touch on her belly making her muscles go tighter in amplified awareness.

"Relax," he said quietly, leaning closer across the console. "I've seen breasts before."

I've seen yours, many times.

Her gaze zoomed to meet his stare. He hadn't said it out loud, but it'd *felt* like he did. She saw the slight tilt of his mouth. His fingers found the zipper. Gia stared down at his large, dark hands moving on the white fabric of the binder, speechless.

"I think I can do the whole procedure under your T-shirt, if that'll make you feel better."

"What a skill to possess," she managed dubiously.

He chuckled. "Every high school boy learns how to maneuver under the clothes. We haven't talked about who you are yet," he said, pulling on the zipper. It inched up above her belly button.

"Who I *am*?" she squeaked, surprised by his turn of the topic during such a delicate maneuver. Had he said it to distract her from what he was doing under her shirt? He paused and stared into her face. She'd absorbed his scent repeatedly when he'd applied her makeup this morning and done her hair application: clean, spicy, male. It had alarmed her, her body's reaction to that scent. He leaned closer, and she had no choice but to inhale him even more deeply.

"Yeah. Your character. Makeup artists come up with characters and backstories to flesh out a makeup, just like an actress might do for a role in a script. We have to come up with a story for why we're together and traveling across the country. Here's what I have so far. You're from San Diego. You're my nephew, my brother Jake's son. Jake is the manager of the European Formula One racing team. He's a wanderer who has about as much conscience—and control—as a jackrabbit hepped up on testosterone. I always wondered over the fact that he didn't have at least a half dozen children popping out of the woodwork. You were supposed to start at UCLA this fall, but instead you decided to postpone college for a semester while you discover yourself. You badgered your mother until she finally told you Jake's name. In a fit of teenage rebellion against your mom—you have those a lot—you traced Jake to the reservation in New Mexico. My relations told you his whereabouts, in addition to mine. Since Jake is in Europe, and almost impossible to track down, you came and found me for the time being. We decided to take a little vacation together to get to know each other. You haven't traveled much, and you always wanted to see the country, so we decided on a road trip."

"Do I love Jack Kerouac?" she asked in an amused, choked voice.

He pulled up on the zipper and frowned. "Sure. And surfing. Adjust your breasts." She was so caught up in his little story, she didn't register his meaning at first.

Coming to herself, she shoved both her hands beneath the T-shirt, Seth's buried forearm between them. She grunted softly, struggling to cram her breasts more securely into the shaper while Seth hovered over her. How ludicrous could this situation be? "We *are* maligning Joy's father with this story, right? That's who you mean?" she asked in a stifled voice, wanting to keep things straight in her mind. "You want me to be Joy's sister?"

"Her *brother*," he said succinctly. She looked into his face, startled. He grinned, white teeth flashing against swarthy skin, at the same moment she laughed.

"Don't laugh. It's no joke," he instructed with amused exacerbation, forcing the zipper up beneath her breasts with brute strength. "I'm proud of your makeup. You're a damn good-looking boy."

That definitely didn't help quiet her giggles. Her jags of laughter *certainly* weren't helping Seth bind her breasts.

"It's no good, I have to lift the shirt. I'm sorry," he said after a moment. He flipped the edge of the T-shirt up beneath her chin. Cool air-conditioned air flickered across the exposed skin in the V of the binder. Seth's stare landed on her chest and stuck. Her mirth evaporated as quick as it had come. It took her a moment to realize his had as well.

"Exhale all the breath from your lungs," he said unsmilingly. His knuckles brushed against the exposed swells of her breasts as he firmed his hold on the zipper. The unintentional caress made her lungs collapse as surely as anything else could. Seth jerked the zipper up to just beneath her collarbone. Any remaining air was expelled from her lungs.

"Mission accomplished," she gasped.

"That's one way of putting it," he replied grimly before he turned toward his door and popped it open.

On the way to the bathroom, Gia worked on her boy impression. It was sort of fun. She'd always thought playing the opposite sex would be a great challenge. Her character slouched a little and possessed that stiff-hipped, hands-in-pocket, slightly awkward gait she'd observed in teenage boys. Her character, she decided, was a late bloomer.

She headed immediately to the bathroom. She extended her hand to open the door, turning in surprise when someone grabbed her wrist from behind. Seth looked down at her.

"Wrong bathroom," he said.

She gaped at the W on the bathroom door and then back at Seth. Despite the shadows in the hallway and her sunglasses, she saw the slight tilt of his mouth.

"Men's bathrooms? *Really?*" she hissed incredulously. "Did you and Charles even *consider* that little detail when you came up with this crazy plan?"

"I'll pick clean spots."

"Men's bathrooms are *never* clean."

"How would you know? Now who's being prejudiced?" he asked quietly. He cast a wary glance down the dim, deserted hallway and exhaled. "There's practically no one in here. Go on into the women's. I'll keep watch and say the men's was out of order if someone comes. But you'll have to dare the men's room at some point on the trip. The last thing we need is for you to get arrested."

She threw him a dark look—which he stoically ignored—and plunged into the bathroom.

He was waiting for her at the entrance to the bathroom hallway near the hostess station, a newspaper in his hand, when she exited. Seth asked the waitress to seat them at a specific booth. Gia wondered if he had chosen it because it gave him a good view of the road and the diner entrance. She studied him surreptitiously over the top of their menu after they were seated, trying to picture him in espionage work. She had no problem doing it. Seth Hightower looked like he could hold a bunker full of secrets inside him.

Another slap of reality hit her when she went to order her food. She hadn't practiced a boy voice. But she was an actress, wasn't she? She was delighted to see the waitress mostly ignored her as she jotted down Gia's order, although she did keep casting speculative glances at Seth.

Her attempt had worked.

She noticed Seth examining her closely when the waitress moved out of hearing distance.

"What? Wasn't I convincing?" she whispered.

"No. It's not that," he replied, his expression stony.

"Well? What?" she prodded.

"If I didn't know better, I would have sworn I was sitting across this table from an eighteen-year-old boy."

"Well, that's good," she said, muffling her pleasure at his compliment. She noticed his continued sober look and wilted a little. It *was* a compliment, wasn't it? "Isn't it, Seth?"

"Yeah," he said, opening up his paper.

She mentally rolled her eyes at his laconism. Determined to be as calm about the situation as Seth, she looked around with veiled interest. He had been right about one thing. The gazes of the few people inside the sleepy diner slid right off her as if she were about as interesting as the paint on the wall. Anonymity was familiar to her from her younger years, of course, but an extremely rare experience recently. It was *nice*.

She found herself breathing easy for the first time in months, despite all these new realities and the cursed binder she wore. The binder, she discovered, might restrict deep breathing, but it was no dieting device. She ate more than she had in months, willfully ignoring Seth's small grin as he watched her wolf down a double cheeseburger and fries.

"You don't have to be so patronizing-looking. I was hungry," she told him stiffly as she ate her last fry with relish.

His dark brows arched. "Is that how I looked? I'm just glad to see you eating. You've lost weight since . . ." He abruptly wrapped his hand around his coffee cup and took a sip. "Is that because of all the crap going on in your life, or Hollywood having its effect on you?"

"Do you mean is it making me anorexic?" she asked scathingly.

"Yeah. Because that's something I've never seen: an actress with an eating disorder."

She blinked at his quiet, dripping sarcasm.

"I'm not eating disordered," she hissed under her breath. "I've just been . . ."

"Run ragged?" he asked levelly, taking another slow sip of his coffee.

"You should try keeping all the balls in the air that I have lately."

"Not a chance," he replied with quiet conviction.

Gia opened her mouth to respond, but the waitress returned.

"Are you two an item?" the chesty waitress asked as she began to clear. She waved her hand between Seth and Gia significantly. Gia froze in the act of setting her napkin on the table. *Crap.* Had the waitress seen through her disguise all along?

"He's my nephew," Seth said, giving the waitress a stare that would have sent a less determined woman running for the distant mountains. The waitress was made of strong stuff, apparently. She blanched, but rallied.

She winked at Seth as she took Gia's plate. "Just double-checking. I knew God couldn't be so cruel as to make a man who looks like you gay. Boys are a bottomless pit at this age, aren't they?" she asked Seth, glancing at Gia's polished plate. "But a big, strong guy like you definitely needs his energy as well," she added with a warm downward glance at Seth's chest. "That salad isn't enough to power up muscles like those. How about a slice of cherry pie?"

Gia watched in openmouthed amazement as the waitress continued to flirt outrageously with Seth for the next half minute. She seemed to consider Seth's occasional grunts and brief, uninformative replies to her comments and queries as some sort of challenge to try harder.

Finally, Gia's amusement waned and she stood, mumbling an excuse. She checked out the tiny on-site gift shop. Seth joined her a minute later.

"Are you a gambler in addition to being a surfer?" Seth joked a few minutes later as they walked through the parking lot back to the SUV. He nodded at the pack of playing cards she'd bought; they featured Route 66 streaking through the desert like a black-paved path to adventure.

"I thought we might need something to do while we're in exile. Do you play?"

"A little," he replied with typical brevity.

"*Hmmm.* You sound like you're still talking to the waitress. Could you *believe* her?" she asked as they got into the SUV. Seth had indicated he wanted to keep driving until he got tired.

Seth started up the vehicle. "Believe what?"

"That waitress! The way she was coming on to you like I wasn't even there," Gia said with incredulous amusement.

He shrugged. "She thought you were a guy. She didn't bother to put on the dampers."

Gia absorbed this bit of information in fascination. "You mean that when you're not with another woman, women flirt with you like that as a matter of course?" Weird. There was a whole other world out there to which she had previously had no access.

He pulled onto the highway. "I wouldn't say as a matter of course. If they're prone to flirting, they certainly tone it down if there's another woman around."

"She really *did* think I was a guy," Gia said, the reality of her appearance striking her again. She looked down at her boyish figure with renewed interest. When she focused on Seth, she saw the amused tilt of his mouth as he stared at the road.

"I'm good," he said.

She laughed at his atypical cockiness. "What about my acting? You have to admit my boy voice was good," she challenged, pointing a finger at him.

He nodded once in uncontested agreement. "And your walk was inspired. Smart of you to keep your hands in your pockets as much as you can. You definitely have the hands of a girl."

She grinned because he'd noticed. A flash of guilt went through her when she recalled she'd refused to say anything about his disguise because she was feeling a bit prickly and vulnerable about these circumstances.

About being with Seth.

"If I was inspired, it was by your work. I didn't tell you after you finished the makeup in L.A. I couldn't believe that was me in the mirror. You *are* good," she conceded, her gaze glued to his compelling profile. "I'll give you that."

Good at quite a few things.

His smile faded. Damn. Why did she feel like he could sometimes read her thoughts?

"So what's my name?" she rallied, trying to turn things light again. He was going to think she was as flirtatious as that waitress. "My boy name, I mean."

He seemed to consider for a second. "Jessie? Jessie Bauer."

She tried out the name in her head and nodded in agreement. "And should I call you Uncle Seth?" she teased.

His swift, dark glance made her clamp her mouth shut.

"Let's not make this any weirder than it already is," he stated flatly.

After another couple hours on the road, he found himself glancing over at Gia's hands again. She had a restless habit of moving her fingers on her thighs in little squeezing movements. He found her short fingernails scraping against the denim—and imagining her firm, supple thighs beneath the fabric—highly distracting.

He wished like hell he were one of those people in the diner who had been fooled by her skillful acting and his makeup. Having prior knowledge of what was under those slouchy jeans and the shapeless shirt was like a splinter under his skin. Something about covering up Gia rubbed him the wrong way. The idea of ripping through the disguise to the real woman kept creeping into his mind, unwelcome.

The fact was, the stupid fantasy of exposing the real Gia underneath the very disguise he'd engineered was turning him on, and that irritated him a lot.

"What do you suppose the weather will be like in—*what* did you say the name of the place where we're going was?" she interrupted her own thought abruptly.

"Vulture's Canyon."

"Weird name for a town."

"It's a weird town, so it's fitting," he assured her. "And we probably won't go into the town itself much. We'll be pretty isolated at John and Jennifer's house. It'll probably still be warm. October stays warm there, although there might be some cool fall days."

"You sound like you've been there a lot."

"I have. Remember—"

He halted abruptly.

"What?" Gia asked, sitting forward. She'd caught his mistake. He'd been about to mention something they'd talked about during their first meeting. That, in turn, had reminded him of something else that annoyed him. He felt her gaze on his cheek. "Seth? Were you going to say something about that night?"

"Yeah," he admitted gruffly after a tense pause, requiring no further clarification as to which night she meant.

"Do we really have to tiptoe around it?" she asked, sounding a little exacerbated. "We slept together. It's not the end of the world."

"Yeah. You're right. Just forget it."

"No," she said. He exhaled irritably, tightening his hand on the wheel.

"I thought you just said it wasn't the end of the world, and we should just forget it," he said.

"*You* said we should forget it. I just asked if we had to walk on eggshells about it. What were you going to say?"

He frowned at the road. The sun was starting to dip behind them, giving the pavement and the surrounding desert a rosy tinge.

"Fine. I was going to say, 'Do you remember when you asked me if I'd ever worked with the director Rill Pierce?' I hadn't then, but I have now. That's who I visit a lot in Vulture's Canyon. He's married to Katie Hughes, who is the sister of Everett Hughes, who married—"

"Joy. Your niece," Gia finished for him, her voice sounding thoughtful all of a sudden . . . tentative. "I knew you did *Razor Pass* and *Keeping It Light* with Pierce since we met a couple years ago," she said, mentioning two of Rill's recent films.

"And I know now that the person whom you mentioned *knowing* that had won the Pierce scholarship to UCLA was *you*," he said.

Her hands moved on her thighs as if she was trying to dry them.

"You were a theater major at UCLA, not a history major. Why'd you have to lie about *that*, in addition to everything else?" He gave her a hard glance. She was watching him, but he couldn't read her expression with her makeup and sunglasses. "Never mind," he said when she didn't respond immediately. "It doesn't matter."

She made a sound of disgust.

"*What?*" he asked sharply. What right did she have to be annoyed? *He* was the one lied to, not her.

"I was a double major in history and theater, for your information. I wasn't lying about loving history. At the time I met you, I was doing an adaptation of *Nine Days a Queen* and was playing Lady Jane Grey."

His annoyance swelled at her uptilted chin and regal manner. She was such a damn riddle box. Only Gia could suddenly make him bizarrely imagine Lady Jane Grey being portrayed by the beach-bum teenage boy sitting in the passenger seat.

"I often choose historical roles," she continued. "As for Rill Pierce, his scholarships are for theater and film students. I didn't want you to find out I was an actress back then. If I'd told you *I* was the one who had won a Pierce scholarship, you would've asked me *which* scholarship I'd won. And in case you've forgotten, we've already established that I knew at the time you possessed this unreasonable prejudice against actresses," she finished with force.

"Unreasonable to you, maybe."

"Tell me why it's reasonable to *you*."

"You've worked in this business a while now. You must realize that it's common for makeup artists to avoid actors and actresses. There's often a clash between us."

"That's a lame reason to judge people without knowing them."

"But why did you have to mislead me when it came to the scholarship? I felt like an idiot when Rill happened to mention that the blazing comet of the film business—Gia Harris—was a recipient of his scholarship."

"Is *that* what this is really all about? You don't like having the wool pulled over your eyes? Ex-intelligence operative and Hollywood special effects–artist bigwig doesn't like being out of the loop."

"Nobody likes being misled. Why should it have mattered if I took a dislike to you that night?"

She made a sound of bitter disgust and crossed her arms above her waist. "You are such an idiot," she breathed out as she turned away from him, mutely staring out at the stark desert landscape.

He simmered in the silence for the next several minutes, undoubtedly grinding some enamel off his back teeth. Curse him for having the idea of driving to Illinois. True, he thought it was a better idea for security, but the memory of Gia lighting up as she'd told him about the cross-country trip when she'd been sixteen might have nudged his decision a little, as well.

Nothing good ever came from being sentimental.

Gia lowered her seat to a full reclining position. When she squirmed to get comfortable, while still keeping her back stubbornly to him, his attention was caught. She'd scooted up the chair and pulled her knees up onto the seat. The seat belt lowered over her hips, the seat strap pressing against her loose, low riding jeans and cupping her ass.

As if a guy would ever have an ass like that. Arousal tickled the root of his cock. She wiggled impatiently, still struggling for a comfortable position. This time, lust roared instead of whimpered. He hardened with vigor.

With effort, he jerked his gaze off the appealing sight of her ass.

This trip with Gia was going to be a trial all right. In more ways than one.

Maybe she slept. He thought she did, not only because of her stillness but also because the anger and tension that had seemed to pulse in the air between them seemed to slowly dissipate. Seth started to feel guilty for taking his irritation out on her. He didn't want to reveal his frustration; it just seemed to pop out of him at times.

Best to face the fact. His sexual attraction to Gia Harris had been—and still was—uncommonly strong. He'd been more disappointed than he'd cared to admit when he discovered she was something different than he'd been led to expect that night years ago. He'd thought her a fresh, sexy surprise, one of those moments in life when you think, *Jesus, what did I do to deserve something like this?* Realizing she was a twenty-two-year-old ingénue with the flame of fame burning bright within her had made him more bitter than he already was.

And he'd been pretty damned cynical on the topic even then.

But Gia wasn't the one responsible for his original jadedness when it came to actresses. She didn't deserve the weight of his experience and history.

Admitting that made him feel steadier. Almost as if the landscape were mimicking his calming mood, they entered the environs of Flagstaff. He turned the heat on to low as the temperature plummeted in the refreshing mountain oasis. Gia squirmed a little in the seat next to him and turned over on her other hip, facing him. Her lip paint had nearly faded away. She yawned widely, the glimpse of her pink, full lips and red mouth making him want to stare at her instead of the road. For a full moment, he sensed her studying his profile, but neither of them spoke. He felt it for the first time since that night two years ago, that ephemeral, magical spell settling on his tingling skin.

"Where are we?" she murmured sleepily, her low, smooth voice causing his forearms and neck to roughen.

"The outskirts of Flagstaff. Do you need a break?" he glanced at her as he came to a stop at a light. It had grown overcast as he wound up the mountains to Flagstaff. He'd taken off his sunglasses, and so had she. Her eyes were like a clear spring day.

"Yes, please. I'm sorry I called you an idiot," she added quietly.

He nodded. "I'm sorry for getting irritated at you for something that happened a long time ago."

Her gaze flickered over his face. She started to speak but then hesitated.

"What?" he prodded.

"It doesn't really seem like a long time ago," she murmured.

"No. It doesn't," he agreed, studying the sublime curve of her jaw and the sweet target of her mouth.

A horn honked loudly. He cursed and drove through the green light. Neither of them spoke for the time it took him to pull into the parking lot of a roadside log-cabin restaurant and gas station that had Route 66 memorabilia and signs plastered all over it. The charged atmosphere didn't dissipate though. He whipped the SUV into an empty spot at the side of the building. Slowly, he twisted the keys in the ignition.

"Do you need to retouch me before I go inside?" she asked.

Her words struck him as potently sexual. Naturally. Everything was striking him as sexual, ever since he'd seen Gia sitting in that conference room yesterday. He wanted to touch her all right, and retouch her, and squeeze her . . . and consume her. He looked over at her. Her lips parted beneath his stare. Prodded by instinct and simple, unmitigated lust, he gave up the fight for the moment. He leaned toward her.

"I need to do something first," he rasped before he covered her mouth with his own.

He knew the moment her warm breath rushed against his lips and her mouth softened beneath his kiss it wasn't *just for a moment* though. She was under his skin, and good. He'd wondered if he had fooled himself into thinking that being with her was much, much better in memory than in reality.

No. He'd had it right from the first.

He heard her soft whimper as he slicked his tongue along her lower lip and felt her inner heat. Right here, right now, only the naked truth existed. He dipped his tongue between her lips, the act of piercing into her sweetness striking him as intensely erotic.

He knew he should stop. But he couldn't. Especially when she slid her tongue against his, and her flavor fully penetrated his brain. He framed her face with his hands and delved his tongue between her lips hungrily. When she gripped his hair and her short nails scraped against his neck, his cock jerked viciously.

He wanted inside her again, and his craving was sharp and cutting.

He tore his mouth from hers, grimacing at the harsh depravity. Sitting up, he inhaled, straining to clear the fog of lust from his brain.

"Sorry. I don't know why I did that," he said, scraping his hair out of his face in a frustrated gesture.

"Yes, you do," she replied softly.

Seven

For a few seconds, he just stared at her.

"Things are different now than they were then," he said.

"Because you know the ugly, horrible truth about me?"

"Because of the circumstances. We shouldn't make this situation any more complicated than it already is," he growled softly, pulling the keys out of the ignition and avoiding her stare. He twisted around and found his makeup kit.

"Maybe it would be best if I showed you how to do your mouth," he said quietly as Gia started to raise her seat.

"Yeah, maybe it would be."

Damn. He knew by her cool tone he'd offended her.

Gia applied her lip makeup as Seth had instructed her, trying to ignore the potent combination of anger and lust simmering inside of her.

So what if what Seth said was true? The reasonable thing to do would be to rein in this teeth-grinding attraction they had for each other. She *knew* that. But that didn't make it any easier to hear him say it. Instead, it just brought back all the reminders of why he'd never called her to begin with.

You had my number as well.

The memory of his saying that this morning popped into her brain, unwelcome. She irritably shoved the thought aside. He'd been changing the subject to derail her.

She knew she shouldn't care what he thought of her. But no one liked being stereotyped, being seen as something they weren't. Being seen incorrectly by Seth Hightower especially grated on her already raw nerves.

"Go on inside. I'll follow you in a minute," she told him coolly as she painted the neutral shade on her lips.

"Gia, I only meant—"

"I know what you meant," she said crisply, studying her reflection in the mirror. "It wouldn't be smart for us to give in to it."

"That doesn't mean I don't want you like hell."

She blinked in surprise at his harsh statement and turned to him. His face looked rigid, his eyes glittering.

"But not enough. Isn't that right?" she asked quietly.

His mouth tightened. For a second, she thought he was going to curse. She wished he would, for some reason. It would be nice to see him lose control for once. Instead, he turned suddenly and whipped open his door, got out and slammed it behind him hard. She watched his long-legged saunter across the parking lot in the makeup mirror, her anger amplifying to a low burn.

When she followed him a minute later—perfecting her slouchy boy walk—she noticed him standing in the checkout line, holding two cups of coffee and several bottles of water tucked beneath his forearm. She hesitated outside the bathrooms, inhaling for courage before she plunged into the men's. Thankfully, there was no one inside, and it was reasonably clean.

When she reached the parking lot after leaving the bathroom, she didn't see him in the SUV. He must still be inside. As she approached the vehicle, however, she spotted him in the distance. There was a small playground in the back of the establishment, built to give car-confined kids an opportunity to expend some youthful energy. Seth was the only one using it today. She leaned her hip against the car and watched, openmouthed. He hung off an iron horizontal ladder, knees bent to keep him suspended, doing pull-up after pull-up, his precise, rapid strength and obvious pent-up power stunning to observe.

When he straightened, feet on the ground again, Gia turned away abruptly and got in the car. She felt rattled by the vision. It took her a few seconds to realize why. In her mind a moment ago, she'd accused him of not wanting her, of possessing annoying amounts of sexual restraint.

But the truth had just been right there in front of her. Seth Hightower wasn't impervious. Far from it.

He was burning just as much as she was.

They didn't talk much as Seth drove for the next several hours, and dusk slowly began to settle. What had happened in that Flagstaff parking lot seemed to hover like a dense cloud inside the SUV, making the atmosphere crackle with tension. Seth showed no sign of tiring, even when full night fell. Curiosity pierced her ruffled emotional state after they paused for gas and a quick break on the outskirts of Albuquerque.

"Do you miss it? Living here?" she asked him, once they were on the road again.

"Yeah. The wide-open spaces. The quiet." He lifted two long fingers off the wheel, gesturing to the midnight dome of millions of bright stars above them. "The night sky."

She loved the sound of his deep, rough voice in the darkness.

"I recall you mentioning college once when . . ." She cleared her throat remembering too late the circumstances where he'd mentioned it. She'd been in his arms, following a particularly fulfilling round of lovemaking, their breaths and hearts slowing. Blinking away the potent flash of memory, she rallied. "Did you go to school around here?"

"Yeah. University of New Mexico. Jake and I both went there on football scholarships."

"Is Jake big like you?"

He nodded. "Jake's the one who played four years though. Made Defensive Player of the Year two years in a row. I quit late in my freshman year."

"College?"

"No, football."

"Didn't like it?" she asked, turning slightly in her seat, her interest caught. She could perfectly imagine Seth as a football player, given his size and athletic grace. She could imagine one big problem with the scenario, though, given what she knew about him.

"I like football okay, but it's a game."

"It got in the way of your art, didn't it?"

He looked over at her swiftly. She gave him a small smile.

"Yeah. That's the reason I jumped at the scholarship," he agreed quietly, his eyes back on the road. "I couldn't have studied art any other way. We didn't have the money for school. But being an art student isn't like being in your typical liberal arts program. It's very demanding. I started to resent all the practice hours and travel time required for the team. So I joined ROTC and got my free ride that way."

"I was wondering how being an artist and the whole Army intelligence thing went together," she mused. "But I suppose military intelligence could use a master of disguise."

"The military taught me almost as much about makeup as a special effects internship I did for a couple years in college. Maybe more."

She wanted to ask him about some of his assignments but figured perhaps they were confidential, so she refrained. The mood in the vehicle had segued from tension-filled to mellow, and she didn't want to ruin it.

"It's certainly a beautiful place to call home," she said, gazing out her window onto the dome of stars.

"Yeah. But ever since my mom passed, it doesn't feel as much like home to me."

"She was the artist."

Gia blinked. Somehow, her words sounded more significant than she had meant them to be. She had meant it generally, but also specifically. Seth's mother was *the* artist of Gia's sculpture. Seth didn't respond immediately. She shifted uncomfortably in her seat.

"Do you still have it?" he asked after a moment, his casualness sounding a little forced.

Her heart leapt at his quiet question. She didn't need to ask him what he meant. Somehow, they both had been thinking about her favorite sculpture that had bizarrely been modeled after Seth himself.

"Yes," she replied in a hushed tone. She felt too vulnerable to tell him it still sat in a prime space on her mantel. "I thought about getting rid of it after that night."

"Why didn't you?" he asked, his profile rigid, his gaze never wavering off the road.

"Your mother's sculpture didn't do anything to me."

She'd said it matter-of-factly, but realized he might have thought she was being petulant. She shifted in her seat again restlessly, scratching under the wig.

"Is it starting to bug you?" he asked her, noticing her scratching. She nodded.

He swiftly checked behind them, but the empty road disappeared into the blackness of a desert night. He pulled over to the side of the road and put on the hazards.

"We can take it off for now. Do you want me to take off the cap too?" he asked, leaning toward her and peeling off the wig. She heaved a sigh of relief. He placed the wig carefully in the backseat.

"No," she said, touching the brown skullcap that closely bound her hair to her head. "It's not bothering me. It's the hair that was hot and scratchy. The binder *is* uncomfortable though. Can I take it off?" she asked, waving at her torso.

"You don't want to go inside somewhere and eat soon?"

"I'm not that hungry," she said honestly. "But maybe you are? You only had a salad at lunch."

He shook his head. "We'll stop somewhere in a couple hours and get a snack for the road. I'd just as soon get there as quickly as possible."

She nodded in agreement. He didn't move.

"Do you want help?" he asked, nodding at her bound torso.

"No, I can do it," she said, glad the dim dashboard lights were the only source of light in the vehicle. Heat had rushed into her cheeks when she recalled that, while she might be able to get the zipper down on the stiff garment, getting it back up would require Seth's help. She probably shouldn't loosen the binder in order to prevent that agitating scenario again, but it was so *uncomfortable*.

"Do you want me to drive?" she asked as he shifted the SUV out of park and glanced into the mirrors in preparation to return to the road.

"No. I'm fine. You can rest if you want to."

"All I've done is. rest," she said ruefully. "I haven't slept this much during the day since . . . *forever*."

"You must have needed it. Sometimes, you've just got to let your body tell you what's right."

His words seemed to hang in the air and vibrate in her ears. She thought maybe he noticed the charged, potential double meaning of his statement because he inhaled sharply and shifted in his seat as he got the SUV up to speed on the highway.

Sometimes, you've just got to let your body tell you what's right.

The image of his long body stretching and flexing as he'd pumped off those pull-ups jumped into her head. His body was telling *him* something. So was hers. Seth didn't want to hear the message. She wasn't sure she was comfortable giving in to that primal mandate either. Indulging in desire with Seth Hightower might set her off-track. It might make her waver from what had once been a well-planned life and career. She longed to have her orderly life back, not to send it into further chaos.

Despite her cautionary thoughts, she reclined the seat and reached beneath the T-shirt. Seth glanced sideways at her, then quickly returned his gaze to the road. Her breasts felt achy, her nipples chafed and sensitive from the stiff restraint. She found the tab on the zipper and exhaled. They hadn't turned the radio on when they returned after their short stop. The metallic sound of the zipper lowering sounded far too loud and illicit in her ears.

She finally got it all the way down to her belly and inhaled a full breath of air. Seth opened his mouth as if he were going to say something, but then pressed his lips together, his jaw rigid. She turned on her side toward him, crossing her arms beneath her breasts. He didn't fully look at her, but she sensed he was very aware of her watching his profile.

For a moment, the silence seemed to pulse with unsaid words. Gia longed to voice some of them, but dread mingled with the urge. Still . . . maybe loosening the binder had released more than the constriction on her lungs.

"I didn't keep the truth from you that night because I'm a liar by nature," she finally dared softly. "I wanted you to like me because I thought you were the most attractive man I'd ever met."

He looked over at her.

"If that was wrong of me, I'm sorry," she continued in a hushed tone. She waited for a moment for the hot, thick feeling in her chest and throat to recede. "You said on that night that the only rationale for us getting together so impulsively was that we wanted each other. Period." His hand tightened on the wheel. "I understand that the circumstances have changed. I understand that there are things that make me objectionable to you."

"I find you far from objectionable, Gia," he grated out, still staring fiercely at the road.

"Let me finish. I was only going to say that I don't think all those things make the original reason why we got together invalid. In fact, that reason seems as valid to me as it ever did. More so."

His hands tightened on the wheel. "You want to give in to it?" he asked tensely through gritted teeth. "All in the name of a few fucks?"

Her heartbeat started to throb in her ears at his crudeness. She understood he was purposefully trying to put her off. It wasn't going to work. She thought Seth knew that too.

"I don't know. Maybe. We did that first night. Do *you* want to? Maybe you think it'll mean more than just a few fucks, and that's why you're balking? It would be horrible, wouldn't it?" she needled with quiet sarcasm. "Finding yourself wanting to be around an actress? Around *me*?"

A muscle jumped in his lean cheek. She almost felt the curse he restrained blistering his throat. The silence pounded in her ears. She sighed. Sensing his guard all too perfectly at that moment, she turned away from him and closed her eyes.

Maybe you think it'll mean more than just a few fucks, and that's why you're balking?

Her voice kept replaying in his head, taunting him. His head started to throb with it. His cock had been intermittently throbbing with something altogether different, and even more incendiary.

Damn. The fact of the matter was, he had sensed it was something more than just a few fucks on that night two years ago.

That's the truth he was guarding himself against. And Gia had guessed that.

He glanced sideways for the hundredth time in the past several hours at her still form. She said she'd withheld the truth from him about her age and about her profession because she'd wanted him. Plain and simple.

For once, while she slept, he raised the barricades on his memories. He recalled in graphic detail how good it had been with her. She'd been so sweet and generous, letting him devour her, and clearly loving it. He knew he was very demanding in bed. He knew what he liked and wasn't afraid to voice it. Gia had been right there with him, even though he'd been more demanding and challenging with her than he had been with some long-term lovers.

More insistent, because his lust had never been as sharp as it had been for that fresh, beautiful young woman with a smile that pierced straight through him.

That *still* pierced.

He'd grown hard again. He hadn't bargained on how brutal the impact would be when he combined memories of that night with Gia's nearness to him in the vehicle. Even though he'd drunk two large bottles of water since that kiss, her taste still seemed to linger on his tongue.

He winced and glanced aside again at Gia's silent form. The forbidden image of making love to her that first time flamed into his head, her fascinated gaze and vividly red cheeks in the mirrored reflections as she observed him watching, as his cock had plunged in and out of her. He'd always been a very visual person. It was part of who he was, a characteristic reflected in his near-photographic memory, his career, his aesthetics, his sexual preferences. Some women found it offensive that he liked to watch lovemaking. He understood that they might feel objectified by it, but that was never his intention. He'd learned to tone it down, depending upon his lover's temperament.

But Gia had liked watching them together, almost as much as he had.

She'd liked a lot of things.

Blood pulsed into his cock.

He checked the rearview mirror. The highway had been mostly desolate. He'd taken Historic Route 66 intermittently because he thought Gia might like it, but he also knew that it would expose any followers more quickly than a busy interstate might. If he had to guess, he'd say their mission thus far had been successful. One of the most recognized faces in the country had vanished off the map. He felt safer about switching to the major highway in Amarillo, which would be soon.

Making sure Gia was still turned away, he tried to shift his aching cock to a more comfortable position. If she woke up anytime soon, he doubted he could hide his arousal from her. He was hard as a stone, the rigid column of his cock pressed against his jeans at a slanted vertical angle along his pelvis and lower belly. The outline of it was obvious in his jeans. He managed to shift it, but the stimulation didn't help matters. Gia moved restlessly.

He grimaced, experiencing quiet, simmering agony. So *this* is what the road to hell looked like.

"Gia."

She opened her eyes, immediately recognizing Seth's voice. The car was dark and stationary. In the distance, she saw the glow of neon lights. She spun around in the seat. Seth was watching her, his face tense, long legs bent directly in front of the seat, his wrists draped over the wheel.

"Where are we?" she mumbled, starting to sit up. She looked behind her and saw a large gas station–convenience store in the distance. As she turned back to him, he quickly dropped his arms to his thighs.

"Outside of Amarillo, Texas. It's two in the morning. I need a break."

"Okay," she said, rubbing her eyes. "I should go too."

"Okay. But do you think you could get yourself together while I go ahead inside? The gas station looks deserted. You shouldn't have much of an audience."

She blinked in surprise at his quiet, pressured tone. He must really need to go.

"Sure. The wig won't be a problem, but I'm going to take off the binder. I'll put on my jacket," she said quickly when he looked doubtful.

He nodded, although discomfort shadowed his face. "It'll do for now. Don't forget to do your lips and put on the powder."

He got out of the car. Her brow crinkled in confusion as she watched him in the rearview mirror walk toward the entrance, his quick acquiescence to her disguise shortcut striking her as odd indeed. He usually had a sexy, loose-hipped saunter, but his long, lean form looked especially stiff at the moment. Poor man. She suddenly was very regretful for being so confrontational with him earlier. His muscles must be starting to seize up on him. He'd driven for nearly sixteen hours straight. She would insist on driving when he returned so that he could stretch out. This time, she wouldn't take no for an answer.

She got on the wig without mishap and quickly reapplied her makeup. The finished result wasn't as good as when Seth did it, but it was sufficient for a dark night and nearly empty gas station. She put on her sunglasses. If she looked a little more hermaphroditic than when Seth took charge of her disguise, Gia doubted it would matter here. One thing was certain: She *didn't* look like Gia Harris. She shrugged out of the hated binder and found her jacket in the backseat. She also spotted the toiletry kit Seth had packed and grabbed it. She longed to brush her teeth. Flinging open her door, she got out of the SUV to join Seth inside.

* * *

He couldn't take it anymore. Desperate times called for desperate measures, and Seth was ready to break apart from acute desperation at that moment.

Desperate, nagging, biting arousal.

He couldn't get back in the close quarters of that vehicle with Gia with his ponderous erection harassing him every fucking second.

He stood in the closed bathroom stall facing the door and unfastened his jeans hastily. Not bothering to remove his underwear, he pulled his heavy erection through the slit in his boxer briefs, wincing as he cupped his balls and lifted them out as well. Furious at his inability to control his arousal, he slapped irritably at the jutting stalk, but even that stimulation excited him. He'd never felt so sensitive, his nerves leaping with excitement. The last several hours in that SUV inhaling Gia's scent had been a living torture. He needed relief.

He craved *her*.

Gia wanted to give in to it. He'd never wanted to submit to his need more in this life. He suspected what Gia had said was true though. Once he surrendered, instinct told him he might not be able to leave her without regret.

None of that mattered. Not now. He parted his thighs, taking a firm stance. He fisted himself and began to pump midstaff to just below the swollen head, single-minded and greedy. Only his need to empty himself of this painful craving counted. He closed his eyes and gripped onto the top of the door with his left hand, vivid memories bombarding him: holding Gia naked against him while he sucked on her beautiful breasts, of laying her on that couch and driving into her tight, sweet body while she stared up at him with helpless arousal.

Of course he'd have her again eventually, he thought wildly as he jacked his cock faster and faster, feeling that inevitable truth rising in him as surely as his impending, explosive climax. Could any man hold out with such a bounty of sexy, hot sweetness taunting him at every turn?

Inside the gas station, Gia passed a sleepy-looking attendant and found the corridor in the back leading to the bathrooms. Figuring Seth was in the men's room, and seeing not a single female—or anyone—in sight, she ducked into the women's. She exited several minutes later, assuming Seth would either be out in the car or getting gas. Walking out to the SUV in the back parking lot, she realized he still wasn't there though. She turned back around and backtracked, thinking she could help him carry the snacks and beverages. The attendant must have been in the back room, because she didn't see him behind the counter. She started to get a couple bottles of water when she noticed the toiletry bag in her hand.

Maybe Seth wanted to use it?

A moment later, she walked down the corridor that led to the bathrooms again. It suddenly struck her that she was treading very quietly as she approached the men's room. What was she thinking? Seth had told her he thought she should use the men's room on the trip. But she couldn't go in there while *he* was in there, boy disguise or no. She was being ridiculous.

Yet she drew closer to the wooden door, the skin of her neck and forearms roughened with awareness. Maybe he wasn't even in there? He could have been in a part of the large store where she couldn't spot him? Somehow, though, she didn't think so. He was *in* there. She was always very aware of him, but that awareness at the moment seemed to swell and vibrate.

Very softly, she opened the swinging bathroom door. She immediately recognized his black leather work boots in a stall. No one else was in there. She ducked back hastily, but halted her exit just as abruptly. He wasn't back in the stall, as if he were using the toilet. Instead, he stood close to the stall door, feet forward. Then she noticed his large hand—along with the signature silver ring—gripping the stall door at the top.

As if in a trance, she entered the large lavatory and closed the door silently behind her.

Her heart started racing in her chest. Adrenaline poured into her veins, causing her flesh to tingle. For an eternal second, she remained unmoving. Then she heard a rough, muted groan, and she was moving toward him as if in a dream.

The crack between the stall door and the metal surround wasn't large, perhaps a quarter of an inch. It was enough for a voyeur—which is what Gia had apparently transformed into in the past few seconds. Of course, she'd guessed what he was doing in there. She'd witnessed his mounting tension. Felt it . . . Shared it . . .

Despite her suspicion, when she saw the fast, pistonlike motion of his arm through the crack, an electrical shock seemed to go through her body. It was enough to mainline a jolt of arousal straight through her. Seth was a very powerful man. To witness him using all his innate force, to sense the tight coil of his arousal unraveling in a frenzy of raw need, was the most forbidden, thrilling thing she'd ever seen.

His pumping grew even faster. She heard him hiss furiously. His hand clenched the top of the door tighter. She stepped closer. Her mind and body had gone tight with anticipation and a purpose that was as single-minded as his apparently was.

She wanted to see his rigid restraint shatter.

She longed to see him erupt in pleasure.

Moving her head in a darting motion, she tried to get a better angle on him. It took her a moment to realize she no longer saw his frantic pumping motions.

The lock clicked. She barely backed up in time before the metallic door swung open. She jumped when it clattered loudly against the next stall. Her breath froze in her lungs. Seth stood there, arms at his side, his face the vivid picture of a dangerous storm about to break. Her gaze dropped to his crotch. His jeans were still unfastened and bunched around his hips. His cock was inside his briefs, but still flagrantly obvious. It tented the front of his white boxer briefs, huge and intimidating-looking. Her stare locked with his.

Oh my God. What should I say? What should I do?

It wasn't as if a person was ever taught to deal with a situation like this.

Then he was stalking past her, jerking up his jeans and fastening them as he went. She heard the water start to run at the sink. When she mustered enough nerve to move, she peered around the bank of metal stalls and saw him standing at the sink. He washed his hands vigorously with soap and water, then leaned down and splashed his face repeatedly. She could tell by his stiff, forceful movements he was furious.

He shut off the tap and turned to retrieve several paper towels from the dispenser. After he'd thrown away the damp towels, she finally found her voice.

"I just thought you might want this," she said lamely, holding up the toiletry bag. Her gaze kept bouncing off him, like he was a fire too hot and radiating for it to rest for long. "I'm . . . I'm sorry," she said in a choked voice. "I didn't mean to—"

"Gia."

She blinked and gaped up at his face when he cut her off harshly.

"Give me the bag, and go out to the car and wait for me."

Her mouth fell open in disbelief. His eyes were molten. With that ominous pronouncement, did he mean what she thought he meant? One dark brow quirked as he stared at her stunned face. "Why are you surprised? You're the one who won't give me a second of rest. You should be the one to give me a moment of relief, don't you think?"

His quiet, grim voice echoed in her head repeatedly. Her skin tingled beneath his scoring stare. She said nothing when he reached out and took the bag from her frozen, clawlike hand, setting it on the counter.

"Go on. I'll be there in a moment." She started to move toward the door, her heart beating uncomfortably hard in her chest. "Wait," he barked.

She turned abruptly, surprised by his command. He tore off a paper towel and walked over to the sink. He wetted the towel. Without uttering a word, he stepped over to her. He cupped the back of her head with his palm and began to rub the towel over her lips, wiping off the paint there. Her lips parted when he moved the wet towel in the slit. His gaze narrowed on her mouth. He pushed with his hand at the back of her head gently and with the towel firmly, her soft flesh molding and succumbing to his touch.

"There's a surveillance camera aimed at the cash register and the front door. Keep your head down when you pass. Go on," he said gruffly as his hand lowered.

Eight

Gia swallowed thickly. Something ought to be said in these circumstances, but for the life of her, she couldn't think *what*. She was feeling too much to talk. She took one last look into his gleaming, pantherlike eyes and stumbled out of the bathroom.

The trip back to the SUV was undertaken in a fog. She sat in the passenger seat, her gaze trained on the path to the store, breathing in ragged anticipation. He came within a minute of her, his stride long and rapid.

Hasty.

He clambered into the SUV. His scent followed him: soap, the lingering fragrance from his hair.

Male arousal.

He twisted the keys in the ignition. Her buzzing confusion mounted.

"What are we—?"

"Just a second," he growled, swinging the vehicle around aggressively. He drove to a rear part of the parking lot that was deep in shadow. The car came to an abrupt halt. He threw it into Park. Then he was reaching for her.

She supposed some people might have called his kiss angry, but Gia understood it wasn't. It was wild and furious, yes, but with need, not anger. She shared in his mood, so his mouth seizing hers single-mindedly only felt right. Delicious. He wasn't going to hold back this time, she knew. His need had finally torn through his rigid defenses and irrational prejudice.

He tasted like peppermint and Seth. He'd held back in the bathroom to brush his teeth, she realized with amazed excitement. That knowledge struck her as poignantly sweet, especially in the fury of the raging storm of his lust. He ate her with focused fervor, biting at her lips, slicking the sting with the tip of his tongue, plunging into her mouth with unapologetic greed, and applying a slight suction that made her desperate. She sunk her fingers into his hair, straining to meet his powerful hunger.

He ripped at the button fly of her jeans and spoke next to her lips between small, lustful bites of her flesh.

"You're killing me." He shoved his hand into her underwear and her eyes sprang wide. His fingertip found her clit with unerring accuracy.

"No. You're killing me," she whimpered, kissing him back feverishly. "Oh God," she moaned, because the ridge of his finger was rubbing her with a friction that made her eyes cross. Reality trickled into her rabid excitement. She reached across the console for that sexy belt buckle. "Let me first," she hissed against his lips. "I'm the one who interrupted you."

He growled in protest, pushing her back slightly with the mass of his solid body, continuing to agitate her clit in a bull's-eye fashion. His hand opened at the small of her back, where he applied a slight pressure, pushing her against his agitating hand between her thighs. She writhed against him, struggling to reach him again. It was a wrestling match, but a hot, tense, sweaty one. She found the column of his thick, rigid cock pressing against his jeans and rubbed it with single-minded purpose through the fabric.

"Jesus," he muttered. His head thudded against the back of the seat. She saw the pain on his face. She loved the evidence of his stark need and hated it, all at once. She released his belt, ripped at his button fly and tried to get the denim over his hips.

"*Help* me," she insisted.

Gritting his teeth, he raised his head. With the aid of the dim dashboard lights, she thought she glimpsed grim resignation etched on his rugged features. He lifted his hips, assisting her in shoving his jeans down his thighs. She banged her elbow against the console when she jerked at the stretchy fabric of his boxer briefs.

"Ouch," she mumbled, but she hardly registered the pain.

"Maybe we should get a room," he said thickly. He inhaled raggedly when her fist enclosed his cock. "Jesus," he gasped.

He was enormous with need, teeming with pulsing life.

"I don't think this is going to wait for a room." She began to pump him, if not as forcefully as she'd witnessed him pounding himself in the stall, every bit as fast and twice as eager. This wasn't a moment for lingering caresses and foreplay. He was in a fever of need, and she was rabid to bring him relief.

With a choked sound, he pushed his underwear down below his balls, cupping them as she pumped the rigid staff. She felt his stare on her as he watched her, hell-bent on jacking him. Her awareness of his observance made her clit prickle with amplified excitement. He lifted his hand and covered hers, guiding her, showing her exactly what he wanted without words. When she followed his lead, tightening her strokes on the stalk just below the fat, delineated crown, his hand dropped to his testicles again. It aroused her, the way he touched himself in front of her without a trace of hesitation. Her pumping grew more forceful. He growled tensely and cupped his balls, massaging them. Wild with arousal at the viral image he made, she strained toward his lap, but the console got in her way. She hungered to feel the rigid, warm flesh parting her lips, the hard pressure of him straining in her mouth. He groaned and halted her with one hand at her nape.

"Not now. It's too late. I'm going to come," he grated out, sounding agonized. He groaned and grabbed at the hem of his T-shirt, jerking it up his taut belly. He began to ejaculate as she pumped him, white jets of semen spilling down to her fingers and shooting onto his belly. Just when she thought he was slowing, his muscles tensed again hard. She jerked his cock with force, and he heaved a guttural moan. Another jet erupted and fell back onto the swollen crown, seeping onto her fingers. His male scent entered her nose, slightly salty, musky . . . heady.

She stared up into his face while he panted and his muscles clenched, continuing her strokes with force until he was emptied. He finally sagged in the seat, the tangible tension in his big, long muscles dissipating at last. His eyes were closed.

He opened them slowly as her movements gentled.

"So much for not giving in," he said.

She smiled. "Restraint is overrated." She glanced down to his come-damp belly and cock. "Highly."

His mouth quirked slightly in amusement, but she still sensed his grim resignation. As always, she experienced the strength of his character. He was not a man used to submitting to need once he'd decided there was reason for restraint. Maybe that's what had made his surrender to it so intoxicating to her.

He reached around the seat with one arm and retrieved a box of tissues from the backseat floorboard. She took several and mopped up her hands, his belly, and then, very gently, his cock. When she'd finished, she lifted herself slightly over the console to get the angle she hadn't achieved earlier. She pressed her lips against the moist, pulsing shaft. He made a rough sound in his throat, and his hand cupped the back of her skull. His fingers clutched at her head when she slid her lips over the still turgid, moist crown.

She leaned up, slicking her tongue along her lower lip, capturing his taste. "I hope that means that my boy look isn't what got you all hot and bothered," she told him. His nostrils flared slightly and that lean, hungry look—the one she most associated to Seth—shadowed his face again.

"You hardly need a 'look' to get me there," he declared grimly.

He reached across the console and rapidly unfastened her shirt. The cool air of the cab tickled her sensitive nipples when he pulled her T-shirt up her chest unceremoniously. He jerked the fabric of the shirt and her jacket open forcefully, exposing her bare breasts to the dim light and his blazing, possessive stare. "It's knowing what's under the disguise that's making me crazy."

Gia held her breath as one hand shifted, gliding across her heaving rib cage and caressing the side of her right breast. His other hand rose. He cupped her breasts from below and massaged them firmly in his big hands. She whimpered, as aroused by his deft hands as she was his fixed stare while he watched himself touch her.

"You're more beautiful than I remembered. Which I would think was an impossibility," he muttered. All ten of his fingers slid to her nipples. He rubbed at the tightening crests and pinched them lightly. "Such pretty nipples."

"Seth," she whispered tensely.

He glanced into her face and something shifted in his expression.

"Are you hurting as much as I was?" he asked, a trace of incredulity in his tone.

She nodded. "I think so, yeah," she replied with a shaky laugh.

Without another word, he lowered his hand over her ribs and belly and slid it into the opening of her jeans. He continued to watch her face as his fingers slipped beneath her underwear. A spasm of sensation tightened her face as he began to rub her clit.

"Christ, you're wet." She moaned as his finger agitated her. The sound of him moving in her lubricated flesh reached her ears . . . his, too, she guessed, because that feral expression tightened his face again as he stared at her. She reached for him, overwhelmed by the intimacy of what was happening, but he backed away slightly, eluding her. "No. I'm going to watch you come."

His proclamation amplified her arousal. He continued to rub her clit until she burned and clenched her teeth. The sound of him moving in her lubricated flesh was subtle, but seemed to roar in her ears. She bit off a cry when he massaged a breast in his hand and plucked at the nipple with his fingertips, making it pinch tight in pleasure. "That's right," he said quietly, leaning forward and nipping at her lips with his. "That's what I remember. Too well. How responsive you are. There was never really a chance of me being able to resist you, was there?" he said in a harsh tone, as if he were questioning himself and resigning himself to his weakness all at once. She strained toward him, trying to deepen their kiss. She'd be cresting soon—it felt so good.

"No, lean back," he instructed. She followed his demand, groaning in mounting agony, her head thumping against the back of the seat.

"I burn," she mumbled.

"I'll say. Lift your hips for a moment. I want to feel that heat."

Gritting her teeth, she complied. What he did next made her eyes spring wide. He palmed her entire sex, sending his forefinger into her channel. She gripped onto his shoulders, her mouth gaping open. He moved, shifting his hand, vibrating it very subtly. The pressure on her clit made her eyes spring wide. It took her a dazed second to realize why it felt so good. He was agitating her most sensitive flesh with that half-inch round stone at the bottom of his ring, the one he used so deftly to smooth his makeup applications. The pressure wasn't hard, but it was firm, precise . . . sublime.

"Feel good?"

"Oh my God," she exclaimed, stunned by the concise, imperative pleasure. "Yes."

"What a sweet little pussy," he growled, his face tight with frustration. "Damn this situation. I want inside this," he grated out thickly, plunging his finger into her slit for emphasis. He pushed his finger in and out of her as he made tiny vibrations on her clit with the round stone. He watched her face closely, perhaps taking cues from her expression. When she gasped and her head jerked forward, he increased the pressure.

"*There*. Are you going to come for me?" he asked after a tense moment.

She had no choice. Her fingers sank into the dense muscle of his shoulders. He pinched at her nipple as his hand continued the small, but tense and fast movements between her thighs. "Answer me," he demanded, the stone's pressure and speed on her clit optimal.

"*Yes*. Oh—God yes." She shuddered as the first wave of climax struck her. Pleasure pounded through her. She cried and his lips were on hers, as if to capture her bliss.

"*Shhh,*" he soothed when he lifted his mouth a moment later and she shook. He gave her nipple one last taut caress and transferred his hand to her shoulder. Leaning closer, he spread his hand at her back and kissed her lips greedily while she whimpered. He kept stimulating her, nursing her through her climax, his big hand absorbing her shudders. After a mindless moment, she gasped and tilted her head forward, her forehead bumping against his.

For a moment, their breaths mingled as she panted, and his hand began to slow between her thighs.

Finally, he lifted his hand from her sex, dragging his palm over her heaving belly, his fingertips leaving a trail of wetness on her skin. He stroked her sensitive sides with both hands, his touch soothing and exciting her at once. He cupped both of her breasts and his head lowered.

She stared out of the front windshield onto a star-filled desert sky, while Seth held up her breasts and buried his face between the flesh. He turned his head, his whiskers pleasantly chafing her sensitive skin. He kissed and stroked and sucked her nipples with a breathtaking sweetness. Her lungs grew tight as she reached up and delved her fingers into his smooth, thick hair, the moment sweet and taut and almost painfully arousing, despite the fact that she'd just come.

"We should find a hotel," she murmured, her voice thick with satiation and reawakening need.

He kissed a damp nipple and laved it with a warm tongue. "Are you tired?" she heard him ask before he surrounded the crest with his lips and applied a suction that made her clamp her legs closed to alleviate the pressure growing there.

"Tired?" she asked incredulously. "Are you kidding?"

He lifted his head slowly. His face was shadowed but she saw the glint of his eyes. "Because if you're not tired, I'd rather push through."

"You would?"

"Now that this has happened once," she sensed him glance down at her bared torso, "do you want it to happen again?"

His deep voice echoed in her ears.

"You mean . . . just while we're on this escape mission?" she asked wryly. But Seth's serious expression didn't flinch. He nodded.

"Yes. I mean . . . I *think* so," she said honestly. She wanted to do things like skydive someday, too, but that didn't mean she wouldn't be nervous as all hell and having second thoughts standing on the edge of that plane, considering a free fall to earth. "Do you?"

The two simple words sounded very vulnerable to her, hanging in the air between them, exposed. His head tilted downward. Her naked skin prickled with awareness at his stare.

"I can't imagine not touching you, now that I have. I'd rather get to a place that I know you're safe, though, before . . . indulging."

A spike of excitement went through her at his words.

"You can think about it? While we're on the road?" he asked with a pointed glance when she didn't answer immediately. She swallowed thickly and nodded. He was asking her if she wanted to indulge in phenomenal, no-strings-attached sex while they were on the lam together for the next few weeks. She thought she knew her answer, but maybe he was right. She shouldn't decide when her flesh still sang from his touch and the scent of Seth and sex filled her nose.

"Okay. I'll think about it," she said, brushing back his hair with one hand. "But you shouldn't worry so much. I'll be safe, no matter what, as long as you're there."

He caught her brushing hand with his. "Do you really believe that?"

She started in surprise at his intensity. She weighed the question. "Yes," she said with conviction. "I'll drive. You should rest, and I'm wide awake." She bit her lip when he didn't speak, one hand still shaping and caressing her breasts gently. "Are you starting to regret it already, Seth?" she asked shakily.

He smoothed one hand on the skin above her left breast. She wondered if he felt her heart bumping. "I don't think it's possible to regret what just happened," he said gruffly.

"No?" she queried softly. "Not like what happened two years ago?"

He exhaled heavily and dropped his warm hand from her breast. His fingertips traced her eyebrow. "A big part of me didn't regret that, Bright Eyes. You're too smart not to realize that."

A pressure swelled in her chest. *Bright Eyes*. He hadn't called her that since that night two years ago.

She believed him wholeheartedly in those sweet moments after the rapture of the storm. Still, reality crept in slowly once they were on the road again. They'd been in a fever of lust and had given in gloriously.

But surrendering to the inevitable and liking it were two very different things.

*   *   *

Seth instructed her to get onto I-40 toward Oklahoma City. She'd been highly aware of him studying the mirrors for the past hour as she drove.

"Do you think we're being followed?" she asked anxiously. She hadn't noticed him watching so closely before, but he'd been driving when glancing into the rearview mirror was more usual.

"No. I'm almost one hundred percent certain we haven't been," he said at the same time he reclined the passenger seat. "That's why I took parts of Historic 66. It's hard to tail someone on a road like that for long distances and get away with it. Now that we're on the main interstate, just be mindful of any cars that travel for long periods behind you and don't pass, even ones that are two or three cars back or ones that pass you but still stay in proximity. I know it's hard in the dark, but take note of colors and makes of cars, if you can. Just be alert."

"Okay," Gia agreed, glancing in her mirrors. "I can't believe anyone would invest so much time and energy to follow us this far, though."

"For the money they could get selling an exclusive story? A reporter would follow you much farther than this," Seth stated flatly. "Quite a few people would. Or they could call ahead and have a tail pick us up once they sighted us."

She glanced aside. Had he meant someone else might follow them beside the press?

"Do you mean McClarin's people?" she asked him.

"I doubt it, but anything's possible. Has there been *any* contact made between him or one of his followers and you? Even something remote, like an e-mail?" She felt his searching stare on her cheek.

"No. I think you're wrong to be concerned about it. Madeline and Charles agree with me. They're just playing it safe with this whole escape from L.A. thing because they're worried about the press. Do you really feel that differently about it?" she asked bemusedly, frowning at the road. "I happen to know that Jeannie's mom has had Jeannie sent away to relatives in South Carolina until the trial, but no one thinks it's because of a danger thing. That poor girl just needs a break from this crap."

"I'd be a fool to act like I know everything. I'm just being careful. I don't think there's a bodily threat against you, but I think Madeline and Charles are right to want you away from that press zoo. I also agree that the chances are excellent nothing will happen in regard to McClarin influencing you."

"*Attempting* to influence me," she corrected.

"Don't be so certain a man like McClarin wouldn't find a way into your cracks," Seth said. "Everyone has a weakness or an insecurity. Everyone. McClarin thrives off information like that. He preys on the weak and vulnerable and emotionally unstable."

"You think I'm *emotionally unstable*?" she demanded, insulted.

"No, I don't. I *do* think McClarin's more dangerous than a lot of people realize though."

"You don't have to convince me," Gia assured, gripping the wheel harder. Her muscles always went stiff at the disturbing memory of walking down the hallway in the Salinger home and opening that bedroom door. McClarin hadn't realized Gia would show up for an emergency hair appointment with Mary Salinger, her hairdresser, that day. He'd known Jeannie was alone and vulnerable. Gia had made the plans with Jeannie's mother over the phone. When Gia arrived, Mary hadn't reached home yet. Her fourteen-year-old-daughter Jeannie had been there, though.

If only I'd gotten there sooner.

An ache went through her at the familiar thought. At least she had *been* there. Mary was an avid follower of the New Temple and in awe of Sterling McClarin. If Gia hadn't witnessed McClarin's crime firsthand, she feared McClarin would have hushed Mary. And Mary, in turn, would have silenced her daughter. It was just one more reason Gia was determined to testify and do her part.

"McClarin is finished, Gia. It's just a matter of keeping you safe and counting off the days."

Gia blinked in surprise at Seth's quiet intensity. She saw the gleam in his eyes and knew he'd noticed her anguish at thinking of the rape. At Charles's request, she had briefed Seth on what she'd witnessed.

"You all right?" Seth asked.

"I'm fine," she insisted.

"Okay. I'm just going to rest my eyes for a few minutes. Wake me up in an hour?" Seth asked.

"In an hour? That's all?"

"That's all." He crossed his arms below his waist and went still.

She checked the clock, but told herself she'd let him sleep longer than an hour if nothing unusual happened on the road. She was sure nothing would. Something told her that Seth wouldn't "rest his eyes" if he weren't confident all was well.

In the silence, her head filled with the volatile memories of what had just happened at that roadside gas station. Her sex still felt overly sensitive and damp, the nerves tingly with continued arousal. She turned the radio on a very low setting, hoping to distract herself as she drove.

Her resolve not to wake Seth went untested. After an hour, he uncrossed his arms and shifted his long legs. Gia glanced at his face and realized his eyes were open. He seemed completely alert. She looked at the digital clock on the dashboard.

"How did you do that?" she asked, amazed. He'd awakened exactly one hour from when he'd shut his eyes.

"Internal clock. It got honed in the Army," he said, raising the back of the seat and finger-combing his longish hair. He checked his surroundings in the mirror and then picked up his cell phone and began briskly checking messages.

"How long did you serve in the Army?"

"Five years of active duty after college, two years of reserves," he said distractedly. "Your driver's name is Jim, isn't that right?"

"What?" she asked, startled by his question. She grew concerned when she saw he was still peering at his messages. "Yes, Jim Adair. Is everything all right? Did you get some kind of message about Jim?"

"Not at all," he said, making a scrolling motion with his thumb. His cell phone looked oddly small in his big hand. It was strange, the contrast of his largeness and the subtlety of his touch. "I'm just asking because I forgot to ask during our planning session. How long has Jim been with you?"

"Eighteen months," Gia said, giving him a wary sideways glance.

"Do you trust him?"

"Completely," Gia stated with force. "He lives on the grounds in the carriage house. I wouldn't have anyone live so close that I didn't trust completely."

He nodded. "But we're still in agreement that it would be best for you not to be in contact with him, or anyone at all, for the next few weeks?"

"Seth," she said, exasperated. "Did you get a message that relates to Jim or not?"

"No," he said with emphasis, setting down his phone. She caught a glimpse of his expression and sensed he was telling the truth. He quirked his dark eyebrows expectantly, and she made a frustrated sound.

"*Yes*, I agree that I won't be in contact with anyone. I wrote my parents and a couple friends and told them I was okay, but off the map for a few weeks, just like we talked about. Jim and my housekeeper have been told something similar, except that Jim knows a little more since he was driving during the switch-off with Leti. You really are the suspicious type, aren't you?"

"Now is not the time to be blindly trusting."

"Am I supposed to read multiple meanings into that?"

"No," he rumbled, the vision of him spreading and planting his long legs distracting her. "It's just common sense in this situation."

She scowled as she stared at the road. "Talk about doublespeak. You really are a trained spy, aren't you?"

"Not anymore."

"*Hmph*. Once a spy, always a spy," she said under her breath. She felt his stare on her face in the darkness. It caused her neck to prickle in awareness. It was as if she could feel his hand pressing against her breast and beating heart and hear his roughened voice.

I don't think it's possible to regret what just happened.

She experienced an irrational desire for him to touch her. She tamped it down with effort.

"It almost sounds like when you talk about McClarin, it's personal," she said, rallying. When he didn't respond—or even move—in the passenger seat, she shut off the radio. "Seth?" she prompted. "Do you *know* Sterling McClarin?"

"No, not personally," he said after a pause. "Let's just say I know of his type."

She glanced at him expectantly. "What do you mean?"

He exhaled and raked his fingers through his hair in an impatient gesture.

"There was a girl who was an extra on a film I did a few years back. She was new to the area and the industry. She was young. Too young. Dharma came from a fucked-up family in a tiny town in Maine and had just come to Hollywood in hopes of healing all her scars by seeing her name in lights. She didn't know anyone in L.A. and was excited and scared and just plain lonely. You know the type," Seth said gruffly.

Gia clamped her mouth shut and stared at the road. Yeah, she knew the type, all right. Sad, sweet, naïve men and women who craved acknowledgment and self-esteem so much, they would do practically anything for the mother lode of the stuff: Fame.

Is that how Seth saw *her*—Gia? The thought made her vaguely queasy.

"She got mixed up with a new-age cult at the same time we were working on the film," Seth was saying.

"The New Temple?" Gia asked.

He shook his head. "No, a smaller organization run by a Rasputin-type character named Vladimir Tomoriv, a Russian import with all of McClarin's charisma and sex appeal, but not as much smarts for the financial side of swindling. I tried to warn Dharma off, but Tomoriv's church—it was called God's Chosen Few—promised her a place to belong and told her she was unique . . . one chosen out of many. She lapped up their attention and the special treatment built into the psychological mind-fuckery of a cult because she was starved for it. Long story short, she was dead within six months."

"How?" Gia asked, startled.

"Exposure was the official cause, although when she was found dead in Franklin Canyon Park, she was also extremely malnourished and dehydrated. I noticed her losing weight, even while we were still filming. But according to her, this organization had her going through some kind of 'purification' ritual in order to reach the 'next level,' " he muttered derisively, anger edging his tone. "It was just a way to break her down psychologically, make her more malleable to their indoctrination. When I informed the police about her involvement with the organization, they dragged their feet about investigating. The cause of death wasn't murder, and no members of the cult could be linked to her presence in the canyon. I tried to confront Vladimir Tomoriv myself once, but he just spouted some new-age fiction at me and ran. It really galled me, to think of them getting away with the murder of an innocent girl. It was like . . ." he faded off, frowning, "she was disposable goods. Her death meant she hadn't passed the test or something. They professed to be her mother, father, brother and friend. When she died, the God's Chosen Few acted like Dharma Jana had never existed. They figured she hadn't really been one of them after all."

She glanced aside, her heart seizing slightly when she noticed how rigid his profile and posture looked. His regret over Dharma's death was palpable, despite his even, matter-of-fact tone. No wonder he'd understood her without words earlier when they'd spoken of Sterling McClarin. He seemed personally affronted by the cult leader's antics.

"I'm sorry," Gia said sincerely. He waved his hand as if to say *that's life, right?* But Gia wasn't buying his nonchalance. "It wasn't your fault, Seth."

"I know it wasn't. But you can't help but wonder if you did enough, that's all."

This was the real reason he'd sacrificed his time and put up with the inconvenience of their trek across the country. Of course, it hadn't related to her personally, she acknowledged with a sinking feeling.

"Were you involved with her?" she asked.

"Who? Dharma?"

Gia nodded, her gaze glued to the road. Why had her heart started to beat uncomfortably fast upon asking the question?

"You mean was I sleeping with her?"

"Yeah."

"Of course not," he said with quiet disdain. "Haven't you been listening? I don't get involved with actresses, *especially* a fragile one like Dharma. I tried to be a friend to her. Not that it worked."

A silence settled between them. He seemed as thoughtful as she was.

"But Dharma, and other women like her," Gia said after a while. "Are they the reasons you routinely don't date actresses? Because they're vulnerable and needy, and often don't show the best judgment?"

He exhaled, making a frustrated sound. "No. Not entirely. I know you say it's prejudice on my part, and maybe it is," he said stiffly. "But it's my *experience*. I'm not saying every actress is as fragile as Dharma. Far from it. It's more than that."

He glanced aside and noticed her raised eyebrows.

"Personalities and weaknesses of character aside, two people who are both part of this business shouldn't be involved. It's too much craziness and not enough reality."

"That seems like way too rigid a rule."

"Do you really love it that much?" Seth asked her. She blinked at the unexpected question.

"Yes," she replied without hesitation. "Sure, it's crazy at times, but acting has been my passion since I was in middle school. I thought the theater was everything to me, but I'm finding film to be fascinating too. It's stretching me creatively. I'm not power or fame hungry, and I think my feet are planted solid on the ground. But that doesn't mean I don't want to take my career as far as I can."

He didn't reply for a moment.

"You should be careful what you wish for," he said somberly. "This business can eat people alive or take you bit by bit until there's nothing left. You're young. You still have a lot to learn about it."

"Do *not* throw my age in my face again, Seth Hightower," she said, pointing at him accusingly. "You're only ten years or so older."

"That's a hell of a lot of years of experience."

"I'm old enough. I was then too," she grated out. Her words

echoed in her brain in the tense silence that followed. She hadn't meant to bring up what had happened two years ago. Seth's calm know-it-all attitude had pricked her temper. Again.

"Fine. I didn't intend to argue with you about it. You're the one who asked why I'm offended by assholes like McClarin," Seth said, staring out the passenger's-side window.

"Is it that surprising that I'm annoyed? You're labeling me as an emotional simpleton on the sole basis of my career and the number of years I've been alive." How could he be so clueless as to not realize how insulting that was?

"I said no such thing," he shot back with force, making her jump. "How can you imagine for a second I think you're an emotional simpleton? You're smart as a whip and courageous as hell. Look at what you're doing, testifying against McClarin despite every obstacle being thrown in your path? Most people who have far less at stake than you do would never put themselves on the line like that."

She glanced at him, her mouth sagging open.

"Why are you looking at me like that?" he demanded sharply, seemingly as aghast by her incredulous reaction as she was by his passionate declaration.

"Because I didn't know you thought those things of me."

"Jesus, Gia. I can't keep my damn hands off you. Do you think that's all because you've got a pretty face and phenomenal body? I see gorgeous women every fucking day," he said, his deep, rough voice pressured and beleaguered.

"Well, I'm so sorry to be such a distracting . . ." She fumbled for the right word. "*Nuisance*. You're sort of a nuisance yourself, you know," she added under her breath.

She listened to her heart throbbing in her ears in the strained silence that followed.

She reached for the control button on the radio and turned up the volume on a pop song. From the corner of her vision, she saw him open his mouth as if to say something, but then he seemed to think better of it. Instead, he picked up his cell phone and resumed checking his messages.

Gia wondered furiously if the atmosphere inside the SUV could spawn lightning.

Nine

~~~

They stopped at a roadside gas station and restaurant for breakfast three hours past Oklahoma City. Gia was feeling prickly and edgy, but not for the same reason she had been in the early morning hours when she and Seth had argued. Well, not argued, really. Disagreed.

Heatedly.

Her edginess now came from what had happened before they got to the restaurant. In short, Seth had gotten her into full disguise again, and that process was always a trial on her senses.

"So when we get to this house, what are we going to do?" Gia asked him as she spread some jam on her toast. She paused in her actions when she met his stare. Instead of looking grubby and sweaty as she did—after nearly twenty-four hours without a shower, wearing a hot, itchy wig and constrictive binder—Seth looked rugged and a little dangerous. His jaw was shadowed with whiskers, and his amber eyes seemed to glow in his swarthy face. His longish, smooth hair was made for road trips, looking best when swept back from his face in finger-combed carelessness. She scowled at the appealing sight of him and shoved a corner of the toast into her mouth.

He shrugged and picked up his coffee. She'd learned already that he didn't hold the handle of a coffee cup, but instead gripped the whole thing in his large hand. She found the habit extremely sexy, which only amplified her current annoyance.

"I think we should stay in as much as possible. And it's not like there's much to do around Vulture's Canyon anyway. As long as you're in full makeup and character, we can go out now and then. If that's what you want," he added very quietly.

She realized she was staring at him, thinking about what he'd said after they'd given in to their feverish libidos in that parking lot outside of Amarillo.

I can't imagine not touching you, now that I have.

Ever since their disagreement on the road, Seth certainly hadn't touched her. Gia wasn't sure if he even wanted to proceed with his suggestion that they carry out a sexual affair while hiding out from the world in the forest. She wasn't sure *she* wanted to. He took a sip of his coffee, holding her stare over the rim of the cup.

"Do you want to test out your role on someone?" he asked, setting down his coffee cup.

Gia blinked. "Who?"

"Rill and Katie Pierce live close by to where we'll be staying. If Katie knows we're there, she'll probably extend an invitation."

"And you think it would be okay for us to go?"

Something about his certainty when he nodded made her realize he'd thought about it. "Yeah. I trust Rill and Katie completely. I'd have to tell Katie not to say anything about this plan to Joy though. Joy and Everett are in Mexico right now. If they talked, I wouldn't want Joy to actually *believe* she had a half brother." He paused, his flickering gaze over her face made her go still in awareness. "You said that you'd seen Rill do a presentation at UCLA. Did you ever meet him in person then, or have you met him since?"

"No. His scholarship recipients were supposed to meet with him after he spoke, but he was called away on some emergency."

"So it'll be a good acting challenge for you, won't it? To see if you can fool Rill and Katie?"

"Don't you think they'll be insulted when they eventually find out the truth about us tricking them?"

"I don't think so. Not if we explain. But we don't have to see them if you don't want," Seth shrugged. "It was just a thought. I can think of plenty of other things I'd rather do," he said frankly. The sunglasses she wore didn't provide any protection from the lancing quality of his stare. She felt herself going warm beneath it. Her chewing slowed. "I was just thinking about how you hate being confined. Have you been thinking about what I suggested?" he added so quietly, for a few seconds she thought she had misunderstood him.

"What?" she asked, although her prickling skin warned her of what he meant.

He didn't respond, his answer clear in his heavy-lidded stare, despite his impassive expression. She looked unseeingly at her half-eaten bowl of oatmeal.

"I really didn't mean to insult you earlier, Gia," he said, his hoarse voice just above a whisper. "Do we have to agree on everything in order to—"

"Have meaningless sex?" she finished for him as calmly as she could muster, looking up.

They faced off, the din of the restaurant fading to distant background noise.

"I was just being honest by saying I've never met an actress I thought wouldn't be more trouble than pleasure to get involved with."

"Including me."

"That's the whole point, isn't it? You *are* different. I clearly can't abide by that rule when it comes to you." He glanced around tensely, assuring himself no one was listening. "And don't act like this is all on me, Gia."

"What do you mean?"

"Like I said yesterday, you had my number two years ago. Why didn't *you* call *me*? This isn't the 1950s. Women call men all the time. Did your not calling have anything to do with the fact that starting a relationship would have broken your career focus at that point in time? You've skyrocketed to fame. I admire your single-minded ambition, but I don't think having someone like me hanging on your arm at every turn would have served your purpose very well."

"You would hardly *hang on my arm*," she snapped, finding the idea of a clutching, insecure Seth ridiculous. She met his solemn stare and swallowed back her flash of irritation.

It wasn't as cut-and-dried as he was making it sound, but there was *some* truth to what he said. Gia had always been a planner. If you didn't set goals, it was hard to focus on the desired outcome. Things that didn't blend with her goals—things like Sterling McClarin or her off-the-charts attraction to a gorgeous, blatantly independent man like Seth—tended to sidetrack that focus.

Still . . .

"It would have made a difference if you'd contacted me after that night. I wanted it," she said honestly.

"Yeah. But not enough to potentially screw up your carefully made plans and call me yourself."

She opened her mouth to argue, but he held up a hand, stilling her. "I'm not mad about it. I understand. I'm just pointing out that we *both* have histories. We *both* have reasons to be wary about this. I've learned that a Hollywood relationship is a hell of a lot more complicated than most people could even begin to imagine. *You* learned early on from your mom that you were never going to let a man sidetrack your career."

It was like he'd applied a mild shock to her skin. She stared at him, tingling, left stunned that he recalled that small detail from the night they'd spent together. His words replayed in her head.

"Is *that* what you really think? That I didn't try to contact you, because I didn't want to repeat my mother's mistakes?" she breathed out, amazed. Unsettled.

Disturbed.

Was he right?

"When's the last time you were in a serious relationship?" he asked quietly.

"I . . . I've been in plenty," she sputtered.

"Really? The press isn't doing its work for once? You've hidden *that* from your adoring public?"

"I assume that means you're one who's checking?" she challenged.

He threw her a dark look that somehow conveyed her attempt at sidetracking him was beneath her. Damn. She was a glass surface to him. It wasn't as if she was *lying* or anything, it was just that she was a little worried he was right. Sort of. She'd had two involvements with men in the past couple of years that lasted more than six months, which was her record for relationship length. The problem for Gia was that she was always so busy. She seemed to match up with men who initially seemed comfortable and secure with her hectic schedule but in reality were just taking advantage of the fact that she wasn't around enough to interfere with their typical tomcatting activities.

God. She hadn't matured a bit since catching that moronic rock star Tommy Valian in bed with another woman and whining about it to Seth.

She exhaled, feeling drained suddenly.

"Yeah," he said, as if he'd noticed she had finally gotten what he was trying to convey. "It's complicated," he told her pointedly, reaching for his wallet. He dropped some bills on the check resting on the table and met her stare again, his gaze unflinching. "The fact that I want you, though? That's as simple as it comes."

Losing several hours because of the time zones, they reached the Shawnee National Forest in the afternoon of a cool, brilliantly sunny day. Seth drove the last leg of the trip with familiar ease. They passed St. Louis and finally were traversing a narrow, twisted country road that meandered through hills and forest. Gia didn't speak for the whole forty-five minutes before they came to a halt, awed by the beauty of the rolling land and woods decked out in brilliant hues of yellow, orange and vivid red. It was a shock to her city eyes, but a wonderful one. She lowered her window all the way and inhaled deeply of the crisp, spicy air rushing across her face. It was like the cobwebs of the past several months—the anxiety of the McClarin trial, the hounding reporters, the worry of completing *Interlude* without creating a scar on her work record—slowly melted away. The road trip had succeeded in one thing; it made Los Angeles seem distant and small.

She glanced sideways at Seth's bold presence behind the wheel of the SUV. *He* seemed even bigger and more vibrant since their cross-country escape. Her uncertainty about how she should proceed with Seth Hightower in a secluded forest home remained, but the lessening of her other anxieties at least made her feel clearer . . . lighter.

That incident in the parking lot had vividly brought back his dominant manner of making love. She'd found it intensely arousing, which had surprised her a little. Two years ago, she hadn't had enough experience with men to know she would like having someone call the shots in bed. Certainly, she'd never been with a man—then or since—who was as physically powerful as Seth. He could so easily optimize her pleasure.

There had never been a doubt in her mind that Seth enjoyed sex. A lot. He was clearly practiced at getting it precisely the way he wanted it.

She shifted her hips restlessly in the seat, her thoughts arousing her more than was appropriate, given the circumstances. But where was the harm in giving in to her desire full throttle? She'd been banned to the forest for three weeks by circumstances beyond her control.

Why couldn't she turn it into a sex-drenched, indulgent getaway with Seth Hightower? Most women would leap at the chance.

They traversed down a two-lane country road that was shrouded by trees on both sides and from above, creating the feeling of traveling down a sun-gilded, leafy tunnel. She leaned out the window slightly, curious when Seth turned off the road onto a long drive. In the distance, she saw a log home cozily situated on the side of a hill.

"Is that it?" Gia hoped. In her almost twenty-five years of existence, she'd never stayed in a forest retreat, so remote from the rest of the bustling world.

"Yep."

"It's lovely."

A moment later, he brought the SUV to a halt. The forest crowded around the log home from the back. When she stepped onto the leaf-strewn driveway a moment later, she filled her lungs with fresh, cool air.

She slowly spun around in a complete circle, absorbing her surroundings. The trees blazed with color. The forest seemed alive with the sounds of birds chirping and leaves rustling and falling to the ground in the soft, cool breeze. The house looked new. The back of it and part of the sides nestled inside the hill, but the front was almost all windows, giving it an airy, modern feel.

"John had it built fairly small, better for security," Seth said as he popped the trunk and began to haul out luggage and duffel bags. Gia hurried to help him. "Because of the way it's dug into the hill, I only have to be worried about a few exposures as far as a potential security breach."

Gia smiled but held back her teasing. He couldn't help it if the lessons of security had been ground down into his bones. That's why the FBI and Charles had been comfortable sending her away with him, after all, even if everyone agreed there was no likely threat.

"I'm just excited about a hot shower," she said longingly. She glanced up at him. They hadn't stood side by side much on the trip. When they did, she was always a little surprised at his height. The top of her head was only a few inches past his nipple line.

Excitement bubbled up in her. The trip had seemed so interminable, she hadn't really allowed herself to dwell much on the bliss of arriving. It rushed her now, making her feel a little giddy. Maybe Joshua Cabot was right. As unlikely as it would have seemed just days ago, she suddenly found herself smack dab in the middle of a picturesque getaway with an extremely sexy, attractive man.

There were much worse things in the world.

She took her favorite suitcase from Seth—a small vintage leather steamer trunk that she'd had updated with roller wheels. He continued to rustle around in the back of the SUV, seemingly deciding what to grab now and what to take later. He'd packed a hell of a lot more than she had, she realized for the first time. She spotted some sketch pads, art supplies and his large makeup kit. He'd packed dry goods and groceries. She saw a case of bottled water. In a paper bag she saw coffee, paper towels and a loaf of bread.

"I can't believe you brought so much stuff. Are you going to work on a project while you're here?" she asked, nodding at his sketch pads.

"Nothing specific. Just messing around."

She nodded and scratched hard under the wig before she reached for a grocery bag. "No more wearing this damn thing for hours on end. Heaven," she mused to herself. The idea made her smile hugely. "I can let my hair down and live a little while I'm behind closed doors."

Seth glanced at her and did a double take.

"What?" she asked, noticing his narrow-eyed gaze. A strange expression settled on his face, one she couldn't quite read. He turned back to his task, his face averted from her.

"Nothing. Just . . . your smile."

Gia opened her mouth, but nothing came out. It was hard to put a name to what she'd heard in his deep, gruff voice just then.

Whatever it was, it had struck her temporarily mute.

Seth deactivated an elaborate alarm system before they entered the snug, pretty house. They paused at the threshold of the vaulted living room. Gia removed her glasses, pleasure warming her. She set down her bag and walked into the large space with the vaulted timber ceilings and fieldstone floor-to-ceiling fireplace. The décor, bright, tree-dappled sunlight and a warm color scheme of golds and dark reds made the room extremely welcoming and comfortable.

"I love it," she said, spinning around to look at Seth. He'd set down the bags and items he'd been carrying, too, and was watching her.

"We should talk about the sleeping arrangements," he said.

Her mouth snapped shut. She'd been both dreading and excited for this moment. Now it had come.

"Okay," she said, taking a step closer toward him.

He just quirked up an eyebrow. "Do you want to sleep with me while we're here, or not?"

Leave it to Seth to get right to the point.

Not that he had much of a choice, she reasoned. He had to know where to put the suitcases. Her desperate gaze landed on the carton of water he'd carried in and set on an entryway table. "Do you think I could have one of those waters?" she asked.

"Sure." He stepped over to the table and extricated one of the bottles from the plastic. He cracked open the lid and handed it to her. She drank, glancing furtively at his face while she did.

"No strings attached? We both walk away afterward?"

"It would be for the best. But God knows that while we're here, I'll want you," he said, his simple, primal honesty sending a thrill through her. His gaze sunk over her face. "Again and again."

She spilled some of the water on her chin, set off balance by his quiet, restrained intensity. "It's like I told you in that parking lot. Now that it started, I can't imagine stopping until this thing has played out."

"What if I'm not fully convinced, like you are, that it's 'for the best' to keep it to mere getaway sex?" she asked frankly, wiping her chin.

"You mean because you feel I'm unreasonable about thinking we wouldn't work in the real world?"

She laughed. "In the *un*real world, right? Hollywood? Yeah. That's what I mean."

"I told you we don't have to agree on everything to enjoy each other. It's up to you whether or not you want to explore this . . . heat between us. If you think it would be a bad idea, then we'll sleep in separate bedrooms. I'd understand completely." He paused, considering. "I wouldn't like it though."

Some of the heat he'd referred to seemed to rush through her now. Her cheeks burned. Her sex tingled.

Don't agree. You know what might happen.

But what if that dreaded thing had already occurred, and she was just blinding herself to that fact? Her work wasn't available here in these woods to distract her. It was just Seth and her.

She agreed with Seth though. She wasn't a coward. If she left this "heat" between them unexplored, she'd regret it. A lot.

"It all seems a little mercenary, the way you talk about it." She met his stare unflinchingly. "But maybe you're right to be straight-forward. What's more honest than wanting someone? And I think we both know that applies to us, in spades," she added wryly under her breath. She inhaled for courage. "So I guess that's it. It would be stupid for us to sleep in separate rooms. Stupid and dishonest."

He nodded once, unsmiling. He looked quite formidable.

"Since we're being honest, I want you to know that I'll use protection when we're together," he said. "But I'm healthy. I just had a physical a few weeks ago, and I haven't been with anyone else since then."

She gave him a grateful smile, appreciating him bringing up the topic. His straightforward candor. "Yeah. I'm healthy too. My physical was more like months ago, but I haven't been with anyone since then, either," she admitted, hating the rush of color in her cheeks at the admission. She cleared her throat. "Plus, I'm on the pill." He remained unmoving. Unsmiling. "Don't look so serious, Seth," she chided lightly, even though deep down, she was a little intimidated by her agreement to his proposal . . . by the laying out of the rules and boundaries. She started to peel the wig off, wincing. "It doesn't match a sexy, no-strings-attached situation, you know."

"That's what you keep calling it, not me," he said, picking up four large bags at once.

"What do *you* call it?" she demanded, freezing in her task.

He cast an amused, resigned glance her way as he straightened. "Trouble worth risking."

She stood there, speechless, watching him saunter away.

Ten

He put away the supplies and re-familiarized himself with the property. Afterward, he made several calls, including one to Charles to update him on their arrival. While he did so, he closely studied the entrance to the property and the surrounding woods. He'd been certain no one had followed them from St. Louis. He was alone in these woods.

Alone with Gia.

When he'd spoken to John Corcoran, the owner of the residence, while they were stopped on the road earlier, John had encouraged them to choose any suite they liked, including the master. Seth had put their things in a large guest suite, however, not wanting to infringe too greatly on John and Jennifer's hospitality and privacy. The suite was nearly as large as the master, and equally as comfortable. Plus, it possessed one feature he found extremely appealing . . .

Gia was showering when he finished his call. The thought of joining her in the shower tempted him—a lot. But she would be clean and sweet by now, while he still felt grubby and stiff from the long drive. Instead, he grabbed some clothes and showered in the bathroom of a second, smaller guest room.

Gia was standing in the well-appointed, modern kitchen when he entered it a while later. She pulled her hand back hastily from a teakettle when she saw him, as if she'd been caught red-handed at something. He came to a standstill several feet into the kitchen when he took in her appearance. She stared at him with huge eyes, her self-consciousness obvious.

Endearing.

Yet, she was Hollywood's sweetheart, a woman who could expertly transform into someone else at a second's notice. He'd come to learn that actors were an odd lot. Many of the best gave too much of themselves to roles, sacrificed themselves to the flames of a brilliant performance. They won accolades, but lost a bit of themselves with each role.

But as he examined Gia standing there, looking nervous and excited at the same time, Seth suspected there was something different about her. When she wasn't acting, Gia possessed one of the most candid, pure spirits he'd ever witnessed. It'd been what had drawn him to her from the start, even though he hadn't fully understood it at the time. Was that why she could absorb a role so utterly? He wasn't saying she was a blank slate, far from it. If anything, her strength was the one clear, steady note of her character. Maybe *that's* why she could transform at a moment's notice, and then bounce back so quickly to being the hardworking, practical girl with a plan?

Thinking about her career aspirations to become the biggest and the best struck a bad chord, creating friction in him. Maybe he was kidding himself by imagining her as an exception.

It was so damn hard to say with Gia, because she was so *exceptional*.

There was one thing that was certain, and that was that he wanted her like hell.

She wore a white belted robe and her hair was down, falling around her back and shoulders in loose waves. Her feet were pinkish-hued from the hot shower, the vision of their nakedness surprisingly sexy. It looked like she'd taken a blow-dryer to get most of the wetness out of her hair, but some strands were still damp. Her full breasts looked soft and inviting beneath the terry-cloth robe. Seeing her lush, natural feminine beauty exposed after it had been under wraps for so long sent a jolt of lust through him. His cock twitched. He took a step toward her, his nostrils flaring slightly when he caught the fresh, citrusy scent from her washed hair.

"Uh . . . tea," she said awkwardly. "I found some tea bags in the supplies you brought. I just put on the kettle. Do you want some?"

"No. Not tea," he said. Her eyes sprang wide when he placed his hands on her waist and lifted her. She made a startled sound as he plopped her down on the granite countertop across from the stove. He immediately reached for the belt of her robe and unknotted it. He had a sharp urge to see her exposed. Undone. When he glanced up at her, he couldn't help but smile when he saw her stunned expression.

"No time like the present," he told her before he deliberately parted her robe, still holding her stare. He glanced down. His smile evaporated in a second. She was naked. "You are *such* a good girl, Gia," he murmured, arousal pounding through him when he saw her smooth, glistening skin and svelte curves. It was like opening the most erotic, beautiful gift in the world. She might have been startled by his actions just now, but she'd known what was going to happen after they both showered.

"No time like the present," she whispered. He glanced swiftly into her clear, shining green eyes, seeing the reflection of his own need there. Parting her legs with his hands, he stepped between them. He nuzzled her neck.

"Your hair is so beautiful," he said distractedly, surrounded by her scent. He delved his fingers into the thick, soft waves, gathering it at her nape with one hand. He tugged gently. Her head fell back, bringing her ripe, pink lips within striking distance. His cock stiffened with amazing haste.

Jesus. Gia's mouth. For the past two years, every dream and fantasy lover's mouth always took the shape of it.

"I can't believe some jerk actually encouraged you to cut this," he added thickly, squeezing her hair in his fist, his stare glued to the target of her mouth. His cock throbbed when he saw her small smile.

"He's not really a jerk. He was just acting like one at the time," she said throatily.

"He was probably struck stupid because he was in the presence of an amazing, gorgeous woman," he muttered before he seized her mouth forcefully. She whimpered when he penetrated her depths, suddenly voracious for the sensation and taste of her . . . abruptly starved to experience full possession when it had been denied to him for excruciating hours.

For years.

Her fingers delved into his hair and clutched at one of his shoulders. Gia's mouth was not a thing a man could take in half measure. Kissing her was a pleasure akin to much more flagrant sexual acts.

Kissing Gia was as serious as it gets.

Realizing he was getting drunk on her, he leaned back, his gaze latched on to her parted lips. He let go of her hair and grabbed the collar of her robe. Slowly, he eased it off her shoulders and arms, hearing his heartbeat in his ears, feeling it throb in his cock. He dropped the robe in a pool of cloth around her ass.

Anticipation building in him, cutting at him from the inside, he opened his hands along her firm thighs and skimmed them over her supple hips. He molded his palms around her taut curves.

"I forgot how well you fit me," he said, spellbound. His hands glided up to her narrow waist and delicate rib cage.

"I forgot how well you touch me," she whispered. He glanced up into her face, snarling slightly when he saw her dazed eyes shiny with arousal. Jesus. She was real and she was *right here* and she was the most beautiful thing he'd ever seen. Lust lanced through him, too powerful to contain. He cupped her breasts from below. The globes were round, but extremely firm and thrusting. Her nipples were large and pink, the vision of them like a distilled sexual stimulant.

"You use a body double for your sex scenes."

"Yes, for the full-on nudity," she admitted shakily. He shaped her breasts to his palm, his sexual focus intense . . . rabid. She cried out softly when he lightly pinched both nipples at once, loving watching the delicate crests tighten and feeling the sensation of them hardening beneath his fingertips. He'd never seen nipples this large that were so sensitive.

"I knew it," he said starkly. "I knew that wasn't you I saw up on that screen."

She made a soughing sound when he circled her nipples teasingly with his fingertips. "I didn't realize you'd ever seen me in a movie."

He glanced up and met her stare. He'd seen her all right. Only because he hadn't been able to stay away, despite his self-lectures to do precisely that. His restraint had worked at times.

Other times, he had succumbed.

"Not all of them," he said honestly. "A few. It wasn't easy, seeing you so close when you were so far away. It was weird, but it gave me some measure of peace that you didn't share everything with the whole world . . . some measure of *satisfaction*," he growled softly, molding her breasts to his hands for emphasis, making the nipples protrude between his fingers. He barely noticed her lips falling open in amazement at his fierce declaration before he leaned down and inserted a crest into his mouth. He closed his eyes and drew on her.

A ripple of pleasure went through him when her fingernails scraped against his scalp. God, she was sweet. His tongue laved and pressed, hungry for the sensation of her beading flesh. She clutched his hair and moaned when he drew on her, suckling her greedily, then pausing to soothe her with his tongue. His hand lowered and caressed a smooth thigh. He reached, his fingertips seeking glory. He groaned, deep and primal, when he dipped his fingers between her labia and found her sweet and warm, her arousal wetting his fingertips.

A storm seemed to settle on his brain, an uncompromising need to mate, hard and fast. It wasn't logical. It was the direct opposite of making sense. It was a primal directive. He slid his fingers lower between her thighs, palming her entire outer sex possessively. She said his name and clutched at his hair, hurting him a little. The evidence of her returned desperation only fueled his rampaging lust. He moved his hand in a tight, small circle, stimulating her clit. When she started to gyrate her hips in a subtle, erotic movement, pressing against him frantically, he saw red.

The next thing he knew, he was extricating a condom from his wallet and panting while Gia ripped at his button fly. She scooted forward on the cabinet, the tiny twitching of her hips and the slight sway of her breasts killing him.

She reached between his opened fly and found the outline of his erection straining against his boxer briefs.

"Christ," he grated out when she flicked her fingernails against the stretched fabric, erotically scraping his aching cock. Shivers rippled through him, tightening every muscle in his body. He grabbed her wrists, pushing her hands down to her thighs. He shot her a fiery glance when she started to reach for him the second he let go. Her hands moved anxiously on her thighs, but she stayed put. Their stares held as he jerked down his jeans and underwear and extricated his cock. He winced as he rolled on the condom, his gaze straying like a bee to honey to the vision of Gia's pussy. She was spread for him, but not as wide as he wanted her.

He looked up at her as he took his sheathed cock in one hand and cupped her hip with the other.

"I'm going to have you again and again in the next few weeks," he told her as he guided his cock to her pussy, pushing her closer to the edge of the counter with his hand. "Sometimes it's going to be slow," he grated out when he felt the tip press against her clasping warmth, "and sometimes it's going to be fast, but right now, it's going to be *furious*. I've waited for too long to get back inside you, Gia."

She cried out when he flexed his hips and her softness parted for him. The counter's height was perfect for the maneuver. His cock entered her at a horizontal angle from his body, and she was *so* damn wet and warm and tight. He clenched his teeth. She was so sweet, and she was squeezing him mercilessly.

He grabbed both her hips and sank into her. Their stares held as he bumped his pelvis against her outer sex and ground his hips lightly against hers. Her beautiful face tightened. She looked anguished. Wild. He stroked her cheek soothingly.

"There, you can take that, can't you?" he muttered thickly, pulling lightly on her long hair. Her head fell back, and he bit gently at her pink mouth and fragrant neck. It was delicious, staying still while the ache in him mounted. A siren was starting to wail in his brain, a distant claxon approaching. "You *have* to take it, sweet girl," he said between ravishing her mouth. "Because I'm about to lose it. You feel so fucking good."

"Yes," she hissed. Her fingers flexed into his ass, begging him, taunting him. "Give it to me hard."

He drew his cock out of her and rocketed back inside, using his hold on her to keep her still for his possession. It was madness. It was fantastic. He groaned gutturally at the brutality of the pleasure. He held her tighter, grimacing, powering his hips. She shook every time he crashed their flesh together, but he brought her closer, holding her tight, absorbing the blow.

It took him a moment to realize that wailing alarm of excitement wasn't just coming from inside his head. The hissing teapot on the stove had escalated to a shrill whistle, the sound of it blending with Gia's high-pitched keening as they crashed together. He straightened slightly, never ceasing his ruthless plunging into her body. She stared at him, and it all came rushing back to him, that wild, helpless expression she got on her face when he took her.

"You always liked it hard, didn't you?" he rasped, holding her hips and driving into her.

Her breasts trembled with each forceful thrust. He spread her pale thighs wider and pushed her closer to the edge. He caught sight of her slick, swollen clitoris. A madness struck him at the flagrantly erotic vision, and he was charging at full steam. The teapot was screaming, that claxon now upon him, blaring, insistent.

Stupid, to believe this rabid, feral need for Gia was something he could control.

He reached with his thumb, rubbing her slick clit. He powered into her with short, forceful thrusts, watching her intently. Their gazes held as cruel pleasure sank its talons deep. The pressure in her taut muscles broke, and her nails dug into his hip and buttocks. She began to shudder, her helpless whimpers barely audible against the screech of the steaming kettle. Her climactic convulsions pushed him over the edge. He thrust high in her.

He roared as the climax hit him, blistering. Scalding. He locked gazes with her again as he came. Grinding his teeth, he used both thumbs to part her labia wider. Instinctively, he pushed closer, circling his straining body subtly against her exposed clit, demanding she join him full force in his pleasure. Her whimpers escalated to a scream. They shook together in the kind of tense, mindless bliss that for better or worse, was bound to incinerate everything in its path.

Eleven

~~~

She stretched luxuriously next to him on the bed, feeling wonderful and liberated in their nakedness, her body still chafed and tingling from their frantic lovemaking. And why shouldn't she feel free? True, they'd both struggled over the wisdom of giving in to lust and need, but that fight was over now. Who could struggle for long against the type of attraction that throbbed between her and Seth?

"You must be exhausted," she murmured, seeing his eyelids growing heavy as he languorously stroked the curve of her hip. They were lying on their sides, facing each other, the duvet and sheets drawn down around their ankles. "You've only slept for an hour since the night before last."

"I'm okay," he assured shortly. She loved the sound of his gruff baritone. She loved exploring his beautiful, hard body. He so often restrained her hands during sex, something she adored and hated in equal measure. But he wasn't restraining her now. Her stroking hands on him mimicked his movements on her. She caressed a lean hip. When he cupped an entire buttock in his large hand, she grinned and leaned forward, reaching around to do the same to him. She grasped a hard, smooth ass cheek and squeezed.

"God, you feel good," she whispered, awe spicing her tone. She nipped at his mouth, massaging his ass. In her closer position, she felt his cock flick up against her pelvis. Excitement tingled through her as she shaped the dense muscle lasciviously. "How do you keep so hard?"

"I work out, like most people," he said, kissing her back with a strange paradox of idleness and focus that made her think of a big cat lazily playing before it pounced.

"You'd have to do more than just 'work out' to have this butt," she remonstrated lightly, squeezing him. "How will we exercise here?"

"There's a nice workout facility in the basement."

"There is? Can we . . . go jogging . . . in the woods, as well?" she asked distractedly, plucking at his mouth, most of her attention held by his spicy, clean scent, delicious ass and his firm lips.

"We can. If you're in disguise."

She pulled back at that. As he looked at her face, his slow smile caused a sensation in her sex like a flame flickering up to a steady glow.

"What?" she demanded.

"That look on your face. No one does outrage better than you, Gia." He leaned up and captured her protest with his coaxing lips. Her flash of irritation evaporated like steam, next to his kiss. She struggled not to forget it.

"I wasn't *doing* outrage. I'm pissed. No one will see us around here!" she insisted, backing away from his logic-evaporating mouth. "If you haven't noticed, we're in the middle of the woods, Seth."

"It's a national forest to the south and east of us. Anyone can access those woods, and they do. True, this property and the woods to the north are private, but John told me hikers or hunters occasionally wander onto it. Not often, but it's been known to happen." He raised his eyebrows at her stubborn expression. She felt like one of those poor deer in the woods. Hunted. "You have one of the most recognizable faces in the country. All it takes is one person. *One.* And our cover would be blown."

She exhaled slowly. "I guess you're right. It *would* be a shame if our time together was cut short." She sounded breathless to her own ears as she resumed massaging his ass.

She glanced over his shoulder, her eyes widening when she saw their reflection in a row of mirrored doors on the closet. The entire bed was displayed in them. She squeezed, her breath catching at the exciting feeling of Seth's dense muscle combined with the vision of her hand on his gorgeous ass. Her clit tickled with excitement. She kissed his shoulder, but continued peering past him curiously, watching her hand massaging a buttock. His body was so male, so thrillingly different from hers. He was a long stretch of corded sinew and lean, rippling muscle. His skin color was beautiful, swarthy with a warm, gilded undertone. She smoothed her hand along his strong-looking, sculpted back and swept it back down, her palm itching to cup his ass once again. She was pale next to him. Never once had she considered herself delicate or small, but that's how she felt next to Seth. That's how he made her feel. His opposite. Feminine.

Desired.

Maybe he noticed her stillness and distraction.

He calmly lifted his head off the pillow and looked over his shoulder. Their gazes locked in the mirror. A flash of excitement went through her when something sparked in his sultry, amber eyes.

He turned back to her.

"You like to watch," he stated gruffly.

Her mouth fell open in surprise, but a rush of heat went through her as well.

"I remember. From that night we were together a few years back," he explained, stroking her shoulder and back with his opened, massaging hand.

Her hand fell away from his ass like it had burned her. A desire to deny it leapt up in her. She felt very exposed beneath his steady stare. It was a little embarrassing, having him say something so baldly, something so personal. His gaze flickered over her heating cheeks.

"There's nothing to be embarrassed about."

"Says you," she mumbled, keeping her gaze lowered. Didn't that make her some kind of narcissistic nympho, that she found the image of her and Seth together highly charged and erotic? She found *lots* of things about Seth charged and erotic. The vision of them was just one of *many* things.

For a moment, he neither spoke nor moved. Then he resumed caressing her, warmly stroking her back and the side of her waist.

"It's an unusual situation. Us having these weeks here together. We're very attracted to each other. On my part, it's unprecedented."

She glanced into his face, her embarrassment forgotten in the face of his honesty. "Me too," she admitted truthfully, studying his sober expression.

He nodded. "If we wanted to, we could take advantage." She arched her eyebrows in interest. "We could be honest about what we like. We could indulge every fantasy."

A smile flickered across her lips. "Sort of like a sex-cation?"

His mouth tilted. "If you want to call it that. But it would require complete honesty. Because otherwise, what's the point?" He ran his first two fingers over her pulse. She realized her heart was throbbing in excitement.

"That sounds very risky."

"You don't have to do anything you don't want to do. Or admit anything you're not comfortable admitting. I won't judge," he said, meeting her stare.

"Okay. I won't judge either. I don't want you to think I'm a narcissist," she said in a whisper. "Especially knowing what you think of actresses. I'm not that fascinated by looking at myself in a mirror when I'm alone. But it excited me . . . excites me, to watch us together."

His narrowed eyes made a frisson of excitement go through her.

"Your *honesty* excites me," he stated bluntly. He put his hand on her back and urged her closer to him. The tips of her breasts brushed against his rib cage, her nipples tightening at the contact. He lowered his head and spoke near her ear, his hoarse voice causing shivers to course down her spine. "You're the most beautiful woman I've ever seen. I like watching myself touch your beautiful body. I love seeing my cock in you. I'm becoming addicted to seeing that wild, helpless look on your face when you're about to come. I'd look at those things from every angle available to me, if I could. Does that make me sound like a narcissistic pig?"

"No," she said starkly. *It makes you sound sexy as hell.* She leaned back and looked at his face. "What . . . what else turns you on?"

"Lots of things."

She couldn't help but laugh softly at his wry reply, as if he were saying, *Do you want the CliffsNotes, or the fully annotated edition?*

"How about something for starters?" she suggested.

His expression hardened. "Okay," he said suddenly. He pushed her onto her back and hovered over her. His warm hand drifted down her bare belly and skimmed lightly over her sex. Her body went tense with excitement. "Spread your thighs," he murmured. She widened her legs. "That's *one* thing."

He began moving just the edge of his hand flirtingly along the crevice of her labia, up and down, up and down. That teasing caress in combination with his lambent stare down at her had her tingling in anticipation. She realized belatedly she hadn't understood what the *one thing* was. He noticed her raised brows. "When I ask you to do something, and you do it without questioning me," he explained.

"Are you saying it turns you on when I'm a pushover?"

"No. It turns me on that we're so in sync."

"Oh," she whispered, a little stunned. Was that the key to why things were so boiling hot between them? That they were so attuned to one another?

"But I'll admit, it does turn me on when you submit. That's far from being the same thing as being a pushover," he added gruffly. "It's a much more complicated, charged dynamic than that."

She felt her pulse thrumming wildly at her throat. What he'd said had excited her. She wasn't sure that she liked the fact, but his primal masculinity and dominant manner of lovemaking *did* turn her on.

And she had said she'd be honest . . .

"At the risk of having you boss me around for three weeks, I'll admit it turns me on when you take control."

A smile flickered across his hard mouth. His sawing hand lowered. The ridge of his finger burrowed just a fraction of an inch between her labia, creating a light, flickering pressure on her clit. She bit off a whimper.

"I'm not going to boss you around outside of sex," he said, amusement tingeing his tone. She gave him a skeptical look. "And outside of concern for your safety."

"From the description of this little sex-cation we've come up with thus far, that pretty much covers all the bases, doesn't it?"

His low, rough laughter was delicious.

"Knowing you, you'll have no problem putting me in my place if I get away from myself. And remember. You can always say no. Spread your legs wider," he murmured, his mirth fading. He moved his hand when she opened even farther for him. She burned beneath his stare as he idly rubbed the cream that had gathered on the edge of his forefinger onto her hip while he stared fixedly between her legs.

"It would turn me on if you shaved," he said, his gaze leaping up to her face. "You're so beautiful. I don't like your pussy being hidden from me in any way. But it's up to you."

Well. They had agreed to no-holds-barred honesty. Gia forced her mouth closed.

"Okay. Lots of women shave or wax, right? And you do. I like it. That you do, I mean," she finished clumsily. She *more* than liked his round, full testicles. She recalled how he'd cupped and massaged them gently in his hand while she'd jacked his staff. "It would be a real shame to hide those." She said her last thought out loud, her gaze flickering down his ridged abdomen to his cock. He'd hardened again. Her body quickened in excitement. She reached for him instinctively, but he caught her wrist and pinned it next to her ear on the pillow.

"I'm glad you think so," he said amusedly. "I feel the same way about this," he said, letting her wrist go and cupping her sex. Heat rushed through her. She just stared up at him. He was so big. It turned her on when he held her like that. Better not to think of how much it aroused her when he held her that way with his left hand and stimulated her with that wicked ring. "I admitted to you earlier I'd seen a few of your movies. You may not be aware of it, but you regulate what you give away to the world. Just a hint of you is enough to have people lining up on the streets to catch a glimpse. I want all of you, Gia. I want you completely exposed to me."

She glanced at his face, surprised by his sudden intensity. His hand shifted between her thighs.

"You don't ask for much, do you?"

"I'm sorry. I don't like things in half measure. In your case, that preference seems exponentially strong."

Her gaze stuck to his amber eyes as his deep voice reverberated around in her head.

"Okay. I'll go shower now and shave."

He leaned down and pressed his small smile to her lips.

Twelve

Seth told her he had new razors, scissors and high-quality shaving cream in his bag. She'd never shaved before, so she took her time in the hot shower. Thinking of Seth's reaction when she was completely naked for him added an element of excitement to the focus and care required for the procedure. Maybe she'd get a Hollywood wax at some point. It had been something she'd considered in the past anyway. Although she supposed she couldn't get one during her current predicament. Seth wouldn't let her go out without her disguise, and the beauty technician surely would be shocked to find out her male customer wasn't a male at all.

By the time their sex-cation was over, getting a wax might just depress her though. Seth wouldn't be in her life anymore, after all.

She suppressed the disturbing thought determinedly. That time wasn't now.

Finally, she was clean and smooth. Before she got out of the steaming shower, her curiosity got the better of her. What did Seth see that gave him that hot, rabid expression every time he stared between her thighs? She'd been looking at her sex closely while she shaved, of course. But now she took a moment to inspect herself objectively, something she'd rarely ever done. The hot shower combined with her previous arousal and orgasm left her labia plump and soft. She spread her sex lips. She looked vividly pink and glossy next to the pale, smooth skin of her thighs. The vision was surprisingly delicate and beautiful, but also flagrantly sexual at once.

Oh. So *that's* what he saw.

Her excitement mounting by the second, she toweled herself off and applied a lightly scented moisturizer over her whole body. She donned her robe and went in search of Seth.

She found him in the living room making a fire in the huge stone fireplace. At first, he didn't hear her silent approach in her bare feet on the soft carpet. She took a moment to study him while he was turned away, watching the kindling he'd laid begin to catch fire. He wore a pair of dark blue cotton lounging pants that were held by a drawstring at his narrow hips. She took a moment to admire the phenomenon of his slanting, muscular, corded back. His skin took on a reddish-gold tint in the light of the flickering fire.

Such a beautiful man. And he was hers.

For now.

He turned and regarded her soberly, and she realized he'd known she was there all along.

"You have eyes in the back of your head," she murmured, stepping toward him.

He stood from his crouching position before the massive field-stone hearth. Her gaze caressed his powerful chest before her chin tilted back to look into his impassive, handsome face.

"If you're so intent on what's in front of you, you'll forget what's creeping up behind. I haven't stalked in years, but that's one lesson my father taught me that's served me well over the years," he said quietly.

"I've never heard you speak of your father," she said, taking another step toward him.

"He wasn't a big part of my life. He and my mom separated when I was six. He's an alcoholic."

"I'm sorry," Gia said, compassion rushing through her.

"Jake, my older brother, got the brunt of it. He lived with my father for all of his childhood. It was a lot worse for him. I was an unexpected accident. My mother had me when she was forty-three.

She'd learned to deal with my dad a lot better than when Jake was young. She and I got along really well, so I never felt any great absence without Dad being there. As things stood, my dad would show up occasionally—once in a while sober, even. When he was clean, he used to take me stalking with my two uncles. It was one of the few occasions where none of them would drink. I think the memory of *their* father influenced them in that, and even they had to admit drinking was counterproductive to stalking. Those memories with Dad, Uncle Mac and Uncle Gill are few and far between, but the ones I have are all good."

"Stalking?"

He nodded. "For deer and elk."

"So . . . hunting," she clarified.

He shook his head. "We rarely went for the kill, unless Uncle Mac hadn't worked for a while and needed the food. The challenge was to get within shooting or bow-and-arrow distance of the animal without it being aware of your presence. It required swiftness on the land and wits for tracking, but most crucially of all, truckloads of patience just to keep still for interminable periods of time."

"Oh," she said, thinking. "I like that. It certainly sheds light on your control."

He studied her for a moment, the fire popping and crackling as it caught hold fully behind them.

"I don't get why you think I have control. I don't have an ounce of it when it comes to you."

She couldn't think of how to respond to such a blatantly sweet compliment.

"The fire is getting warm," he said, stepping back and sitting on the stone hearth before it. "Do you want to take off your robe?"

Her heart jumped. She nodded.

"Come here. I'll take it off," he said quietly, putting out a hand for her. She stepped in front of his long, bent legs. He opened his thighs and pulled her between them. He untied her robe, his brisk matter-of-factness about his task once again sending a jolt of arousal through her. When he parted her robe, she felt the heat of the flames curling against her naked skin. She found his slow, deliberate gaze moving down her body almost excruciatingly arousing.

By the time he stared between her thighs, her clit pinched in acute anticipation. What did he think of her naked and shaved? It was hard to read his rigid, still expression. She was about to say something—she wasn't quite sure what, but she couldn't stand the heavy tension crackling in the air between them—when he reached with one hand and parted her flushed sex lips. Heat licked at her exposed outer sex. His impassive expression broke slightly, and suddenly he was leaning down, nuzzling her smooth labia with his lips and nose, inhaling deeply.

She made a broken sound of surprise and arousal, her fingers running through his fire-warmed, smooth hair. Then he sent the tip of his tongue between the crack of her labia and agitated her clit, and she clutched onto his head as a wave of sensual heat rushed through her. She stared down at him, entranced, watching as his dark pink tongue laved her with a tight focus. He cupped her left buttock and pushed her closer, increasing the pressure of his stiffened tongue. She gasped and moaned, her fingers tightened on his head. His single-minded hunger left her speechless and completely at his mercy.

He slicked his tongue along her labia, as if trying to capture her essence. He pressed avidly against the sensitive folds, as if learning her flesh. She moaned in rising arousal when he swiped his tongue down toward her slit, teasing her with the tip. He lifted his mouth and again nuzzled the slit of her labia. He parted her sex lips with his fingers and sat back, his stare burning her.

"Look at that," he said thickly, awe tingeing his tone. "You're so damn pretty. So sexy."

Gia didn't know if she was really trembling, or if it was just some invisible, internal quaking from excitement. She watched him avidly as he leaned down and lapped at the moisture next to her thigh and labia. It was the most incendiary, erotic moment she'd ever experienced. She almost begged him to put his tongue back on her clit—the pleasure had been that sharp—when he pushed her back slightly and stood.

"Oh," she muttered in dazed surprise when he lifted her into his arms and started toward the bedroom. Her robe was falling off, the belt trailing behind them on the carpet, but Seth seemed impervious. He glanced down at her swiftly when they entered the bedroom. He looked beautiful to her in that moment, his face set and hard, her arousal glossing his stern mouth.

When he set her down, it was on her feet before the large vanity in the luxury bathroom. She was about to ask him what he was doing, but he was busy briskly pulling her robe off the rest of the way. His thighs bracketed her right hip and buttock, cupping the side of her with his large body. He reached around her with his left hand and parted her sex lips with his thumb and forefinger. With his other hand, he ran the ridge of his forefinger between the flushed valley of her sex lips.

"Look at that," he rasped next to her ear. "Look how beautiful you are."

She gasped at the precise stimulation, having no choice but to stare wide-eyed and mute into the mirror before them. It was a brazenly sensual vision, his dark hand between her thighs, his finger moving so surely in her exposed flesh. She'd grown very wet. His low, rough growl in her ear sent her arousal even higher. Her clit began to burn beneath his rubbing finger. She moaned and flexed her hips against the pressure.

He grunted in satisfaction, and her gaze darted to him in the reflection. He was watching his hand move just as avidly as she was. Her clit sizzled. "I have something you'll like," he said near her ear.

Then his hand was gone. She whimpered softly at the depriva-
tion, feeling just as undone and aroused as she appeared in the
mirror. Her cheeks were vividly pink and her nipples had grown
erect. Her breasts heaved up and down as she tried to recover from
the jarring absence of his rubbing finger. He was digging in his
leather toiletry bag. He removed a cylindrical case and tipped out
a bluish-purple metallic tube, about the size of a cigar but a little
thicker. Next he took out a small bottle of clear liquid, his actions
precise and rapid.

"Is that a vibrator?" she asked, stunned, watching him closely
as he hastily ripped off the plastic seal on the cap and flipped up
the tiny nozzle.

He made a gruff sound of affirmation as he again curled his
large body around her hip. She realized the position let him embrace her in a sense while leaving the front of her body exposed to
the mirror . . . to the image of him making love to her.

"Do you use one?" he asked gently. At the same time he brushed
a few tendrils of hair away from her breasts, fully exposing her. He
picked up the bottle of lubricant.

She cleared her throat uncomfortably. Again, he was asking her
to be honest about things most human beings just never said out
loud. Gia had found dating since she moved to Hollywood challenging for several reasons, the most crucial of which she just
hadn't had time to devote to a relationship. Her little vibrator had
become a necessity.

"Yes. Not like that, though," she admitted, nodding at the blue
metallic tube he held in his palm. "Mine is a bullet vibrator."

"So it's okay if I use this on you?"

She nodded. He placed his lips briefly on the pulse fluttering at
her throat, his pressing, warm lips making her heart leap. Desire
swelled in her. She started to reach for him.

"Keep your hands at your sides."

She made a muffled sound of combined arousal and frustration, but followed his demand.

"You really do blow me away, Gia."

He squirted some of the clear liquid from the bottle onto the crevice of her labia. Her eyes sprang wide in surprise and interest at his action. Her outer sex glistened. "I know you're very wet already, but I want to make sure I'm not abrading the skin too much, since you just shaved," he said, his matter-of-fact explanation and hoarse, deep voice in her ear causing her nipples to tighten even further. She licked her lower lip in mounting anticipation as he turned the power on the vibrator. It was nearly silent, but she could hear the slight buzz. He swept one hand along the side of her body that was farthest from him, caressing her at the same moment that he pressed the purple metallic vibrator between her labia.

"Oh God" leapt out of her throat. She quaked in his hold. Her own arousal and the squirt of lubricant from the bottle had made her very wet. The vibrator buzzed energetically on her clit. But it was the vision of Seth sliding the tube up and down between the sensitive lips that left her wide-eyed and spellbound.

"Feel good?" he asked, his stroking hand cupping her breast and massaging it.

"It feels . . . amazing," she managed breathlessly.

"Is the pleasure a little sharper, now that you're all clean and naked?" he murmured in her ear.

"Yes," she grated out between clenched teeth, because it was *definitely* true. She winced in excitement when he lightly pinched at her nipple with thumb and forefinger. He continued to move the vibrator up and down in the valley of her sex lips, the vision lewd and beautiful and compelling.

"I like watching your face while you watch me touch you," he said thickly, nipping at her earlobe. She trembled in his hold. He shifted his hips and stepped closer.

"Seth," she muttered in mounting excitement. The weight of his cock thumped against her right buttock. He pressed closer, letting her feel the full extent of his arousal. He held up her breast and squeezed it gently. She felt his heavy erection jump against her skin.

"See what you're doing to me?" His eyes looked liquid and hot as he held her stare in the mirror. "It's going to feel so good inside your little pussy once you come for me."

The vibrator was ruthless, but so was Seth's deft skill at using it. "I'm going to come," she said shakily after a while.

"In a moment," he said, kissing her ear. She realized he had used a soothing tone with her because he'd slid the lubricated vibrator out of the cleft of her labia. She watched in a rising agony of pleasure as he dragged the vibrating missile over her belly and heaving ribs. Gia knew what he was about to do, reading the hot intent in his hungry gaze as he watched in the mirror. Knowing made the anticipation cut at her.

He lifted her breast and used the tip of the vibrator to stimulate her nipple. She moaned at the erotic sensation and potent image. His cock lurched against her ass. She was so aroused, she dipped her knees and pressed closer to him, stimulating him with a subtle up-and-down motion.

"Hold still," he told her tensely, his jaw rigid.

She gasped and went still, choking back a cry.

He resumed circling the tip of the lubricated vibrator around the crown of her breast. Arousal spiked through her, causing her clit to pinch in pain. She clamped her thighs shut to alleviate the friction. "That's right," Seth said near her ear, moving his hand in a gentle massaging motion as he stimulated the nipple. "That's what I remember most about you. How sensitive you are." He kissed her ear. "How sweet."

She moaned in anguish.

"Do you want to come now?" he rasped.

"Yes. Please."

He removed the tormenting vibrator from her nipple and picked up the bottle of lubricant again. She gave a plaintive whimper as she watched him squirt a small amount of the clear, silky oil directly on her labia again. Her naked outer sex glistened in the mirror. Every muscle in her body grew tight, and she held her breath as she watched him lift the metallic vibrator to her pussy. He began to slide the buzzing missile up and down in the juicy cleft of her labia directly onto her burning clit.

"*Shhh*, that's right," she heard him say, as if from a distance as she broke in orgasm. His arm surrounded her from the back, his hand bracing her at her waist as she shook in release. As pleasure pulsed through her, she was aware of the arousing sensation of his heavy cock pressing tight to her hip and buttock, the full, vibrant sensation taunting her even in the midst of breaking bliss.

He withdrew the vibrator when her cries softened and she sagged against his weight.

"Can you walk out to the bedroom?" he asked.

She blinked dazedly and focused on him in the mirror. She understood why he'd asked. Her reflection looked sex-flushed and thoroughly dazed. It had been one hell of an orgasm.

"Of course," she said.

She thought she saw his hard mouth curl into a small smile before he took her hand and led her out of the bathroom. She sat down at the edge of the bed at his urging. He remained standing. Her mouth dropped open, and she went still when he stepped closer, parting her thighs with his body. His cock tented the loose cotton pants he wore. It filled her vision. Moaning softly in desire, she cupped him through the fabric, gripping him and sliding her fist up and down the thick shaft. He groaned harshly. Her excited actions pulled the waistband down closer to the root. She impatiently jerked the pants forward over his long, suspended cock and shoved the waistband down to his hair-sprinkled thighs.

"Ah," she muttered in supreme satisfaction as she held the

warm, heavy shaft from below and brushed her cheek and sensitive lips against the swollen crown. His low growl from above her sounded ominous and thrilling. She'd taken him into her mouth only once briefly on that night they'd been together years ago, but the experience remained scored in her memory. Gia wasn't inexperienced when it came to sex, but she wasn't exactly worldly either. She'd had a few lovers, but not a lot. She'd only had one serious boyfriend when Seth and she had fooled around that night years ago. Her scorecard hadn't filled up by much since then—her career had occupied almost all her time—but still, she had enough experience to know that Seth's cock was uncommonly beautiful.

She let her hunger for him guide her, immediately sucking the flushed, mushroom-shaped cap into her mouth. She glanced up his considerable length to his face as she moved her hand up and down the shaft and bathed the delicious head with her tongue. Every muscle in his lean, strong body looked rigid and strained. Still holding his magnetic stare, she held up his cock and wet the pulsing shaft with her tongue. His expression looked like it might break, it grew so tense. His arousal was palpable, so she was confused when he backed away slightly, taking her treat from her greedy hands and laving tongue.

"Open your thighs wider," he demanded.

"What?"

He held up the glistening vibrator. She'd been so focused on touching him she hadn't realized he carried it still. Her lungs locked, she did what he asked, parting her thighs. The sound of the vibrator's light buzzing penetrated her awareness as he lowered it to her slit. He pushed it into her pussy. She moaned loudly. When he'd inserted it several inches, and the little vibrator was buzzing her energetically, he grabbed her left hand and placed it where his had been.

"Make yourself feel good while you suck me."

It sounded like an inspired plan to her. She pushed the vibrator in and out of her pussy, sinking into a cocoon of pleasure and sexual hunger as she lifted Seth's damp cock and took it between her rigid lips. He made a rough sound and cupped the back of her head as she sucked him deeper.

He was a mouthful, but she was too aroused to consider whether or not she was skillful at her task. She lost herself to pleasure. Her fist moved along his lower shaft in synchrony with her plunging lips. His cock grew rosy and engorged beneath her eager ministrations. Given his gruff, taut moans of pleasure and the way his fingers tightened in her hair, she would have to guess he was pleased.

Very.

His arousal was hers. It swelled into an orgy of uninhibited need. She grew shameless in her desire to please him and pleasure herself. Her head bobbed faster over his cock, her hand moving between her legs at the same pace. She was the conduit of their mutual pleasure, the link that joined them. Her pleasure felt so fused with Seth's in those taut moments that she relished the moment when his hold on her grew more forceful and he began thrusting more demandingly between her lips. She cupped his balls like she'd seen him do while they were in the SUV, begging him to let go, spurring him to the finish line. He gave a blistering curse.

"I'm going to come, Gia," he growled, and she heard the dark warning in his tone. He was giving her a chance to come off him if she chose. But she didn't choose. Sensing glory within her reach, she sank him deep and pulled the vibrator out of her slippery sheath. Reacting on pure instinct, she pressed the buzzing missile against her clit.

She screamed onto Seth's cock as she began to climax. She heard Seth swear. His cock swelled in her mouth, making her eyes spring wide.

The next few seconds were a haze of pounding pleasure. She shook in orgasm as he held her head steady and thrust in her mouth shallowly but forcefully, coming on her tongue. She couldn't keep up with him. His semen spilled from her lips, but he kept erupting. It felt overwhelming and frantic as she strained to keep pace while her own climax held her captive in its clutches.

Later, she thought of how messy and unrestrained it all was as they both abandoned themselves to the moment.

She wasn't regretting a second of it though. As for Seth, well . . . she doubted he was regretting a single thing.

A minute later, he held her in his arms as she lay with her cheek on his chest. Both of them still panted softly, undone by the storm that had shook their bodies simultaneously. She stroked the side of his ribs, and he moved his fingers in her hair, massaging her skull languorously. She heard his strong heart thumping into her ear. It began to slow its frantic pace.

"That was . . ." She faded off breathlessly. "There're no words for what that was," she said sincerely, after doing a mental search for apt descriptors and coming up short. His low chuckle felt delicious in her ear.

"You're incredible," he said, stroking the back of her shoulder. "I think I blacked out for a second there . . . short-circuited."

She grinned and lifted her head from his chest. He wore a small smile. It faded as he traced her jawline. "You're very beautiful. And generous. Thank you," he murmured. Something in his tone made her heart pause and then surge faster. He traced her lower lip with his thumb and she let her mouth fall open slightly, granting him full right to touch her in any way he liked. "Are you glad you shaved?" he asked, his sexy, amused expression returning.

"You better believe it. Not to mention happy as hell you brought that vibrator."

She suddenly went still as a thought struck her.

"What?" he asked, his dark brows slanting as he stared at her face. He'd noticed the change in her.

"That kind of vibrator isn't for you, is it?" she asked slowly. His stroking thumb on her lip stilled. "It's for a woman. Why did you bring something like that if you didn't want us to be together? Did you bring it for someone else?"

"Of course not," he said, scowling.

"Then why did you bring it, Seth?" she demanded.

He closed his eyes briefly and exhaled. Her curiosity amped up. Was that vague guilt she saw on his handsome face? He clearly had been swept away by lust and hadn't thought out his actions very well in regard to revealing the vibrator and a bottle of lubrication in his bag. She wasn't blaming him for that.

Still, she wanted an explanation.

He exhaled and met her stare. "I brought a lot of things I knew I probably wouldn't use. It was . . . wishful thinking." He noticed her bemused looked. "I told you earlier that I would tell myself not to go to your movies. Sometimes my self-discipline worked. Sometimes it didn't," he added with a hard look. "I wasn't sure what it would be like, being with you again. I knew I still found you attractive, but face it: Hours alone with someone in a car can amplify an attraction just as easily as dampen it. I might find you less attractive than I had two years ago, or you could be as turned off by me. Memory and imagination are rarely as good as reality." His glance lowered over her face slowly. "I was certain I could resist you, but at the same time . . . I hoped I couldn't," he said slowly, as if he admitted the truth for the first time to himself.

Gia swallowed thickly. "I understand. It's okay," she said shakily.

He blinked and focused on her face, obviously surprised that she wasn't yelling at him.

"It is? After I told you I thought we should try and resist it?"

She thought of what she'd packed in the secret locked compartment of her suitcase, her cheeks heating. She examined his wide chest, avoiding his gaze. Seth had told her point-blank not to pack anything girly or feminine, an order that she'd willfully rebelled against, telling herself she would never put the items to use anyway. She was as guilty as he was.

"I kind of experienced similar flashes of hope and combined with absolute denial. I was convinced I was being ridiculous and adolescent, and yet . . . I kept thinking . . . *wishing*," she admitted softly. "That night we were together years ago was incredible enough to inspire a weird combination of expectations when it came to you. It's funny, the things we can hide from ourselves, isn't it?"

Something entered his expression she couldn't quite identify. He touched her cheek, his caress tender and cherishing for such a big, virile man. "The truth is, part of me knew I was a goner from the second I saw you again. Even when I allowed myself to imagine giving in to this thing I have for you, it was never like this. Never this strong. Even more crazy than the night we were first together."

She nodded.

"Thanks," he said with a pointed glance.

"For what?"

"For understanding that it's complicated. And for not getting pissed."

"Seth," she whispered softly, again at a loss for words. She was as illogical and confused as he was by the power of their attraction for each other.

"Come here," he said quietly, palming the back of her head. She went to him, their mouths fusing in a kiss that was both rife with sensual promise and tender at once. At some point, she broke it and kissed his cheeks and neck hungrily. When she lifted her head, she saw him watching her with a warm, heavy-lidded stare.

"You're exhausted, aren't you?" she whispered regretfully, thinking of his long, uninterrupted hours driving. She glanced at the clock on the bedside table. "And *hungry*, I can imagine. It's almost eight o'clock, and all you've had all day is breakfast," she said, realizing belatedly there was no sunlight peeking around the curtained windows. Night was falling. "I'll go out to the kitchen and whip something up for you," she said, starting to scurry off the bed.

"I brought some supplies, but Jennifer said we're free to use whatever is in the freezer. I figure we can go shopping before we leave and replace anything we use." He started to follow her off the bed.

"Uh-uh," she warned, giving him a hard glance from where she sat at the edge of the bed. "Stay put. I'll go get it and bring it to you. I owe you, for doing all that driving."

At first she thought he would argue, but then he settled back on the pillows, his exhaustion more apparent with every passing second. She felt his gaze on her back, and she rushed to the bathroom for her robe. She glanced back after she'd covered herself and was walking to the kitchen. He hadn't moved, but she saw the glint in his amber eyes as he watched her from beneath heavy eyelids. He was still gloriously naked, a gape-worthy landscape of muscle and brawn and relaxed male virility. Her feet flagged as she experienced a strong urge to get back into bed with him and cuddle up to his hard, warm body.

"Hurry back," he said gruffly.

"Oh, I will," she assured.

He smiled tiredly.

In the kitchen, she found that the freezer was extremely well stocked. Along with the dry goods and fruits that Seth had brought, they could stay well fed for quite some time. In her brief observations of his eating habits on the road, not to mention his hard, lean physique, she had a feeling Seth ate healthy. She hoped he would stay awake long enough to partake of the turkey burger, baked potato and sliced pears she'd prepared.

She wasn't at all surprised, however, when she walked into the bedroom later and saw that he was utterly still and fast asleep. For a few seconds, she just stood there and admired his form and face. The years hadn't changed the fact that she found him compelling and beautiful.

She set the plate and glass of ice water down on the bedside table and gently covered him with the sheet and a light blanket.

She wasn't that tired yet, having slept so much on the trip. There was a large entertainment center in the bedroom suite that included a stereo and TV, but she didn't want to risk waking up Seth. She'd go out to the living room and watch television there while she ate the turkey burger she'd made for herself.

Instead, she found herself sitting cross-legged on the bed next to him.

She never told herself to linger there. It was just that watching Seth's strong, typically impassive features give way ever so slightly as he slept was a hundred times more fascinating than anything the television could offer.

Thirteen

She awoke to the sensation of him kissing and nuzzling her breast. Her eyelids fluttered open.

"Seth," she murmured, her consciousness hovering in the vicinity between sleep and waking. Nevertheless, she wasn't disoriented. She'd immediately recognized him and relished what was happening. He answered by drawing sweetly on her nipple. His hand cupped her sex in that tender, possessive manner he used. Slowly, she felt him circle and press, ever so carefully penetrating the cleft between her sensitive sex lips and treating her clit to a subtle little polish with the smooth stone on his ring. Not too hard, not too soft. She moaned. It felt even more imperative and exciting, now that she was shaved clean for his masterful stimulation.

If she was sleeping, this was a sweet dream. It was a wonderful feeling, to wake to the sensation of being made love to by Seth Hightower. Yes . . . a very sweet dream indeed.

The king-size bed faced the wall that consisted almost entirely of windows. Although the blinds were lowered on the entire east-facing set of windows, she could see morning sunlight peeking around the edges. She saw the dark shadow of Seth's chest and shoulders as he hovered over her.

He paused to run his tongue over her pebbled nipple as if to test her swelling arousal, and then he lifted his head.

"Do you mind?"

His deep, rough voice sounded delicious in the hushed semi-darkness.

"God, no."

"Good. Because I woke up hurting for you."

He shifted on top of her, bracing his upper body on his elbows. He rolled slightly to one side, reaching between his legs.

Then he was coming over her and sliding his cock between her thighs.

Her eyes sprang wide at the sensation. Hurting *indeed*. He *must* have been aching. He was huge with arousal and had already sheathed himself with a condom. She loved the evidence of his impatience. She shifted her hips to better accommodate him. He groaned as he sank deeper, her flesh giving way and melting around his hardness. Gia whimpered at the sensation of him filling her. She was a little tender from his forceful lovemaking in the kitchen yesterday, but somehow that only added to her arousal.

"Okay?" he asked tensely. "You were warm and wet when I touched you."

"Yes. It feels so good."

She wasn't sure why they kept their voices so low and furtive, except to say that the unfolding moment felt uncommon somehow . . . sacred. He pushed his hips, and she felt him slide into her to the hilt. He paused with his cock throbbing high and hard inside her and leaned down to brush his lips against hers. She gasped against his mouth when he circled his hips slightly, pressing on her clit.

It felt so full, so incendiary.

"As if it was ever a remote possibility for me to resist this," he said quietly. She knew what he meant. They fit so well, like their bodies were designed to lock together. Made to fuse.

He began to move. She said his name shakily, her hands moving over his muscular back and flexing hips, caressing him, urging him. His strokes were firm and forceful, but measured as he built their pleasure. She moved in synchrony, letting desire guide her in this tight, fluid dance with him. His outline above her looked shadowed and mysterious. She brushed her fingertips over his face as he thrust into her, wishing she could see his face. He paused with his cock high inside her.

"Put your hands above your head on the pillow."

Her fingers stilled their anxious search. "Don't you like me touching you?" she whispered.

"No. I love it." She felt his cock lurch inside her and understood. He wanted this to last. He wanted to be in control. She dropped her hands over her head, exposing the sensitive skin on the underside of her arms. He began to move again. The morning light was growing brighter as it glowed around the curtains. She could make out the rigid angles and planes of his face as he fucked her more forcefully.

"God, you're beautiful," he muttered thickly, and she realized that her features were also resolving out of the darkness. She was growing hot from her arousal. Sweat sheened her upper lip and the valley between her breasts. He plunged into her, rocking her body, her breasts bobbing at the impact. She moaned, lost in the glory of the moment.

A beeping noise tickled the edge of her fevered awareness. Seth cursed and drew out of her. She gasped, his sudden loss like a slap to the face, it was so harsh and unexpected.

"Seth?" she asked, disoriented. He was clambering off the bed so fast, she thought she was hallucinating. She saw his large shadow fly across the room. He stood behind the edge of the blinds. She heard the distant sound of a car engine.

"What's going on?" she hissed.

He didn't reply. His form remained eerily still, adding to her bewilderment. A tiny bit more light seemed to enter the room. He peered into the crack he'd formed. For a brief second, she'd seen his profile perfectly. There was tension in every line of his tall body.

His cock protruded between strong thighs, flagrant and huge. She blinked, her anxiety fracturing for a second at the erotic picture he made.

"Seth? Who is it?" she asked, starting to get up from the bed.

"Stay there," he said. His voice was very quiet, but there was a thread of steel in it that made her pause and stay put. A doorbell rang, and Seth's shadow disappeared. The beeping alarm silenced, and she realized he'd shut it off at the control panel on the wall next to the bed. "There's a hundred-foot-security perimeter around this house. The beeping was an alert that someone had broken it," he said quietly. Then he was touching her lower leg.

"Lie back," he directed in a gruff voice. She followed his command, dazed. He came over her once again. In the distance, she heard someone start to knock on the front door.

"But . . . who is it?" she asked in a strangled voice. She felt him gently touch her slit and then his cock was entering her again. She groaned, her formal arousal leaping back to the surface of her consciousness.

"Sherona Legion. Well . . . Sherona Hathoway now that she's married. A friend. It's nothing to worry about," he murmured as he resumed fucking her like they hadn't been interrupted. "*God*, you feel good."

"But . . . shouldn't we answer the door?" she mumbled, her swirling confusion fading under the power of Seth's possession.

"No. You aren't in disguise, and I'm not presentable to the public at the moment," he grated out. He thrust into her and circled his hips slightly, emphasizing his point while she was filled with him. Overfilled. Overwhelmed. She vividly recalled that compelling image of him standing at the edge of the curtains, his cock distended, heavy and glistening. Of course he couldn't answer the front door to a guest in *that* condition.

He put his hands at the back of her thighs and rolled her hips back.

"Put your hands over your head, Gia. Now spread your legs nice and wide," he directed darkly, coming up on his knees, his hands bracing his weight on the mattress.

She opened farther for him, her legs splayed, her feet suspended in the air. She felt totally open to him. Vulnerable. She whimpered in acute anticipation. He drove into her, his deep growl of pleasure thrilling her. Her world began to rock. All thoughts about the early morning visitor flew straight out of her head as she abandoned herself to pleasure. To Seth.

After their lovemaking, they rose in preparation to shower. Gia flipped on the bathroom light.

"Gia," he said slowly, an edge to his tone. "Look at me."

She turned to him, a question in her clear, shining eyes. His gaze moved over her. Her mussed, golden brown hair spilled sexily around her shoulders and back. A still semi-erect nipple poked coyly through some tendrils of hair, a pink, mouthwatering tease. Her breasts and cheeks were flushed. Her legs looked long and supple, making him recall all too well how strong they'd been squeezing him to her when he'd ridden her just now. Her naked labia were still swollen slightly and glistening from her recent arousal.

He felt his cock stir.

She looked fresh and yet decadently wanton at once. Suddenly, all he wanted to do was debauch her all over again. Would he ever get enough of her? He somehow doubted it.

He jerked his gaze off the arousing image of her newly shaved, flushed sex and grabbed his toiletry bag.

"I'll shower in the other room," he said.

"Oh . . . okay."

He winced slightly when he heard the uncertainty in her tone. He gave her a small smile and glanced down significantly at his reanimating cock. "I think it'd be best," he said simply before he kissed her mouth and left the room.

He finished showering before her.

"Coffee?" he asked when she entered the kitchen a while later.

"Yes, thank you."

He paused in the action of pouring coffee into two mugs, his gaze moving over her appreciatively. She noticed his warm stare and smiled.

"*What?*" she asked with a small laugh.

"Just the obvious," Seth said shrugging. What man wouldn't pause to eat up the sight of her? He resumed pouring the coffee and handed her a cup. "You look pretty. I was appreciating seeing you in girl clothes." He dropped a kiss on her parted lips. She looked up at him, a little dazed. Adorable. "I don't get how you do Jessie so well. You're a miracle worker. There isn't a masculine thing about you," he said, stroking the taut curve of her hip.

"Thanks," she said, looking both pleased and slightly off balance, which pleased *him*. She was a movie star, after all, one of Hollywood's elite. It did something to him, to know he had the power to make her blush.

To give her pleasure.

"They're hardly girly clothes, though," she said, glancing down at herself with a frown. "You told me not to bring any."

She looked as if she regretted that fact when she met his stare again. He idly moved a strand of damp hair away from her cheek, glancing down over her. She wore a pair of jeans and a Jessie-worthy button-down plaid shirt. Her unbound breasts looked soft, firm and touchable beneath the cotton fabric. She wasn't wearing a bra, which was highly distracting. She had the most beautiful breasts. He could make out the outline of her nipples through the thin fabric. The scent of tangerines tickled his nose. Everything about her teased him. Tempted him. "You could make a paper bag look sexy," he muttered before he leaned down and kissed her temple.

His kisses on her fragrant skin were becoming more avid when he heard the spring on the toaster release. He grunted in irritation at the interruption, but he supposed he *should* feed her. He gave her one more kiss and reluctantly went to remove two pieces of thick multigrain toast from the toaster.

"That smells great," Gia said from behind him. He heard a drawer slide open as he opened the lid on the margarine. When he turned around to get a knife, she was there handing him one. "So, who is Sherona Hathoway?" she asked as she watched him butter the toast, leaning her hip against the counter.

"She owns the diner in Vulture's Canyon," Seth explained. "John is blind, so when he came up here for getaways, Sherona used to bring him supplies. That was before he met Jennifer. Sherona's a good person. John told me on the phone yesterday he was going to tell her we were staying up here—me and Jessie, that is. Sherona is kind of the hub of the Vulture's Canyon social network—a term I use lightly. People around here love their solitude and isolation too much to ever behave too socially. Sherona left us this bread. Here, I already ate mine. This is yours," he said, lifting the buttered toast toward her lips. She looked surprised by his actions, but took a bite. Her eyes went wide in pleasure.

"This is delicious." Before he could place the toast on a waiting plate, she caught his wrist and sank her teeth into the toast again. Their gazes met. She smiled. Only Gia could make chewing the height of sexy.

"Yeah. Sherona is one of the best cooks I know," Seth said, blinking to bring himself out of his feral focus on Gia's mouth. "She left us three loaves of bread, a dozen eggs, two jars of preserves, two pies, some fresh vegetables and a bag of apples. Plus, she brought us two pumpkins, which I left on the front porch. All of the fresh stuff will be from the co-op in town. Sherona's a big backer of it. Local people work the communal farm, and they distribute the food to families who might not be able to get fresh, healthy produce because they're isolated. Or poor. It must be a familiar routine for Sherona to come up here when someone's in residence, because John has an animal-proof wooden box out on the stoop with a lid. That's where I found all the food after I read the note Sherona left."

"That was so sweet of her," Gia mused. "Vulture's Canyon sounds like quite a unique place."

"The people here are artsy, quirky. Fiercely independent. They're generous and warm, too, once they get used to you, that is. They tend to be a little standoffish and suspicious of strangers."

"Sounds like you'd fit in perfectly here," Gia said dryly, taking another bite of toast.

"What?" he asked, wondering if he was misreading the sparkle in her springtime eyes.

"Most of those descriptors fit you, as well," she said.

"I suppose you're going to leave me to stew about which ones apply and which ones don't?"

Her smile was an innocent tease. "Can we go down to the diner later, so we can thank her in person?"

"It would require you getting into makeup," he said with a significant glance. "And putting on the act."

A shadow crossed her luminous face. She stared at the toast in her hand.

"You really hate it, don't you? My acting, I mean," she said slowly, examining the toast in her fingers like she found the vision fascinating.

"I only meant that if you want to make a trip into town, you have to be in full disguise. I thought you might not want to, once you realized all the effort involved for a casual visit to the Legion Diner," he explained.

"No. I realize what you meant. Still," she murmured, "there's something about me acting that . . . rubs you the wrong way. Not just in a general sense. On some personal level."

He absorbed what she said while he put away the margarine and opened one of the jars of Sherona's preserves. He really didn't want to get into this with her. Not now.

"You're good at it," he said shortly, opening a drawer to retrieve a knife. "I've never told you. You'll end up being the best of your generation. Maybe of several generations."

Neither of them spoke as he handed her the knife and nodded at the opened jar of preserves. She took the knife, but didn't otherwise move.

"Coming from most people, that would be an incredible compliment. Somehow, when you say it, it sounds a little like an insult."

"I didn't mean it like that," he stated flatly.

Her gaze narrowed on him. "What *do* you mean, exactly, Seth?" she prodded when he glanced away, wariness prickling through him.

"I know it's your art form," he said gruffly. How had they gotten here? He suddenly wished they were talking about anything but this.

"*But?*" she pushed.

He shook his head, exasperated she wouldn't let the topic go.

"Seth? I want to know what you think."

"It's just . . . how does a person ever know what's real and what's not?"

Regret swept through him as his words seemed to echo around the sunny, still kitchen, and he took in Gia's frozen expression.

"A person," she repeated in a hollow tone. "By person, you mean *you*? How do *you* know when *I'm* ever being real or not?"

He shrugged irritably. *No*, that wasn't what he meant. He made a sound of frustration, struggling to find the right words. "That night . . . when I opened that door and saw you standing there, I thought you were the freshest, least contrived, most unexpected person I'd ever met in my life." He raked his hand through his hair, feeling prickly under Gia's stunned stare. "When I found out you were an actress, it was like . . . discovering something that didn't *fit* with everything else."

"What?" she asked, clearly confused.

"I don't know how to explain it." *I don't really want to explain it, even to myself.* He knew he had no choice, however, when she continued to stare at him, silently entreating him to clarify. "It was like . . . finding out the most natural thing in the world wasn't what you thought it was, like being blown away by the immensity of the Grand Canyon or stunned by the beauty of a night sky, and then realizing it's a movie set."

"Fooled," she said sharply, putting down the knife on the granite countertop with a clanging sound. "You were fooled by me. I wasn't that natural, unaffected woman you thought I was. I was really a fake."

"*No*, Gia," he grated out, halting her by grasping her upper arm when she started to turn away. Jesus, how had this moment plummeted from heaven to hell so damn fast? He saw her proud, hurt expression and experienced a sinking sensation. "I mean yes, to be honest. That's what I thought *then*." He tightened his hold slightly when she started to go. "I don't now," he added grimly. "I was *wrong*. You really are uncontrived and fresh. I don't know how this business hasn't spoiled you, but it hasn't."

"Still, there's a chance it still will. Isn't that what you think?" she asked in a low, vibrating voice. "Isn't that why I'm a risk? And even though you say I'm uncontrived, you can't trust *entirely* that I'm not faking. Right?"

He winced. He didn't want to tell her he *did* find it damn unsettling, the way she could alter right before his eyes into Jessie, for instance, or the way she could so brilliantly transform on the screen until the woman he thought he'd known disappeared. Maybe that had been part of his wild need to have her while they'd been on the road together. He'd been desperate to see the woman beneath the façade, to touch her, to possess her, to assure himself of her existence.

He exhaled in temporary defeat at the realization.

"I'm sorry," he said, releasing her arm. "You said you wanted to know, so I was trying my best to tell you. I guess I didn't say it right. I didn't mean to insult you." He hesitated. "It's hard sometimes, figuring out what's real when you do the work we do."

He walked out of the kitchen, knowing he'd ruined the brilliant morning with her by being honest about his doubts. He regretted it like hell, but was clueless as to how to make it right.

Fourteen

❦

Gia told herself to stop being so hyperaware of Seth's where-abouts and actions in the house that morning and a better part of the afternoon, but she couldn't seem to stop herself. After he'd walked out of the kitchen earlier, she'd sat down at the kitchen table, determined to eat her breakfast and sip her coffee as if everything was normal and that charged, bewildering, hurtful exchange hadn't taken place. Or that it didn't matter.

Even though it *did*.

At some point, she'd heard him moving in the hallway and then a door opening. She'd paused in the act of smothering her toast in Sherona's delicious strawberry preserves, her ears keyed in for any hint of noise. Sure enough, she'd made out the distant rumble of rapid footsteps. He'd mentioned a lower level area with a workout facility. Maybe that's where he'd gone.

After she'd cleaned up her breakfast, she added a log to the fire Seth had started that morning and found her tablet. She managed to lose herself for ten-minute stretches in the Eleanor Roosevelt biography she was reading for the third time, but that was the extent of how long she could focus. A producer had approached her about the possibility of playing a young Eleanor in a movie based on the same book. She was very interested in both the book and the possibility of doing a movie version, so her difficulty in concentrating was unusual and annoying.

She would intermittently look up when she heard a slight sound of Seth moving in the distance, wondering what he was doing, then becoming irritated with herself for caring one way or another. Too many times, his words would rise in her consciousness, batting aside her focus on the book.

"*It was like . . . finding out the most natural thing in the world wasn't what you thought it was, like being blown away by the immensity of the Grand Canyon or stunned by the beauty of a night sky, and then realizing it's a movie set.*"

What an awful thing to say, she thought, scowling as she stared blindly out the windows onto a glistening autumn day.

"It wasn't horrible. It *was* honest," she mumbled irritably to herself. Hadn't she begged him to explain his reservations about her career, about her? There was little doubt he hadn't relished telling her, or that he was bewildered by his own feelings on the matter.

Still . . . to compare her to an artfully contrived movie set, a skillful facsimile of the real thing. *That* stung.

She exhaled her irritation with effort. He'd also told her he didn't feel that way anymore. He'd said he was wrong for judging her as a fake. But he was also still struggling with his thoughts and feelings when it came to her.

She couldn't alter that. He'd have to deal with it on his own. *She* had nothing to prove.

When she heard his solid step on the stairs a while later, she focused on her book with determination. He didn't come into the living room though. Tracing his movements through the comfortable, but small home, she suspected he was in the shower. Taking her opportunity, she furtively entered the bedroom they shared. Sure enough, the door to the bathroom was shut and the shower was running.

She grabbed some workout clothes and her tennis shoes. Now that Seth was finished in the facility, she was eager to get out some of her frothing feelings with a good workout.

John and Jennifer's workout facility was much larger and more sophisticated than she'd anticipated. She discovered the lower level also featured a den, a bathroom and a wet bar. Because John was blind, the treadmills and cardio machines in the exercise room all possessed video and tactile monitors, and audio prompts as well. Spurned on by her volatile mood and a smooth-voiced female occasionally goading her to move faster, Gia got in a good sweaty hour-and-twenty-minute workout.

When she entered the bedroom later, she saw no sign of Seth. By the time she'd showered and dried her hair, her thoughts and emotions were a little calmer. It wasn't that she thought Seth's attitude toward her was fair. It wasn't. She wasn't going to apologize to him for being an actress and loving her job.

But her reality didn't negate his. He probably *had* seen a lot of things she hadn't, despite the fact that she hated when he mentioned her youth and inexperience. He'd never struck her as intolerant or bitter. If he had strong opinions, he'd likely come by them honestly.

Yet, that didn't make them right.

She dressed in the jeans and button-down shirt she'd had on before her workout and stepped out of the bathroom. Seth had raised the fabric blinds. Afternoon sunlight turned the bedroom into a cozy, golden haven. He'd also made the bed. For a few seconds, she just stared at the neat bedding, imagining their unrestrained, wild . . . and, yes, soulful lovemaking last night and this morning.

It had been a mistake to expose herself. Hadn't it?

Her heart seemed to swell painfully.

No. She might not have liked what he'd said this morning, but being with Seth didn't *feel* wrong. This whole conflict between them *did* though.

She grabbed the remote control and curled up against the pillows, her knees drawn up, her back to the door. She turned on the television and flipped through the channels, desperate to distract herself.

A quick flash of her own pale, averted face on the television screen stilled her impatient punching on the remote. The curvy, brunette hostess of *Hot Topics* continued to talk as clips of Gia avoiding cameras played in the background.

"Despite being one of the most sought-after faces in both celebrity and legal circles these days, Gia Harris seems to have dropped off the radar. An inside source reveals that the popular star of *Fatal Honor* and *Glory Girl* has insisted that shooting on her new blockbuster film *Interlude* be postponed due to heavy media coverage of the Sterling McClarin trial, where Harris will be a key witness against the defendant. It seems that the onetime film ingénue has officially moved up the ranks to diva status, given that she's calling the shots with such Hollywood power players as director Joshua Cabot and the money men at United Studios," the hostess finished with a knowing grin.

"Don't pay any attention."

Gia turned around, startled by Seth's calm, gruff voice. He stood several feet inside the bedroom. He'd been stalking again. She hadn't heard him come in, but he'd obviously just heard the incendiary bit on the cheesy entertainment-news show. She glanced over at him. He wore jeans and a simple gray T-shirt that showed off his muscular arms and skimmed his strong chest. He'd been even longer in the workout facility than she had. Had he grown even *more* carved, just from one rigorous workout? It seemed like it. His casual dress only emphasized how hard he was underneath, how essentially male.

How beautiful.

"At least they're saying you're off the radar," he said quietly.

"And that I'm a power-hungry diva," she added neutrally, turning her back to him and hitting the Off button on the remote. It figured, Seth had had to hear *that* piece of salacious gossip about her.

"You okay?" he asked.

She tossed the remote control device on the mattress.

"Are you asking because of what that twit just said on that show?" she asked.

"Not really, no. But I suppose it applies."

She wasn't looking at him, but she could tell by the distance of his deep voice, he'd stepped closer to the bed.

"Because that show and the millions of people who watch it share your opinion that movie stars are narcissistic, fame-starved idiots? Is that what you mean?" she asked, unable to keep the trace of bitterness from her tone.

"No," he said. "But I can understand why you might think that, given what I said this morning."

She rolled over on her opposite hip. The hint of regret in his deep voice made her curious.

"I know that ninety percent of that crap the entertainment news slings around is just that. Shit," he said. "You don't think I'm that shallow, do you? I was there when Madeline and Joshua told you about your scenes on *Interlude* being postponed, remember? I know how insulted you were that the decision was made without you. I know the last thing you wanted was to have the schedule thrown off because of your situation."

"Not that what I thought made any difference," she mumbled.

"Yeah. Well losing control of your life is another upset all to-gether. Can I sit down?"

She glanced at him doubtfully when he pointed at the edge of the bed. After a pause, she nodded. He sat a foot or so away from where she lay on her side.

"About this morning," he began.

"You were just being honest," Gia replied resignedly, staring at the dark green duvet.

"No. I wasn't."

She glanced into his face, surprised by his stark reply. She tried to read his impassive expression, but the only thing she sensed was his somberness.

"I've told you I have a hang-up about actresses, and I confessed my doubts about relationships between two people both working in show business. It's not only you I've expressed this attitude to. People I work with are aware of it. My niece, Joy—whom I consider my closest family—is aware of it. I tried to warn her to stay away from Everett Hughes."

Gia bent her elbow and propped her head up on her hand. "Joy and Everett are both in the business. Joy is your partner in Hightower Special Effects, and Everett is arguably the most famous actor on the planet. Are you saying that their relationship is doomed to failure?"

"No. They're disgustingly happy together."

"So?" Gia asked slowly, confused as to why he'd brought up Joy and Everett.

"I wanted to be honest with you about my doubts. But in fact, I was only being half-honest, and maybe in the end, that's the same as being dishonest."

"I'm not following you, Seth."

He exhaled. "Not even Joy knows my original reason for avoiding actresses in the dating arena. I've never told her." He gave her a quick, fierce look. "I've never told anyone that I was married before."

"What?"

"It lasted all of ten months. I got married when I was twenty-three years old. I was still twenty-three when I was divorced."

A tingling sensation started down her spine as she stared at him in the taut silence that followed his revelation.

"And she was an actress?" Gia whispered, already knowing how he'd reply.

He nodded. "Not at the time, but she became one. Not just any actress. An actress you know. An actress everyone knows," he added, his mouth slanting grimly.

"Who?" Gia asked warily. Did she really want to know? She sensed his hesitation. "I'll take this to my grave, if that's what you want, Seth. You've never even told Joy, and she's like a sister to you." A flicker of unease went through her. "You *do* trust me, don't you?"

"Zoe Lindsay," was his blunt reply.

The name seemed to echo and vibrate in Gia's head.

Zoe Lindsay was in her mid-thirties, but already she'd reached legend status. She had starred in not only commercial blockbusters but also highly acclaimed independent films, and even on Broadway. She was drop-dead gorgeous—a true Hollywood siren—intelligent, savvy and highly respected by her peers. Gia's heart began drumming loudly in her ears.

Seth's eyebrows pinched together in puzzlement.

"What's wrong, Gia?"

"She's my idol," Gia mumbled under her breath, stunned. She blinked, immediately regretting saying her thought out loud. Had Seth heard her? She saw his expression stiffen and feared he had. "I'm sorry. I'm just kind of . . . shocked," she tried to explain her dazed reaction.

"Yeah. It's kind of hard to think of the two of us together."

She sat up slowly, studying his face. "No, it's not that. It's just . . . *unexpected* to suddenly pair you two together. You and Zoe Lindsay."

He nodded. "For me too. Of course, she wasn't Zoe Lindsay when we met. She was Lindsay Callahan, a waitress in a dive bar in Barstow, California, not far from the National Training Center at Fort Irwin where I was based for a while. She was a force to be reckoned with, even then." He gave a mirthless bark of laughter and shook his head. "I never stood a chance."

"She must have thought the same about you," Gia said. She felt a little dizzy, considering it. Dizzy and *heartsore*, somehow. Funny, she'd always known Seth was older than her, more experienced, and just worldlier in general. But to think of her—Gia Harris— involved with the same man Zoe Lindsay had married? To learn that Seth and her career idol shared a past?

Well, it was jarring, bewildering, and just plain unsettling on so many levels.

"Why did the marriage end so soon?" Gia asked.

"We were young and stupid. We got married in Las Vegas one weekend while I was on leave after a crazy summer infatuation. It was destined not to work from the start. I wouldn't have been able to last long myself in the heat of Zoe's fame fever . . . under the camera lens always trained on her world."

He gave her an uncomfortable glance.

"It was a mistake, Gia. Plain and simple. We *knew* I was going to ship out overseas within weeks, but we did it anyway." He shook his head. Even though he was often so impassive, she sensed his feelings clearly at that moment. He was disgusted at the memory of his weakness. His vulnerability. Compassion swept through her, a clear, concise note that pierced her stunned confusion at his ad- mission. She put her hand on his. He glanced into her face.

"We're all young once. It's not a crime. That's what you told me once," she said softly. His hard mouth tilted slightly. It felt like a band was constricting her chest, and she realized why. "You really loved her, didn't you?"

"I *thought* I did, yeah. I was wrong. I barely knew her," he finally said gruffly. Something about the stiff manner in which he said it made Gia suspect that not only had he never admitted it out loud, he had rarely allowed the truth even to himself. He inhaled slowly. Her clasp on his hand tightened. "Have you ever met her? In your work?" he asked after a tense silence.

"I met her briefly at a Screen Actors Guild luncheon last year," she admitted, cringing inwardly when she thought of how awe-struck she'd been upon meeting Zoe. She recalled all the idiotic praise that had come rushing out of her in the presence of her patient, forbearing idol.

"You must know how magnetic she is, then. She was every bit as potent at age twenty-three. I couldn't resist her. Most men couldn't, and she couldn't resist the ones that could help her with her dreams of getting out of a little town in the middle of the desert and into the Hollywood limelight. I must have seemed a likely can-didate in the absence of any better options. But I was off for a tour of duty in Iraq within eight weeks of our marriage. I couldn't get her out of Barstow fast enough. Nor could I do it in the grand fashion she wanted. When a movie producer wandered into the bar where she worked one day, scouting out territory for a shoot, her fate was sealed. So was mine. She got out of Barstow the second the producer twitched his finger," Seth explained flatly.

"She went with him?" Gia asked, dread settling in her stomach. "Even though she was married to you?"

"She not only went with him, she married him a few weeks after our divorce was finalized. If you look up her bio, the man who walked into that bar in Barstow is the one listed as her first hus-band and the man who gave her her first break in Hollywood. She's on husband number three presently—according to her official bio, anyway." He glanced at her face and must have noticed the compas-sion she was feeling for him. He turned over his wrist and grasped her hand. "Don't look like that. It's not some dramatic tragedy. I was a kid. It stung for a while, especially when I started seeing her movies. Luckily, I had a life of my own, and I lived it fully. I was halfway across the world. Time and distance taught me how naïve I'd been. It wasn't an easy lesson to learn, but I learned it."

"You learned it so well, you avoid all actresses," Gia said hoarsely, staring blankly out the wall of windows.

"It wasn't just because of Zoe that I have that attitude," he said sharply. "I worked in the industry when I left the Army. I entered it knowing full well it was a world of grandeur, but illusion as well. I've learned how to navigate it, over the years."

"You've learned how to *thrive* in it. But you keep yourself at a distance from many of the people in it," Gia said, nodding her head. Finally, she understood. She didn't like it, but she understood. Something struck her and she laughed bitterly. "Why couldn't you have fallen in love and married some crackpot I could disregard? I mean . . . *Zoe Lindsay*. She's such a class act. I thought she was, anyway," Gia added, frowning. "The way she ran off on you was about as classless as it gets."

"We were young," Seth repeated tiredly.

"Were you faithful to her while you were married?"

"Yes," Seth replied calmly.

Gia just arched her brows significantly.

He twitched his shoulder. "None of it matters now. I just . . . wanted to tell you."

"I appreciate it. I do," she repeated when he met her stare. "I know it wasn't easy for you to talk about. I get that you never *do* talk about it." He nodded and pulled her hand onto his thigh. Both of them stared at their hands as he idly stroked her wrist with long fingers for several seconds of silence.

"Do you guys ever see each other?" Gia asked suddenly.

"Rarely. We're always polite when we do. Lindsay—Zoe, I mean—has made it clear she doesn't want the press to know she was married to someone else when she ran off with her producer. Image and all," he said, giving her a dry glance.

"Do you mind? Playing along with her story?" Gia asked cautiously. She really couldn't get a bead on whether or not Seth was still torn up from a youthful infatuation with a Hollywood goddess or if he was truly cynically disinterested.

"No," he said. "I don't like to think of myself being so stupid. Colluding with her helps me not to have to think about it."

"And you're such a private person. I'm sure the last thing you'd want is to have your name linked with hers." She sighed heavily. "I think you're far too forgiving of her though. She sounds like a real bitch."

"She's ambitious. That's one of the things you admire about her. Isn't it?"

Her mouth fell open at his quiet question. So, he *had* heard her say Zoe Lindsay was her idol.

"I do. I *did*, I mean," she amended. "Isn't it possible to be ambitious and decent at the same time?"

"Maybe."

"You are," she whispered fiercely.

He squeezed her hand. She lifted her face. He watched her with a sober focus. Her heart seemed to spasm in her chest. She held her breath when he leaned down and brushed his lips against hers. "I'm not as close to the fire as you are," he said against her mouth. "And in case you haven't figured it out yet, you have the power to catch hold and burn brighter than even a Zoe Lindsay."

A sense of helplessness went through her.

"Don't worry," Seth said firmly, dropping a kiss on her brow and then her cheek. He stood suddenly. She watched him in bemusement as he went and pushed the button to electronically lower the blinds.

"Why shouldn't I worry?" she asked when he turned and headed back to the bed.

"Because those things are all thousands of miles away from us," he said as he lay down on the bed next to her. "It won't do any good for us to worry about them now. Let's take a little nap." His arms came around her. She gaped at him, but instinctively rolled over at his urging. He scooted behind her, his front to her back, spooning her.

"You want to take a *nap*?" she asked incredulously.

"Sure. Why not? We're on vacation."

Her chest felt very full, her throat achy. It seemed like such an unsurpassable breach had opened between them. He couldn't trust what she was. She would never sacrifice her career goals, not that Seth was asking her to.

But nothing felt more tangible and more real in that moment than his embrace. How could she think he was so far away from her, when he was right here?

He began to stroke her hair, as if he sensed her unease and attempted to soothe it. His heat began to resonate into her. She wasn't sure how it happened, but the knot in her chest slowly began to unwind. Her eyelids grew heavy as he caressed her shoulder and upper arm. Her flesh melted against his solid length.

"But nothing has been solved," she said, resisting letting go. She wasn't used to leaving things hovering in midair. She was a problem solver.

"Nothing is going to be solved in a day," he rumbled from behind her. "You can't force it. We'll just have to wait and see what happens. Right now, relax," he said before he kissed her ear and she shivered in pleasure.

It wasn't as if she entirely agreed with him. But his deep, rough voice always reassured her . . . compelled her, the truth be told. She curled up closer to him, and succumbed to sleep.

Fifteen

When she opened her eyes later, the room was filled with slant-ing slivers of gold-red light and deep shadow. Evening was falling. Seth didn't move from behind her, but somehow she sensed he was awake. Maybe it was the tension in his body.

"If I don't watch it, I'm going to get used to falling asleep in the middle of the day," she said in a hushed voice, just in case she was wrong about him being awake.

"It's good for you. You need the rest," he said, sliding his hand down the side of her body, cupping her curves lightly. She went still in awareness as he rubbed her hip in a small circular motion.

"It's good for you too. You work just as hard as I do. Harder, no doubt, being the owner of your own company."

He flexed his hips slightly, and her eyes sprang wide. No won-der she'd sensed tension in him. He must have awakened from his nap aroused. He buried his nose between her shoulder and neck and grazed his lips across her skin.

"Yeah. Hard," he muttered near her ear, and she heard the thread of amusement in his gravelly voice. She burst into soft laughter, and he pressed his smile to her neck. "That's nice," he said, kissing her throat. "Can we go back to being not so serious?"

"Can you do that so easily?" she wondered.

"Maybe I want to stop thinking about what might not work between us and focus on what *does*."

"Sex, you mean?"

His lips lingered on her pulse. "Yeah." He lifted his head, but she felt his warm breath brush her neck. "But not just that."

"What else?" she asked, glad his lips weren't on her skin at the moment, lest he feel the leap in her pulse.

"Just being with you."

She clamped her eyelids shut as emotion rushed her. He'd said it so concisely. She loved being with him too. His absence would hurt. She didn't want to think about that now.

She turned partially onto her back, opening her eyes to study the shadowed angles and planes of his face. "You're right." She laughed to ease the tightness in her throat. "'Not so serious'—is that what you said? What do you have in mind that's nice and frivolous?"

His gaze traveled over her face, neck and chest. "Did I say 'not so serious'?" he mused. "Wrong word usage. Completely," he added, lifting his hand to her shirt. He began to unfasten the buttons, his patience and somber purpose making it hard for her to catch a full breath. He stopped at her ribs and deliberately moved back the plackets of the shirt, exposing her breasts. His nostrils flared slightly as he stared down at her. Her sex seemed to flex inward. She suddenly felt empty because he wasn't fused with her.

"If this isn't serious, I don't know what is," he growled softly.

His hand cupped her right breast. His head lowered. She sighed at the sweetness of the sensation of his warm, suckling mouth and pressing tongue on her nipple. They shifted in unison, seeking each other out like an invisible cord that joined them had just been drawn tight. She flexed her hip against his cock. He ground against her. He groaned low in his throat, the vibration resounding into her breasts, thrilling her.

He lifted his head and kissed her damp, erect nipple. Her fingers threaded into his hair at the tender, erotic gesture.

"You have the most beautiful breasts in existence."

"I suppose that means a lot." She gasped when he rolled the sensitive tip against his lips. "Since as you so unkindly reminded me in the car, you've seen your fair share of breasts before." He took her back into his mouth and sucked firmly. Her hips jerked, her clit twanging with pleasure as he rolled his warm tongue over the crest, then sucked again. Her fingers clutched his hair.

"That *was* unkind," he agreed a moment later, massaging her breast in his hand while he ran his lips against the inner swell of flesh. He was always so single-minded in his actions, so pure in his greed. She loved it. "Let me make it up to you," he said next to her skin before he again plucked at her nipple.

"You're doing a pretty good job of it," she admitted, highly distracted by what he was doing.

"In the hot tub."

Her eyes opened. "There's a hot tub?"

Much to her disappointment, he lifted his head. She saw the gleam in his eyes, in his otherwise shadowed face. "Yeah. It's outside, on the hill. John has walls built around it, but it's open to the sky."

"You're not going to worry about some horny hunters or paparazzi hikers sneaking up on us?" she teased him.

He shook his head without hesitation.

"Are you becoming a little more trusting?" she asked.

"With that security perimeter, we'll be alerted if anyone approaches."

She smiled. "Of course. I should have known you were as suspicious as ever. John certainly is diligent about protecting Jennifer."

He planted a firm, too-short kiss on her mouth. "He's smart enough to protect what's important," he said before he sat up, pulling her along with him.

Seth punched in a code on a keyboard next to a door in the kitchen. They walked up a flight of stairs and stepped into a chilly autumn night. The hot-tub area was spacious, enclosed by wooden walls that matched the timber of the log home. Above them, the night sky was filled with more stars than Gia had ever seen in her life. The outdoor area featured not only loungers and a bubbling, steaming, spacious tub, but also two outdoor showers and a wide polished bench that looked like it might open for storage. It was lit by ambient outdoor lamps. Her eyebrows shot up in speculative interest when she noticed that the far wall was adorned with three mirrored panels, each about three foot in width and nearly spanning the height of the ten-foot-tall wooden wall. Seth noticed where she was looking. His small smile made excitement spike through her.

"John has the wall heated, so the mirrors don't steam."

He set the two large towels he'd retrieved from the bathroom a moment ago on the bench and immediately began to strip. She blinked, distracted by the sight of his flexing, taut abdomen muscles, hard chest and bulging arm muscles as he whipped off his shirt and tossed it aside.

"So John and Jennifer have a thing for mirrors?" she said as she kicked off the flip-flops she'd donned to walk outside.

"That would be my guess," he replied dryly as he attacked his button fly. Gia quickly used the elastic band she'd wrapped around her wrist to tie back her long hair into a haphazard bun/pony tail.

"But isn't that a bit . . . unusual?" she asked, unbuttoning her jeans, her gaze following Seth's progress with a tight focus as he jerked down his pants and boxer briefs at once. She caught a glimpse of his cock and long, strong, hair-sprinkled thighs before he bent to pull the garments over his feet. He wasn't as erect as he'd felt in bed a few minutes ago, but he was still long and firm and quite an eyeful. She moved her feet restlessly. The slate stone floor was very chilly.

"I don't see anything unusual about it," Seth said, tossing his jeans and underwear on the bench. "I thought you liked them too."

"But . . . didn't you say John was blind?" she asked awkwardly, discombobulated by his casual reference to a topic she'd never admitted to anyone but him. She shimmied out of her jeans.

"Yeah," Seth said. He grabbed the folded towels and sauntered naked across the terrace and set the towels close to the tub. She watched him as he lowered into the pool, regretting when his strong legs, muscular ass and cut torso were submerged in the bubbling water, depriving her of the awesome sight. He sat on the circular bench and looked at her with his eyebrows raised in droll expectancy.

She hastened to draw her jeans and underwear off her legs.

"Leave the shirt on," he called.

"What?" she asked, confused by his request.

"Yeah," he said thickly, his gaze between her thighs making her feel like she was in the steaming water already. Except for her feet, that is, which were quickly turning to blocks of ice. "Leave it."

"All right. Whatever. I didn't realize it was so cold out here," she muttered, hurrying across the deck and shivering. "Oh, that feels *good*," she mumbled earnestly when her icy feet hit the hot water. She settled on the lower bench next to Seth, sighing with pleasure. Water bubbled energetically around her chest. It felt divine. She saw her smile through the rising steam in the reflection of the mirrors, reminding her of their topic.

"If John is blind, why would he think mirrors are important?"

"Maybe they're for Jennifer," Seth said.

Gia considered and nodded.

"Maybe he likes Jennifer to tell him what she's seeing."

Her eyebrows went up in prurient interest. "How would you know something like that? Locker-room talk between guys?"

Seth shook his head. "No. Just something John joked about once when we were together. He mentioned porn for the blind." He noticed her dubious expression. "It's basically people describing other people having sex. It's on the Internet."

Her mouth fell open in amazement. She glanced at the mirrors again, assessing. She could see her and Seth's reflection quite well, despite the curling steam. "Oh, I see," she said slowly.

He laughed quietly and knelt in front of her in the water. "Do you?" he asked amusedly, a god-awful sexy smile lingering on his firm lips. He was usually so somber, intimidating even. To see him laugh and smile and joke with her was a potent aphrodisiac. She could get used to a playful Seth. Of course, she was kind of partial to a stern Seth, as well . . . given the right situation.

He put his hands on her waist and lifted her body to the upper bench. The water sloshed around her, the waterline lowering to her ribs. She glanced down and saw that the wet cotton shirt was plastered to her breasts. The night air was cool. Her nipples were clearly defined against the clinging wet cloth of the shirt.

"Lecher," she joked softly.

His grin widened. She'd hastily buttoned up the shirt earlier when they'd gotten up from bed to come outside. Seth cupped her breasts in both hands and shaped her to his palms, examining her with salacious intent. She whimpered softly when he ran his thumbs over the beading nipples, outlining their circumference, rubbing the distended tips. "You didn't think I was done playing with you, did you? I was just getting started."

His inspection of her breasts in his hands had her steaming more than the hot water. When he leaned down and inserted just the tip of one between his pursing lips, then gently scraped his straight front teeth front over the cloth-covered tip, she squirmed in arousal on the hard bench. He kissed the crest through the wet fabric, and she saw his smile.

"Hold still," he murmured, backing away slightly. His gaze on her was smoky as he began to unbutton her shirt. When he'd finished, he pulled on the end of the plackets, exposing and bracketing her bare breasts. He tied off a snug knot beneath the bottom curves, and then reached into the pocket he'd formed and lifted the globes of flesh higher over the cloth. Gia glanced down in amazement.

The taut fabric pulled tight, lifting and emphasizing her thrusting breasts. They were shiny with moisture from the steam. It looked very . . . naughty.

He glanced at her and smiled. He'd highlighted her in just the way he wanted.

"I can practically see the canary feathers hanging out of your mouth," she murmured.

"Don't blame me for thinking you're beautiful."

He leaned down and sucked a nipple into his mouth with hot, unapologetic greed. Air soughed out of her lungs. Arousal shot through her, hot enough for her to feel, even in the steaming pool of water. He was a little more ruthless than usual with her, drawing on her with a firm suck that had her eyes crossing. After a thigh-clamping moment for Gia, he lifted his head and lifted her breast with his hand, inspecting her nipple closely. It had grown rosy, the tip defined and stiff. His mouth shaped into a snarl before he bent and gave the other nipple the same treatment, seemingly utterly focused on his task.

"Seth," she muttered after a minute, her fingers tangled in his steam-dampened hair. She couldn't take this anymore. He lifted his head after a moment, her nipple popping from his sucking mouth with a lewd sound.

"Tell me what you see," he demanded.

Her gaze drifted over to the mirrors. She saw his dark head hovering close to her flushed, damp breasts. He'd made the nipples look large and vividly pink with his attentions, the contrast stark in comparison with the surrounding pale, curving flesh. And the shirt . . .

"You made me look like some kind of X-rated Daisy Duke," she muttered.

He chuckled and slowly kissed the nipple nearest to the mirrors. "You can do better than that," he chastised her for the description. He began to slide his pursed lips up and down over the erect crest, using the tip of his tongue to flick the center nubbin. Her clit pinched tight. She moaned and clasped his head to her as frissons of excitement and pleasure coursed through her. "I like how different you look than me," she said, her gaze now locked to the erotic image of his mouth and hand on her breast.

"*Hmmm?*" he asked, sounding both interested and preoccupied, as he used his hands to plump her breasts together and continued to suck her nipple in and out between her lips.

"You're so . . . masculine," she whispered. "Your hands are so big. You make me feel—" She gasped when he drew on her nipple more firmly, suction hollowing out his cheeks. "So feminine next to you. So *wanted.*"

"That's because you *are* so wanted," he told her as he molded her breasts more firmly into his hands and brought her nipples together, licking and kissing them both at once with feverish intensity. She put her hands between her legs to stifle the ache that flamed high there, and then she reached for Seth's cock. She made a sound of frustration when she couldn't reach him, because he knelt in front of her, his knees on the bottom of the pool. He wouldn't let her alter her position as he sipped and sucked at her breasts with avid intent. An anguished sound left her throat. His head rose. He nipped at her neck and then plucked at her parted lips. His hand closed on hers as she rubbed her clit. His eyebrows went up when he realized what she'd been doing. "Are you playing with yourself while I play with you?" he asked with fond amusement.

Her cheeks burned. "*No.* I mean, yes. But I was trying to reach you and couldn't, so . . ."

His smiled widened as he bit gently at her lower lip. "Don't be embarrassed. I don't want to be reached at the moment. I like finding you with your hand between your legs too much." Her head fell back, and she moaned when he used his finger to press hers between her labia and they both rubbed her clit in the warm water. He dropped heated kisses on her mouth, but it was the way he watched her with such hungry focus that undid her.

"Your cheeks are turning red, Bright Eyes," he said, his deep, gravelly voice rushing over her wet, naked skin like a rough caress. Her eyelids drifted closed as their hands began to move in synchrony between her thighs. "No. Keep them open," he demanded. "I told you I love that helpless look you get in them before you're about to come."

"I'm not helpless," she muttered thickly. Oh God, she was hot, and her clit was starting to sizzle from Seth's deft maneuvering between her thighs. Even though water surrounded her sex, their fingers moved with slippery ease. He rose slightly in the pool, his muscles flexing and gleaming with moisture.

"No?" he asked. She blinked dazedly because his hand had left her. He was reaching behind her. When his hand returned, she saw the purple tubular vibrator in his hand. He must have secreted it in the towels. Immediately, he turned it on and plunged his hand into the water. "If you don't want to call it helpless, fine, but you *are* about to come."

She cried out shakily when he pushed the vibrating tube between her labia and began to slide it up and down against her clit. It must have been waterproof, because it was working just fine underwater.

"Nice?" he asked.

"God, yes," she moaned, panting. It was too much. She was drowning in thick, hot pleasure.

"Here," he said, grabbing her hand hastily. "You do this."

She took the vibrator from him and continued manipulating it over her clit. Part of her couldn't believe she had become so shameless with him, but most of her didn't care. It felt so *good*. Seth rose out of the water suddenly, the image of rivulets of water rushing off his naked, awesome form scoring her consciousness. Her face was at the level of his long, strong thighs sprinkled with wet, dark hair. His cock was fully erect, springing from between his thighs. The long, thick staff was flushed dark pink from the heat and his arousal. The fat, defined cockhead was the very image of temptation. She opened her lips and leaned toward him, but he stopped her with his hands on her shoulders.

"No. Lean back as far as you can," he said, and she could tell by the roughness of his voice that he was nearly as excited as she was. She leaned back against the smooth cement surround, her gaze never leaving his cock. "Farther. Arch your back and stretch your throat back. That's it," he acknowledged when she rested the crown of her head on the terrace surface and arched her spine, sending her breasts high. Excitement and anticipation pounded through her. She thought he was going to kneel over her and push his cock into her mouth.

But that's not what he did.

Instead, he plumped her breasts higher in the pocket of the tied-off shirt and placed his foot on the bench below where she sat. He braced himself with his arms on the side of the pool, his big body tenting her, and pushed his protruding, swollen cock against the cleft of her breasts. Gia cried out in sharp excitement at the sensation of his heavy, warm cock against her skin.

"Look in the mirror," he growled from above her as he thrust and sent his cock deeper into the cleft of flesh. She rolled her head sideways and watched, spellbound as he sawed his hips back and forth, his glistening buttocks flexing magnificently as he rubbed his cock between her breasts. "You said you liked how different we are," he grated out as he thrust, and the swollen cockhead popped up between her breasts. She pushed one breast closer to his thrusting cock, cushioning his hardness in her softness. He groaned roughly. The image of Seth naked and hovering over her in such a dominant position, of his flagrant, ruddy erection against her pale, curving flesh—all of it overwhelmed her with excitement. It would be stamped in her brain forever. She felt herself cresting against the vibrator. She cried out and shuddered in pleasure.

"You can't get much more different—or beautiful—than that," she heard Seth say as she moved the vibrator rapidly between her thighs and rode the hot waves of orgasm.

Her eyelids had clamped closed while she came thunderously. She raised them sluggishly when she felt Seth gently lifting her out of the water. The smooth tile surround felt cold and delicious against her steaming flesh. She stared into Seth's face, her brain and flesh heavy with satiation and heat.

"I think I overcooked you," he said, his handsome mouth quirking. Despite his smile, he looked concerned, she realized. "Are you okay?" he asked her gently.

She blinked, trying to muster her brain into working. The cool air against her wet, hot skin was helping clear the heavy sensual fog.

"Yeah," she swallowed. "That was . . ."

"Nice?" he murmured, leaning past her. His movement caught her attention. His cock still looked huge and heavy between his strong thighs. She sat there, panting softly, her focus now entirely snagged, as she watched him efficiently roll on a condom. He sat on the deck next to her, their feet both still in the bubbling water.

"Gia?"

"Huh?" she asked, dragging her stare off his cock and gazing up at his face. His brow quirked in mounting concern, and she gave her brain a vicious mental prod. "It was *so* nice. I don't know how you make me so . . . different."

"Different?"

She nodded, licking her bottom lip. "You take me out of myself," she whispered.

His slow smile made her cooling skin prickle, bringing her back to the moment, surer than anything. "Maybe you just are being *more* yourself." She blinked as she took in his words.

"I'm going to try and make this easy on you," he said, urging her to stand with his hands on her shoulders. "Come here," he directed gruffly, guiding her between his spread thighs, her back to him. She felt his cock brush against her ass and glanced back. He was holding it up, aiming it between her thighs. Understanding his intent, she braced her hands on his solid thighs and lowered. He found her slit. She bit her lip hard at the sensation of him flexing his hips and pushing the plump head into her. Gritting her teeth, she dropped lower onto the rigid stalk.

"Yeah, that's right," he groaned roughly, transferring his hands to her hips. He took the majority of her weight, lowering her slowly onto his cock. When she sat in his lap, he circled her hips in a taut little circle, his thumbs sinking into her buttocks. Gia hissed at the incendiary sensation of him stretching her and throbbing deep inside. Glancing aside, she saw how tense his big body looked in the mirror, his biceps and shoulder muscles strained hard and round as he contained his arousal. She sat forward slightly to accommodate his cock inside her. He opened his hand along her hip and stroked her from ass to rib, his actions deliberate and focused. Her vagina flexed inward at the vision of his dark hand sliding against her skin. She moaned and began to lift over him, but he placed both of his hands on her hips and kept her nailed firmly to his lap.

"Hold still while you cool off a bit." Despite his command, his cock lurched inside her, and she heard the hard edge to his tone. As always, she loved the evidence that he wasn't as cool and in control as he seemed most of the time. He began to stroke her again while both of them watched in tense fascination in the mirror. "What do you see?" he asked her, his deep, rough voice causing her spine to prickle.

She said the first thing that popped into her brain. "My ass looks white as a ghost next to you," she said, frowning slightly. She saw him smile. He caressed the buttock closest to the mirror.

"I like it white," he told her warmly, shaping the flesh to his palm. "I'd like to turn it pink . . . and hot beneath my hand."

Her gaze flew to his in the mirror. He was watching her with a steamy focus. "Don't worry," he told her, restrained amusement in his tone. "I'm not going to spank you now. You already look wrung out as it is."

"I'm fine," she said quickly. She replayed what he'd just said in her head. Her clit pinched in excitement. Instinctively, she tightened around him. He grimaced and suddenly pushed her up on his cock then hauled her back again, grinding up on her and circling her hips subtly in his hands. She whimpered at the incendiary, unexpected stroke.

"You're not fine. You're fucking fantastic . . . and a *trial*," she heard him say darkly. She saw his broad chest expand as he inhaled slowly. A thrill shot through her to see him fighting for control. He seemed to come to himself and saw her greedy gaze on his face in the mirror. "You're still holding the vibrator," he said, stroking her hips. She blinked in surprise and glanced down. She hadn't realized she still clutched it. Had Seth turned it off when she was short-circuiting in orgasm?

"Turn it on and press it against your clit," he instructed warmly.

"No," she said shakily. He'd seen her come undone enough for one night. She wanted to see him unwind. "Fuck me."

She saw his mouth harden in the reflection. He sunk his fingers into her ass and rubbed her lasciviously.

"Turn on the vibrator, and press it against your little clit," he repeated. He hadn't increased his voice volume, but he gave her a dark, significant glance in the mirror. She sighed and turned on the vibrator. It buzzed energetically. "I don't see why I have to be the one to always lose control," she muttered under her breath.

"Do you want to bring me pleasure?"

"Yes, that's my point."

"Then do as I say," he said gently, but succinctly.

He was trying to tell her that seeing her in the clutches of pleasure is what aroused him. Slowly, holding his stare, she brought the vibrator between her legs. She tensed and shuddered slightly when it vibrated into her most-sensitive flesh.

"*Ohhh,*" she moaned. It felt so decadently good, to have Seth stroking her with his big hands and filling her up completely with his cock while the vibrator buzzed away at her clit and labia.

"That's right. Move it up and down now. Let me see," he was saying behind her. She realized he was straining to see in the mirror because her forearm was in the way. She moved the vibrator to her left hand and began to push it up and down in the cleft of her sex lips, letting him observe her naked hedonism. What use was there in hiding it, when it seemed to crave the spotlight in Seth's presence? He clutched at her hips and ass and began to rotate her subtly in his lap. "Yeah, that looks so beautiful," he said thickly, and she felt his hot gaze on her almost as surely as the vibrating metal tube. "Lean forward a little and ride it."

She blinked, a little unsure of what he meant. Then she realized that if she braced herself more securely on his thigh and leaned away from him an inch or two more, it really was a little like she was riding the thrusting little vibrator.

It was so naughty. It felt *so* good.

She did what came naturally. Taking just a little of her weight on her bent legs, she began to ride the vibrator and Seth's cock at the same time.

He groaned roughly, like something had just been ripped out of him. He popped her ass with his hand, but it was a love slap more than a punishment, and she knew it.

"Dirty, adorable girl," he accused with rough fondness before he grabbed her hips and drew her up the length of his cock several inches. He crashed her back down onto him, his biceps flexing hard, their damp skin slapping together. "What a sweet little pussy," he grated out.

Almost immediately, he was urging her up again, and she knew by the way he clutched her back to him, skewering her with his cock, he was becoming as unwound as she was.

She gloried in it.

Her thigh muscles tensed as she bobbed her hips up and down over his cock, but he took a good portion of her weight. They found a taut tempo that had both of them clenching their teeth in pleasure. Gia felt it happening all over again as she lost herself to the hot, mounting bliss of the moment. She stared in awe at the image of their mating. It was lewd, and vivid, and magnificent. His cock looked intimidatingly big and flushed with his blatant arousal next to her pale curves, his hands holding her at his mercy.

She *was* at his mercy, and she loved it.

"I love seeing my cock in you," he said darkly.

She bounced on him more forcefully and he groaned. He lifted his hand and swatted her ass, and then grabbed her to him again, smacking their skin together.

Excitement tightened every muscle in her body. She couldn't take it anymore. She had to give in.

"Seth," she cried out in anguish. He fucked her at a relentless pace, never once breaking stride. She was starting to shake.

"Go on. Come," he said tensely.

He'd issued an order and expected her to comply. She moved the vibrator frantically between her creamy labia, bobbing up and down in his lap like a cork in a wild, seething sea. He spanked her bottom again briskly for emphasis, but she was already following his command.

"Oh," she cried out wildly as orgasm hit her. Her muscles seized.

"That's right," he said, his voice thick with triumph and lust. It was a little hard to keep up their frantic pace while she shuddered in pleasure. Seth took most of her weight, settling her into his lap. He continued to fuck her while she came, every muscle in his powerful body straining tight as he controlled her movement on him. He stabbed his cock into her with short, hard strokes, racing for his own release. It was such a discombobulating rush of pounding pleasure and straining sinew, for a moment everything blurred in Gia's consciousness.

She finally focused on the reflection of Seth's profile. He didn't make a sound as he watched himself—not in the mirror, but in real life—drive his cock into her with ruthless abandon. In the mirror, she saw his rigid face, blazing stare and bulging muscles. Suddenly, a great shudder went through him and an ominous low growl escaped his throat. A thrill of anxious excitement went through her.

Talk about sitting on a bomb.

He pulled her down in his lap, and she felt his cock swell. His growl escalated to a roar. She felt him pulse high in her as he ejaculated. He kept her nailed to him as he came, the only exception being the way he pushed her buttocks together and circled her hips tautly in his lap. It was overwhelmingly thrilling.

Finally, he lifted her once and crashed her back to him.

He made a harsh, ragged sound. Instead of slowly fading, all the tension seemed to fall out of his big muscles. He encircled her waist and brought her against his torso tightly, his face pressing to her shoulder blade, his powerful chest heaving against her as he fought for air. He clutched her like he was afraid to let go.

Gia just stared at him in wonder in the mirror, as moved by the vision of him frayed and undone as she was by the ruthless, powerful lover.

Sixteen

Gia was beginning to get used to a vacation schedule, as new and alien as it was to her. She was starting to love the long, sweet hours filled with nothing but relaxation and discovery and pure, golden pleasure with Seth.

They spent the next week in a cocoon of warm intimacy, sitting in the hot tub under a dome of stars, talking, playing cards and watching old movies in bed far into the night. A few times, Seth brought some blankets onto the deck and they would lie on the wooden bench, snuggled together and cocooned beneath the covers.

"Do you like to go camping?" Seth asked her once as they had stared up at the beauty of the night sky.

"You mean sleep in tents and make campfires?" Gia asked doubtfully.

He lifted his head and peered at her closely. "Never mind," he said, smirking, letting his head fall again. "City girl disdain is written all over your face right now."

She laughed. "I'm not that bad. I've never been camping, so I don't know if I'd like it or not. Maybe I would," she said, touching his naked chest. "With you."

Seth could make anything appealing, after all.

He smiled and pushed a tendril of hair behind her ear. "I'm thinking the best we could hope for in your case is glamping."

"*Glamping?*"

"Yeah. Luxury camping. You get all the benefits of the beauty of the outdoors in addition to five-star restaurants and spas."

"I don't need a spa and restaurants," Gia insisted. "I just want a clean bed and a lock on the door."

Seth shrugged in a concessionary gesture. "Yeah. I can see how those things would be a necessity in your case."

Whatever activity they undertook during those sweet, sensual days and nights, it usually never reached full completion because they couldn't keep their hands off each other and ended up making love.

During that time, she found out that Seth possessed a shockingly accurate photographic memory, something that guaranteed she lost at poker every time they played. She discovered he ate his eggs over easy and liked English period dramas, even though he refused to admit it. He *would* admit to a penchant for sci-fi and horror movies, which she said she hated. Then she proceeded to grow enraptured with the genre while in the circle of Seth's arms, listening to him explain the fascinating details of the special effects makeup on the screen. She learned his stamina for both exercise and making love was gargantuan.

They didn't speak of their relationship beyond the days in the brilliant autumn woods, but instead did as Seth suggested, focusing on what worked between them instead of the obstacles.

And there was so much that *did* work.

Seth got up from bed one early afternoon, insisting she stay put while he made them a *real* lunch. They had subsisted almost entirely on easy meals thus far: Sherona's delicious breads, fruit, eggs and some frozen chicken breasts and vegetables from the freezer that they would replace before they left. She hadn't eaten all day and was both curious and starved by the time Seth entered the bedroom a half hour later, carrying a large tray.

"I didn't know you could cook like *this*," she said in amazed pleasure as she set aside her book, her gaze caught by the delicious-looking contents of the tray. She sat up against the pillows, drawing the sheet up to her chest, her appetite piqued.

"I'm a single man. If I don't cook, I starve most nights. It's nothing fancy," he downplayed, handing her first a cloth napkin and then a plate.

She disagreed and told him so several times in the midst of wolfing down sesame-citrus halibut, wild rice, green beans and a warmed piece of Sherona's delicious cinnamon-raisin-walnut bread. This bounty was accompanied by a lovely dry chardonnay.

After Seth had taken her empty plate and glass and set it down, along with his, on the tray, Gia fell back on the pillows in content, sensual lassitude.

"I'm going to make you dinner tonight for payback," she sighed dreamily, thinking of what she'd stowed away in the locked compartment of her suitcase. She smiled to herself.

"What's got you looking so smug?" Seth asked.

"Nothing," she said, meeting his stare. "Thanks again. That was the best meal I've ever had."

Seth gave her that amused, fond glance she was starting to recognize and cherish seeing. "Right. Never a better meal, even though you've lived in restaurant meccas like Manhattan and L.A."

"None of those were made by you," she said quietly, her cheek on the pillow as she studied him. He was reclining on his hip, elbow bent, his head resting on his hand. Unlike Gia, who was naked under the sheet, he was partially dressed in a pair of black cotton pajama pants that he'd donned before cooking for them. She languorously followed the beautiful upward slant from his narrow waist to his wide chest to his face. "I mean the whole experience, not just the food, although that was delicious. I'm not used to having someone cook for me."

"Are you a cook yourself?"

"When I focus on it. Which is never," she added under her breath, grimacing slightly. "I've been so busy lately, I live off catered food from a movie set or I order in. I try to eat fairly healthy, but still . . . there's something less fulfilling about the experience of eating food like that, you know?"

He nodded. "Impersonal. The person preparing it doesn't know you."

"Yeah, exactly. The ingredients are first-rate, and the preparation is skilled, but there's no love or caring, no acknowledgment of you as an individual." She realized how wistful she sounded and blinked, darting an anxious glance at Seth. She'd probably freaked him out by suggesting he'd prepared her meal with *love*.

He didn't look at all ruffled by what she'd said.

He *did* change the subject, however.

"Is this good?" he asked, picking up the book she'd been reading and had discarded on the mattress when he arrived with the food.

"Excellent. Do you know much about Eleanor Roosevelt?" she asked, drawing the sheet more firmly around her breasts and sitting up against the pillows.

"A little. I had to write a paper about her in a college history class."

"Could you do me a favor?" she asked, taking the book from him and setting it down between them on the mattress, still facing Seth. She rifled through the pages to a series of photos. "These are of her in her late teens and twenties." She said, leaning forward as they both studied the pages. "There's a producer interested in adapting this book into a movie, and he's asked me if I'd be interested in playing a young Eleanor. Cecilia doesn't think my looks are at all suited for the part," she said, referring to her agent. She frowned. "Actually, she also thinks it won't have a wide-enough commercial appeal, but I don't care about that. Eleanor has been an idol of mine for a long time. It'd be a dream to play her. But I *am* worried about if I could pull it off, from a physical-appearance standpoint. There's no one better to ask than you. What do you think?" She tapped her finger on the page of a young, quite pretty Eleanor with dark blond hair styled in a poofy upsweep. She had a pensive face and intelligent, soft eyes. "Could I become her?"

She waited anxiously while Seth flipped through a couple pages, studying the images silently. She trusted his opinion completely. If he said it was impossible to transform her physically into Eleanor, it was. He finally glanced up at her, his stare moving slowly over her face. She experienced, not for the first time, his intense focus and that cool, penetrating . . . *all-seeing* gaze that defined his genius.

After a tense pause, he nodded once. Her heart leapt with excitement.

"It would be a subtle, but complicated, makeup. A mouth insert would have to be used to shape your lower face, and it would have to be a really good one, sculpted to not only Eleanor's facial features, but yours as well. Your lips are usually a problem—not in everyday life, or for *me*," he added dryly, "but to disguise." Gia smiled. He nodded at the page. "Eleanor has a nice, full mouth, though, and it was much softer-looking when she was young. It would mostly be your acting that counted for embodying her, though. Roosevelt had very characteristic mannerisms and voice intonation."

She nodded eagerly. "I think I could do it."

He gave a small smile and glanced back at the page. "I'm sure you could. The face would be easier than her body though. Wasn't Eleanor one of the tallest first ladies?"

"Five eleven. I'm barely five six," Gia admitted.

"Well . . . the trick of film and costume could diminish that, and the way you move your body, of course," he said slowly. "I can make some sketches, and I brought my kit. Do you want to experiment a little with it while we're here?"

"Yes," she enthused. "That'd be amazing. But only if you want to. It's supposed to be a vacation for you too."

He didn't speak for a moment, and she wondered if indeed he'd only offered to be polite. Then she noticed his quirked brow as he studied the book intently. She could almost hear his brain whirring.

"Seth?"

He glanced up distractedly.

"Oh . . . sorry. Yeah, I definitely want to do it," he replied simply.

His phone buzzed on the bedside table. He twisted around and snagged it with his left hand. She saw a small smile shape his lips as he read the message once he faced her again.

"Apparently even the gossip grapevine is slower moving in the vicinity of Vulture's Canyon than the rest of the world. Katie Pierce has just found out from Sherona that I'm up here."

"Rill's wife?" Gia asked.

"Yeah." He glanced up at her. "She's asking us to come to dinner tomorrow night. They just got back from Los Angeles. Do you want to go?"

"As Jessie Bauer?"

He nodded. "As my nephew."

She bit her lip, considering. It would be interesting to meet Rill in person. He was one of the youngest, most respected directors in Hollywood. Seth seemed to notice her hesitancy.

"What are you thinking?" Seth asked her quietly.

"I'm not so sure I feel like sharing you with anyone else," she said impulsively.

Something flickered into his amber eyes. He reached out and cupped her waist warmly in his hand. "I know what you mean. It's nice alone up here on this hill with you. Should I tell Katie no?"

"Well . . . maybe we *should* wander out tomorrow?" she asked, her heart not in what she was saying. She realized that a dark, murky cloud of emotion was hanging at the edge of her consciousness. Maybe that unnamed emotion was fear, that if they left the little world they'd created between themselves, the magic would be broken. What if they could never return?

Gia mentally rolled her eyes. Her anxious, unrealistic thoughts weren't at all in sync with her practical planning self. She reined in her disquietude.

"Yeah . . . we really *should* get some groceries, venture into the real world, I suppose. I wanted to thank Sherona for all the supplies, although I suppose it'd be more in character for you to want to go do that, since I don't think it'd be typical for Jessie to return social calls. We could walk through one of the local towns, check out the sights, and then go to Katie and Rill's for dinner?"

"Sounds like a date."

"Except that you'll be dating a boy," she said drolly. "But would that be so bad? A date, I mean?"

That sexy smile tugged at his mouth. "Not in the slightest."

"I mean, if I have to be in disguise, we might as well get it over with all at once, right?"

"Get what over with?"

"Halting cabin fever from ever setting in?" she suggested, shrugging.

"A preventive measure?"

"Exactly."

"Fine with me either way. You're the one who hates being confined."

"That was before," she admitted, touching the side of his ribs. She thrilled to feel his skin roughen beneath her stroking fingertips. He growled softly when she touched his stiffening nipple. He promptly dropped the phone behind him on the bed.

"Before what?" he asked, suddenly dead serious. He pulled the sheet down, exposing her bare breasts. Without pause, his head lowered. He pressed his mouth over her heart and softly cupped a breast.

"Before being confined with you," she whispered, enthralled by the sensation of his light, brushing lips and the slight abrasion of his whiskers on her skin. He found her sensitive nipple, his warm mouth enfolding her.

Gia closed her eyes and forgot Rill and Katie Pierce. Nothing existed but Seth and the new, amazing world he was opening up to her.

Later, after they'd made love, Seth held a warm, supple, dozing Gia in his arms, her cheek against his chest. He thought she'd fallen asleep until she spoke.

"Do you know what would be amazing?" she asked, her voice dreamy and slurred with sleep.

"*Hmmm?*" he asked, running the soft coils of her hair idly between his fingertips.

"If you could work on the Eleanor film and do my makeup."

The citrus fragrance from her hair and the unique scent that came off her skin after orgasm filled his nose in the silent seconds that followed. He couldn't think of how to respond to her sweet words. He lifted his head to peer into her peaceful face.

By the time he quietly said her name, she'd fallen asleep, a small smile on her lips.

Later, Gia cuddled against the pillows and watched a local St. Louis television broadcast of the news while Seth sat in bed next to her, making sketches of her face. At first, she felt a little self-conscious knowing he was making such an intent study of her. Eventually, she sank into relaxation, however, lulled by the pressure of his gaze on her cheek and the subtle scratch of his pencil on the pad. After he set down his pencil and stretched, Gia roused herself from her lassitude.

"You should go and do your workout while I make you dinner."

"You weren't serious about that, were you? You don't have to cook anything," he said, scowling slightly as he landed one final kiss on her shoulder before he got out of bed.

"Of course, I was serious. I'm making you a special dinner, and you better shower after your workout and dress nice for it, or I'll be insulted. Go along," she teased, waving her hands in an "away with you" gesture. He gave her a slightly amused, speculative glance. He knew she was up to something, but couldn't guess what. She watched him saunter over to the bathroom, as insouciant and comfortable as a god in his nakedness, and twice as gorgeous because of it. Gia leafed through her book, waiting impatiently for him to go downstairs so that she could set her plan into action.

She was sick of either appearing to Seth as a teenage boy or a frump in a robe with wild hair and not a smudge of makeup. The fact that she was going to go out with him tomorrow as Jessie Bauer only solidified her determination. Tonight, she was going to remind him—and herself—that she was one hundred percent female.

When she finally heard the door to the lower level close behind him, she sprang up from bed and extracted the skeleton key from a pocket in her purse. She hurried over to her small antique steamer trunk and opened it.

Seth's secret had been exposed when she confronted him about the vibrator he'd brought on their trip. Part of him had wished something would happen between them, even if most of him had warned him it was unwise to hope. Gia hadn't blamed him for that because she was similarly guilty.

She unlocked the secret compartment, withdrew the delicate, feminine items inside and smiled.

*   *   *

When Seth came upstairs after his workout, he heard the sound of pans rattling in the kitchen. He thought about going and stealing a kiss from Gia before he cleaned up, but he was really sweaty from his workout. Best just to get his shower out of the way before he joined her.

Or maybe it was the memory of what she said as she'd drifted off to sleep that kept him away. He remembered it, although Gia didn't seem to after they'd awakened.

He probably shouldn't dwell on it. Hadn't he told her they should just focus on the moment instead of worry about the future?

But he had thought about it this afternoon and all during his workout.

A lot.

The bathroom smelled good, like Gia's tangerine-scented shampoo and something else that appealed. He picked up a bottle of perfume that sat on the counter. He'd never seen it there before. After taking an appreciative sniff, he set it down, smiling to himself. Seeing and smelling the uncustomary bottle of perfume had reminded him that Gia had teased him about dressing for her dinner. He noticed an unplugged flatiron on the counter that he'd never seen before either. She'd clearly made an effort with herself. It would be impolite of him not to reciprocate.

Several minutes later, he realized he was still grinning slightly as he showered. Gia had that effect on him. Thinking about her made him horny as hell and just plain *hungry* for the sight of her, for her taste, for the sound of her sighs and whimpers as she succumbed to pleasure. He was growing addicted to her honest, uninhibited reaction to his touch.

The thought of her also just made him smile though. Sex aside.

Despite his earlier misgivings about Gia's dreamy statement about them working together in Hollywood, a pleasant sense of anticipation started to build in him, making his skin feel prickly and his cock to partially harden. Instead of ignoring his arousal at the idea of spending the evening with Gia and losing themselves once again in erotic pastimes, he encouraged the taut expectation, teasing himself, letting the suspense build. He soaped up his cock and balls and stroked himself idly, vividly picturing the way Gia had looked earlier this afternoon as he'd lapped and licked at her smooth, sweet pussy, bringing her to climax twice before he'd finally given in to his need and sunk his cock into the heaven of her. He imagined doing it all over again, except this time, her arms would be restrained to the bed. Yes, he thought as his fist moved faster on his now-stiff cock. That's what he would do to her tonight. He'd already admitted he was addicted to that helpless expression that overcame her lovely face when he made love to her and her climax loomed.

He wanted to see her helplessness in the face of desire even more closely. He wanted to wrap himself in her total surrender.

The fact of the matter was, he wanted Gia to become as hopelessly addicted to him as he was becoming to her.

That jarring thought pierced his intense autoerotic fantasies about restraining Gia. He dropped the hand that had been cupping his balls as the other jacked his shaft.

He frowned at his reflection a moment later when he stood in front of the mirror, naked. His erection hadn't dissipated, despite the unsettling thought he'd had about needing Gia so much. His cock sprang between his thighs, heavy and ready. Hungry.

He was letting his cock rule him in this. He'd known that from the moment he ordered Gia to go out to the SUV and wait for him while they'd stood together in that gas station restroom, both of them strung tight as piano wire by lust. His cock jumped in the air when he recalled that tense, delicious moment when he'd finally given in and exploded with Gia's small hand pumping him so eagerly.

It was heaven to indulge himself, to drown in Gia for these

stolen moments. But it wouldn't last forever, Seth thought grimly as he drew on a pair of boxer briefs, wincing in aroused discomfort as he forced his erection into the clinging cotton. They would return to Hollywood, that world of illusion, and Gia would resume her place as its charmed, adored princess. There was no place for him at her side. Seth despised the limelight.

Why the hell did Gia have to adore it so much? He knew she wasn't like some of the fame-starved waifs he ran into daily with his work, but she certainly didn't avoid the blinding spotlight. She accepted it as one of the hallmarks of success. And there was no doubt Gia *did* seek success. Accolades, fame and public adoration were the equivalent of a raise and a good review from a boss in the everyday work world. Of course she would seek out those measures of her success.

Sometimes it was easy to forget when Gia was in his arms that he existed in a temporary heaven. The sweeter it got with her, the harder it was going to be to exist without her.

By the time he turned the corner into the kitchen several minutes later, his arousal and his anticipation and his doubts had created a taut tension in him.

He stopped dead in his tracks the second he saw her. She stood next to the counter and was in the process of adding some cherry tomatoes to a salad bowl. She looked around when his boots scraped on the tile floor as he halted.

"Where'd you get that?" he asked, gaping at the short, champagne-colored silk robe she wore. The robe outlined her feminine curves, flirting with his senses. His brows drew together in stunned disbelief when he realized she was also wearing pale stockings and a pair of taupe-colored pumps. Her shapely, long legs looked mouthwatering. His erection, which hadn't really dissipated much in the past few minutes, now tightened again with alacrity. The caveman in him urged him to rip off that silk robe to see what she was hiding from him.

She was his, after all. For now.

Her golden brown hair looked drop-dead sexy, falling in a gleaming, straight curtain to the middle of her back, strands of it whisking against her high, firm, silk-covered breasts. He could see her nipples pressing against the silk, which definitely piqued his curiosity about what was under the robe. She wore a tasteful amount of makeup, mascara and subtle shadow accentuating her large, light green eyes. A tinted lip gloss transformed her always sexy mouth into a decadent sexual confection.

She looked extremely pretty, feminine and . . . downright edible.

"It was a little secret I brought along," she said, turning toward him, her gaze lowering over him with warm appreciation. Her eyes widened slightly when her stare landed in the vicinity of his fly. She blinked. "Now you know why I wasn't mad at you for presuming to bring that vibrator."

Her voice was like smooth, warm honey. It ran over his skin, awakening his nerves. It did something to him, having her admit that she'd hoped enough to plan, as he had, that they would rekindle their attraction for one another. Seeing her looking so feminine and sexy, so *available* to him when he'd just been experiencing the friction of having her here in the woods, yet knowing she was out of his reach in reality . . .

Well, it made him a little crazy. In Hollywood, she belonged to the world.

But right here, right now, she was *his*.

"Seth? Is everything okay?"

He blinked, realizing he'd been staring at the appealing sight of her breasts pressing against soft silk while his cock twitched and ached.

"Yeah. It's great. Take off the robe."

"But I have the steaks ready to broil," she said, pointing at two rib eyes on the broiler pan on the counter.

"The steaks will wait," he said gruffly. He touched his raging erection where it pressed against his jeans. "This won't."

Color rushed into her cheeks. She began to untie the robe, her gaze glued to where his fingers stroked the rigid staff of his cock through his jeans. She hastily slipped the robe off her shoulders and tossed it onto the counter.

His stroking fingers froze. His hand dropped to his side.

"Holy Jesus," he muttered, staring at her, spellbound.

She stood still beneath his avid perusal of her beautiful body, but her breathing became ragged. He knew this because the lacy, white "shelf" bra that she wore lifted her delectable breasts, highlighting them to perfection and making them heave slightly as she panted. The revealing bra supported her breasts from below, but left her large nipples completely exposed over the edge of the lace. The vision of her was like mainlining arousal straight into his racing blood.

His gaze lowered over her. Her belly looked pale and taut. He wanted to bury his nose in the soft, feminine expanse. She wore a white garter belt that held up pale stockings.

She wasn't wearing any underwear.

He ripped his gaze off the mesmerizing vision of her naked labia framed by the elastic straps of the garter.

"Turn around," he said.

He saw her wide eyes before she followed his instructions, turning her back to him. His mouth went dry as he stared at her curving hips and the white garters bisecting her plump ass. He stepped forward, acting purely on instinct. She squeaked in surprise when he flicked the garter, popping her ass, before he landed a taut spank on a firm, smooth ass cheek. His conflicting feelings and raging lust reached the boiling point.

He stepped back and picked up a dish towel from the counter. He dropped it on the floor between them.

"Come here," he said. She approached, a man's fantasy come to life. *His fantasy*. It was too much to take, given the friction of his emotions and his furiously aching cock.

"Don't be mad at me for this, Gia." He ripped at his button fly. His gaze fixed on her sexy lips as they parted in surprise. He hastily shoved his jeans down to the top of his thighs and extracted his cock from his underwear, exposing his balls.

"The thing of it is," he explained, stroking his erection and reaching for her face to caress her soft cheek. "If you don't take the edge off now, I'm never going to make it through dinner without throwing you on top of that dining room table and making a mess of all your hard work."

Her small smile belied her innocent face; it belonged to a temptress. He let go of his cock. He slipped a finger beneath a tautly drawn garter and snapped it against her thigh. Arousal shot through him. Gia flinched slightly and bit at her lower lip, suppressing a whimper. He held her jaw and brushed his lips against hers hungrily before he pulled back.

"Okay?" he asked, glancing at the floor between them.

"Oh, yes," she whispered without hesitation.

He brushed his fingertip across her smooth eyebrow. "Then on your knees, Bright Eyes," he urged quietly. He took her hand, guiding her as she lowered before him.

He knew it was crude of him. The knowledge didn't faze him. His need for her was cutting and cruel. Normal rules of sexual etiquette didn't apply.

Not with Gia, they didn't.

He cupped her head and brought his cock to her lips with his other hand. She parted for him sweetly.

"No. Stay still," he growled when she leaned toward him, her eyes staring up at his face, a brutal tease.

"You try me constantly. How dare you tempt me even more

with this getup," he said, his stern act ruined by his fond tone as he watched himself tracing her plump, parted lips with the flaring crown of his cock.

"I'm sorry," she whispered.

"No, you're not. So I'm going to have to punish you later." He saw the look of trepidation and excitement in her eyes. "Spread your lips wide."

He couldn't help but smile when she immediately did as he asked. He pushed the head of his cock into her warm, wet mouth, gasping as she clamped him tight with the rigid ring of her lips.

"Oh, yeah. Such a hot little mouth," he snarled at the sensation of penetrating her heat and sliding against her tongue. She began to bob her mouth along the shaft, but he tightened his hold in her hair. "Hold still," he rasped.

For a delicious moment, he fucked her mouth shallowly while she applied an eye-crossing suction and stared up at him with shiny, beautiful eyes. He cupped his balls, watching her unflinchingly.

"Your eyes are going to kill me." He backed up slightly, extracting his cock from the sweet, warm haven of her mouth. The slick head bumped against her lips.

"Polish the head with your tongue." She glanced down to target him before she slicked her tongue across the swollen crest. He grasped the throbbing shaft, adding friction to her pressing tongue by pushing his cock against her. "Now, look at me again," he demanded, his voice harsher than he'd intended. Her wide-eyed gaze rose to his face again while she continued to polish him. She was so lovely and generous. If she had any idea of the things he wanted to do to her at that moment, she'd probably run for the woods.

No. Not Gia, he admitted to himself as he reinserted his cock into her mouth and proceeded to debauch her sweetness.

Gia didn't run from much of anything.

* * *

She didn't know what had gotten into him, but Seth was a lit
fuse during those tense, electrical moments while she knelt before
him and he took his pleasure unapologetically. It took only minutes
before he was coming fiercely in her mouth, giving himself completely. His blatant, honest expression of his need, the wild beast
breaking free of its restraints, aroused her immensely. His manner
mystified her, too, although she wasn't complaining. Not in the
least. His intensity of need aroused her more than she expected. He
was typically more controlled in the early stages of lust. He enjoyed
building not only her pleasure but also his until they reached com-
bustible levels.

She sucked and swallowed repeatedly as he came, eager to consume the evidence of his unchecked desire. There were ample
amounts of it, that much was certain. Had it been her lingerie that
had turned him into a single raw, throbbing nerve?

She didn't think so, Gia realized dazedly as she cleaned his cock
with her tongue, and his low grunts of satiation rained down upon
her. There was a tension in him that seemed to surpass the merely
sexual, although it had certainly found a conduit for release in lust.
One thing was certain, she thought as she touched his rock-hard
thighs, inserting his cock into her mouth for one last, thorough
sucking.

The tension hadn't fully evaporated, even with his powerful
orgasm.

A frisson of excitement and anxiety went through her when he
bent to help her rise from the kitchen floor. His expression was
rigid as he pulled her against him and dropped small, hot kisses
along her jaw and neck.

What sort of emotional brew created this degree of friction in
him?

And did she *really* want to know the answer to that question?

Seventeen

Gia remembered on that first night they had met years ago, she had naïvely called him "simmering" out loud. The descriptor had never fit more aptly than it did tonight. After his fierce display of need, Seth seemed subdued, but only by comparison to that flash explosion of feral lust. His intensity and broodiness remained.

Despite his odd mood, he helped her on with her robe and assisted her in preparing the rest of the dinner. Gia had set the dining room table earlier with china, wineglasses and some candelabra she'd discovered in a cabinet. Once the steaks were ready and the rest of the food was on the table, she lit the candles, casting the comfortable dining room in a romantic, golden glow.

"Thank you for doing all this," Seth said as he sliced his steak a moment later. He took a bite and shot her an appreciative glance, giving her a small smile as he chewed.

Gia grinned back, taking a bite of her own steak. *Whew.* Relief swept through her. She'd cooked them perfectly.

"Do you want to tell me what that was all about in there?" she asked nonchalantly as she took a bite of salad.

His chewing slowed. He glanced into the kitchen to the spot where she'd just gone down on him with gusto and loved every second of it. Something sparked in his golden eyes.

"Do you really need an explanation?" he rasped, taking a swallow of ice water. "You look like sin walking in that getup."

"You like it then?" She smiled smugly as she tore apart a slice of Sherona's multigrain bread.

His gaze narrowed on her. "What do you think?" he rasped dryly. He speared another piece of steak with his fork, watching her distractedly. "I'd like to see it again."

She paused with her fork in midair. *"Now?"*

He nodded, a glint in his eyes.

"Okay," she replied slowly, her low voice vibrating with excitement. She untied the silk robe and drew it off her shoulders, letting the material fall in a pool around her naked hips. Her heart started to drum against her breastbone as she watched Seth's gaze sink over her. She shifted restlessly in her chair. She was sitting at a candlelit dinner with a very sexy man, and she was essentially naked.

More than naked.

"Push back your hair," he said.

She pulled the strands that fell over her chest to her back. Highly aware of Seth's palpable stare, she arched her spine slightly, sending her breasts into further pronouncement. He paused in his chewing, his slightly bulging eyes making her worry for a second that he had choked on something. He took a swift swig of water and resumed eating, his stare returning to her unerringly, however.

The lingerie made her feel like she was on display, she realized. She admittedly liked the feeling of power it gave her. She liked giving *Seth* that hot, rabid look in his eyes.

Arousal spiked through her as she witnessed his rising lust. He took a bite of his potato, never removing his hot stare from her nipples where they protruded over the edge of the lace shelf bra.

"Touch your nipples," he said gruffly.

She dropped her fork, reaching for her nipples with both hands. She touched herself for him, but she had to admit, it felt good. His unwavering stare seemed to mix with the pleasure of her touch, optimizing the sensation. Her nipples grew stiff and beaded between her rubbing fingertips. Seth just watched her, eating his meal distractedly.

"Pinch them," he directed hoarsely.

She did what he asked. His jaw clenched hard.

"That's enough. Go ahead and eat. You'll need your strength."

She picked up her fork and regarded him in the candlelight. She thought she looked calm outwardly, but her heart was racing. The tension in him tonight both thrilled and intimidated her. It had excited her so much to have him use her for his pleasure there in the kitchen. Maybe she should be ashamed for wanting to do it again, but that didn't make it any less true.

"Tell me what you thought about when you packed that lace-and-air costume," he said. "Did you think about this? Did you think about parading around in front of me as a form of torture?"

"Of course not," she chastised, taking a bite of steak. He raised his eyebrows expectantly and she sighed, recognizing his nonverbal command to answer his question. "You told me not to bring any girly clothes. I thought . . . what if things did heat up between us? They had in the past. Of course, I didn't really believe anything would happen. It was just wishful thinking, at the time. I warned myself they wouldn't. I reminded myself that you weren't interested, and that I wasn't going to go chasing after a man who didn't want me."

"How could you have thought I wouldn't be interested, after that night we spent together? I took you like an animal, over and over."

"And I loved it," she replied quietly.

Her nipples prickled when his gaze sank to her breasts again. Liquid warmth surged at her core. It seemed impossible for him to stop visually devouring her.

"In some corner of my brain, I thought that if we did end up getting physical, I'd like to have something pretty and sexy to wear for you." She leaned forward slightly, showing off her breasts to him at a new angle, smiling when his eyes widened. "I wanted to seduce you," she whispered dramatically.

"*That's* not a seduction," Seth replied grimly, setting down his fork and reaching for her. She gasped softly when he pinched a nipple gently between his thumb and forefinger. "That's like blasting a guy to bits with some kind of sex-ray gun or something. God, you're soft," he said almost as an afterthought under his breath, as his fingertips swept over the top swell of her breast. He dropped his hand and stared at his plate for a second like he didn't know what it was.

"Eat," he said under his breath, picking up his own fork with determination.

She laughed softly and obeyed. "I wasn't imagining my candlelit dinner to be so . . . perfunctory."

"Then you shouldn't have put on that," he said grimly, nodding at her exposed nipples. He suddenly shoved his fork down impatiently on his plate with a loud clattering sound. "Who am I kidding? Move your chair toward me. Show me your pussy."

A frisson of excitement went through her at his hard, determined manner. She scooted her chair around the corner of the table.

"Open your legs," he demanded. She parted her thighs, letting him look his fill. Her clit twanged in excitement as his stare fixed on her. She was glad she'd started shaving. It made her feel exposed and very sexy. With Seth it did, anyway.

"Run your fingers between the lips." He groaned roughly when she did as he asked. "You're wet. I can see your juices on your fingers," he mumbled, transfixed on her pussy.

She moaned, her excitement mounting. It felt good, touching herself in front of him. She rubbed her slick clit firmly, watching him closely, fascinated. His gaze flickered to her face.

"You're an exhibitionist, Gia Harris," he said. Her fingers faltered. From the tone of his voice, she couldn't tell if he'd meant it as a compliment or not.

"Don't stop," he said, picking up his fork. "Rub your little pussy. Put on a show for me."

She did it, mostly because she found that she couldn't stop. It felt very naughty to sit there and masturbate while Seth mechanically ate his meal and watched her like a hawk. Her own appetite for food had fled. She thrived on Seth's hot, focused attention.

Her hand moved more quickly between her thighs. She moaned shakily. He set down his fork.

"You're not allowed to come yet," he said abruptly.

"Not *allowed*?" she panted, her heavy eyelids flickering open at that ultimatum. Seth gave her a small smile.

"You heard me," he said with a pointed look.

Her chin went up. She dipped a finger from her other hand between the slippery folds of her sex. She traced her nipple with it, moistening the erect crest. His gaze grew fierce.

"Don't test me, Gia."

She thrust her breasts higher in the air, pinching at the damp nipple, glorying in the effect she was clearly having on him. She gave him a defiant look, taunting the beast. Loving it.

"Don't look at me like that, little girl," he breathed out ominously.

"Why not? What are you going to do?"

"You *know* what I'm going to do. You know because you're asking for it, clear as day," he replied grimly.

She rubbed both nipples at once. Her eyes went wide when he rose from his chair with breathtaking speed. He loomed over her, sliding his hand beneath her thighs. Suddenly, she was airborne. He looked as hard and untouchable as her wooden sculpture as he carried her down the hallway to the bedroom, his stride so long and rapid, it was like they were flying.

Her heart was threatening to leap through her skin by the time he set her down next to the bed. She just watched him warily, knowing what was coming, dreading and craving it at once. It would have helped if she'd known what to expect.

But she'd never been spanked before. Would it hurt?

Seth walked past her toward the bathroom. When he returned, he carried the purple vibrator and the bottle of lubricant. His expression was as fierce and intimidating as ever. She had a wild urge to run, which she stilled with effort. He sat at the edge of the bed, fully clothed, and set the vibrator and lubricant next to his hip. He put his hands out for her in calm expectation.

"You're going to spank me?" she asked shakily, thinking it was best to clarify.

"For starters." She swallowed anxiously. "It's been my fantasy to spank you and restrain you, then to take you hard . . . make you know you're mine and no other's."

Her heart pounded in the thick silence that followed, his voice resounding in her head. Had he really said that? He always turned her world upside down when he was honest about his desire. "But of course, it's up to you. Just say no if you don't want the same thing, and we'll stop now."

She nodded, her mouth too dry to speak, and stepped toward him. She gave him her hand.

"Lay across my lap," he instructed.

She felt a little awkward coming down over his thighs. He guided her, though, with words and his touch. When she was finally settled, the lower curve of her breasts pressed to the side of his thigh and her bottom was draped over the edge of his other thigh. She could feel his cock pressing against her upper belly. She lay her cheek next to the mattress and watched him in the row of mirrors.

He stared down at her as he ran his hand along her ribs, hip and buttock, making her shiver in anticipatory pleasure. He cupped an ass cheek and she stiffened.

"Two years ago, I would have sworn you'd never been spanked before. That's still true, isn't it?" he asked. She watched in the mirror as he slipped his long forefinger beneath the white garter on her ass cheek and caressed her skin beneath the strap, up and down, up and down. Her clit pinched in arousal.

"Yes. I don't think I'd ever let anyone but—"

"Me?"

"You," she admitted, shooting him a stubborn, anxious glance in the mirror. Why did he have to make her say it? He was watching her in the reflection and noticed. He gave her a small smile and rubbed her bottom with his big, warm hand. Her heartbeat redoubled.

"I'm in a mood," he said, staring at his hand on her ass. "This will probably sting."

"You're in a mood? Really?" she feigned innocence, and then rolled her eyes.

"But I don't want your first time to be too trying," he continued as if she hadn't spoken. He picked up the vibrator from the bed and flipped the top on the lubricant. She watched, her breath stuck in her lungs as he rubbed a thin layer of the sheer liquid onto the metallic tube. He put out his hand. "Here. I want you to vibrate your clit while I punish you. I won't have a spanking be paired in your mind merely with pain."

Her mouth fell open in disbelief. Arousal. Feeling a little overwhelmed, she reached for the lubricated vibe. Pushing herself up with one hand, she tucked her arm beneath her body before she settled again in his lap. It was a little awkward. She wriggled around to adjust herself to a comfortable position, finally settling her arm at the side of her body next to Seth's taut belly. She felt his cock leap against his jeans as she writhed in his lap. Aroused by the sensation, she prolonged things.

Until he cracked her ass with his palm, that is.

She went still in shock, her eyes springing wide, the electrical popping noise of skin against skin replaying in her head like a gunshot. He'd slapped her ass playfully before, but this was a more precise, stinging stroke. Her butt cheek tingled and burned. What's more, she had seen his reflection in the mirror as he did it—first his dark frown as she wiggled around in his lap, then the decisive, quick rise and fall of his hand.

He needn't have applied the lubricant. Things were very wet between her thighs.

"Turn on the vibrator," he said, resting his hand again on her ass, just above where he'd spanked her. She pushed the little metallic tube between her labia and flipped the switch. She moaned, squirming her hips slightly against the buzzing pressure. Seth's cock jumped again next to her skin. His hand rose and fell again in quick succession, landing several slaps on her ass.

"Your first lesson is that you have to keep still during your spankings," he rasped. "You're teasing my cock when you do that," he said, flexing his hips up slightly and letting her feel his erection. "You make me lose control a little, so it'll go harder on your ass when you squirm."

He finished the lesson with a firm spank on the lower curve of her buttocks.

She bit her lip to keep from crying out and forced herself to be still. Her bottom stung, but the vibrator was making her clit sizzle. The heat from her arousal was mixing with the stinging burn from Seth's spanks. It felt very exciting and bad, but in the best kind of way. He began to rub her ass where he'd spanked her, soothing the skin. She couldn't remove her gaze from the erotic vision in the mirror of his large, dark hand on her blushing ass.

"I shouldn't let you watch." He had noticed her avid stare as he rubbed her bottom. "But I love that look on your face when you do," he admitted gruffly. "Hold still."

He lifted his hand and peppered her bottom with brisk spanks. She moaned, shifting the vibrator subtly up and down against her labia and clit, watching him raptly. She found it exciting. Especially when he used both hands to mold her buttocks into his palms, a snarl shaping his handsome mouth. She whimpered, her hips riding the vibrator a little more forcefully. She felt his cock swell. The price of her lack of control was to have him squeeze one buttock taut between his fingers while he spanked the captive flesh repeatedly.

"If you don't hold still, I'm going to have to take away the vibrator," he told her when he'd finished the flurry of spanks. She panted raggedly as he massaged her buttocks in a lascivious manner, straining to keep still for him. "You're turning nice and pink," he murmured approvingly. He flicked her garter against her tingling skin. She whimpered in arousal at the sting.

He raised his hand and spanked her several more times, the sound of taut flesh smacking taut flesh ringing in her ears. It stung, but wonderfully. Her clit was on fire. Her cheeks and lips looked vividly pink in the mirror. She made a sound of misery, and he ceased spanking her.

"What is it?" he asked sharply, meeting her stare in the mirror.

"I'm going to come," she gasped.

"Go on, then. Do it," he insisted, lifting his hand.

He waited until she shuddered in his lap, then spanked her tautly as she climaxed. Gia had never felt so out of control during sex. There was only that pulsing, heart-pounding moment. She burned so badly. All she could do was quake in helpless pleasure as Seth's hand rose and fell, pinkening her ass while she surrendered every last trace of inhibition.

If he'd wanted her to pair pleasure and spanking in her mind, he couldn't have done it any better. She gasped, collapsing in Seth's lap limply. She moved the vibrator off her clit. His cock throbbed against her skin as he massaged her bottom.

"Your ass is beautiful. So tight and round." Gia bit her lip when he parted her ass cheeks. Cool air licked against her sensitive asshole. "I can't believe I've held out this long in doing this," he muttered thickly.

"Do . . . doing *what*?" she gasped, still turned inside out by her climax.

He glanced at her face calmly in the mirror. Wariness prickled through her.

"What do you think?" he rasped, still holding her buttocks in his palms. His gaze slid down her back to her ass.

"You . . . you want to fuck me there?" she asked.

"Oh, yeah."

"You'd like it that much?" she asked, fascinated by his feral expression.

"I'll love it."

"Then yes," she replied simply.

Something flickered across his rigid features as he met her gaze in the mirror. Then he was reaching beneath her. At first, she thought he was rubbing his raging erection, but then he extracted his hand, holding the vibrating tube. Anticipation choked at her throat as she watched him lubricate the tube again. He parted her ass cheeks.

"Is my spanking finished?" she asked anxiously, half-hoping to distract him as he brought the buzzing vibrator to the crack in her ass.

"For now," he replied calmly, intent on his task. She moaned when he pushed the round tip of the vibrator against her asshole. He kept it there a moment, vibrating the sensitive ring of muscle. "I know you can't see it in the mirror, but your asshole is pink and pretty. It's going to be so damn good fucking you there."

"Seth," she groaned, her muscles tensing when he pushed the vibrator into her ass.

"Don't resist it," he urged softly. "Press back against it. It'll go in better that way."

Within seconds, he was pushing the five-inch tube smoothly in and out of her ass. Gia's fingers clawed at the duvet. It not only looked highly illicit and sexy in the mirror, it *felt* that way. Forbidden and dark and very arousing.

He plunged the vibrator all the way into her and held it there. She moaned helplessly. His face tightened in a grimace, and he reached beneath her, stroking his swollen cock.

"Enough. I can't take this anymore," he said abruptly. He drew the vibrator out of her and lifted her legs and hips over him, setting them back down on the edge of the mattress when he stood. Gia scrambled up on her hands and knees, dazed with arousal.

Seth attacked his button fly. "Stay there. On your hands and knees."

They watched each other in strangling excitement as Seth stripped off his clothes. When he finally stood before her naked, she stared at his awesome erection springing between his strong thighs.

"Don't look at me like that, Bright Eyes," he coaxed as he reached for the bottle of lubricant. "You know I'm not going to hurt you."

"So it won't hurt?" she asked, relieved. Her mouth grew wet with saliva as she watched him matter-of-factly lube up his erection. He looked awesome and even a little fearsome in that moment.

"It might a little. Just at first," he admitted, coming up next to where she was perched on the bed. He adjusted her hips so that her knees were still on the mattress, but her legs and ass were slanted toward the edge of the bed and his jutting, shiny cock. "You're a virgin here, right?" he asked.

"Oh," she cried out when he pierced her ass with a lubricated finger. It had felt very dirty watching him penetrate her ass with the vibrator, but having his finger in her felt that much more sharp and intimate. What would it be like to have his big, beautiful cock thrusting in and out of such a private place?

She moaned uncontrollably as he continued to push his finger in and out of her. He cupped a suspended breast with his other hand and rubbed her nipple with his fingertip.

"Gia? You're hot and very tight. Are you a virgin here?"

"Yes," she gasped.

"Good. I like hearing there are parts of you that are mine alone," he said darkly. "Would it be too much for you, since this is your first time, if I restrained your hands behind your back?"

"Why do you want to?" she mumbled, highly distracted because he was finger-fucking her firmly now.

"Because I want to know you're completely mine for a few blessed moments," he grated out, his nostrils flaring. "I'll probably want that a lot, in one way or another. I've been reining myself in so far with you. The truth is, I don't like sharing you, Gia. Do you think you can accept that?"

She glanced back and met his fiery stare. Her heart throbbed in her ears' taut silence.

"Yes," she said.

He nodded once, and she sensed his respect in that brief acknowledgment. He understood that while all this excited her, it was new and overwhelming too. She blinked in surprise when he abruptly leaned forward and unfastened her bra. His cock brushed against her naked hip as she lifted her hands off the mattress so that he could remove it.

"Put your cheek and your breasts on the mattress, leave your bottom high in the air," he instructed. "No. Other cheek down," he said, halting her with a touch on her shoulder. "I know you'll want to watch in the mirror."

Her cheeks were already on fire, but they scalded as she turned her head so that she faced the mirror.

"Hands at the small of your back," he said gently.

She watched, biting her lip as he used her lace bra to tie her wrists together at the small of her back. When he'd finished, she looked utterly vulnerable in the mirror, her ass in the air, her hands restrained at her back.

She also looked beautiful, Gia admitted, her face flushed, her bottom rosy next to the lacy, feminine garter and hose. Seth's hand began to move and she forgot all about how she looked. She stared at him hungrily in the mirror. He was pumping his lubricated cock and staring at her with rigid intensity.

He stepped behind her.

"This is going to take a little doing," he said gruffly. "I'll do my best to go easy on you. I don't want to hurt you, but at the same time," he spread her ass cheeks, opening her, and presented the fat head of his cock to her asshole. "This is going to feel so fucking good," he growled tensely. He gripped her hip and pushed with a gentle, but relentless pressure. "Don't fight it," he bit out through a clenched jaw. "Push back against it, like I told you."

She released a trembling cry as the crown of his cock slipped into her ass. Pain shot through her, but it was gone almost immediately. His hold on her hips tightened. "I'm not moving," he assured. "Are you okay?"

"Yes," she said. She keyed into the sensation of him being in her. It felt very strange . . . illicit and incendiary. She felt him throb next to the nerve-packed flesh and instinctively tightened around him. He sank deeper several inches and groaned roughly.

"I told you that your spanking was over, but if you keep that up, you'll have another, Gia. You have no idea how good you feel. If you knew what I was thinking about doing to you right now, you wouldn't tease."

She pressed her hot cheek next to the soft duvet, panting, mesmerized by the vision of him in the mirror. This is why he'd angled her body in this direction, slanting her so that she could see him penetrating her. He was so *dirty*. She loved it. His muscles were tight and delineated, his cock ruddy and shiny, piercing her pale flesh. He was the image of primal sex in that moment, beautiful and flagrant. He began to pulse his hips, his hard buttocks flexing in a subtle, controlled movement, as he fucked her shallowly.

A howl of excitement left her throat, the sound surprising her. He clutched both her hips in his hands, his cock half buried in her.

"Are you okay?" he demanded anxiously.

She answered him by bouncing her bottom slightly, pulsing his cock in her. He lifted a hand and swatted her bottom in gentle remonstrance before he firmed his hold on her and continued to fuck her with quick, shallow strokes. She groaned roughly. She couldn't shut up. Her reaction to this whole thing was unprecedented.

"God, you're so damn hot," he growled.

With each firm pass of his cock, he sank deeper, until his pelvis popped against her buttocks as he fucked her. He paused with his cock fully sheathed, his arm muscles bulging tight as he held her against him.

"Gia," he said sharply, piercing her haze of lust. She gasped wildly for air.

"What?" she asked weakly. He was filling her completely, his cock throbbing deep inside her. She was going to burst into flame any second.

"You're screaming nonstop, baby. Are you okay?"

"I am?" she moaned feverishly. "Oh, God, Seth, help me."

He cursed and reached beneath her, rubbing her clit firmly. She exploded like a cache of dynamite. The next few moments were a haze of pounding pleasure and pressure and unchecked carnality. She opened her eyes to see Seth standing over her, one of his feet on the mattress next to her hip, his knee bent, the other foot on the floor. He was fucking her with long, firm strokes, his ridged torso tight and gleaming with perspiration, a snarl on his handsome mouth.

He had said he was holding back with her before. This was the real Seth, savage and unbridled, fearsome and beautiful. Gia watched him in that mirror and knew she was witnessing a claiming in some sense. She didn't want to be claimed by a man or any person.

But she *did* want to be by Seth.

He was the exception to the rule.

"You're mine. Say it, Gia," he grated out as he thrust, and she wondered if their minds were fused in that volatile moment as intimately as their bodies.

"I'm yours," she affirmed shakily. Because in that moment, she was.

Her face convulsed with some mixture of awe, longing and amazement when she felt him swell inside her and saw the wild expression on his face. Then he was holding her to him, every muscle straining in his long, powerful body, desperate in his need. The sound he made as he came was fierce and plaintive, as if he gloried in that brutal, slashing pleasure and hated it at once, because it signaled the end.

His head fell forward as he gasped for air. Slowly, the hard tension in his body started to dissipate. The sounds of their rough, uneven breathing filled the room. Something had altered deep inside her, and it both frightened and awed her.

Gia glanced at her own face in the reflection for the first time in minutes, not at all startled to see that her cheeks were damp with tears.

Eighteen

Seth never said so in specific words, but she sensed he'd been as moved by their raw, powerful lovemaking as she was. He couldn't keep his hands off her for the rest of the night. Gia would remember the sound of his hoarse, quiet voice in her ear, murmuring sweet, unexpected praise as well as tense, erotic tributes for the rest of her life. After that heated, raw joining, they'd showered and then returned to bed, too involved with each other to worry about everyday matters like their discarded meal or cleaning up the kitchen.

Or unpleasant ones like the clock slowly ticking away their time together.

The next morning she rose at nine, strangely bright-eyed and energized, even though she and Seth had slept little. He was already gone from bed. She pulled on her robe and wandered out to the kitchen in search of him.

"Coffee is ready for you," he said when she rounded the corner. He sat at the kitchen table, shirtless. One of the pumpkins from the porch sat in front of him, and he was utterly focused on carving it.

"What are you doing?" she asked, grinning as she approached him.

"It's for Daisy," he said. He looked up and saw her confused expression. "Daisy Pierce. Rill and Katie's little girl," he explained. He hitched his head slightly in a "come here" gesture and she leaned down to kiss him. He smelled and felt wonderful. She lingered, plucking at his lips. He became the aggressor, and their kiss deepened.

"Morning," she breathed out next to his mouth a moment later.

"Morning," he replied gruffly. He shifted his face, burying his nose in her neck and nuzzling her with his lips and mouth. "You smell like sex."

She laughed softly and ran her fingers through his soft hair. "You got that straight. Lots of it. You certainly are energetic after sleeping only a few hours." She glanced at what he was doing to the pumpkin and gasped. She straightened, staring in amazement. "Oh my God, that is the coolest thing. I can't believe you can do that. Is that *Daisy*?"

She was referring to what he was subtly carving on the pumpkin. It was clearly the face of a little girl with twin curly pigtails on either side of her head. Most of his marks didn't fully penetrate the pumpkin. Instead, he'd artfully cut just past the skin, revealing the paler inner surface. The contrast between the bright orange skin and the paler flesh-colored interior of the pumpkin was what created the surprisingly detailed image.

"Yeah. Daisy loves to wear pigtails. I thought she'd like a pumpkin," he said, resuming his carving.

"She'll love it. I forgot that you're a sculptor too," she mused, watching in fascination as he deftly moved the small carving knife according to some master plan in his head. She'd not yet worked on a play or film that required Seth's level of expertise with special effects makeup. What he'd explained while they watched movies about the basics of special effects required a shocking level of artistry and minute detail.

Seeing him creating something spur of the moment for the thrill of a child was no less eye-opening.

"Sculpting and carving were my first mediums," he said, working intently.

"Your mom taught you?"

He grunted an assent.

"And you sculpt all your facial and body prosthetics first in clay for work, isn't that right?" she asked, remembering his explanations about makeup as they had watched sci-fi and horror flicks together.

"Yep," he said, again fully immersed in his task. Gia didn't mind his preoccupation. She liked to watch him work. He was always sexy, but she found him exponentially so when he was focused on creating something. It only added to the appeal that he worked shirtless. She sat down across from him, comfortable in the silence. He finished while she was on her second cup of coffee. Gia started to stand to admire the finished product, but he directed her to sit back down.

"You can see it when I get it ready for Daisy tonight," he said as he retrieved a large bag from the pantry. He noticed her disappointed look. "It's a surprise for you too. I would have done you on the other pumpkin Sherona brought, but your face is top secret at the moment."

Appeased by his explanation, she watched him carefully place the jack-o'-lantern in the bag.

They worked out and showered, and then Seth began the process of doing her Jessie makeup. It felt strange to don the disguise of the boy again. They'd only been in the Shawnee National Forest for eight days, but it felt longer . . . certainly more *significant* to her than that. She hadn't experienced any of the feelings of claustrophobia she'd thought she would. Seth was an antidote against it.

He explained that he'd be using contacts this time, as it would have been rude for her to wear her sunglasses the entire time she was a guest in Rill and Katie's home. Gia told him truthfully that she had no problems with contacts. He proceeded to turn her light green eyes into an unremarkable hazel. She was startled at how different the small detail made her look.

"But surely Rill and Katie will suspect something, despite how good the makeup is," Gia said as she watched Seth begin to apply the subtle hair prosthetic that gave the impression of whiskers. "It's not like while we were on the road, when strangers got brief glimpses of me as we crossed paths at a gas station." She noticed Seth's small smile as he worked.

"Are you looking *forward* to trying to fool Rill?" she asked, grinning.

He shrugged. "It's a professional challenge. Actually, I think Rill will eventually figure it out. He's got a great eye. I'm measuring success by how long it'll take him to figure it out, not whether he does or not. I'm putting a lot of faith in your acting skills."

"Thanks," she said, amused to know he was plotting to trick a friend. She liked the revelation of that playful side of his character. "And you're comfortable with the idea of Katie and Rill realizing I'm Gia Harris?"

"I'm not going to give it away. But if they do figure it out, I'll give a brief explanation. If they don't realize this evening, I'll eventually tell them the truth, once you're back in the public eye again." He met her stare in the mirror. "I trust Rill and Katie completely, or I wouldn't be allowing them to see you for any protracted period of time."

Gia nodded in understanding, giving him a small smile, and he resumed his meticulous application.

She watched him closely in the mirror as he transformed her into Jessie. Once again, his singular focus and consummate skill seduced her. But it was more than just sexual, what she was feeling. Unable to get up or distract herself, Gia was forced to acknowledge that she'd fallen in love for the first time in her life. Part of what she felt for Seth had been present from their first meeting and their impulsive, uninhibited lovemaking. But the seeds of her feelings had burst into flower, the roots burrowing deep.

The thought of not seeing him, of him not being a regular part of her life, made her lungs lock uncomfortably. It was like her brain would freeze at the possibility . . . the probability?

And that frightened her on some deep level that she desperately tried to ignore.

Seth was so large. Not just his physical appearance, his uncompromisingly quiet, yet forceful character. He would never fit into her world. He didn't *want* to.

What were they going to do?

Not sure how to answer in the present moment, she forced the uncomfortable question out of her mind.

"What if we go to Sherona's diner and then do a little grocery shopping in Prairie Lakes. We'll get the stuff into the refrigerator back here, and then head back out again. We can wander around Prairie Lakes a bit before we go to Rill and Katie's? Do you think that'd inoculate you against cabin fever?" Seth asked her once she was in full Jessie regalia, and they met up in the living room.

"Sounds good to me," she said, her gaze dropping over him appreciatively. He exuded masculinity and vitality, looking very handsome in a pair of jeans, a white fitted T-shirt and a denim overshirt. Just beneath his partially untucked T-shirt, she spied the sexy, silver belt buckle. She reached out and touched it.

"Did I ever tell you that this thing drove me a little crazy with lust while we traveled across the country together?" she asked quietly.

"No," he said, reaching out to rub her hip. He drew her closer and spoke hoarsely near her ear. She resented the wig she wore at that moment, wishing she could feel his lips brush against her skin. "But I'm glad to hear it now. It only seems fair I was driving you a *little* nuts because you were making me stark-raving mad." She smiled, warmed by his words, and traced her finger along the top of the sexy buckle and his warm, taut belly. He squeezed her hip and rubbed her.

"That's a very non-Jessie look, Gia. Do you want to go out, or not?"

She looked into his face bemusedly. It was a good question. She suddenly wasn't so sure she did at all.

"Well, I *do* have on the disguise, and you put so much hard work into it. And we really need some fresh food," she sighed resignedly.

"Wow. This town is amazing," Gia said several minutes later, staring out the window as Seth drove into Vulture's Canyon. To call it a town was being liberal. She stared at the ancient, weathered storefronts that looked as if they might have been built in the 1800s. It brought to mind Western ghost towns—or it would have, if there hadn't been several long-haired, free-spirited types standing next to paintings that were leaned against the graying storefront of the Dyer Creek Trading Company. Apparently they were the artists who had done the paintings. Since Main Street was otherwise completely desolate, Gia wondered if the artists weren't one another's best customers.

Seth parked in front of the Legion Diner, and they both got out. Some bells tinkled as they walked inside the neat, nearly empty restaurant. An older couple sitting at a booth to the right of them looked around.

"Monty. Olive," Seth said cordially. The grizzly-looking man named Monty nodded his head while the gray-haired woman called out a pleasant greeting. "Hey, Errol," Seth said quietly as he passed the next booth, where a dark-haired man wearing a grimy hat sat studying something in his hand. Errol didn't respond, but Seth didn't really seem to expect him to.

"Well, if it isn't the world traveler," Seth said as they approached the long Formica-topped bar that ran the length of the diner. He put out his hand to a good-looking, tanned man with tousled ashy blond hair who looked like he could have modeled for a rugged-outdoor-clothing company.

"Seth. Good to see you," the man greeted Seth in an Australian accent as he shook his hand. "Yeah, we just got back from a trip to Australia, New Zealand and Japan. It was only partially business. I took Sherona home to meet my dad for the first time," the man said, a twinkle in his eye.

"How'd that go?" Seth asked dryly.

"Brilliant, considering the old man was on low boil ever since he heard Sherona and I eloped. Sherona had him purring in the palm of her hand in no time though. Who's your friend?" he asked, glancing at Gia.

"Chance Hathoway, meet my nephew, Jessie Bauer."

"Nephew? Nice to meet you," he said, extending a big paw across the counter. Gia practiced her man shake for the first time. "I didn't know Seth had a nephew."

"I'm sort of newly discovered," Gia said in her boy voice, glancing aside with Jessie-awkwardness and shifting her feet. She noticed Chance's slightly bemused expression. "It's a long story," Gia added under her breath.

"Those are the best kinds. You'll have to settle in and tell it sometime," he said, giving Seth an amused glance. "You a surfer, then?"

"Yeah. How'd you know that?"

Chance just nodded at the T-shirt she was wearing beneath her plaid overshirt. She'd forgotten that the small logo on it was of a popular surfwear company.

"Oh. Yeah," she grinned sheepishly, hunching her shoulders with her hands in her pocket.

"Where do you surf?"

She noticed Seth giving her a wry glance. She resisted frowning at his subdued amusement while she was put through the paces of her role.

"Mostly near home in La Jolla. Scripps Pier, Oceanside, Swami's, Trestles, when I'm feeling ambitious," she grinned.

"Did you do Lower Trestles?" Chance asked.

"Yeah, it rips."

"I was there once when the water was like glass. It was pure magic. What kind of a board do you—hey, babe," he broke off, glancing over his shoulder when a pretty auburn-haired woman stepped out of a swinging door.

"We wanted to stop by and thank you for dropping off the food. It was a lifesaver," Seth said. "Sherona Hathoway, this is my nephew, Jessie Bauer."

"Hi. Yeah, the food was great. Thanks," Gia said.

"No problem," Sherona assured them warmly, coming to stand next to Chance. "I know how isolated things can get up there in the forest." Chance put his arm around her familiarly, rubbing the curve of her hip. Clearly these two were crazy about each other. Sherona glanced up fondly into Chance's face. Gia saw the warm amusement in her eyes.

"And how did that conversation end up getting them a front-row seat to the Great Surfing Moments of Chance Hathoway?"

"I wasn't spouting off. Jessie's a surfer too," Chance said, shrugging insouciantly.

They talked with the nice couple for several minutes, Gia becoming more relaxed when they seemed to accept her Jessie character.

"I should turn you over my knee for that," Seth muttered when they returned to the truck and started down the deserted Main Street. She could tell by the slight quirk of his lips he was kidding.

"Twice in twenty-four hours? Is that going to be customary?"

"I had no idea you really surfed. I just happened to have some outfits in my costume collection for a surfer boy that I thought would work for your size. I was wondering how you were going to work your way around Chance's questions."

She chuckled, enjoying putting one over on him. "I learned to surf when I lived with my mom and stepdad."

"That's what I get for underestimating you."

"Exactly. So . . . what's the story with Chance and Sherona? They seem crazy about each other. He's a nature photographer and has to travel a lot for his job, but I got the impression that Sherona's roots run deep in Vulture's Canyon."

"They do. Chance is a wanderer by nature and feels comfortable in every corner of the globe. Sherona is the heart of this community. For a while, it looked like their differences were going to keep them apart, no matter how crazy they were about each other."

Her skin prickled with awareness. "What happened?" she asked intently.

"They figured it out. Sherona travels with Chance for half the year, while that other woman in the diner—Olive Fanatoon—looks after the diner for her. Chance takes a few necessary solo trips, but otherwise, he's here with Sherona the rest of the time. They decided what they had together was worth some compromises and sacrifices."

Gia cleared her throat in the uncomfortable silence that followed. Maybe it only seemed charged to her. She couldn't be sure if Seth had noticed the potential parallels between Chance and Sherona's vital differences and theirs.

"Why do you have that look on your face?" Seth asked her twenty minutes later when he parked at a grocery store in the small town of Prairie Lakes.

"I was just thinking that at first, being Jessie made me feel freer. No one recognized me. I blended into the woodwork, and it was nice," Gia reflected as she took off her seat belt. She glanced at Seth and gave him a small, wistful smile. "Now . . . well, I can't even touch you while other people are around."

"And you being Jessie suddenly feels like a trap. Yeah," Seth agreed with his typical laconic preciseness. He seemed to hesitate.

"Seth?" she prompted.

"It'd be like that for us in L.A. too. You realize that, don't you? It'd be for different reasons, and you wouldn't be in disguise, but we'd always have to be careful of showing too many displays of affection. We'd always be in front of the camera's eye."

Gia inhaled slowly, trying to ease the sudden tightness in her chest. *She* could bear that, even if she didn't love it. Seth was a privacy hound though. She realized she cared about him too much to force him into the spotlight.

"Do we have to talk about it right now? Can't we just enjoy this beautiful day?" she hoped.

She felt his stare on her cheek as she averted her gaze.

"Yeah. Let's do that," he said.

While they were in the grocery store, Seth picked up a celebrity gossip magazine as they stood in the checkout line, reading the pages with seeming bored idleness.

"What did that magazine say?" Gia asked when they returned to the SUV and were driving back to the house. "I saw my picture on the front, but it looked like it was a small feature."

"Yeah. You're shrinking a bit in the tabloids because the press doesn't have any new gossip or photos to feed to your hungry public. That's just what we wanted to do. We cut off their supply by making you disappear. I spoke with Charles yesterday, and he and Madeline are pleased with the way the mania is dying down. Madeline certainly would like the eye of the world turned away just a bit while she finishes up on the last touches of her case."

"And McClarin?" Gia asked tensely. "Is there any news of him or his camp's maneuvers?"

"Just the usual hogwash about how you're an unstable, hysterical, attention-seeking movie star."

"Someone tried to leak a fake story that I was a drug addict a while ago. I'm sure it was someone related to McClarin," Gia stated flatly. "So does Madeline, because the rumor started flying around just before jury selection. After jury selection, the jurors are told to stay away from all media outlets, so there was a higher chance of it reaching potential jurors and alternates."

"Yeah. It was definitely a purposefully leaked story. But they had no proof of those rumors about you. The story died out."

"A bit of a slow death for my comfort," Gia mumbled.

"Yeah, I know," Seth commiserated, reaching across the console and squeezing her thigh. "All we have to do is keep quiet and wait. Once you get on that stand, McClarin is screwed and he knows it."

"Thanks for the vote of confidence," she said, rubbing his hand with hers.

"Anytime."

After they'd stored all the food at the house, Seth retouched her makeup and they headed back out again. In Prairie Lakes, they parked and walked. It was another pleasantly cool, crisp, brilliant fall day. Prairie Lakes was a picturesque small town, especially with all the trees dressed out in brilliant autumn regalia. It was no Vulture's Canyon, but it was far from bustling. Walking from the car down Main Street, they passed all of four people.

They stopped in a pharmacy on Main Street to pick up some supplies, including some battery candles Seth wanted for Daisy's jack-o'-lantern. Gia nudged Seth with an elbow to the ribs when she spotted the old-fashioned soda fountain on the far wall.

"Would it be too un-Jessie-like if we went for a sundae?" she asked under her breath.

"Yeah," Seth murmured. She nodded in understanding.

"But it would also be Uncle Seth–like to ignore Jessie's cocky attitude. Jessie really needs to work on that. So we're going," he said without a break in his stony expression. He handed her a pack of razors. She barely hid her grin as she examined the package with undue fascination and followed him out of the aisle.

They ate lunch at the nostalgic diner, where they were the only patrons. Even on weekends, traffic downtown was probably slow, but on a weekday afternoon with school in session, Main Street seemed cast under a sleepy spell. Afterward, they ordered coffees to go and wandered through a nearby wooded park. Spotting a bench near a burbling spring, they sat down, inhaling the crisp fall air. She noticed Seth unobtrusively scanning the entire area for possible observers. When he relaxed his militant tension ever so slightly and took a sip of his coffee, Gia assumed that he saw no potential threats to their privacy.

"Did you like being in military intelligence?" she asked him quietly.

"I would have liked it better if my skill for disguise and makeup was used one hundred percent of the time. Whenever the opportunity came up, I thrived on the challenge. That's how I knew for a fact I wanted to work in special effects makeup full-time when I left the Army. But I do miss the . . . *substance* of the disguises I did while I was in the military."

"Substance?"

"Yeah. Knowing that my makeups really meant something important—an individual's safety, a successful mission, people's lives."

"Is that why you still do consulting work for people like Charles and Madeline when you get the chance?"

He nodded.

"Do you really think of film work as substanceless?" she asked hesitantly after a moment.

His gaze flickered over her. "I think it has substance. Entertainment is important. Creative expression is important. I'm just glad I had the opportunity to use my art to help people as well."

Gia nodded. She understood what he was saying, but it unsettled her for some reason. What had *she* ever done to directly help people? She did some charity work but always felt on the fringes, distanced from the possibility of making a concrete, measurable difference in someone's life.

"What you do is important, Gia," Seth said forcefully under his breath. She blinked, realizing he'd noticed her bereft expression. "You shouldn't listen to half the things I say about Hollywood. I'm old and I'm cynical."

"You're not *old*," she chided.

"I see you don't correct me about my cynicism though," he added wryly, taking a sip of his coffee. "The truth is, someone like you influences tens of thousands of people every day. Maybe in subtle ways, maybe in not-so-subtle ways. Certainly in ways you're likely never going to know about firsthand. I think movie stars have a huge potential for making a difference."

"Really?" she asked, doubtful not for her own part, but as to whether or not *he* truly believed it.

He nodded soberly. "Look at the fact that you want to play Eleanor Roosevelt, for instance. Given your status with young people, you'll expose a generation of females to an important, powerful woman. You'll make someone who formerly seemed like a boring history lesson approachable and interesting by mixing some of your magic with hers. You could have just listened to the naysayers and your agent and dismissed the role as not commercially viable, but you didn't."

She made a face. "I didn't insist on the part because I wanted to

make a difference in young women's lives though," she admitted
with a sinking feeling.

"Why did you then?"

Gia thought for a moment. "Because her story inspired me."

He shrugged and leaned back on the bench. "Exactly. And your
inspiration in combination with your talent will inspire others."

"Do you *really* think that?"

"I do," he replied simply.

"But you look down on actresses and actors so much," she said.

"Not all of them. There are a few I respect." She studied his
stoic profile anxiously. He must have noticed because he turned
and met her stare. "One actress in particular. More and more so
every day."

Even though he couldn't touch her while they were out in public
and the bright light of day, his words and small smile felt like the
equivalent of a caress.

Later, they walked down Main Street and wandered into a
nearly empty antique store. Gia found herself resenting the disguise
more and more as they perused the contents of the aisles. It was so
nice to be out with him in public, idling away the afternoon. She
very much wanted to touch him, and the prohibition not to do so
only seemed to sharpen her desire. When they entered a particularly
dark, dusty corner aisle of the store, she realized Seth must have
felt the same way. He suddenly halted her by grabbing her hand.
Then he was leaning over her and brushing his lips against hers.
He was careful not to smudge her lip makeup, but he wasn't so
subtle with his touch. He didn't bother caressing her torso, knowing the rigid shaper was beneath her shirt. Instead, he cupped her
ass possessively and gave it a firm rub.

"I didn't know it was going to be so hard not to touch you in
public," he said next to her lips.

"Me either," she whispered, touching his hard abdomen greedily.

She cupped his rib cage, a thrill going through her, and went up on her toes to nuzzle his chin with her nose. An aisle away, they heard a woman making a comment about an antique baby carriage and a man replying. Gia guiltily backed away from Seth, her heart racing from his touch and nearness. Her longing to touch him openly felt even sharper than before.

"Look what's at the theater," Seth said under his breath when they returned to the sleepy, sunny street.

She blinked in surprise when she read the marquis. "They must not get many first runs in Prairie Lakes. It's been out for over a year." She gave Seth a small smile. The film was *Shadow Mistress*, the first movie she'd done following the success of her Hollywood debut. Unlike *Glory Girl*, *Shadow Mistress* was a sexy, dark, very adult thriller. It had immediately smashed the stereotype of her created by her role in her debut young adult film. She'd been lucky that the thriller had been a success. Instead of alienating her youthful following, it had amplified it, plus added an older generation to her fan base.

"Do you want to go? There's a three thirty matinee." Seth checked his watch. "We'll only miss the first few minutes."

She did a surprised double take at his suggestion. *"Really?"*

He looked completely serious. "Yeah. We don't have anything better to do until we're due at Rill and Katie's at six." He gave her a dry glance. "And I doubt there's another theater in town."

She laughed dubiously and shrugged. "Okay, if you really want to." His suggestion and the circumstances were unexpected. She wasn't sure how she felt about sitting side by side with Seth—of all people—and watching herself on the big screen.

The theater was one of those old, large, ornate structures that were disappearing too fast from American cities in the modern age. The movie had already started by the time they bought their tickets and entered.

"We can have our pick of seats," Seth muttered under his breath as they assessed the near-empty theater. There was a couple seated several rows back from the front and another couple in the middle-right.

"There goes my ego," Gia said humorously. "I'm really roping them in around here."

"Seriously? The whole town has probably seen this movie three times over by now. They can likely recite your lines better than you," Seth said dryly. "Can we sit in the back?"

"Anywhere," Gia agreed.

He waved her ahead and followed her into the very back row. They took their seats.

"This is weird," she whispered once they sat and she trained her gaze on the screen. The scene depicted the tense discovery of a murder, and Gia was in it.

"Why?" Seth asked. "Because you're watching one of your movies while you're disguised as someone else?"

"No," she fumbled. "Well, not *just* because of that. Because I'm watching it with you." She felt him look at her in the darkness and sensed his question. "It's . . . *awkward*."

"You shouldn't feel self-conscious," he whispered, spreading his long legs slightly so that his knee bumped into hers. He opened his hand on her thigh. He must have noticed her arched brows. "No one can see us back here. And as for feeling awkward, don't. I've heard this movie was great, and you're a fantastic actress."

"You haven't seen it?" she hissed.

He merely shook his head, his attention on the screen.

For some reason, his admission made her feel even pricklier with awareness. As one scene ended, she started to realize why. The next part of the movie was one of two pretty intense love scenes. She swallowed uneasily and slunk down in her seat. The experience was a new one for her. She'd never been embarrassed watching one of her movies with company before, even with a few short-lived boyfriends. She hadn't treasured the idea of her father or mother watching her love scenes, but they hadn't made her cringe like she was at that moment. She and Seth had already discussed the fact that she used a body double for nudity though. Maybe it wouldn't be so bad.

She held her breath as Scott Barrett, the male lead, leaned down to kiss her on the screen. Was it her imagination, or did Seth stiffen in the seat next to her? She glanced anxiously at his face in the darkness. No, it wasn't her imagination. He peered at the screen with narrowed eyelids as Scott unbuttoned her blouse and the kiss turned torrid. The critics had labeled her and Scott's chemistry electric. The tabloids had falsely reported a secret romance between them. Did Seth realize those reports were false? She and Scott had little in common, although she'd found him to be a nice enough coworker. The whys and why nots of onscreen chemistry remained a mystery to Gia, as they did to most actors.

Maybe Seth wouldn't find that reassuring, though, given the heat escalating on the screen as Scott came down over her on the bed.

How does a person ever know what's real and what's not?

His voice replayed in her head, along with the vision of the tense frustration in his expression when he'd said it.

An eternal moment later, the camera angle tightened on Gia's face as they enacted intercourse. It was unbearable. Seth prized her sexual honesty, just as she prized his. It was one of the magical things about their being together. Gia had never experienced true intimacy in her life until she'd been with Seth. She knew that now. It was ridiculous, but she felt guilty somehow, watching the scene. Not because she'd acted out intimacy with Scott Barrett, but because Seth stared at her giving away a tiny part of what she gave him when they made love.

He would always think he shared her with the world.

She opened her mouth to suggest leaving, but his hand tightened on her thigh. A knot had formed in her throat. She exhaled in relief when the scene came to an end. If she thought the charged atmosphere would ease when the scene ceased, she thought wrong. Heat emanated from Seth's large hand onto her thigh. He squeezed the muscle and rubbed her. His hand slid higher. Arousal prickled through her, the unexpectedness of it in this situation taking her by surprise. She squirmed slightly in her seat to alleviate the pressure growing at her sex.

Suddenly his hand was gone and she felt his fingers near her ear.

"What are you doing?" she whispered.

"Exposing your ear," he replied very quietly. He pushed the edge of the wig over the top of her ear.

"Why?"

"Because I'm going to talk dirty to you," he said very quietly right next to her ear.

Excitement jolted through her, sending shivers of sensation rippling through her body.

He cupped her sex through her jeans. Gia went dry mouthed as she stared blindly at the screen, and he moved his hand in a subtle circular motion, stimulating her. Gia bit her lip. It felt *very* good.

"Unfasten your jeans," he breathed out near her ear.

She glanced over at him. She could see the determined gleam of his eyes in the flickering shadow. "Are you sure it's okay?"

"No one can see us. I want your pussy. Now. You'll have to keep very quiet."

His incendiary words thundered in her consciousness.

Keep quiet? Given what Seth typically did to her? She hadn't realized she could be so noisy in bed until Seth had made love to her.

He removed his warm hand from between her thighs. She missed his touch. She glanced aside anxiously to make sure no one had walked into the theater. The aisles on both sides were empty, the row of seats shadowed and dark, and the other movie watchers were far away. The risk was worth it . . . to her it was. But that didn't mean her heartbeat didn't start to slam in her ears.

She unfastened her button fly. Seth immediately sank his left hand into the opening and beneath her underwear. His gaze remained on the screen as he moved his fingertips deftly against her outer sex, parting her labia.

At first, it felt like he was tickling her eager, sensitive flesh. His touch was dead-on, but he kept it light, building the burn in her until she squirmed in her seat. She placed her hands on the chair arms and subtly bucked her hips against the pressure of his hand.

He lowered his mouth near her ear.

"Do you need it harder?"

"Yes," she whispered emphatically. She turned to him, blindly seeking his mouth with her own.

He backed up slightly. "No. Don't tempt me."

Gia suppressed a sound of frustration. She understood. He would ruin her lip makeup if they started kissing. Besides, if someone looked back, they'd see them making out. They *couldn't* see what Seth was doing to her below the seats. Lots of people made out in movie theaters, but Gia wasn't so sure of how fond Prairie Lakes would be of two males doing it in the local theater.

"Slouch down in your seat some and spread your thighs," he said into her ear. She did as he directed. There was a chase scene going on in the movie. Not that she cared. She lowered in the seat and opened her legs, giving Seth more access. He palmed her outer sex, his fingertips rubbing her entrance teasingly. He pressed the round stone of his ring between her labia and began to rub her clit in a subtle circular motion, occasionally pressing it like a little button. For the next several minutes, she just slouched there, tense as a coiled spring, staring straight ahead with glazed eyes as he played with her and whispered illicit things in her ear, and she burned.

"You're so fucking creamy. Your pussy kills me," he whispered hoarsely, his mouth caressing her ear as he spoke. Gia realized muzzily that he'd turned her ear into a sex organ, exposing it the way he had. He was a precise devil when it came to sex. He stirred his hand a little more forcefully and the sound of him moving in her wet flesh reached her ears, highly charged and erotic. "Do you hear that? You're so warm and wet. I wish I could slid my cock into that tight little pussy."

His dirty talk sent her over the edge.

"Seth—"

"Come against my hand," he demanded, intuiting what she was about to say.

She bit her lip and began to climax. The need to be silent—the entire situation—seemed to make her orgasm all that much more tense and forbidden. Delicious.

"That's right," he hissed as she shuddered. He used his other hand to move her right knee toward him, parting her wider. He removed the hand with the ring and shoved his other hand down her pants. He thrust a finger into her slit. She didn't succeed in silencing her cry entirely this time as her orgasm ratcheted up momentarily. Fortunately, her low bleat of excitement was lost in the swelling music on the screen. She was slouched very low in the seat now. The chair in front of her was obscuring half the screen. Instead of giving her a post-climactic break, Seth began to power his finger in and out of her, his actions deliberate and forceful. Again, the sounds of him moving in her wet pussy reached her ears, not loud enough to carry far, but electrical in their impact.

He dipped his head.

"I can smell you. You're so sweet," he grated out. He pushed another finger into her. Her face tightened in pleasure as he finger-fucked her, and his thumb began to rub her clit. Her body tensed. She shouldn't be doing this. This was getting out of hand.

"Don't fight it, Gia," Seth whispered near into ear. He'd sensed her second-guessing herself. "If I can't fuck your little pussy with my cock right now, I sure as hell will with my fingers. Give in to it."

His entire arm moved tensely over her now. Gia grimaced as the friction took over and she felt herself rising again toward climax. She felt completely helpless, vulnerable and open to his insistence upon pleasuring her.

But it was Seth's touch, and it was so good.

"I'm going to feel you tighten around me this time," he said very quietly with his lips touching her ear. "You wouldn't believe how good it feels when you squeeze my cock when you're coming."

She clutched onto his thrusting forearm as she came again.

"Yeah, I can feel your heat. Give me more of that."

She lost herself for a moment, coming violently against his hand.

When she came back to herself, he'd removed his fingers from her and was spreading her abundant juices all over her labia, anointing her.

Making a point.

"That's not something that can be faked," he said darkly near her ear.

Gia wasn't sure what to think about him saying that, fogged with lust as she was. He removed his hand from her pants and closed the button fly partially.

He took her hand in his and placed it on his crotch, and her thoughts about his tensely uttered words vanished. His cock rode horizontally along his pelvis and was pressed tightly against the fabric of his jeans, furiously erect. She tightened her fingers on the shaft. He moved his hand, forcing hers to move with it, grinding her hand against his cock and jerking it up and down several inches so that his cock rose and fell, his actions forceful and crude and exciting. Wordlessly, he let go and began to unbuckle his belt and unfasten his jeans.

A moment later, she held his naked cock in her hand. He felt warm and deliciously hard.

"Watch the movie, Gia," he ordered near her ear. "Stare at the screen and jack me. I want you to remember this."

"I'm not going to forget it," she whispered shakily, training her gaze on the flickering screen. Her image was up there, huger than life, but it was the experience of pumping Seth's cock, of holding his pulsing flesh in her very hand that was real. In her peripheral vision, she saw him cup his balls as her fist flew up and down his shaft. She looked into his lap, hungry for the familiar, yet always compelling, vision.

He lifted his hand and tilted her face gently back to the screen. "Faster," he hissed into her ear. "I'm about to come, and you're going to swallow what I give you. Aren't you?"

"Yes," she whispered, her mouth salivating at the thought.

Her arm muscles ached as she pumped him for all she was worth. He made a low, rough sound in his throat. Unable to keep her gaze locked on the screen, she looked into his lap again. His hand lifted his clean-shaven testicles, cradling and squeezing them while she furiously jacked the long, straight shaft.

"I'm about to come," he said into her ear, his breathing rough. "Slide my cock into your mouth, but you don't need to suck. Don't ruin your makeup."

She bent, fitting the fat, succulent head between her spread lips, her hand still jacking him. He jerked when she defied him, tightening around him and bobbing her head up and down just a few inches. She sucked, prodding him to give her what she wanted.

He complied silently, every muscle in his body drawn tight. His cock swelled huge. The musky taste of his come spread on her tongue. He clutched her head. She remained still while she pumped him and he ejaculated into her mouth.

It was dark in the theater, but the moment was lurid. Brilliant. Intense. Gia knew it would be indelibly pressed into her memory for as long as she lived.

Nineteen

They left the movie a little early and returned to the SUV, where Seth retouched her makeup. He seemed especially focused on his task, and Gia thought it was because he considered it a professional victory if he could fool Rill Pierce's sharp director's eye.

She was still a little dazed by what had happened in the movie theater, mostly because she wasn't sure *what* had happened. She wasn't sure if it was just an impulsive, incredibly charged erotic interlude—a product of their having to restrain themselves from touching each other—or if there was something more to Seth's intensity.

Had she been right in thinking he'd been making some kind of point by making her surrender to him sexually in front of the big screen, that blatant symbol of her career and the life she'd chosen?

Had he been subtly insisting she give herself to him completely after watching her give a small part of herself to millions of people?

She'd participated eagerly. The sex had been charged and deeply erotic. But what had happened in the movie theater seemed somehow ominous, too, like a dark cloud had begun to cast a shadow on their idyllic time together. Maybe she'd been right in fearing that their intimacy would be ruptured if they left their private sanctuary in the woods.

She grew quiet on the way to Rill and Katie's, thinking. If any aspect of her concerns were true, why did she love submitting to him so much? Shouldn't she be worried she would sacrifice personal goals in order to be with him . . . especially given how hard she was falling for him?

That thought made anxiety flame higher.

Her sense of unrest didn't really leave her, but she subdued it as they drove to Rill and Katie's house. While they climbed a long road up a hill, Seth briefed her about why a top movie director–screenplay writer and a former tax lawyer from Hollywood lived a good part of the year in remote Vulture's Canyon. It seemed Rill had gone through a particularly dark period after losing his first wife in a car accident and had ended up in Vulture's Canyon, licking his wounds and sinking into a deep depression. Rill was Irish, but had come to UCLA for undergrad, where he'd become good friends with Everett Hughes and been adopted by the entire Hughes family. When Katie had come to Vulture's Canyon to "save" Rill, at first he had strenuously resisted the overtures of his longtime friend. Katie refused to be scared away, however, goading Rill out of his funk with her stubbornness and determination. With her love. Finally, he'd wised up, realizing he wanted Katie even more as a partner than he had as a friend. They lived simply and happily up on top of the hill in the midst of the forest, where Rill could focus on his screenplay writing, Katie could work as a tax consultant for a local social service center, and they both could raise their little girl, Daisy, in peace.

The Pierces lived in a handsome, sprawling farmhouse. Through encroaching dusk, Gia saw the large front porch was decked out with pumpkins, corn sheaves, and purple and orange mums in pots.

"It's already near sunset," Seth said quietly as he parked the SUV in the driveway at the front of the house. "The shadows are in our favor as far as your makeup, and their interior lighting is soft." He removed the keys and looked at her. "Are you ready to do this?"

Her excitement about meeting someone so respected in the film

industry—not to mention the benefactor of her college education—
had turned her anxiety in a new direction. "You're really looking
forward to this, aren't you? Maybe we should make a bet on
whether or not they figure it out to make things more interesting.
I'll take Rill figuring it out; you bet on your powers of deception,"
she told him humorously, watching as he unwrapped the package
on the battery-operated candles.

He shook his head. "Your acting is the key to it all. I don't want
to weigh the odds against a bad performance." He squeezed her
thigh warmly. "Break a leg," he said amusedly before they got out
of the car and retrieved the bag holding the pumpkin from the
backseat.

Rill stepped onto the front porch to greet them. He was a big
man with the shoulders of a linebacker. He bent slightly, holding
the hand of an adorable toddler sporting two dark, curly pigtails
behind her ears. Daisy watched their approach up the stairs with
enormous eyes. Gia recognized the immediate challenge to enact-
ing her role. Her heart melted at the sight of the little girl. Gia had
been her neighborhood's favorite babysitter. Maybe it was because
she was an only child, but she'd always loved kids. She doubted
Jessie would fawn over a two- or three-year-old though. She'd have
to ignore her cute button being pushed.

Pushed ruthlessly.

Things only got worse when Seth climbed up the stairs before
her. He laughed and greeted the little girl, who grinned up at him.
He set down the bag he carried and swept her into his arms.

Oh no. Adorable emergency.

Seth was so big and masculine, and Daisy was so tiny and feminine. Something swelled tight in Gia's chest, her unexpected reaction making her panic a little. Would she give herself away to Rill
so early on?

"This is Daisy," Seth told Gia. His usually impassive features
cracked open into a wide grin that made Gia's heartbeat quicken.

"You've grown since I saw you two months ago," he told Daisy. "How old are you now? Twenty-one?"

"She's not allowed to ever turn twenty-one. We've already discussed it," Rill said, his Irish accent perfectly suiting his brawny handsomeness. "Hi. I'm Rill Pierce," he said, sticking out his hand.

"Sorry," Seth said, pulling his gaze away from Daisy, who was soberly holding up two pudgy fingers to tell him her real age. She heard the screen door squeak open behind them. "This is my newfound nephew, Jessie Bauer."

Rill gave her a hearty handshake, which she returned with boy gusto.

"I can't wait to hear this story," a woman said from behind Rill. Rill turned and Gia saw Katie Pierce. She thought she saw the resemblance between Katie and her celebrity brother, Everett Hughes. Katie was beautiful, with long, wavy blond hair that almost reached her waist and delicate features that her daughter had inherited. Something about her face suggested she loved to laugh. Seth bent down to give her a kiss on the cheek, still holding Daisy. Despite her mother's arrival, Daisy seemed quite happy to stay in Seth's arms.

"Uncle Seth," Daisy interrupted as Seth made introductions.

Katie gave Gia a wink. "Her aunt Joy calls him Uncle Seth, so Daisy thinks it's her right as well." Katie blinked and her smile faded. "I'm having an awful hard time keeping the secret of Jessie under wraps from Joy," she told Seth.

"I'd rather break the news to her in person," Seth said evenly. "It's not really the sort of news she should hear over the phone, do you think?"

Katie gave a concessionary nod, then seemed to realize something. She looked at Gia. "Oh my gosh, if you're Joy's half brother, then that means we're family as well, right?" she asked Rill, her brow scrunched together.

"It's a bit convoluted," Rill said.

"Isn't family always?" Katie replied with a grin at Gia.

Daisy patted Seth's shoulder to get his attention. She pointed wordlessly at the large sack he'd set on the porch.

"You think that's for you?" Seth asked Daisy teasingly. Daisy searched his face somberly and then nodded her head, her pigtails bobbing. Seth laughed and set her down on the porch. He reached into the bag, and Gia knew he was turning on the candles before he withdrew the jack-o'-lantern.

"*Ohhh,*" Katie said in amazement when he withdrew the pumpkin. "It's *you*, Daisy."

"Would you look at that," Rill said in quiet admiration.

Gia couldn't help but grin at Daisy's huge eyes and rapt expression as she stared at the glowing pumpkin with her face carved on the side. She hadn't realized when he was doing it, but Seth had altered the thickness of how much he cut into the skin of the pumpkin. In some places, the candlelight barely showed through, but in others, the pumpkin was nearly transparent. It created a subtle shading to the carving. The only place where he'd cut all the way through was at the opening of Daisy's mouth and two specks in her eyes, which gave the impression that the face was full of life and laughter. It was a skillfully done piece of art.

She met Seth's stare. She shook her head slightly in amazement. He really was brilliant.

"It's a Daisy pumpkin," Seth told Daisy when she stepped toward the carving, her small hands outstretched eagerly. "A Daisy-kin."

"Mine," Daisy said.

"It is definitely yours, but it's too big for you to hold. How about if we set it out here on the porch."

But Daisy was having none of that. She kept trying to grab the large pumpkin until Katie laughingly took it from Seth, assuring Daisy they would take it inside and put it in a well-deserved place of honor.

* * *

A while later, the five of them sat around a large antique oak table in the dining room. Rill was at one end of the table, the Daisy-kin at the other. They'd all done some serious justice to the smoked chicken that Rill had cooked in his outdoor pit cooker, homemade macaroni and cheese, salad and baked apples. Without her sunglasses on, Gia felt very exposed in her Jessie disguise. Especially when she had to rein in her stare from sticking on Seth, who was sitting across the table from her, looking very appealing in the glowing, soft lighting of the dining room.

"That was really good," Gia said in her boy voice, thinking that was probably high praise coming from Jessie.

"Thanks," Katie replied.

"More," Daisy insisted from the chair next to Gia, where she sat in a booster seat. Without thinking, Gia sat forward and filled a spoon with macaroni and cheese and plopped it on Daisy's plate. The little girl gave her a dimpled smile before she dug in with her spoon.

"How did you know what she wanted more of?" Katie asked, laughing.

Gia shrugged. "It was her favorite. Mine too."

"You must have little brothers or sisters at home," Rill said. She and Seth—mostly Seth—had provided their cover story and brought it off without a hitch. Seth had already given Katie a brief overview on the phone, so it wasn't as if they weren't prepared. Apparently Rill and Katie had heard about her supposed father, Jake Hightower, both from Joy and Seth. They didn't seem to find the idea that Jake had fathered a child and not known of his existence all that surprising.

"No. I was an only child," Gia said.

"It's a shame that Joy and Everett are in Mexico," Katie said, sipping her remaining chardonnay. "Even though I know both of them have been working nonstop and deserved a vacation, Joy will be sorry she didn't get to meet you right away. If you were to hand-pick a sister, you couldn't pick a better one than Joy," Katie told Gia. "Trust me, I know."

Seth nodded soberly. "Too true," Rill murmured. Rill set down his water goblet and leaned forward. "I hope you don't mind me asking, Jessie. I don't want to pry. But how'd you figure out Jake Hightower was your dad?"

Jessie hesitated for a split second. Rill must have sensed it because he rushed to explain.

"I'm only asking because . . . well, I never knew my biological father either. Or his identity. I've been doing my own search for him, using both government agencies and a private investigator," Rill said. "I'm assuming my dad was Irish, although I'm not sure if that's even true. It makes things a bit more complicated. I was just wondering about your search. I've never talked to anyone in person who's gone through something similar."

"Oh," Gia said, relief sweeping through her. She had thought Rill's sudden intensity related to suspicions about their cover story. She glanced at Seth furtively. He raised his eyebrows slightly, and she immediately knew he was asking if she wanted him to take over. "No . . . I didn't have to do any searches like that. I mean . . . I *did*," Gia stuttered. "But only after I found out my biological dad's name. I did computer searches for him. That's how I found out he still had family members living in Isleta Pueblo. His relatives told me about him living in Europe, and also about Uncle Seth. Since I'm from southern California, it was a lot easier to contact Seth than my dad. After we met, we decided to come here to get to know each other. I'm starting college in a few months, so it was now or never." Gia noticed Rill's pinched brows and realized she hadn't really answered his question. "Oh, sorry—my mom told me his name when I turned eighteen."

"Ah, well, that explains it," Rill said, seeming to deflate a little.

Gia noticed Katie's worried glance at her husband. "When you don't have a name, you're sort of screwed."

"Rill's mother absolutely refuses to breathe a word about his father's identity. So Rill decided a couple months ago to start seeing what he could find out on his own," Katie explained quietly.

"And no luck so far?" Seth asked.

"I keep running into dead end after dead end," Rill said, shrugging broad shoulders.

"You have your birth date and place of birth?" Gia asked, her heart going out to him. Something told her this was a very old, haunting question for Rill Pierce. Katie must have seen that look, too, because she reached over and covered Rill's hand with hers. He glanced at her and gave her a small special smile before he took her proffered hand in his, squeezing it.

"I have a birth certificate. My mother said the father was unknown," Rill said heavily, brushing the back of Katie's hand with his fingertips.

"Didn't you tell me once that you had two uncles still living in Ireland? Your mother's brothers?" Seth asked. "They can't provide you with any leads?"

"Just speculations. Besides, Ray and William are currently on sabbatical."

"In jail, in other words," Katie told them under her breath.

Gia decided there was a little of herself in Jessie. He was also an only child; he might have a weakness for children too. Besides, he was still close to boyhood, wasn't he? This rationalization gave her an excuse to volunteer to watch over Daisy in the living room while the others cleaned up in the kitchen. While they were playing blocks together, Daisy got up and unceremoniously dropped a book in Gia's lap.

"Read?" she asked hopefully.

"Okay," Gia said gamely, standing and sitting on the couch. She beckoned Daisy, lifted the little girl into her lap and began to read.

Several minutes later, Gia looked up toward the end of *How to Catch a Star* to see Seth leaning against the entryway, watching her broodingly. For once, she'd caught him in an unguarded moment. She paused, her mouth falling open when she took in his expression. It was some strange combination of conflict, frustration, longing . . .

. . . And heat.

For some reason, seeing his feelings so clearly on his face acted like a lit match to her own emotions. All the uncertainty she'd experienced after they'd made each other burn in the movie theater flamed high inside her once again.

"Jessie, you're a godsend," Katie said, walking into the room. Seth straightened, his expression going stony. Katie looked back at him. "He's so good with kids."

"Yeah. He is," Seth muttered, holding Gia's stare.

"Mommy and Daddy will finish the star book with you. It's bedtime, Daisy girl," Katie said, lifting her daughter into her arms.

"No, *Jessie*," Daisy said, stretching her arms out to Gia.

"You've made quite the impression," Katie told Gia approvingly. She turned back to Daisy. "Daddy will start your book over from the beginning. That's *two* whole readings of the star book," Katie bargained.

"*No.*"

"Those are the terms. Do you want to say good night to Jessie and Uncle Seth?"

Daisy bumped her cheek against her mother's chest, an adorable scowl on her face.

"We should be going anyway," Seth said, stepping fully into the room. Gia stood up from the couch. "Thanks, Katie, the dinner was delicious."

"Oh, please, don't go yet. It won't take us long at all. *Rill reads really fast*," Katie mouthed over her daughter's head. "I wanted to talk to you about the birthday gift I'm thinking of getting Joy, and I need an artist's opinion."

Seth agreed.

"Don't pout, Daisy. Don't you want to thank Uncle Seth again for the Daisy-kin?" Daisy hesitated, but then turned suddenly, her arms extended toward Seth. He leaned down and received a wet kiss on his cheek. He twitched a pigtail fondly. Seth looked like he thought the kiss more than adequate payment for his pumpkin carving. Gia said good night to the sleepy-looking, too-cute little girl.

She looked up at Seth once they were alone in the living room.

"What were you thinking?" Gia whispered.

"When?" he asked blankly.

"When you watched me reading to Daisy a little bit ago."

His mouth slanted. "Nothing," he said, but she knew he was lying.

In the distance, she heard Rill's deep voice. She exhaled in frustration. "Right. Nothing. Just like you weren't thinking anything in particular in the theater today."

"What's that supposed to mean?" he asked, an edge to his tone.

She threw him a dark glance, suddenly feeling very vulnerable. Volatile. From Seth's sudden fierce expression, she guessed he was too.

"Come here," he said quietly, grabbing her hand. He led her through the kitchen and opened the front door, pulling her onto the front porch. Even through her sudden storm of uncertainty, Gia acknowledged it was a beautiful night. She inhaled a breath of cool, crisp, leaf-scented air.

"What's wrong?" he asked her once they stood on the porch steps, millions of stars sparkling above their heads.

"I don't know exactly," she said honestly in a choked voice.

"Why did you do that? Why did you seduce me in that movie theater?"

"Because I wanted you. Why do you think?" he bit out quietly. He paused and turned to her midway down the steps, still holding her hand. Gia pulled it from his hold.

"It was like you were trying to . . . tell me something. *Prove* something," she hissed. She felt strangely out of control and embarrassed about it. Why had her unrest chosen that moment to break free? It had something to do with the unguarded conflict she'd seen on his face as he'd watched her reading to Daisy.

"I don't know what you're talking about," he said with infuriating calmness.

"Don't give me that shit. I know you don't like actresses, but it's like . . . it's like you're *mad* at me for being one. It's like you wanted to trump my job. That's what you were doing in that theater!"

A gust of wind made the woods seem to sigh around them. His silence in the face of her outburst made her uncomfortably aware of how stupid she sounded.

"What do you want me to say, Gia? That I'm happy you're an actress? Because that's not true. Things would be a lot simpler if you were an accountant or a lawyer or just about *any* goddamn thing but a movie star living in the spotlight. Thriving in it," he added darkly under his breath.

"For a decent guy, you can be a real ass sometimes."

"Were you acting in there?" he asked, seemingly unaffected by her accusation. He pointed to the living room.

"What?" she asked, furious and confused.

"With Daisy. You look like a complete natural with kids," he seethed, stepping closer toward her.

"It wasn't an *act*," she spat. "I love children."

He reached up and palmed her jaw, his fingertips digging slightly into the muscles of her neck. She flinched back, but he tugged her closer, so that their mouths were only inches apart. Her heartbeat started to pound in her ears.

"Do you plan to have kids someday?" he breathed out, his face lowering over hers.

"Yes."

"What are you going to do? Disguise the whole family every time you go out in public?"

"Plenty of celebrities have kids, Seth. Your niece and Everett Hughes probably will someday. Or are you going to try to talk Everett into changing jobs as soon as Joy's pregnant?"

"I probably will suggest it if the occasion arises," he replied sardonically. "He won't listen to a word of it."

"I'm not surprised. He'd be crazy to listen to you. I know *I'd* never sacrifice what's important to me just because of your stupid, smug opinions."

"If you think I'm asking *you* to sacrifice a fucking thing, you're completely misunderstanding me," he said before his mouth seized hers.

His mind had gone blank with a cyclone of fury and want. He knew that as he kissed Gia brutally, but it didn't quiet his sudden flash fire of lust. He wanted her like hell. Not just here in these peaceful woods.

Everywhere.

But it would never work. He'd suspected that as he sat in that theater today, and maybe that was what was making his hunger for her cut at him. He wasn't surprised Gia had told him just now she would never sacrifice her career for him. He didn't *want* her to. How could he? She was like a pure flame up there on that screen, her honesty and beauty and warmth enthralling every watcher.

Did she really think he was so stupid as to ask her to stop acting? Not in a million years. She would just resent him for it. Acting made her happy.

And despite all his misgivings and his biting sarcasm just now, he knew one thing for certain.

He wanted Gia to be happy.

He sensed the moment when their conflicting energies fused into one fire. She began kissing him back furiously, gripping his hair and pressing close to him. He dipped his knees to align them better and palmed her hips and ass. Gia moaned raggedly when he consumed her even more greedily, her back arching to accommodate him. She gripped his ass and squeezed. Hard. Her nails dug into him. Everything faded away for a crazy, lust-numbing moment.

Everything.

"Oh my God," someone said at the far reaches of his brain. "OH MY GOD, stop it, Seth!"

Shit. Katie.

Even as the realization hit him about what was happening, he only reluctantly broke his kiss with Gia and looked around. Sure enough, Katie stood on the porch a few feet away from them looking totally floored. If the situation weren't so serious, Seth would have found her expression hilarious. Rill had frozen in the action of holding open the storm door as he came onto the porch. Seth slowly moved his hands off Gia's ass to her waist, but kept her pressed tight against him.

"I can explain, Katie—"

"What the hell are you doing? That's your *nephew*," Katie accused in a high-pitched voice, shock ringing in her tone.

"That's *not* his nephew," Rill said. Seth noticed Rill was peering narrowly at Gia in the dim light from the porch light. Seth glanced down at Gia's face and knew everything was exposed. It wasn't that some of the pink of her mouth was starting to show through because of his forceful kiss. No, it wasn't Seth's disguise that turned Gia into Jessie. Not entirely. It was Gia's acting that did that. Apparently, their kiss had dissipated the acting magic. It didn't surprise him. There was nothing so honest as what happened when they touched.

Gia stared up guiltily at Rill and Katie, clearly a pretty young woman caught red-handed.

Rill stepped onto the porch and looked down at Gia intently. Seth felt Gia snatch her hand away from his ass and start to back out of his arms. Seth held her fast.

"That's not even a boy," Rill said, frowning. "Jesus. Aren't you Gia Harris?"

Twenty

Seth had left several lights on, but the house in the woods still looked empty and . . . *different* somehow than the house they'd left earlier today.

"Are you sure Rill and Katie aren't pissed at us?" Gia asked shakily when Seth turned the key in the ignition.

They hadn't talked much during the drive home. Both of them had managed to be patient and apologetic, explaining things to a stunned Rill and Katie. But telling their story to the Pierces hadn't really required conversation between Gia and Seth. What had happened on that front porch before they'd been discovered seemed to hover between them like a suspended bomb.

"They're not mad. Once we explained, they got that we were doing it for a good reason," Seth said quietly, his deep, gruff voice in the darkened cab of the car causing her neck to prickle. "And you saw how Rill's brain latched on to the whole thing. It'll be fuel for his writing and directing, trust me."

Gia gave a bark of tired laughter as she recalled what Seth was referring to. In her mind's eye, she saw Rill sitting at the kitchen table, his chin in his hand as he stared at a rumpled, embarrassed Gia. After the kiss and the discovery, they'd gone inside to try to explain what was happening.

"That's amazing. That's *weird*," Rill had said distractedly after they relayed most of the story.

"What's weird—aside from the obvious?" Katie added, rolling her eyes.

"Now that I look at Gia, I can't believe I didn't see it. It's like watching a master magician. First, it was the break in the reality of seeing you two making out. That jarred my brain and signaled something wasn't right. But then you stopped acting, when you two were—" Rill had waved his hand vaguely between them. "Right, Gia?"

Gia had swallowed thickly. "I guess so. I wasn't really thinking about Jessie."

Rill had smirked. "And all of a sudden, the truth was right there, clear as day," Rill laughed, glancing at Katie. "I can't believe I ever looked at her and thought she was a boy."

"Me either," Katie had agreed.

"She cast a spell, some kind of enchantment. It's mind-blowing. I work with actors all the time, and I watch them 'turn on a role' like they're stepping into a costume, but my God . . . I've never seen it done that well before. Don't tell Everett I said that," he'd said under his breath to Katie.

Katie had laughed. "Everett would be the first to agree if he'd been fooled by that spectacle."

"Given Seth's skill and your talent, I'll bet there's no role you couldn't tackle. So far, I've only seen *Shadow Mistress*, and I thought you were really good," Rill had told Gia. "But I'll say this now from firsthand experience: You're an exceptional actress."

"She's only going to get better too. Gia is just getting started when it comes to her career."

Gia had blinked upon hearing Seth's quiet comment. Their gazes met and held. Her chest suddenly got tight. Katie cleared her throat, and Gia had realized she'd been locked in Seth's golden-eyed, somber gaze.

It was like he'd been stating the inevitable.

"You realize Rill will probably be wanting you for his next movie now. I've never seen him so impressed," Seth said presently.

Gia exhaled. At one time, even the remotest chance of doing a movie with Rill Pierce would have sent her into a euphoric mood. Tonight, it felt like a weight was pressing down on her spirit.

"All I realize at the moment is how tired I am," she said quietly, unbuckling her seat belt.

"Gia," Seth halted her when she reached for the door handle. "About what I said on the porch—"

"I don't want to talk about it, Seth. I just want to go to bed."

She turned to look at him as she interrupted. His face looked shadowed and hard.

"Okay," he said. Her heart sank a little when he agreed so readily.

She'd already removed the wig by the time she reached the bedroom. She couldn't wait to take off the rest of the disguise. After everything that had happened that day, Gia felt exhausted, but weirdly agitated, too, like she wanted to jump out of her own skin. It was as if her brain and spirit and body were all in a fight.

All because of Seth.

"Do you need me to help with the binder?" Seth asked from behind her.

"*No.*"

She realized how sharp she'd sounded when she turned to see Seth halt dead in his tracks. She regretted her harshness, but she just wasn't up to having Seth unzip the tight corset. Not now, she wasn't, especially when she considered all those times he'd done it before, and her defenses had crumbled. "It's gotten a little looser since I first started wearing it," she explained lamely.

Seth nodded. "I'll just grab some things and sleep in the other guest room tonight."

"Seth, I didn't mean—"

"You need some privacy," he said evenly, grabbing some clothing from the bureau drawer. He walked toward her, his face a mask, his stare on her unflinching. "Maybe we both could use a little space tonight," he said before he left her standing there alone.

As the minutes passed, she regretted her sharpness with him more and more. After she'd gotten into the large bed alone, her discomfort only amplified. All her thoughts pained her.

If you think I'm asking you to sacrifice a fucking thing, you're completely misunderstanding me.

She cringed internally thinking about the whole volatile exchange. She'd read more than she should have into what had happened at the movie theater. Of *course* he wasn't asking her to change anything about her life. How stupid could she be? He'd made it clear their relationship would last only while they were here in these woods. She wasn't *ever* going to change her acting career for Seth.

So why was she upset about him declaring he'd never ask her to?

Because part of you wanted *him to demand both of you make compromises so that you could be together, not just here, but in Hollywood. Part of you wanted him to suggest that you make concessions on both sides because the relationship was worth fighting for.*

She stifled a moan of misery and moved restlessly on the bed. She'd clearly been influenced by seeing happy couples all day that had overcome obstacles, like Chance and Sherona, and Rill and Katie. It had been her error to put Seth and her in the same category.

It shamed her to think of how stupid she must have sounded to him. Sleep was *not* going to come easy tonight.

She caught a big shadow moving from the side of her vision and stifled a scream.

"*Shhh*, it's me," Seth said.

"Seth?" she asked, startled. Relief and trepidation surged through her. Why had he come? She felt the mattress give as he sat at the edge of it. "What are you doing?"

"I couldn't sleep. I kept thinking about what I said on the porch."

"Me too," she admitted in a hushed tone. She squinted into the darkness. She could just make out the shape of his broad shoulders and head.

"When I said I'd never ask you to sacrifice anything, I just meant—"

"I know what you meant," she said in a rush. "You were reminding me that we'd decided this relationship was going to be about the here and now. Why would you ask me to give up something permanent because of our temporary arrangement?"

He paused. "No, that's not what I meant."

Her heart fluttered. "It isn't?" she asked cautiously, propping up her upper body on her elbow.

"I just meant that I'd never ask you to sacrifice *anything* for me, let alone acting. I've seen how passionate you are about it. You're meant to be an actress. I've never met anyone who was so perfectly destined for something. But more importantly, it makes you happy. And when it comes down to it, I want you to be happy, Gia."

Her throat went tight with emotion. His admission had been so sweet. She felt too overwhelmed to speak, so she reached for him, finding his forearm in the darkness. She slid her fingers over his warm skin and found his hand. He moved in when she pulled him toward her. He came down next to her on the bed. They both lay on their sides, facing each other. She absorbed him with skimming fingertips across his jaw, neck and bare chest. His breath caught when she trailed her fingertips over his taut abdomen.

"I owe you an apology," he said, his low, gruff voice raising bumps on her neck and forearms. He cupped her waist warmly. "I do get frustrated sometimes when I think about your life and mine. I get irritated at your job because it feels like something that separates us. But I realized just now, it's not your job that's doing that. It's *me*."

"But I *like* you," she said in a choked voice. "I like your low-key modesty about your brilliance as an artist and your independence and your need for privacy. I like how you care so much about family and want to keep them safe. I *love* those things about you. I would never ask you to change those things either, because I'd be asking you to be something you're not."

"*Shhh,*" he soothed, because her voice had cracked at the last, and he could probably feel her trembling as she touched him. He pulled her closer with his hand at her waist. Their bodies brushed together, the feeling sublime. Exciting. Her nipples tightened against the thin gown she wore. She pressed them against Seth's hard chest, sighing in pleasure. His mouth found hers in the darkness. He caught her small sob with his lips. As usual, his kiss was deep and possessive, demanding all her attention. He was hot and tasted so damn good. She abandoned her fears and anxieties, sacrificed them to the heat of need. All those insecurities and worries were nothing to the sudden flash fire that leapt between them.

"Maybe it was selfish of me in the theater, but I crave you giving yourself to me, Gia. All I want to do is drown myself in you," Seth said roughly. Her neck prickled as he pressed his lips to her skin.

"I do give myself to you. Completely," she said, her hands moving anxiously over his bare, muscular back. "Here and now, you have *everything*."

He groaned roughly and pressed her closer to him, devouring her mouth. His hands moved down over her body, finding the hem of the short nightgown she wore. She lifted her hips slightly, and a moment later he broke their kiss while he whipped the garment over her head. Then his mouth was back, hot and consuming. His hand moved beneath her underwear, cupping her pussy warmly before he began to apply an ideal pressure and move in little circles. She moaned her pleasure into his mouth.

Suddenly he was breaking their kiss and pushing her onto her back. His shadow rose over her, and he pulled her panties down her legs and off her feet.

"Spread your thighs," he ordered.

When she did, he moved between them on his knees. She saw his shadow lower, a frisson of excitement going through her. He swiped the tip of his warm tongue between her labia.

She cried out, her fingers delving into his thick, smooth hair. He nuzzled her with his nose as he slid his big hands beneath her ass, lifting her slightly to him . . . keeping her in place.

Then he proceeded to hold her at his mercy while he ate her.

After a moment, she shook in climax beneath his merciless tongue. He lapped up her juices like they were his due. He pushed his tongue high into her slit, and then applied a hard pressure on her clit with his lips, amplifying her climax, stretching it out masterfully. He sucked, and her desperate cries grew even wilder.

A moment later, she melted into the mattress, panting.

"That's right," she heard him say, licking her smooth labia in a manner that was both soothing and incendiary. "I'm addicted to your orgasms. I'm addicted to this sweet pussy." She felt him pushing back her thighs, so that her hips rolled back. He held her legs over her body by pressing his forearm at the back of her knees. He immediately plunged his tongue into her slit and fucked her with it, his manner hungry and lewd and forceful.

"Oh God," she moaned, rocking her hips against his mouth. He cupped her ass, holding her in place as he dipped his tongue into her pussy. Every once in a while, he'd focus on her clit, lashing it with a stiffened tongue, before he'd plunge into her again. Gia had no choice but to lie there and accept every ounce of dizzying pleasure he gave her. The moments were so intense, his desire for her so focused and strong, it was like he was trying to tell her something without words, pressing it into her, scoring it into her quivering flesh.

Her nails scraped against his head as she rapidly began to crest again to climax. "Hold on a moment," he said.

She blinked in disorientation, because his heaven-sent mouth was suddenly gone, and her legs were falling as he scrambled on the mattress next to her. She heard what sounded like the bedside drawer open.

"Seth?" she asked shakily.

"I'm coming right back," he said in tense voice.

He meant exactly that. A few seconds later, he'd again pushed his forearm behind her knees and rolled back her hips. She gasped when his tongue immediately was giving her clit a good, hard rub. She furrowed her fingers into his hair and keened. It felt *so* good.

"I'm going to come," she mumbled after a moment, mindless with pleasure.

He cupped her bottom from below, his middle finger burrowing into the crack. Her eyes sprang wide when he penetrated her ass.

"*Ohhh*," she cried out in shock when he began to finger-fuck her smoothly. He'd gotten the lubrication from the drawer. They'd left it there last night. He tongued her clit ruthlessly, shifting his face ever so subtly back and forth. His finger plunged into her ass at a brisk pace.

She screamed as a powerful climax slammed into her.

"I won't make a habit of doing this twice in twenty-four hours," she heard him say through the darkness and her haze of pleasure. "But I've wanted to be naked again inside you all day. All I can think about is coming deep inside you."

She felt his hard cockhead press against her ass. Like last night, when he first pushed his cock into her, there was a flash of pain. She whimpered, pleasure and pain mingling. "Remember what I told you," Seth said from above her. "Push back on my cock." She did it and he slid deeper. "Ah, that's *good*. Stay still a moment."

When he'd entered her, she'd still been in the position she'd been in when he ate her so ruthlessly. Her hips were still rolled back, but now Seth was in a kneeling position behind her, his back straight. He held one of her ankles in front of him, keeping her leg in the air as he began to pump, gently at first.

She moaned shakily, and this time, it wasn't in pain. It felt so good. There was a darkness to his possession . . . a desperation, as if he knew their time together was reaching an end.

She couldn't bear the thought. She reached, finding his hip, urging him with her hand.

"Harder," she pled.

"Jesus, Gia," he grated out. "I don't want to hurt you."

Her nails dug into his tensed buttock. "I'm asking for it. Fuck me hard."

A low growl rumbled in his throat. He swung his hips, his pelvis smacking against her ass. She bit off a scream. He ground his balls against her ass, his cock throbbing deep inside her.

"I'm not going to last," he bit out. "You feel like you've got a fever, you're so hot."

"I don't want it to end."

"Neither do I, honey. Neither do I."

He began to fuck her slow and deep. Her face pulled tight at the pressure and friction. The moment felt electrical, full . . . intensely erotic. His pelvis began to smack rhythmically against her buttocks. She felt him much more acutely in her ass. Despite the fact that she'd said she didn't want it to end, her body strained for release. She urged him with her hand on his ass. He gave a guttural growl and grabbed her other leg. He held both her ankles in the air, keeping her hips rolled back, and gave her what she had begged for.

She screamed, the sound of it vacillating as Seth plunged into her and their bodies crashed together. She hadn't told herself to do it, but her hand was moving feverishly between her thighs.

"I'm going to come," he told her, sounding wretched at the fact.

But she'd already sensed it, they were so attuned at that moment. She felt his cock swell inside her, and she grimaced, her hand moving faster between her thighs. His body went rigid. His groan sounded pained as he began to come. She hated the sound of it. She loved it. His warmth filled her, and she shuddered in her own release.

Afterward, she stared into the darkness, panting, feeling strangely both utterly sated and bereft at the same time.

This thing with Seth was going to kill her. Her desire for him was so sharp, it hurt. Why did the sweetest things in the world also have to be the most painful?

The next day, Seth seemed as subdued as she was. What had happened in bed last night seemed to hover around them, their lovemaking a poignant reminder of what was special between them. Seth was very tender with her all day, almost as if he thought she were ill or something.

Or as if he cherished her very much.

The day was gray and blustery, the wind so fierce it blew half of the leaves off the trees, exposing skeletal branches. Seth made a fire and Gia curled up in a chair near it, reading. He silently worked on sketches of her. Every once in a while, her cheek would tickle from his intent gaze on her face. She would look up, and they would share a smile.

These moments with him were so different from their fierce lovemaking. These, too, she wished would never end.

"Are you working on more sketches for the Eleanor makeup?" she asked him once, while she took a break from reading.

He grunted, scrunched his eyelids together and tossed down his pencil. "It's no use," he said.

"What's no use?" she asked, sensing his frustration.

"I can't get you the way I want you. It's like . . . part of you always eludes me."

"I'm one hundred percent right here. I assure you," she replied softly. He blinked and met her stare, his frustration fading.

"You know what I think?" she asked.

He shook his head.

"I think you're frustrated because you're hungry." She stood briskly. "I'll get us some lunch."

She made them grilled cheese sandwiches and salads. Afterward, they returned to the fireside, the warmth of the fire and the sound of Seth's pencil scratching on his sketch pad lulling her. It felt wonderful, to be so relaxed and yet so aware of his attention focused on her, to have her senses so piqued by his nearness. She leaned her head back and closed her eyes.

"Gia?"

"*Hmmm?*" she purred contentedly, turning her face toward him.

"Would you let me draw you nude?"

Her mouth fell open in surprise. "What does me being nude have to do with the Eleanor makeup?"

"Nothing."

His steadfast reply vibrated in the warm air between them.

"It's just that . . ." He faded off, frowning. Again, she sensed the frustration of a perfectionist who felt he was performing beneath his standards. "Ever since I first met you years back, I've been trying to figure out the magic of you. If I could only capture a hint of it, I'd be a happy man."

"With your pencil, you mean?" she asked, amazement flavoring her tone.

"Any way I can," he replied gruffly. Their gazes held in the taut silence. She sensed he had meant with his powerful lovemaking, as well. "I'll never let another soul see the sketches," he said. "I promise."

"I'm not worried about that."

She stood and began to undress.

"Where do you want me?" she asked awkwardly a moment later, standing before him, naked.

He merely waved at the chair and ottoman where she'd been reclining. She lay back, feeling both exposed and excited by his tight stare on her. Seth stood and moved to the far corner of the couch to get a more straight-on view of her. At first she was tense and hyperaware because of the novelty of the situation. Slowly, the warmth of the fire on her naked skin and the hushed, soothing sound of Seth's pencil made her muscles go soft and relaxed. She studied his face and saw his hallmark rapier focus. She'd been silly to imagine he was considering this situation sexual, just because she was naked. He was an artist, after all, and in those moments, she was his subject. Still, it was a singularly sensual experience for her, to feel herself the target of his gaze and attention. Her eyelids grew heavy, and she drifted off to the sound of his scratching pencil and the crackling fire.

She awoke to the sensation of his hands moving along the sides of her rib cage. Her nipples drew tight.

"Seth?" she mumbled sleepily.

"Your skin is like warm silk," he murmured, his gruff voice washing over her and awakening her nerves. He cupped her breasts from below and shaped them gently to his hands. "Is it all right?" he asked her simply, meeting her stare.

"More than all right," she murmured. He stood and leaned over her, one hand sliding beneath her hips, the other pushing her against his chest. He lifted her. She saw that determined, familiar look on his face as he carried her. He lay her down on her back on the soft couch and began to unfasten his jeans, his gaze on her face.

A moment later, he was coming down over her, his cock slowly sliding home. She panted for air, gritting her teeth. She'd been wrong to think that he'd merely been the cool, detached artist as he drew her. His cock was huge and throbbing and clearly *very* affected. The knowledge moved her.

At first, he remained still while fully sheathed in her pussy.

Then he braced himself on his hands and began to move. She saw so many things in his eyes. They remained silent as he masterfully built the friction between them though.

Words couldn't contain what she felt in those moments.

Twenty-one

Later that afternoon, Gia heard Seth on the phone in the kitchen. Her ears pricked when she heard him say her name. She had a pretty good idea who he was talking to. A minute later, he walked into the living room where she sat.

"Was that Charles?" she asked him.

"Yes."

Dread went though her when his gaze skated off her. "What is it, Seth?"

"The trial is going to begin on Wednesday."

"*This* Wednesday?" she asked, stunned. He nodded. "But . . . Madeline said a week from next Monday at the very earliest."

"I know. But it's like Madeline said from the start, trial proceedings can be erratic in a high-profile case like this. Judge Halloran suddenly got a bee in his robes, apparently, and moved things up. Madeline wants you there as quickly as possible, so you can go over your testimony. The jury is going to be sworn in on Tuesday, opening statements will begin on Wednesday. You're expected to be there, although you probably won't testify immediately."

Gia couldn't speak. It was like something vital had been ripped away from her without warning. She didn't have much time with Seth, save these few remaining days and nights, and then their hours on the road home. And those were going to be stolen from her as well? She turned her head, not wanting him to see the tears welling in her eyes.

"What are we going to do?" she asked, straining to keep her voice even.

"Charles is arranging a flight back to Los Angeles for tomorrow afternoon. I've also put in a special request in regard to you, and Charles told me that request has been agreed to by United Studios."

"What?" she asked, bewildered.

"I asked that during the trial, you be allowed to stay in one of the Bunker Hill condos the studio keeps for visitors. It's situated in a luxury tower, and it's known for keeping its high-profile residents very secure. It'll be safer for your police escort to protect you there. Plus, you won't have to worry about driving back and forth from Bel Air to the downtown courthouse every day. The press is going to be even more rabid than it was before the trial began. I don't want another incident where you're run off the interstate. I spoke to Joshua Cabot about the possibility of you staying there a few days ago, and he arranged it all."

"Will I go back to Los Angeles as Jessie, or me?" she asked, even though what she really wanted to know was, *Are you going with me? Are we never going to see each other again?* It seemed impossible—soul-killing—to consider they might not. Everything they'd shared was about to evaporate into insubstantial memories?

"You'll go back as Gia. A deputy is being sent to the St. Louis airport to escort you back to L.A."

Her lips parted. If a police escort was being sent, then . . .

"You won't be coming?" she asked hollowly.

She was avoiding looking at him, but she heard his heavy exhale. "No. You and I were going to drive the SUV back together before the trial date was moved up, remember? It belongs to a friend of mine. I have to return it. I'll also need to clean the house and restock all the supplies we used."

Her heart throbbed uncomfortably. She'd been looking forward to their return road trip together. That drive had been the silver lining. She'd known it would be an ending ritual for them, but it would have been intimate and special, now that they'd been honest about their desire for each other. Now that they'd stopped fighting it. A road trip between established lovers, the hours of enforced intimacy . . . well, it was the type of experience that could have been a game changer, a last-ditch possibility at saving what was so special between them.

It was the first time she really admitted to herself how much hope she'd been pinning on that return road trip. Now it was being snatched away.

"Gia—"

"No. Don't say anything. We both knew this day would come," she said, cutting him off. "I should go and pack."

When she reached the bedroom, she shut the door, just in case Seth didn't get the message that she wanted to be alone. For a few seconds, she just stood there, fighting down the feeling of misery threatening to choke her throat.

On Seth's orders, she hadn't made any outgoing calls on her cell phone or sent any text messages since leaving Los Angeles. But Seth had just told her the undercover operation was over. She was back to being Gia Harris once again. If she was going to make an exit from this cabin—from Seth's life—she'd do it on her own terms. She couldn't even consider the idea of a tear-filled airport good-bye with Seth tomorrow. It was so cliché and just . . . unbearable to consider.

Aching, but determined, she pulled out her suitcase and retrieved her cell phone and charger.

Gia Harris was back. It was time she took control of her life again.

Gia had just finished her packing when Seth walked into the bedroom. Shutting her suitcase, she stood and faced him. His brows were knitted together slightly as he studied her.

"You okay?" he asked quietly.

She nodded briskly, determined not to melt into a puddle, which is precisely what she felt like doing. "I was just thinking about the trial. It's always seemed so far in the future, I haven't really had time to consider what it'll be like. Or maybe I just didn't want to think about it," she added under her breath with a mirthless laugh.

"You're doing the right thing," he said. Her gaze leapt to his face. "By testifying. By telling the truth. I know it's been a huge inconvenience in your life, but I'm proud of you for doing it."

Emotion tightened her throat. She swallowed thickly and glanced around the attractive, cozy bedroom, willing herself to calm.

"I'll really miss this place," she said.

"Yeah. It's been amazing. Not the place. Being with you."

Unwanted tears stung her eyes. He stepped toward her.

"Let's talk," he said.

"About what?" she asked, frustration and sadness making her sound desperate. "You've told me how you feel about us."

"I don't *know* how I feel about us. If I gave you the impression I have all the answers, I'm sorry. The circumstances have changed all that. You have. I know how I feel about *you*."

She stared at him, aghast. For a few seconds, she just studied his bold features. They had become so familiar to her. She had learned to read him so well. Despite his words, she sensed his ambivalence, that same conflict she'd witnessed on his face when he'd been watching her reading to Daisy.

Her heart sank.

"The circumstances haven't changed, Seth," she said quietly. "You don't think it would work between us in L.A., and I have my doubts too. I would shake up your whole world. And I don't want to give up my work ethic or my dreams because you're uncomfortable with them." She threw up her hand and gave a sad bark of laughter. "It's a catch-22."

His face turned stony, but she sensed his anguish. Maybe it was because she'd fallen in love with him that she was so attuned to him, despite his impassive expression.

"When we started this, you said it would be best if we went our separate ways after it was all over," she said, straining to keep her voice from shaking. "We both knew it would end." She met his stare determinedly. "Well, the end has come."

His mouth twisted slightly, like he'd just eaten something bitter. *He's worried he's hurt you . . . damaged you somehow.* The thought leapt into her brain, and she somehow knew it was true. It was so *Seth*, to worry about someone he cared about, to feel responsible for them.

"I'll be fine, Seth. I'm not one of your vulnerable, fragile actresses," she said gently.

"Jesus, Gia—"

"Listen to me." He blinked, startled at her interruption, giving her a fierce look. "I'll be fine. And so will you."

She wasn't sure she believed it, at least on her part. But she was an actress, wasn't she? What else was there to do but say the words, keep breathing, and put one foot in front of the other. She didn't completely agree with Seth's estimation of whether or not Hollywood romances were advisable, but she understood his doubts. She respected his history and his choices.

"I think, under the circumstances, I should sleep in the other room tonight," she said, staring at the carpet. When he didn't respond, she started for the door, rolling her suitcase behind her.

"Gia."

She spun around, unable to disguise the tear that had fallen down her cheek.

"I've fallen in love with you."

She closed her eyes and several more tears fell at his stark admission.

"I know," she said in a strangled voice. "I've fallen in love with you too. That's what makes this whole situation suck so much. Because unlike in the movies and in make-believe, it's not enough. That's one thing in common you and I have. We work in the industry, but we can tell the difference between reality and fantasy. You don't want me to change for you, and I would hate it," she clenched her teeth, struggling to find her strength, "so *hard* if you changed for me. See . . . I think you're perfect the way you are."

He looked like the weight of the world had just dropped on him, but he didn't stop her this time as she walked away.

Seth had a rough night.

He lost count of the number of times he stood to go and confront Gia in the bed where she slept. Soothe her. Hold her. But it would just turn out like it had the night after they'd gone to Rill and Katie's. They'd smoke up the sheets. They'd feel this incredible connection.

And then they'd be right back where they'd started.

Maybe it would be better if he insisted they talk in the car on the way to the airport. Sex wouldn't be a factor then. It would just be Gia and him and the road, with nowhere to hide and no distractions.

Yeah. That's what he'd do.

At around dawn, he got up and made coffee, setting out a cup, spoon and a packet of Splenda for Gia. He frowned, pain going through him. How she took her coffee was one of the thousands of things he'd learned about her during their time together. He knew there were millions more to learn. And dammit, those little, fascinating things about her, those tiny threads of the tapestry of her character, they were *his* to discover. To cherish.

He grabbed his coffee along with a bottle of water. *If only they could stay in the woods forever, things would be so much simpler.*

He thought he heard Gia rustling around in the bedroom down

the hall. Again, his feet seemed to have a mind of their own, urging him to walk down that hallway toward her. At the last second, he forced himself to take the stairs to the workout facility instead. They would talk on the trip to St. Louis. He would explain that he wasn't the same man he had been when he first laid eyes on that beautiful, glowing girl in the Joan of Arc costume.

Or he was . . . but with Gia, he was different somehow too.

He'd been on the treadmill for nearly an hour when a strange prescience went through him. He slowed to a walk, and then stepped off the machine. The hairs on the back of his neck stood on end. Had it been a sound that had alerted him? He glanced at the security panel on the far wall.

It had been deactivated.

He cursed viciously. Grabbing his phone, he raced up the stairs.

"Gia?" he bellowed down the hallway. There was no response. *"Gia?"* He rushed to the bedroom where she'd spent the night, finding it empty, the bed made. He hurried to the bedroom they'd shared, flinging open the door. There was a bad, hollow feel to the place.

She was gone.

He rapidly grabbed his keys and wallet. He flew out the front door within seconds.

Her red cardigan immediately caught his attention, even though she was quite a distance away. She stood next to a black sedan along with a brown-haired young man who looked unfamiliar. The car was parked on the shoulder of the country road that led to the long driveway of the house.

He started to eat up the distance between them.

Little minx had not only shut down the security alarm on the house, but she'd played it extra safe by requesting that her accomplice not come up the drive.

The man took her suitcase from her and put it in the trunk. Gia walked toward the passenger door. She froze when she saw him storming toward her.

"Get in the car, Jim," he thought he heard her say tensely. She lunged to open the car door, eyeing Seth's approach warily. The man—who must be her driver from L.A.—hurried into the car and slammed his door shut. He revved the engine. Gia started to sit.

"What the hell do you think you're doing?" Seth demanded, still hastening to reach her.

She ignored him, getting in the car and slamming her door shut. Seth thought he heard the click of the automatic lock. The car started to pull away.

"Gia!" he roared.

Her mouth moved. The car came to an abrupt halt. Gia's face looked anguished through the window. The glass lowered.

"Don't come any closer, Seth, or I won't explain. I'll just tell Jim to go."

He gritted his teeth in mounting helplessness and anger. He came to a halt with thirty feet or so still separating them.

"Jim is going to take me to the airport. I called him yesterday afternoon, and he took a flight to St. Louis last night. I called Sherona, too, and asked her for directions for Jim to get here. There's no reason that you should have to take me to the airport. You've done enough."

He goggled at her in disbelief. "Gia, get the hell out of that car. You're my responsibility until I hand you off to Deputy Kildrake. I'm not just your *fucking lift* to the airport."

"Well I'm not a parcel you're supposed to deliver," she snapped, sounding irritated. Overwhelmed. "I'm out of disguise mode, Seth. It's time to go back and do what I have to do. Jim is my driver. This is all perfectly normal. I've just asked him to pick me up here instead of in Los Angeles when I land. I left you a note in the kitchen to explain how I'd gotten to the airport and that I was safe. *Please* don't make more of this than is necessary." She started to say something and hesitated, her anxious expression killing him a little. "I'm not your responsibility anymore. It's over, Seth," she said, her voice cracking. She turned away. Seth recognized that proud tilt to her chin despite her obvious anguish.

The window started to close. He didn't pause to watch the car accelerate down the road. He was already sprinting toward the SUV.

Gia was fighting nausea by the time her driver, Jim, pulled in to the return section of the car-rental facility. In the distance, she saw the familiar SUV she'd taken across the country with Seth come to a halt just outside the car-rental office. Seth immediately got out, his tall, tense body and dark expression striking her as intimidating.

He'd followed them all the way to the airport in St. Louis. Jim had tried several times to lose him, but Seth had followed effortlessly, never crowding their car or creating a potentially dangerous situation, but always keeping her within his sight. Now that they were on the grounds of the airport, Gia was a giant coiled band of tension and anxiety. Somehow, she sensed Seth's simmering anger and eerie focus behind her the entire trip, like a laser pointer on the back of her neck.

"I'm sorry, Gia," Jim said. "He was like a leech. I just couldn't shake him."

"It's okay," she assured, lowering her phone. She'd finally told Jim to stop trying to elude Seth's tail. She didn't want anyone to get hurt. Besides, Seth had called while he was in pursuit and left a message. She'd just listened to it. At least she knew his plan wasn't to throw her over his shoulder and haul her back to the house.

Although that imaginary plan held its appeal, she was fighting against that annoying, unwanted reaction.

Willing down her queasiness, she got out of the car while Jim took care of the bill with the rental-car agent. After she shut the trunk, she glanced around to see Seth standing on the curb in the distance, his muscular arms crossed over his chest.

Waiting.

It was much too cool and cloudy out today for him to be outside in only the training shorts and short-sleeved T-shirt he wore, Gia realized guiltily. Of course he hadn't had time to change clothes before he'd jumped in the SUV and followed her in hot pursuit. Although in truth, he looked too steamed at the moment to even notice the chill in the air.

How in the hell had he noticed she'd gone? She knew well by this time that his exercise routines lasted for almost two hours.

She sighed. May as well get the confrontation over with.

She grimly started to walk toward him. In that moment, Seth was the kind of superstorm there was no hope of avoiding. Jim followed behind her. The closer she got to him, she felt herself cringing a little beneath his white-hot stare. As she drew within speaking distance, a tall man in his thirties approached Seth where he stood on the sidewalk. Seth's wrathful stare on her fractured as he looked at the man.

"Hightower?" the man asked him.

Seth nodded. "Josh Kildrake?"

"That's me," the man said, reaching Seth at about the same time Gia and Jim did. She paused with her hand on her suitcase handle.

"Identification, please," Seth said, extending his hand expectantly. He studied the badge and identification Kildrake handed over with a stony expression. Gia saw the badge. She'd seen enough of them, given all the police protection she'd had in the past. Seth had obviously been in contact with the police escort while he'd pursued them relentlessly. It was just her luck that Kildrake had arrived in St. Louis a few hours before her flight. Seth scrutinized Kildrake's face narrowly before he handed back the badge.

"Here she is," Seth said soberly, nodding in Gia's direction.

"Ms. Harris," Kildrake greeted. "I'll be escorting you back to Los Angeles."

"Gee, thanks," Gia muttered under her breath, avoiding Seth's stare. It seemed to burn her.

"Well, we should probably get going," Deputy Kildrake said, waving in the direction of the transport bus that would take them to the airport.

"I'm ready," Gia said, swallowing back the lump in her throat while Seth remained silent. She hated this. He was clearly furious at her for what she'd done, but she wasn't going to apologize for keeping herself safe from the pain of some dramatic good-bye.

Now they would part with a bad taste in their mouths. *Poorly done, Gia*, a voice in her head said reproachfully. But why did Seth have to be so stubborn and prove a point like this? She wasn't in any physical danger.

Just the emotional variety.

She and Jim started to walk toward the van, Kildrake bringing up the rear.

"Gia."

Her heart leapt at the sound of his deep voice. She spun around, breathless. Hopeful.

"Take off that red sweater," Seth said. "You already attract the attention of every eye within a hundred feet of you. It's stupid to throw a spotlight on a beacon."

As he got into the SUV and slammed the door, she stood motionless, mad at him for having the last word . . .

Missing him already.

* * *

By the time Seth returned to the house in the woods, he was drained and chilled, wiped out after the adrenaline rush. The immediacy and alarm of chasing Gia had made him forget what was about to happen. Now, reality fisted him in the gut.

The house felt as empty as he did when he went inside and locked the door behind him. Gia had shut him down about talking things out last night. He'd assumed he would have another chance during their car ride together to St. Louis. She'd eliminated that possibility too.

For a few seconds, he just stood in the high-ceilinged living room. Gia's reading chair and ottoman were still drawn up to the fireplace, but the hearth was cold. He approached the coffee table and stared down at dozens of sketches of Gia's face. Not just her face. The two nudes he'd done lay on the top. He suddenly dropped down heavily on the couch, his fingers pressed against his eyelids.

He never had been able to capture the magic of her. Maybe his mistake all along had been trying.

Several days later, Seth still hadn't left the woods. It wasn't as if he had planned it that way. He just didn't seem to have the will to undertake the long road trip across the country. The idea of traveling alone in that SUV, of seeing familiar landmarks, of being plagued by memories . . . well, it froze him temporarily. The memories were here in the house too—in spades. It was masochistic of him to stay. He'd go and put all of this behind him.

Soon.

He knew from Charles that Gia had returned to Los Angeles safely and had moved into the studio's Bunker Hill condo downtown. He was relieved to hear that her mother had arrived to stay

with her and offer support during the trial. If he hadn't known from
Charles that Gia was whole and safe in L.A., he would have known
from the nightly news. Gia's return had refueled the simmering,
smoking media fire to a full-out inferno once again. On Wednesday, he saw the same clip of her walking up the steps of the criminal
justice building on a dozen different news shows. He hungrily ate
up the image of her each time. She wore sunglasses and her face was
pale, but she looked calm and resolute in the face of shouting reporters and microphones shoved rudely in her face. The rabid fervor
and callousness of the press's attitude toward her sickened him. He
watched as she ignored the chaos around her, listening and nodding
at something the plainclothes police escort said quietly near her ear.

I'm not one of your vulnerable, fragile actresses.

She wasn't even remotely in the same category.

The trial began.

It was being televised on several stations. Various news pro-
grams speculated that Gia could take the stand as early as Friday.
Privately via an e-mail to Seth, Charles confirmed there was a remote possibility of it, although the following Monday seemed more
likely. "Gia's holding up well under all the pressure, although she
seems strained," Charles wrote. "She asked me this morning if
you'd returned yet, and then seemed a little put out with me when
I said I wasn't sure."

Charles's enigmatic message galvanized Seth for some reason. It
wasn't rational. Gia's query, and Charles's mention of it in the e-mail
were random details. Still, it didn't stop him from starting a major
housecleaning and packing. He made another trip to the grocery store
to stock up the pantry and freezer for John and Jennifer, replacing
any items he and Gia had used during their stay. On Friday, he was
in the midst of his manic attempt to get the house back in its original
pristine condition when the perimeter security alarm began to beep.

A few seconds later, he opened the front door and walked out
into a cool, sunny day.

"What the hell?" he asked, both stunned and pleased to see his niece, Joy, getting out of the passenger side of a sedan. Her hair had completely grown out now after several rounds of chemotherapy. The chestnut strands fell around her shoulders and midback, gleaming in the bright sunlight. "What happened to Mexico?" he asked Everett Hughes, Joy's husband, as he uncoiled his tall body from the driver's seat. He wore a billed Greek fishing cap and a wool sweater that looked like it had fed a few moths some decent meals. Everett always wore hats to cover his signature streaked blond hair and to cast his iconic face in shadow.

"Mexico? Perfect weather and sunshine every day. So over-rated," Everett said.

Seth laughed, confused by their presence, but too pleased to see Joy's beautiful, smiling face and outstretched arms to worry at the moment. He gave his niece a big bear hug and peered down at her for a moment. She looked radiant from good health and her vacation tan. Still, he saw the edge of concern in her hazel eyes as she studied him back.

"You okay?" she asked him quietly before he had a chance to ask her the same.

"Oh. So Katie's been talking," he said, understanding dawning. Katie had obviously observed some of the chemistry and conflict occurring between Gia and him. The sparks between them during and after that kiss were sort of hard to disguise.

Katie had called him three times since Gia had left. Seth had thought he'd explained the circumstances of Gia's sudden absence calmly, but had heard the worry in Katie's reaction to the news. Katie's response had been to suggest that Seth come down to dinner or that they could come up to see him. When he'd refused, saying he needed some quiet time to work, Katie's concern had obviously only grown. Given the anxious look in Joy's eyes right at the moment, Katie had called in Joy for reinforcements.

"Talking is Katie's specialty, haven't you figured that out by now?" Everett joked, coming around the front of the car. He and Seth exchanged a handshake and a half hug.

"Yeah, I'll be talking to your sister about that," Seth told Everett darkly. "What does she think I am, a hysterical teenager or something?"

"It wasn't Katie's fault. She was worried about you," Joy insisted, giving first Seth and then Everett a repressive look. His wife's remonstrance didn't dent Everett's easy confidence in the slightest. He looped his arm around Joy's waist and pulled her against him. "When I heard about my *half brother*," Joy told Seth, resting her cheek against Everett's chest, "I thought a trip to Vulture's Canyon might be called for."

Alarm went through him. "Katie *didn't* blab about that and then not tell you the rest of—"

"She told me *all* about Gia Harris," Joy said. "She didn't consider her promise not to tell me about it until I came back to be binding once the secret of Gia's true identity was out and she had returned to L.A. She knows Everett and I aren't going to say anything about Gia being here with you . . . or about her leaving. And like I said, Katie was worried about you being up here all alone. I'm *glad* she told me."

Seth rolled his eyes.

"I can't believe you cut off your vacation," he said in a stiff tone. Everett's shrug seemed to say it all. *You can't stop family from worrying.*

Knowing it was a done deal at this point, Seth led them into the house. He entered several steps ahead of them and immediately went to the coffee table, where the sketches still lay. For the past few days, he'd found himself adding small nuances to Gia's expression.

Never satisfied.

Missing the real flesh-and-blood woman like hell.

He gathered up the nudes quickly and hid them away in his

leather portfolio before Everett or Joy could see them. Given their expressions, they had noticed his haste, but didn't comment.

Both of them stared down at the remaining sketches on the table though. He saw Joy's mouth fall open in amazement as she moved aside the sheets, studying the multiple sketches with an artist's empathy and skilled eye.

She looked up, meeting Seth's stare. She smiled tremulously.

"We did the right thing to come," she said.

"Well, it's great to see you," Seth sidestepped.

"That's not what I meant," Joy said. "We need to talk."

Everett cleared his throat. "I have a sudden urge to be in the . . . *kitchen*?" Everett asked Seth, pointing, clearly unsure as to where he suddenly needed to be.

Seth gave a tired nod.

"No, Everett. You stay. Seth needs to hear from you as much as he does me."

"*Really?*" Seth asked, unable to hide his exasperation.

"Really," Joy said, grabbing Everett's hand and sitting. Seth lowered to a chair. He really didn't want to discuss Gia with Joy right now, but he recognized that determined look on her typically serene face.

"You've fallen for an actress."

"Don't beat around the bush, Joy," Seth seethed.

"So it's true?" Joy asked, leaning forward slightly. "Katie said she thought she saw the signs. She said you had the look of a man caught in a trap of his own making."

Joy couldn't seem to repress her smile, despite Seth's glare.

"I'm sorry. But you have to admit, it is kind of ironic, Uncle Seth. Out of all the people in the world, you fall for Hollywood's 'It' Girl? *You*—who had all those glamorous actresses throwing themselves at you on movie sets for years, but you always abstained with an almost religious fervor?"

"I didn't laugh at you when you fell for Superstar here," Seth waved at Everett.

"No. But you did try to warn her—and me—off," Everett reasoned.

Seth shook his head wearily.

"I know why Katie blabbed about it," he mumbled. "She thinks it's karma, for judging you," he nodded at Everett. "I can still see her, putting me in my place for doubting you could make Joy happy."

And he *could* envision Katie perfectly in his memory, her stare scoring him:

"Shame on you," Katie had chastised. "You're one of the people responsible for making the fantasy. Surely you know there are real people behind the screen of illusion."

"So caring about Gia Harris hasn't been easy," Joy said quietly. "It would likely continue to be challenging in the future. Good things in life can be hard, Seth. You know that. They have to be fought for."

"I know that's been *your* story," he grated out, referring to their relationship. Everett and Joy had struggled to be together, despite Joy's history of cancer and her constant fear of it returning. No one could guarantee an outcome like that, but Everett had proved to her he wanted to be there, no matter what hurdles life presented. In addition, the couple had to maneuver making their personal life work when Everett was one of the most recognized faces on the planet, a superstar who eclipsed even Gia's meteoric rise. "It's different for me. It's different for Gia," Seth said.

"How?" Joy asked.

"Gia's very ambitious. She should be," Seth said fairly. "She's incredibly talented. She's got the energy to establish herself now, while she's young. She works nonstop."

"And still finds time to testify at that slimeball McClarin's trial," Everett added.

"She would never consider not testifying," Seth said flatly. "She's a workaholic, but she's got ethics that don't crumble when things get tough. And I'm not saying her ambition is a bad thing," Seth defended when Joy opened her mouth. He and Joy had been through a lot together, including her father's abandonment and her mother's lingering, painful death from cancer. They read each other extremely well. "I'm only pointing out that Gia's situation is different than Everett's. He can pick and choose his roles according to what both of you want, he can pace himself and preserve a private life with you."

"So that's it? You wouldn't want Gia to be so busy?" Everett asked bluntly.

"It's her life. I would never want anyone telling me how to run mine, and I wouldn't do that to her."

"Is that really your biggest concern though?" Joy asked. She looked a little confused as she studied him. "You wouldn't want a long-term relationship with someone who was so frequently away and working?"

"No," Seth replied sincerely.

"I didn't think so," Joy admitted. "You're so independent."

Seth just shrugged. He was glad to see Joy, but he felt restless having this conversation. Was there really anything to be gained by it? It was like Gia said. They were at an impasse.

"Can I get you guys something to drink?" he asked, hoping that if he fractured their focus on him, the topic would lose momentum.

"Because I've always been a little curious about your refusal to get involved with actresses," Joy said, ignoring his distraction attempt. "You've been so . . . *militant* about it. Some of those women have not only been very persistent, but extremely beautiful. And we all know you love women."

He gave her an impatient glance.

"I just meant, it seems odd that you never slipped up once or twice," Joy said. Seth looked away. "Or . . . *have* you?"

He cursed silently to himself, avoiding Joy's stare.

But the truth was, talking about Zoe Lindsay seemed nowhere near as taboo a topic as it had been in the past. The forbidden quality of that youthful indiscretion had faded, he realized, once he'd opened up to Gia about it.

"All right, if it's some kind of dramatic confession you want, here goes, detective," Seth growled. "I slipped up once, and it had nothing to do with Gia. Gia wasn't a *slipup*," he added darkly. He launched into a bare-bones explanation about Zoe Lindsay. By the time he was done, both Everett and Joy were staring at him in openmouthed disbelief.

"Why didn't you ever *tell* me?" Joy asked.

"I told you, the marriage lasted nine months. It wasn't worth mentioning," Seth said, grimacing.

"It was the basis for your distrust of actresses—and actors," Everett said. "I would think it's very relevant, especially when the topic is Gia Harris."

"Well, I mentioned it, didn't I?" Seth challenged.

"Don't be upset, Seth," Joy soothed, looking regretful about his agitation. "We're just trying to help. Really."

"I know it. But it's not as if Gia and I haven't discussed all this. We've been through it, and as you can see, we're apart."

"You told Gia about Zoe Lindsay?" Joy asked, amazed. "When you never even told me?"

He exhaled. "And it didn't make any difference, in the end. Zoe isn't the reason I don't think Gia and I would work out in Hollywood together. Gia is no Zoe Lindsay."

He blinked, hearing the bald truth of his spoken words more clearly than his private thoughts.

"I just don't think Hollywood romances work out. For *me*. I'm not talking about for you," he assured, glancing from Everett to Joy. "Everyone is different. You guys have obviously made things work, and I'm happy for you. You know that, right?"

They both nodded.

"This is about me, and I'm trying to take ownership of that. I don't want to have my privacy invaded. I don't want to share Gia with the world when I want to have a private moment with her," he suddenly said emphatically. "There. I've said it. I'm a selfish asshole."

For a moment, Joy just studied him. He felt prickly under her stare.

"You know," Joy began slowly. "I didn't think a relationship was right for me after what I went through with Mom's cancer and Dad leaving, and then being diagnosed myself. It was a personal belief I felt very strongly about. I *still* believe it, in many ways."

Not only Seth but Everett, too, gave Joy nonplussed looks at her admission.

"I'm sorry, honey," she told her husband apologetically, grabbing his hand and squeezing it. "I just mean that a belief like that—or a fear—doesn't just vanish over night. You take one day at a time, and make a vow to have faith with every new day. It still scares me to death," she told Everett quietly, "the idea of the cancer coming back and you having to endure all that with me, like Seth and I did with my mom . . . like Seth did for me. I've learned I can control the worry, and my love for you is thousands of times stronger than the fear," she assured him, her eyes glistening as she locked gazes with Everett. "But even so . . . there's only one thing that could have made me take the risk and enter a relationship, given my misgivings."

"What?" Everett asked intently, staring down into her eyes. Suddenly, Seth felt like a third wheel sitting there.

"You," Seth said, standing abruptly.

Both of them blinked and looked up at him.

"It wasn't just falling in love that changed your mind," Seth said to Joy. "It was falling in love with *Everett*. Because of who *he* is, you took the chance."

Joy nodded, her eyes shining with compassion.

"Yeah," Seth muttered to himself, thinking. He started to walk out of the room. "There's stuff to eat and drink in the fridge. Help yourself. I'm going to take a walk."

"See you in a bit," Joy called.

He walked out the front door and breathed in a lungful of fresh, bracing air.

Seth got what Joy was trying to tell him now. Every rule was meant to be broken.

Once, *maybe* . . . for a very good reason.

And only for the right person.

By the time he entered the house again after a long ramble in the woods, he felt better. Clearer and more resolved as to what he was going to do, at any rate. It was time for him to return to Los Angeles. Gia had left him with the impression that things were over between them, so there was no guarantee of success in trying to see her again. But Seth knew one thing. A big part of the reason she'd agreed that things wouldn't work is because he'd been leading her to believe he wasn't willing to try.

His opinion on that had changed. He wasn't exactly sure *how* they could make it work, but there had to be *something* they could manage. He had the time it took for the return road trip across the country to come up with something to say to convince her that they should take the risk.

The television was on. He came to a halt on the threshold of the living room. Everett and Joy were both still in there, their backs to him. Everett was kneeling before the stone fireplace, rolling up newspapers in preparation to lay a fire. Joy stood next to him, her arm partially extended with the remote control in her hand. Seth's attention was caught by what appeared to be a glitzy celebrity entertainment show when he heard the female host say Gia's name.

". . . just hours ago, the mystery of Gia Harris's location for these past few weeks was solved. But now, *Hot Topics* has the shocking exclusive story revealing how Gia's choice of companion for her getaway may mean trouble for Madeline Harrington, the Los Angeles County district attorney, and her case against mega-billionaire religious leader Sterling McClarin. As KBHT News revealed earlier today, Gia has been snuggled up in a wooded retreat with her secret lover . . ."

A tingling sensation of alarm started down Seth's spine when he saw his own image on the screen—a shot from a documentary he'd been asked to do years back. He tensed into high-alert status.

". . . Seth Hightower, Oscar-winning special effects–makeup artist for blockbuster films such as *Maritime*." The clip altered to him in a tuxedo accepting one of his Oscars along with several members of his team. "Why would the discovery of the identity of Gia's handsome boyfriend be worrisome to Harrington and her team of attorneys?" The video behind the host changed to separate clips of both Seth and Gia. "*Hot Topics* has been working overtime to bring that stunning answer to our watchers," the host said with a seriousness Seth would have found comical in any other situation. "Previously, Seth Hightower was also involved with this woman Dharma Jana—"

"*Fuck* me," Seth muttered viciously when he saw the photo of the young actress he'd told Gia about, the one who had made him extra wary of pseudoreligious organizations that took advantage of the vulnerable. Joy spun around at his cursing. Everett had stood as the salacious news story unfolded, and now he turned to Seth as well.

"Seth! I didn't realize you were back. This is awful," Joy said in a choked voice, but Seth waved her into silence as he stepped into the room, his attention on the television.

"Jana was found dead of exposure in a local park in 2011. Although police saw no evidence whatsoever of foul play, Hightower insisted it was nothing less than murder by the God's Chosen Few Church, a religious organization founded by Vladimir Tomoriv. Hightower reputedly harassed Tomoriv ruthlessly in the months following Dharma Jana's death. According to the minister, Hightower was, quote, 'intimidating and physically threatening.' Only when Tomoriv threatened to go to the police to get a restraining order did Hightower finally stop his relentless harassment."

"*Harrassment* my ass," Seth said scathingly, his incredulity mounting to unforeseen levels as Tomoriv's handsome face appeared on the screen. *Could this fiction possibly grow any more ludicrous?* he wondered in shocked outrage. He'd known the Hollywood entertainment shows thrived on lurid gossip that usually was only loosely based on fact. But *this* was downright lie-mongering.

And all to a purpose, he realized, a chill going through him.

"I didn't put two and two together until I saw the clips earlier today about Gia Harris and Seth Hightower being involved," Tomoriv was telling the camera in his Russian-accented voice, the liquid dark eyes that had mesmerized thousands now holding the attention of millions of viewers. "I'm familiar with Hightower because he was involved with one of the members of my church, God's Chosen Few. When Sister Dharma Jana died under tragic, but accidental circumstances, Hightower irrationally blamed the church that had nurtured and cared for Dharma as one of its own children. He harassed me repeatedly. Seth Hightower has an ax to grind against nontraditional religious organizations. I hadn't really been thinking much about the Sterling McClarin trial—my involvement with my flock and daily solitary meditations in nature keep me away from the clamor and taint of the everyday world—but once I heard Seth Hightower is involved with Gia Harris, I had to consider my obligation to speak out the truth. People like Seth Hightower are enemies against our right to worship as we choose. If he's been involved with Gia Harris, sharing his ideas with her, then . . . who's to say?" Tomoriv arched one sleek black brow. "Maybe there's more to Gia Harris's grudge against the leader of another nontraditional religious group—Sterling McClarin—than any of us had considered before?"

"Holy shit," Everett muttered, looking at the screen with a vaguely sick expression on his face.

"*Nontraditional religious group*," Seth growled, suddenly feeling like he could spit fire. "This is the biggest ocean of crap I've ever heard in my life!"

"I know," Joy said, turning to Seth. Her face was tight with worry. "I remember you telling me about Dharma Jana. You met with the police after she was found dead, right? And didn't a reporter question you about Dharma's death? That article must have been the kernel of truth from where they sprang all these lies. When the police were no help, you *did* go to Tomoriv and confront him with your suspicions, didn't you? I remember how frustrated you were when he fed you a bunch of new-age mumbo jumbo when you asked about Dharma's extreme weight loss and the circumstances leading up to her death," Joy recalled anxiously.

"Once," Seth uttered with a harsh bark of laughter. "I saw Tomoriv *once*, for all of three minutes, before he put a locked door between us. That's the extent of my *harassment* of that asshole."

"Did you threaten him?" Joy asked, her eyes looking huge in her face.

"No. I don't go around threatening people, you know that."

"Tomoriv was likely threatened by the size of your biceps and your scowl," Everett said under his breath, thinking. He blinked, noticing that scowl present now on Seth's face. "What? That's not a real shock, is it? Most men with half a brain are intimidated by you. *I* was when I first met you on the set of *Maritime*. Forget how much it amplified when I started seeing Joy," Everett stated baldly. He saw Joy's disbelieving look. "I just meant that it's not Seth's style to threaten physical violence, but to a weasel like Tomoriv, just his presence can be intimidating enough to prick his pride and put up his defenses . . . and eventually spawn this pile of horseshit," Everett said scornfully, waving at the screen.

"McClarin and his crew are behind this, mark my words," Seth said. "Tomoriv is just their tool. McClarin's back was up against the wall with Gia about to testify soon. She'll be a sincere and credible witness. Up until now, telling the truth is the only reason people could come up with as to why she would testify against McClarin. Now another reason has been planted in their minds, and it'll be hard to make it disappear."

"The jury will be isolated from this gossip, Seth," Joy reasoned.

"Ideally," Seth agreed. "But even if McClarin is found guilty, his lawyers will appeal. It'll be impossible after this kind of exposure to find a jury that hasn't been tainted by false rumors against Gia. They'll linger, even after they're inevitably disproved. And Gia is the linchpin of Madeline's case against McClarin."

"He's right," Everett said, looking unhappy about that fact.

"Somebody leaked that Gia has been here with me, and that was the fuel McClarin has been waiting for," he said distractedly, his mind working. He fastened on possible candidates, ruling out this possibility and that one. When he came up with the likely answer, it didn't help to reassure him much. He'd inform Charles immediately to see if they could contain the threat. "McClarin must have been thrilled when he realized he could link Gia—through me—to even the most bogus, trumped-up insinuation that Gia might have a grudge against *nontraditional religious organizations*," Seth said, his mouth twisting bitterly.

"Where are you going?" Joy asked when he pulled his phone from his pocket and stalked across the room.

"I need to contact Charles," Seth said, pausing and turning back. "I need to find out if this really is a threat to Madeline's case."

"You didn't do anything wrong, Seth," Joy said, stepping toward him. Everett grabbed the remote from her stiff hand and turned down the volume on a loud commercial. "This is all just an outrageous bid for ratings. It'll die down when there's no fuel to back it up. You know that."

"But it's because of *me* this is happening, even if it's in an indirect sense. Maybe I should have mentioned Dharma Jana to Madeline—"

"Why would you?" Everett asked incredulously. "Only a whisper of what was said on that show was true. You had no reason to think this Tomoriv jerk would make your concerned visit about the death of a friend and coworker into a 'harassment charge' or a conspiracy theory," Everett said using air quotes. "There's no proof or witnesses to that supposed harassment charge, right?"

"I don't know how there could be, since it never happened," Seth said.

"One honest reporter is going to discover there's no police report of the incident in about an hour flat. By that time, Madeline will have time to respond with the voice of reason," Everett continued. "*Trust me*, these sensationalistic news stories that have no fuel to back them up flame out fast."

"I know none of it is the truth, but I've still put Madeline in a bad place. And worse, Gia," Seth added with a sinking feeling. What if all this made her hesitant while she testified? What if— God forbid—this whole crackpot incident really did end up spiraling out of control, and McClarin was somehow acquitted?

More than anything, he wanted reassurance that Gia was okay. He *needed* firsthand proof of that.

Fucking Hollywood, land of the vampires and soul suckers.

"What can we do to help?" Everett asked.

He was reminded that as a megastar, Everett had survived his fair share of media shitstorms. Seth was glad of the practical question. It whipped his brain into action mode.

"I know it's a lot to ask, but can you and Joy drive my friend

Alexi's car back to Los Angeles? That way, I can catch a plane tonight."

"Not a problem," Joy said. "We'll return the rental car and take Alexi's back home."

"Yeah, we've still got vacation time left. A road trip will be great. Don't worry about us, or Alexi's car," Everett added.

"Thanks," Seth said sincerely. What the hell would he have done if this bizarre situation had arisen and they hadn't arrived? His phone started to ring. He glanced at the number.

"It's Charles," he told them grimly, bracing himself for bad news.

Twenty-two

Gia studied her phone anxiously for the hundredth time Friday night, but there was no return phone call or text from Seth. The too-familiar ache of worry and panic swelled in her belly. She hadn't been able to eat since Charles had pulled her into a private office at the courthouse during a recess early this afternoon and showed her that outrageous lie being passed off as a news story. They'd exposed Seth's helplessness over that young actress who had gotten involved with a cult. They'd twisted the story until it didn't even vaguely resemble the truth anymore. It was desperate, malicious mudslinging.

God. It was like all Seth's worries about associating with a movie star were coming true. This was a nightmare.

"They can't get away with this!" she'd told Charles, shivers of dread crawling along her arms as the tabloid story concluded.

"Is there any truth to it?" Charles had asked.

"No! Except the part about us being together. Who could have leaked the fact that Seth and I were in the Shawnee National Forest?"

"Only you, Seth, Madeline, Alex and me knew where you went after we engineered your escape. Not even the deputy who came to get you knew your exact previous location in the area. Didn't you tell me your driver Jim came to get you though?"

"Yes, but Jim would never leak that information!"

"Someone did. We compartmentalized the knowledge of where you were. There were some who knew Seth was going to disguise you, but they didn't know why you were being disguised or your final destination."

Gia had thought fleetingly of telling Charles they'd exposed their secret to Rill and Katie Pierce, but immediately dismissed any suspicion in their direction for the leak. Seth was like family to them, and he trusted Rill and Katie implicitly.

"What about this Tomoriv guy and this girl, Dharma Jana? Do you know anything about that?" Charles asked, grabbing a pen and sliding a notebook across the desk. He began to rapidly take notes.

"Yes. I know that Seth knew her from a movie set a few years ago and was worried about her involvement in Tomoriv's cult. She was new to Hollywood and very vulnerable. He'd felt helpless watching her sinking deeper into the cult's clutches. He went to the police after she died to report his concerns about that cult's involvement, but they couldn't do anything, given the circumstances of her death. Seth never threatened or harassed that cult leader though. That's a bald-faced lie. *And*, he never saw Dharma romantically, like they said in that story. You know Seth. He doesn't get involved with actresses. *Everyone* knows it."

Charles had looked up from his rapid note taking when he'd heard her voice cracking.

"Gia, don't let this get to you. This is a sensationalist ploy to divert public opinion, most likely manipulated by McClarin or his followers. The last thing we need is for you to get frazzled by it. That's why they're doing it. Don't give them what they want."

"But Madeline will—"

"Madeline sees this for what it is too. What we need to focus on now is getting all the information we can and coming up with a strategy for how to respond."

"You need to call Seth. *I* need to. He'll hate this. You know how private he is."

"As soon as we finish talking, I will. Until we can figure things out though," Charles had said with a sharp glance, "I don't want you two planning to see each other. Things are too hot for that right now. Do you understand?"

She'd agreed to Charles's request grudgingly earlier that day, only because she didn't think it was an issue. According to what Charles had said this morning, Seth was still in Illinois.

Besides . . . after this whole fiasco, the last place Seth would want to be was anywhere near Gia.

Again, she checked her cell phone then flopped back on the bed, feeling both wired and exhausted. The United Studios' Bunker Hill condominium was comfortable and luxurious, but she missed the familiarity of home.

She missed being snuggled up in the woods with Seth.

Still, she recognized and appreciated Seth's point in having her stay in the downtown tower. Not only was it conveniently located for the trial, her police escorts liked the setup much more in the high-rise. It was easier for them to secure Gia's surroundings there. The word of where she was staying had only started to leak out on their return trip from the courthouse that night. Even so, the building security was keeping the drive and the lobby of the tower clear of reporters. Only residents and guests were allowed on the elevators to the condominiums.

She was secure here. But she was also trapped, she realized miserably.

Seth was right about all this fame and notoriety. Maybe she *was* just too young and naïve to get how destructive a force it could be.

A soft tap came at the bedroom door.

"Come in," she called.

Gia's mother, Susan Moreno, opened the door and stepped over the threshold carrying a tray.

"Room service," her mother said with calm cheerfulness. Gia forced a smile and partially sat up in bed.

"Have I told you how much I appreciate you being here?" Gia asked as her mother set the tray down on the bedside table.

Her mom gave her an arch look. "Several times. More importantly," she said as she poured some steaming water into a cup, "have I told you how proud I am of you for testifying in this trial?"

Gia started in surprise. "You are?" she asked, sitting up in bed slowly.

Her mom nodded. She poured a packet of Splenda into the drink and stirred it before handing the cup and saucer to Gia. "Herbal tea to help you sleep. You're strung tight as a wire," she explained before she sat on the edge of the bed and patted Gia's knee. "In fact, I owe you a lot of 'I'm proud of yous' and just as many 'I'm sorrys.'"

Gia blinked in surprise.

"I know I haven't always seemed supportive of your choice to do films. It seemed different when you were on Broadway. Hollywood seems more . . . *dangerous* somehow. When McClarin was arrested, and all this craziness started, my worry over you being a film actress only amplified. As a result, I know I haven't been very supportive of you. I haven't been fair," Susan said regretfully. "I haven't told you how proud I've been for all you've accomplished in the past few years. But I have been proud. I *am*."

"Why are you telling me this now?"

"Watching you these past few days. Admiring your courage."

"Thanks, Mom," Gia said, moved by the unexpected compliment.

"Your father and I—and Stephen," she added, referring to Gia's stepfather, "we all just worry so much."

"I know," Gia said, her eyes burning. She felt paper-thin after what had happened with that story breaking. Her normal defenses and resilience seemed to have abandoned her. "The truth? On a day like today, I doubt the wisdom of my career choices as well."

"Don't," her mother said resolutely. "*Not* because of that story. After watching these court proceedings over the past few days and seeing that swine Sterling McClarin up close, after witnessing everything you're going through, I know you must feel like you're battling a storm in a ship full of holes. But don't give up. On any of it. I've never been prouder of you in my life, knowing what you're doing, seeing you face this . . . this damn *persecution* by the press. Even though I agree with Charles and Madeline," she added grimly. "It's most likely McClarin and his faction that are behind all that."

Gia smiled at the evidence of her mother's sober fierceness. She hadn't seen her formidable game face since she was a corporate lawyer years ago.

"Now," her mom said, clapping her hands briskly. "Tell me about Seth Hightower." She noticed Gia's stunned look and fading smile at the topic change. "I noticed the expression on your face when we watched that sleazy show's video clip together." Gia exhaled slowly and set her cup of tea on the table. "I assume that part of the story is true? You were indeed in a house in the woods with this man, Seth Hightower, avoiding the press?"

Gia nodded. She pinched her eyelids shut as emotion swelled in her breast. "Oh God, Mom. He must hate me by now," she confessed shakily. Her mother clasped her hand.

"Surely he realizes you had nothing to do with this ridiculous story being circulated."

"He's too smart not to have realized *that* in a split second. That's not why he's probably wishing right now he'd never laid eyes on me."

"Does his opinion mean that much to you?" her mom asked quietly.

The question triggered an unstoppable rush of emotion.

"*Yes,*" she gasped. "I'm in love with him."

Her mother pushed back the hair off Gia's face and said

soothingly, "Okay, this sounds major. Better start from the beginning. Take your time."

The whole story came spilling out of Gia: the strong connection
she and Seth had felt years ago upon their first encounter, his reaction to discovering she was an actress and refusal to contact her
again, the consultant disguise work he occasionally did in legal and
criminal cases, and how he'd been assigned to help her disappear
off the map. She left out Zoe Lindsay's name and provided only the
sketchiest details, but it was enough to give her mother the impression that Seth definitely had his reasons for avoiding actresses. She
described his independence and love of privacy, his determination
not to let the blind greed for power and fame that ran at epidemic
levels in Hollywood taint his creative drive and love of his work.
When she mentioned Seth's contention that because of the clash of
Gia's ambition and his need to protect his private life and artistic
drive, they wouldn't "work" together, her mom paused her tearful
ramble with a hand on her forearm.

"Do you think that's true, Gia? On your part?" she asked.

"I suppose," she said miserably. "I couldn't give up any of my
career dreams for a man. It's not who I am. More importantly, it's
not who Seth is to ever ask or expect me to." She blinked when
there was no response and focused her bleary eyes. Her mother
looked grave.

"Is part of that because you've never forgiven me for giving up
my career . . . for believing I gave *you* up as well, in order to marry
Stephen and move to San Diego?"

Gia held her breath. Her skin started to prickle. She and her
mother hadn't had this discussion since Gia was sixteen. Even then,
it hadn't been as much of an argument as it had been Gia saying a
lot of things she later regretted and her mother reciprocating.

"It's not like that," Gia said. "It was never my place to judge
you anyway. That was wrong of me."

"You're my daughter. You were affected most by my decision. I can't imagine who deserves an opinion on the matter more," her mom responded evenly. Gia opened her mouth to backpedal, but her mother squeezed her forearm gently, silencing her. "My choices were my own, Gia. *I* think I've made the right decision. I'm happy with my life."

"I'm so glad," Gia said sincerely, swiping at a wet cheek.

"I know you are. The thing of it is, I want your choices to be your own, as well."

"They are," Gia assured, a little taken aback. "Who else's would they be?"

"A knee-jerk reaction isn't a choice, honey," Susan said. "Making a decision about your romantic relationship and career based on the fact that it's the opposite of what *I* did isn't the same as a well-thought-out choice. That's being a slave to your past hurts."

Gia just stared for a moment, her mouth hanging open. "You think I should sacrifice my career to be with Seth?"

"*No,*" her mom scoffed. "Not everything is black and white. Maybe you think it was in my case, but it wasn't in my book. You were too young to realize it, but my job was grueling. It took its toll on me. And as far as sacrifices go, we *all* make them in order to get the things we want."

Dread settled on her as she sat there cross-legged on the bed, her thoughts swirling until she felt a little dizzy with them.

"I was wrong to run away from him like that, wasn't I?" Gia asked dully. "He wanted to talk, but I just thought it was postponing the inevitable. I wanted to avoid the pain, but it didn't work. Not really."

"If Seth wanted to talk before, he still will."

She looked at her mom's compassionate face. "Even after what happened today with that story breaking?" she asked dubiously.

Her mom leaned forward and gave her a hug. "I can't say for

sure. But from what I've heard about Seth so far, I'd guess *especially* after today."

Her mother squeezed her extra hard and then leaned back. She became all brisk and businesslike, but Gia hadn't missed the way she had furtively wiped a tear off her cheek.

"Now, you eat this salad, drink your tea and try to get some rest," Susan insisted, fussing with the tray of food. "You said Charles and some of the team are going to be here bright and early tomorrow to go over your testimony again. You need the rest this weekend, given how stressful next week will be."

She followed her mother's instructions, knowing she was right. Next week would be difficult. But after she'd eaten, cleaned up and gone to bed, sleep still wouldn't come.

As she lay in bed, Gia thought about the conversation with her mother, experiencing a mixture of hope, anguish and doubt. She couldn't help but consider how much Seth despised *everything* that news story typified, including the blatant dishonesty and the crass, aggressive invasion of his private life. She'd been the one to make him a target of that, however unintentionally.

There was also the glaring fact that he wasn't returning her phone calls. And that even if the opportunity came up, Madeline and Charles had both insisted that she and Seth not see each other until this media storm and the trial ended. To Gia, that seemed like forever. That gaping period of time would give Seth more time to distance himself and validate his doubts about being involved with her.

Meanwhile, she was stuck here in this condo, trapped in the web of her own life. She had a wild urge to walk away from it all: this tower, where she felt like a prisoner, the trial . . . Hollywood.

You should be careful what you wish for, she recalled Seth telling her with that sober, weighty manner he possessed.

He'd been right.

And she missed him so much.

* * *

The next morning, she felt hollow inside, but her anguish had been contained. All she wanted to do was get this damn trial over with. She had never resented Sterling McClarin more. Instead of being ready when the prosecution team started to arrive at the condominium, she stalled; the motivation she used to feel to get through the gargantuan trial was dwindling to mere fumes. She had asked her mother to tell her when Charles arrived. The meeting wouldn't really get started until he was there anyway.

Gia brushed a little more blush onto her cheeks, but finally gave up. She looked pale from lack of sleep and stress, and nothing in her makeup bag was going to help that. Her mom rapped on the bathroom door. "Charles just arrived, Gia."

Gia opened the door. "Thanks, Mom," she said, giving her mother a brief hug. She felt especially close to her since last night.

Before she left the bathroom, however, she received a phone call from her part-time housekeeper that sent mental alarms going off in her head.

"Hi," Gia greeted Charles anxiously several minutes later when she entered the living area. Charles was talking intently to her mother near the entryway, while several other attorneys were seated in the living room. It looked as if Susan had already distributed coffee to the other members of the legal team and her police escort for the day. Gia felt as if she were surrounded by men and women in dark suits these days.

"Hi. How are you doing? Get any sleep?" Charles asked her.

"Yeah. I'm good," she lied levelly. "Do you think I could have a word in private?"

She was anxious to discuss the troubling phone call she'd just received from her housekeeper, but she also was desperate to ask him if he'd heard from Seth. She pointed in the direction of her bedroom suite. Charles had already become familiar with the layout of the condominium. Madeline and her team had held a few meetings there, before and after trial sessions. As the key witness, Gia had been the focus of a lot of preparation, and the condo where she was staying was centrally located for the prosecution's team meetings.

"Sure," Charles said. "Go on back. I just want to grab my coffee and a file I wanted to show you. Do you want coffee?"

Gia winced. "Better make it decaf," she said before she started back down the hallway.

Charles touched her shoulder. "It's all going to be okay, Gia," he assured her quietly.

Her smile was brittle. She must look like a nervous wreck for him to say that so feelingly.

In the bedroom, she left the door partially open and sat down in one of the armchairs in the sitting area of the large suite.

"Come in," she said when she heard Charles's knock. She heard the door close and looked up expectantly. Her face fell.

"Oh . . . I thought it was Charles," she said, flustered. A slouching, heavy-set blond lawyer with a large nose walked toward her. She wasn't familiar with him. He handed her a cup of coffee, which she took automatically. It wasn't the fact that she didn't know the man that had her puzzled. It seemed as if she'd seen several faces come and go on Madeline's prosecution team. Sometimes lawyers did background work and she rarely saw them, but they showed up at meetings to report on some technical aspect of the case. She was just put off at the moment because it seemed odd for Charles to send a stranger back to her private quarters without an explanation.

"Charles had to step out for a moment. They all did."

A prickle of unease went down her spine. *Something's not right.*

Was it fear she was feeling? *No*, that wasn't it. She looked into the man's flat brown eyes. *What the hell was happening?*

She stood up slowly.

"Gia."

The prickle of anxiety became a cascade of shivers. A shudder went through her.

"It can't be . . ."

"It's okay. It's me," he reached for her.

The man's rounded back straightened. Her eyes sprang wide as he seemed to grow several inches right in front of her. He transformed, and suddenly he wasn't a stranger at all.

"Seth?"

He nodded.

"*Oh my God*." She set the coffee cup down too hard, coffee splashing onto her knuckles in her haste. She rushed to him, clutching him around his waist. His arms surrounded her. If a shadow of doubt lingered, it evaporated at the sound of his familiar, low chuckle.

"Put on a few pounds since I saw you a few days ago, haven't you?" she asked with a hysterical bark of laughter as she squeezed him tighter. He was obviously wearing a body suit that added fifty pounds to his lean frame. A partial prosthetic on his cheeks and nose made him look heavier too. One hand cupped her head.

"Maybe I was binge eating. I was a little upset."

"Seth, I'm *so* sorry," burst out of her throat. She looked up at him. Her brain was still vibrating with shock. "I've been trying to contact you to tell you—"

"I know," he said, cradling her jaw, his thumb wiping away a single tear that had fallen on her cheek. His actions were tender and so familiar, an ache rose in her. He was *really* here. He caught another tear. "And you don't have anything to be sorry for. None of this is your fault. You're the last person who would have wanted this to happen. I know that."

"But if it weren't for me—"

"*Shh,*" he soothed, his warm breath brushing against her mouth. "Everything's going to be all right. Everything."

Her chest swelled with wild hope. Happiness. His lips brushed against hers, and the feeling swelled tight enough to burst.

"I'm so glad you're here," she whispered, catching his scent, something the disguise couldn't hide from a knowing nose. She nibbled hungrily at his mouth. There was no disguise for his taste either.

"I'm glad to see you too," he assured her, dipping his head to deepen their kiss. She moaned, a ripple of pure, powerful euphoria went through her.

"But *how*?" Gia asked when Seth lifted his head.

"After talking things over with Madeline and Charles, they started to get the bigger picture of what was happening. Not only with that story breaking, but what was going on between us. After a lot of back-and-forth on the matter, I managed to convince them it would be in their best interests if they let us see each other."

"As long as you looked nothing like Seth Hightower when you did it?"

"Exactly. Madeline wants to avoid that at all costs. So we came up with this little plan last night to fool any reporters. Should anyone spot us, they would just see various members of the prosecution team arriving for a quick consultation with the witness before her testimony begins. We all took different entrances and left in varying groups in order to throw off any possible watchers. We made sure there was at least one identifiable member of the prosecution team with each group that arrived and left."

Gia lowered her hands to his biceps and squeezed again. Amazed laughter bubbled out of her throat. He wasn't wearing any padding here. The bulging, dense muscle *definitely* belonged to Seth.

"How were you able to convince Madeline? From a couple things she and Charles said, I thought they were dead set against the idea of us seeing each other until after the trial."

"I told Madeline that I thought it would affect your ability to be as convincing a witness as possible. I told her your heart wouldn't be in it if you didn't get a chance to settle your anxiety with me first."

"My anxiety?" she asked shakily.

He nodded, caressing her cheek.

"I know you by now, Gia," he said quietly. "I know you care, even if we'd parted ways. I knew you would be worried."

A tremor of unease went through her when he mentioned their parting ways like it was an established fact. Which it was, she supposed. Still . . . he was here right now.

"Worried doesn't begin to describe it," she whispered. "I feel so miserable about this happening. I know how protective and bad you felt about Dharma Jana. To have her photo plastered everywhere—and her sad story—and all those lies they told about you. It was *obscene*." Her voice broke. "I thought you'd never want to talk to me again."

"Look at me," he said, tilting up her face with his hand. She bit off her anguish. Even through his brilliant disguise, she felt as if she really was looking at Seth in that moment, seeing his quiet, mountain-sized strength. "There's never going to be a time that I don't want to talk to you. Do you understand me?"

She bit at her trembling lip to still it and nodded. He rubbed the pad of his thumb along her cheekbone. Her rising guilt made the caress almost unbearably sweet.

"But you don't know what I know," she insisted.

His caressing finger paused. "What do you mean?"

"This really *is* my fault. Or at least I think it is."

"Are you referring to Jim?"

She blinked in shock. "How do you know about Jim?"

"I know he was responsible for the story breaking. I told Charles I suspected it. Charles sent a deputy over to question Jim."

She took a moment to absorb the news that Seth had already suspected Jim's complicity. "I just spoke to Anna, my housekeeper," she said shakily. "I haven't even told Charles about it yet. Anna arrived at my house today after a two-day absence. She only comes a few days a week. Jim is a live-in though. He's out in the carriage house. Anna cleans out there as well once a week. She told me a few minutes ago that Jim's apartment had been cleared out. He's gone, without even leaving a note."

Seth looked grim. "I'm not surprised. The deputy couldn't get anything out of him, but Jim must have realized someone was suspicious, and it was just a matter of time before you knew what he'd done."

"Charles told me that he, Madeline, Alex, you and I were the only ones who knew originally where we were. But then I gave Jim the information. I trusted him," she said slowly.

"He was probably bribed or blackmailed. I told you that McClarin and his people would find a crack in the armor. That's what spiders do," Seth said, his mouth slanting in anger.

"Then I *am* the one to blame for all of this," she said, the certainty of what was formerly just a suspicion hitting her in a wave of misery. "I'm the one who called someone on the outside when you specifically told me not to, all because I couldn't stand the idea of saying good-bye to you in that airport."

"Gia, it's okay," Seth said, his fingertips moving on her cheek.

"No, it's not. You had things planned so that there was no chance of a break in the security bubble you'd created. I ruined that. I caused your worst nightmare. It's everything you suspected could happen, being with a celebrity. Forget nightmare," she mumbled. "It's like some kind of cosmic joke."

"You trusted Jim. He never gave you any reason not to until now. Jim would have picked you up at the airport in Los Angeles.

There would have been no reason for you to think it would be any different to have him drive you in St. Louis. And there's *no* way you—or any of us—could ever imagine McClarin could twist that relatively innocent bit of information about us being in the woods together into this story. Not even Jim could have ever suspected *that*. He's one of many strands in McClarin's web. As for my supposed nightmare, I'll survive it all. As you can see, I haven't wilted. And I'm standing right here, Gia." She glanced up and met his stare doubtfully. Hopefully. "It's like I said before," he rasped, his fingers massaging her temple in a soothing, circular motion. "There's never going to be a time that I don't want to see you. There's never going to be a time that I don't want to touch you. Nothing is going to change that. Not Tomoriv, not McClarin, not the press or anyone else trying to spin a story to trap us." He touched his mouth to her lips. "Your job isn't going to change my mind about that. Neither is my history," he added steadfastly before his mouth covered hers.

A moment later, they came up for air. Gia realized dazedly she was pressing so close to him, it was like she wanted to crawl inside. She couldn't believe this was happening. She loosened his tie, squeezing at his hard biceps, desperate to feel the real Seth.

"I hate this damn disguise," she said.

"Then why don't I get out of it?"

"But what about the others?" she asked with a mixture of wariness and hope.

"What I said earlier is true. They're all gone," he said. "Including your mother. Only the guard is left, and he's outside in the hallway."

A smile pulled at her lips as she continued loosening his silk tie. "You thought of everything, didn't you? Spymaster to the last. Do we really have privacy for the next few hours?"

"No," he said, his hands moving in a delicious rhythm over the sides of her rib cage, brushing against her breasts. "I've given Madeline and Charles my promise that we won't risk seeing each other after this one time until they agree it's safe or the trial is over."

"*No,*" she whispered heatedly.

"I think it would be best, Gia, and only fair to Madeline. Most of all for Jeannie," he said, referring to McClarin's victim. "We all want to put McClarin away, right? But there is good news."

"What?"

"They agreed to give us until tomorrow morning together. No interruptions. So we have *more* than a few hours of privacy."

Her heart leapt with excitement, but a thought occurred. "What about my mom?"

"Don't worry. I spoke to Joshua. Turns out United Studios owns several units in this building for business visitors. There was an empty one on this very floor. Your mom is staying there tonight. She seemed very glad to accommodate us."

"I can't believe you planned all this," Gia said.

"We've been at it almost nonstop since I saw that damn story on TV yesterday. My disguise must have been the worst of my planning. I fooled Charles and Madeline, but you recognized me right away."

She smiled full-out for the first time in nearly a week, going up on her tiptoes to kiss him hungrily. "I recognized you because it's *you*. The disguise is brilliant, as usual. Now get the hell out of it," she insisted as she jerked his suit jacket off his shoulders.

Seth laughingly restrained her from ripping the disguise off him, explaining he needed to be careful about the prosthetic removal because he had to don it again to leave in the morning. He'd gone to the living room, where he retrieved a soft leather briefcase. He'd retreated to the bathroom to become Seth again.

Now Gia waited for him in the empty living room, her anxiety mounting by the second. She tried to drink her coffee, but it cooled as she obsessed over everything he'd said since he had arrived. He'd said that he was here because of that malicious story. He'd known she'd be worried . . . frantic. It had become his mission to convince Charles and Madeline to let him see her, and they'd allowed it, because they thought her anxiety over Seth might preoccupy her to the point that her testimony was affected.

But Charles, and Madeline, and that damned trial aside, what did his being here *really* mean for Seth and Gia?

She was startled from her ruminations when she heard the bathroom door open in the distance. She stood shakily from where she sat on the couch, her anticipation razor sharp. He came down the hallway and into the living room.

Christ, he was beautiful. He might be the expert on transforming other people, but it was a sin, as far as she was concerned, for Seth ever to be the one disguised. He wore jeans and a simple dark red T-shirt that highlighted his lean, muscular torso and the rich color of his skin. His hair was still slightly damp from his shower. He was barefoot, she realized breathlessly. As if he didn't want to be bothered with putting on socks and shoes when he'd be removing them again so quickly?

"Why are you looking at me like that?" he asked quietly as he approached her.

"You look so beautiful."

One eyebrow went up in a wry expression. He came to a halt with the coffee table between them. His gaze lowered over her. A rush of warmth followed.

"I'm not the one who is beautiful around here." He twitched his hand. "Come here."

She walked around the coffee table, holding her breath the whole time. He put his arms around her waist and pulled her against him. She pressed her cheek to his solid chest, exhaling and then inhaling again choppily. The smell of soap and Seth's clean skin filled her nose. Delicious. She felt his fingers beneath her chin, urging her to look up at him. Emotion flooded her at the vision of his unshielded amber eyes.

"I hated those contacts," she said through a constricted throat.

His gaze narrowed on her mouth, and she knew what he was about to do. She wanted it too. Almost as much as her next breath.

But . . .

"Seth?" she asked, stopping him as he started to lean down, clearly about to devour her.

"What?" he asked.

"Is that . . . is that the only reason you're here? Because of the news story? Because you realized I'd be worried and that it might affect my testimony?"

Her shaky questions echoed in her ears. She saw his face go hard. *Shit.* Why hadn't she waited until later to ask him those volatile questions?

"I was on my way to see you even before the story hit. I needed to talk to you. In person."

Her skin roughened. "You were coming to see me?" she whispered.

He nodded. He pulled her closer against him ever so slightly. His body stirred, and hers flickered with pleasure in answer.

"What . . . what were you going to say?"

"I hadn't really decided exactly," he said. "I was supposed to have the drive across the country to come up with something."

She placed both her hands palm down on his powerful chest.

"I never got a chance to tell you I'm sorry for leaving the way I did, aside from the fact that I ended up breaching security by calling Jim." She swallowed thickly to clear her congested throat. "I couldn't face the idea of telling you good-bye in an airport. It sounded cliché and just . . . too painful."

He opened his hand along her cheek and jaw. She leaned into him instinctively.

"After you left, it gave me time to think," he said gruffly. "Then my niece, Joy, and Everett Hughes showed up." He saw her surprised glance. "Katie told them I was in dire straits, apparently. Long story. Point is, once Joy got there, she made me realize something. You were right. It's not enough just to fall in love with someone in order for you to reevaluate your beliefs."

Tears flooded her eyes.

"No, Gia, you don't understand," he said, touching his forehead to hers. "Sometimes, in extremely rare cases, you compromise and you take risks and you make it work all *because* of one person."

"What?" she asked tremulously.

"You're the exception to my rule," he said quietly. "Once you were gone from that house in the woods, I realized I was willing to bend any number of rules to be with you. Every single one, if need be."

She stared up at him, amazed. It was surreal. She couldn't believe this was happening.

"I'll bend, when necessary. I want to accommodate you into my life. I want to fit into your world. I want to do that for *you*. I'm willing to try, if you are."

"Oh God, I am," she said fervently. "When we were in Illinois, I made it sound like I wouldn't budge about anything in my career or my ambitions, but I get now that it's not a black-or-white situation. I can bend too. I can make exceptions and everyday choices that take into account what's important to me. If I sacrifice some things in my career, it'll be because I want to, not because I feel like I have to because you want it. I want to be who I am . . . not just be some opposite caricature of my mother."

"I don't have all the answers right this second," Seth said. "But I love you. And I'm willing to work things out one day at a time. One hour at a time, if need be. One minute."

A smile flickered across his hard, handsome mouth. His hands moved to her bent arms. His smile faded. "Jesus. You're shaking," he said, eyebrows slanting. "Are you okay?"

She nodded, laughing. "I've never been better. Trust me. I'm shaking in relief. And happiness. I didn't want to *lose* you," she said desperately.

"You're *not* going to lose me." She squeaked in surprise when he put his hands on her waist and pulled her higher against him, her feet leaving the floor. He lifted her until their faces aligned, and then he pressed her to him even tighter. "You're not going to be able to get rid of me," he growled before his mouth covered hers.

His kiss was everything she remembered. More. It was fierce, possessive, demanding. Sweet.

So sweet.

She was drowning in the feeling of his penetrating heat. It took her a moment to realize he'd set her feet down on the floor again and was undressing her. His actions were forceful and hasty. He unbuttoned the sheer blouse she wore and peeled it off her shoulders without breaking their kiss. Gia lifted his T-shirt, running her hands over his taut, rigid belly, absorbing the heat from his skin. She ran a nail over one of his ribs and he groaned deep in her mouth, breaking their kiss roughly.

"This is going to have to be a fast and furious one," he said through a clenched jaw as he whipped her tank top over her head. "I'll make it up to you later."

"Fast and furious sounds perfect," she said breathlessly, helping him push his shirt over his head. It sounded *necessary*, she added to herself before she planted her face against his hard, warm chest, her mouth avid for his texture and taste.

A frantic moment later, he sat on the couch naked, his cock rigid between his thighs. He pulled her down onto his lap, holding it up for her.

"I don't want to be in you any way but raw right now," he said tensely as he guided her onto his cock.

"Yes," Gia agreed, wholeheartedly. She didn't want anything separating them right now either, not even that small barrier.

They stared at each other as she slowly sank onto him. A convulsion went through his rigid face. He held her bottom in both his hands and pushed. She moaned shakily as she sat in his lap, his cock pulsing high inside her.

"This is the way you first made love to me," she said in a tight voice near his ear, her arms surrounding his head so that she felt his ragged breath against her neck. Her fingers delved into his thick, silky hair. "I remember thinking you overwhelmed me. I loved it."

"I want to make this work, Gia."

She leaned back and looked into his rigid, determined features. "We will make it work," she assured. "For each other. Only for each other."

He tightened his hold on her ass and began to move her over him. Her head fell back and she gasped, overwhelmed by Seth all over again.

Epilogue

Joy and Seth were the only ones left with Gia in Daphne DeGarro's gaudy, mirror-filled dressing room. Both Seth and his niece were staring at her fixedly.

"Well?" Gia asked anxiously. "How is it?"

"Eerie," Joy whispered in awe. "I feel like I'm staring at Eleanor Roosevelt when she was twenty years old." She glanced at Seth, who still was peering at Gia with his typical razorlike focus when he was in work mode. "Seth, you're a genius."

"Oh, I can't stand it anymore," Gia said, springing up from the chair. "I need a mirror!"

"You have your pick," Seth said dryly, setting down the makeup brush he held in his hand.

Gia flew over to a nearby gilded mirror. Shivers prickled up and down her limbs at the vision she saw in it. After a few seconds of staring in incredulous excitement, she spun around and smiled at Seth, the sensation strange with the custom-fitted mouth insert she wore.

"She's right. My husband-to-be is a bona fide genius. I can't wait for everyone at the benefit ball to know it tonight. Not that they don't know already," Gia added wryly.

It had been three years since Seth and she first laid eyes on each other in this very room. They'd come back for the Cancer Benefit Ball tonight, Seth's staff working feverishly to do makeups and costumes for over two hundred and fifty benefactors of the cause. Gia had just recently finished filming on *Interlude*. Once the McClarin affair had come to a satisfactory conclusion after a hectic, frenzied trial and McClarin's conviction, they'd gone full steam ahead on filming.

The media flashfire regarding her involvement with Seth, Seth's supposed harassment of Tomoriv and the vague connection between Tomoriv and McClarin, had been just that: a high, sensationalistic inferno that quickly died out when there were no solid facts to fuel it. Seth had calmly but forcefully made a public statement, stating the facts about his brief, one-time meeting with Tomoriv. Tomoriv quickly went into hiding when questioned about his lack of proof of Seth's harassment or any solid connection between Tomoriv's organization and McClarin's. No tangible ties of causality could be made *period* between Seth, Dharma Jana, Tomoriv and McClarin. The lies evaporated beneath Madeline's fierce, relentless challenge for proof from any naysayers and her ruthless determination for justice in the courtroom.

Knowing for certain that Seth was solidly behind her had steadied Gia. She'd taken the stand and told her story with a calm confidence that McClarin's defense attorneys couldn't dent, no matter how hard they tried.

She and Seth had gone *more* than full steam ahead in their relationship once the legal proceedings had concluded. It'd been so hard, to have only a few furtive meetings during the agonizing monthlong trial.

It had been nirvana, after the conviction of Sterling McClarin, both of them defying the tabloids and appearing in public whenever they chose . . . making a point of assuring each other that their reality was the *only* one they'd abide by. It had been a challenging few months of dating, but rewarding too. They'd made mistakes and faltered a few times. Both of them had to make their share of compromises. Neither of them had ever given up, and the lessons they'd learned had only firmed their resolve to make the relation-ship work.

Last month, Seth had asked her to marry him during one of their many compromises—this one about a vacation destination. He'd proposed to her beneath a midnight dome of stars during a luxury glamping trip near the Sierra Aguilada Mountains in New Mexico. She'd agreed ecstatically. It had been the happiest night of her life. Gia had been walking on air ever since Seth had shown up in the disguise during the trial.

These days, she was soaring in the stratosphere.

The producer who wanted to make the Eleanor movie had de-cided to proceed. In a move that both shocked and pleased Gia to no end, he'd asked Rill Pierce to be the director, and Rill had agreed. Gia had insisted upon having Seth do her makeup exclu-sively for the film. Tonight they were trying out the new makeup for the first time at the Cancer Benefit Ball.

Joy hid a smile and replaced several hairbrushes and a container of hairpins into a bag. "Things certainly do change. I can't believe my big, bad uncle is volunteering to wear a tux and escort you to a glitzy Hollywood ball," Joy said. She caught Gia's eye and the two women shared a grin. Gia had found Joy Hightower to be a delight and very easy to get along with. They both loved Seth, and that commonality had been enough to quickly cement a relation-ship between them.

"He's escorted me a lot of times to big events," Gia said lightly. "He's really starting to love them, I think." Joy and Gia both laughed at Seth's "you've got to be kidding me" look. "Okay, so he's extremely forbearing and patient and can't wait until it's all over, but at least he's getting used to it. And I try my best to keep it at a minimum, right?"

Seth grunted an assent.

Joy wished them a nice time at the ball and said her good-byes.

After she'd left and closed the door behind her, Seth gestured for Gia to come over to him.

He dabbed a little extra lip color on her mouth and opened his large hand loosely over her lower face, his fingers on her jaw. She looked up into his golden brown eyes, knowing what was coming next. He rubbed the smooth stone over her lips. Her body tingled with awareness.

"I don't think I've ever mentioned this, but I really wish you wouldn't do that to other women."

"Do what?" he asked, blinking in surprise.

"Use that stone. On other women. When you're doing make-ups."

He opened his hand and stared blankly at the onyx stone. He looked at her face, and she knew he was thinking of all the times he'd made her shake in pleasure with that stone.

"I'd never use it for *that*, with other women," he said dryly. He grew thoughtful and set down the jar of lip color he'd been holding. "Come to think of it, I don't use it much to blend makeup anymore, either." He nodded once. "Okay, I won't use it at all."

"Thank you," she said, beaming. "Another compromise made. I won't forget it."

He walked closer to her, looking somber and handsome as the devil in his tux. Gia had requested that if he did escort her to the ball, he wouldn't wear a makeup. There had been something elementally wrong about Seth being hidden behind a façade that one time. He was the master of disguise, not the wearer. Besides, she liked the idea of him being her cornerstone of reality in this crazy business.

He grabbed her hand and lifted it. His mouth felt warm and firm against the back of her hand. She wondered if the shivers she got from his touch would ever fade.

"It's well worth it, to see you so happy," he said quietly. "Don't forget that we have a private appointment in here after this damn ball. I'm going to peel off this makeup and have you all the ways I did on that first night here, and a few more ways besides." He gave her a sharp, pointed glance that sent a spike of excitement through her. He brushed his fingers over a curl in the wig she wore, and false hair or not, her skull prickled with pleasure.

"I'm glad Joy was here to say the makeup was good because I'm beginning to think I'll never be able to make you up with any objectivity," he said thoughtfully. "I always just see you, whether you're a boy or the first lady."

"That's a good thing, isn't it?"

He examined her closely. "No," he said finally with an air of finality. There was something else in his expression. He was pleased. "It's better than good. I was so wrong to ever doubt you. I used to feel so alone in this make-believe world. I loved it, but I was an outsider. I protected myself against it, like I thought it'd make me unreal somehow if I gave in to it. Now I'm not alone." He pulled her closer against him, his strength and heat resonating into her.

"You're my rock," she told him feelingly. "I want you to know that."

His slow smile made something flicker at her core.

"We may exist in a world of smoke and shadows," he told her, leaning down to touch her lips ever so fleetingly with his own. "But there's *nothing* realer in my world than you, Gia."

All it takes is . . . One Night of Passion . . . Have you read the rest of Beth Kery's irresistibly sexy series?

ADDICTED TO YOU

Irish film director Rill Pierce fled to the tiny, backwoods town of Vulture's Canyon, seeking sanctuary and solitude after a devastating tragedy. Katie Hughes, his best friend's sister, blazes into town determined to save him from himself. Instead, she finds herself unleashing years of pent-up passion. In a storm of hunger and need, Katie and Rill forget themselves and the world. But will Rill's insatiable attraction to Katie heal his pain – or will it just feed the darkness within him?

BOUND TO YOU

John Corcoran loved the isolation of the Shawnee National Forest. Isolation is what movie star Jennifer Turner craved too, an escape that only a weekend away from Hollywood could provide. Yesterday, they were strangers – until a fateful accident throws them together and plunges them into darkness. Now, as intimately close as a man and a woman can be, they find themselves alone. Only an unexpected passion will comfort them – a sensual experience from which neither is certain they want to be rescued.

CAPTURED BY YOU

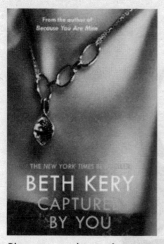

Aussie playboy and landscape photographer Chance Hathoway recognizes a miracle of nature when he sees it. Camera in hand, his instinct is to capture Sherona Legion. But he longs to possess more than her image . . . When Sherona discovers she's being watched she's surprised at her reaction. It's not embarrassment. It's pure, unabashed arousal. Thrilled at having the exhibitionist in her awakened, she agrees to Chance's offer to pose for a series of nude photographs. But how much is Sherona ready to give to a complete stranger? And how much more can Chance take?

EXPOSED TO YOU

It's not often you're hired to paint a body tattoo on a total stranger at a Hollywood film set, and reserved art teacher Joy will never forget it. Certain she'll never see him again, she gives herself completely in a moment of passionate desire. Little does she know the man is film star Everett Hughes. In the heat of an intoxicating affair, Everett endeavours to break down her barriers and gain her trust. But can Joy reveal to him the vulnerable woman who longs to be loved, wanted, and desired for ever?

ALL AVAILABLE NOW FROM HEADLINE ETERNAL

headline
ETERNAL

headline
ETERNAL

FIND YOUR HEART'S DESIRE...

VISIT OUR WEBSITE: www.headlineeternal.com

FIND US ON FACEBOOK: facebook.com/eternalromance

FOLLOW US ON TWITTER: @eternal_books

EMAIL US: eternalromance@headline.co.uk